THE OBJECT
OF
LOVE

THE OBJECT
OF
LOVE

SHARON CULLARS

BRAVA

KENSINGTON PUBLISHING CORP.
http://www.kensingtonbooks.com

BRAVA BOOKS are published by

Kensington Publishing Corp.
850 Third Avenue
New York, NY 10022

All Kensington titles, imprints and distributed lines are available at special quantity discounts for bulk purchases for sales promotion, premiums, fund-raising, educational or institutional use.

Special book excerpts or customized printings can also be created to fit specific needs. For details, write or phone the office of the Kensington Special Sales Manager: Kensington Publishing Corp., 850 Third Avenue, New York, NY 10022. Attn. Special Sales Department. Phone: 1-800-221-2647.

Brava and the B logo Reg. U.S. Pat. & TM Off.

ISBN-13: 978-0-7582-1371-6
ISBN-10: 0-7582-1371-9

First Kensington Trade Paperback Printing: May 2007
10 9 8 7 6 5 4 3 2 1

Printed in the United States of America

THE OBJECT
OF
LOVE

Chapter 1

Through her haze, Lacey barely heard the minister's prayer. Instead, she scanned the bowed heads, still surprised at the number of friends Calvin had made in his twenty-one years. That small consolation did little to ease the ache tearing her apart. All of the platitudes, the well-wishes, even her faith rang hollow at her loss.

She couldn't find it inside herself to pray. She was angry— at God, at life, hell, even at Calvin, who had tempted fate one too many times and now lay enclosed in the ebony coffin half lowered in the crypt. She didn't think she would be able to survive hearing the motorized whirring as the coffin travelled the last distance, or the sound of the dirt thrown on the burnished wood. That was her baby in there. It shouldn't be over, not this soon. Not this way.

Tears blinded her as a tremor shook her body. She fought hard against a total meltdown; Calvin never liked it when she made a scene.

"Ah, c'mon, Ma, you're not gonna start with the tears again," she could hear him saying in her mind.

"No, baby," Lacey whispered to him. "I'm not going to make a scene."

She felt her mother's hand tighten around her own, although the older woman's head was still bowed. Her sister Estelle sat on her other side, tears trailing down her cheeks. She lifted a wadded tissue to wipe them away, but they were quickly replaced with a newer downpour. Calvin's godmother as well as his aunt, Estelle had unofficially adopted Calvin as her own, long ago conceding her own childlessness. Now two mothers sat, feeling barren.

Lacey heard the muffled "Amens," saw heads go up. Distraught faces mirrored one another in various colors and tones, some etched with the wear of age, others still in the smoothness of youth. She saw Ellen, her neighbor, standing across from Calvin's grave, her eyes and nose reddened by grief as well as the unseasonably cold temperature. The climate seemed to be taking issue with Calvin's death, the thermometer having dropped into the forties well into late spring. The cold spell had started almost simultaneously with the first word of Calvin's car crash and still had not broken.

Through her fog, Lacey realized everyone was waiting for her to complete the ceremony. The red rose in her hand was starting to wilt along the edges, but its beauty still held. She stood slowly, walked the long minute to her son's coffin. Refusing to look into the chasm that would forever close her away from her son, she tossed in the flower. The action was duplicated by her mother, her sister, then a line of people forming behind them.

Her first steps were steady as she turned her back on the grave, seeking escape to her car. Her mother and Estelle on either side, she almost made it. Almost. Then, out of nowhere, a sudden deluge hit her. A torrent welled up from within, rushing so fast she had no time to put up barriers to stem the onslaught. The anguish ran through her brain, her heart, threatened to suffocate her lungs.

"Oh, Godddd," she moaned loudly as her knees buckled. She had almost made it. Almost. Calvin would be so disappointed.

Her mother, almost sixty-five and partially arthritic, was hardly capable of holding up a grown woman whose body had given out. Estelle tried to grasp her, but Lacey's strength had silently seeped away during the ceremony, and she collapsed to the ground like a rag doll, sitting on a patch of grass that edged the pathway to the parking lot. She could see the people gathered around her, could hear their voices calling to her.

"Lacey! Lacey!" Her mother's voice barely penetrated her fog. Lacey didn't care now. Didn't care what the others thought of a grown woman sitting on the ground, bawling like a baby. Didn't care that she was making a grand, embarrassing production of her son's funeral, something she had sworn to herself and Calvin's spirit she wouldn't do. She imagined Calvin looking down, shaking his head in mortification as his mother made a fool of herself in front of his friends. But even that image couldn't motivate her to get off her behind, wipe the grass and sodden dirt from her black dress, and grab hold of whatever shred of dignity she had left.

A hand clasped her upper arm, helped lift her, sturdily but gently. She found herself looking into a familiar face, although much older, harder.

"Sean, what are . . . ?"she started, then bit off the rest of the question. Of course Sean would be here. Death had a way of putting pettiness aside. No matter what had happened, Sean would have found a way to be here. If only he and Calvin had reconciled before this, before death.

"Mrs. Burnham, just hold on to me," Sean instructed, his arm going around her shoulder to steady her. For a moment, it felt as though Calvin was there beside her, helping her along. Unconsciously, she leaned into the sturdy body, let his arm lead her.

"Which one's your car?"

He scanned the vehicles as though he would be able to pick hers from among the many clustered along the pathway leading to the cemetery gates. As though he expected to see the old blue Pontiac she used to chauffeur him and Calvin around in to their Little League games. But she had gotten rid of the Pontiac a long time ago. A lifetime ago.

"It's over there," she nodded her head in the direction of her gray Lexus. Although the funeral home had offered limousine services, she had declined the depressing ride. She had escorted both her mother and sister; they were steps behind her and Sean at the moment.

Most of the mourners were heading toward their cars. Some were already pulling off. Still, a few people were standing together in collective angst, talking or just waiting for the crowd to thin. A couple of Calvin's college friends stopped her to give their condolences. One of his former girlfriends, Angie, unceremoniously hugged her, muddy tears streaming down her face. Lacey hugged Angie back tightly, although she barely remembered the girl. She had exchanged many hugs today, accepted kisses from people she barely knew or was only meeting for the first time. They approached her cautiously, wary of her grief, then paused as they searched for appropriate words, settling on safe expressions: "I knew Calvin from the team," or "We used to hang out together." The words she heard the most today were, "He was a really good guy," or variations of the same sentiment.

Some of Calvin's friends from Columbia had flown in to Chicago from New York just to be here. She appreciated these young people. Appreciated the obvious affection they had for her son. Beneath her grief, Lacey felt a small ripple of pride that she had raised a decent young man.

She blinked as Sean recaptured the arm he had let go as people began vying for her attention. She wanted to tell him she was all right, but his expression was insistent. She was feeling foolish now. She didn't know why she had broken down just then. She hadn't cried that hard since the night the police called about Calvin.

When they reached the Lexus, he held the door for her,

then for her mother and Estelle. He hovered near her window, barely peering in.

"It's OK, Sean, I'm fine now. I just want to thank you so much for being here."

He stood there hesitating, suddenly shy, a gust blowing a blond lock across his brow. "OK, then," he said before walking away. She barely had time to notice that he stopped at a motorcycle before she started the car and pulled off. People would already be waiting to gather at her house. She finally prayed for the strength to get through the evening.

Chapter 2

"Where do you want this, sweetie?" Mrs. Hampton asked, standing in the kitchen doorway holding a steaming tureen of her special gumbo in both hands. Lacey smelled the trace of cinnamon and heavy peppers that joined a medley of other smells emanating from containers, plates, pots of donated food sitting on the kitchen counter and table.

Estelle got up from her chair and took the tureen from Mrs. Hampton, one of their mother's oldest friends. "We got a little space right here." She nudged aside the covered plate of knishes that Ellen had brought over before the funeral. Calvin used to love how Ellen flavored the beef with garlic. She pictured the sauce dribbling down his cheek as he sloppily bit into one. Lacey shook the image away.

She knew she was hiding here in the kitchen, that she should make the rounds of mourners in the living room, but right now she didn't have the strength.

Mrs. Hampton beelined around the table, bent to gather Lacey's shoulders in a hug, placed a dry kiss on her cheek. "You hang in there, all right? God's going to see you through this."

Lacey smiled, touched the hand on her shoulder. "I know He will."

She knew no such thing. Didn't know how she was going to get through the next few hours, let alone the next days, months. The intense emotions that had overwhelmed her at the funeral were ebbing back to a small trickle, but she was constantly aware of the pain.

Her mother was in the living room, playing hostess, giving Lacey a reprieve. But it was time to get on with the business of living. She stood up.

Mrs. Hampton and Estelle watched her carefully as she headed out of the kitchen. Both had witnessed her breakdown, and were treating her with more care than she could deal with. She stopped at the foyer, keeping to the shadows as she spied into the living room. Her feet refused to move and she didn't feel impelled to make a grand entrance as the grieving mother. The crowd was thinner than it had been a half-hour ago. Mostly neighbors and friends sitting or standing in groups. Calvin's friends had left to catch flights or clear out of hotels. She watched the guests eating their food, sipping their soda, some talking animatedly. There were even a few smiles. It seemed strange that life was indeed going on, while her son was only a few hours in his grave, cold and alone. Her sadness seemed an intrusion to this parody of a party.

A lone figure caught her eye. Her uncle Joe had parked himself in the big leather chair in front of the television. He had it turned to the news, and seemed engrossed with whatever report was being broadcast. Yet she knew the TV was only a distraction. His weathered expression mirrored her own pain. He seemed shrunken somehow, as though someone had lopped off several feet from his usually six-foot-three frame. Joe had been Calvin's father figure since Darryl died nearly ten years before, leaving her a widow with an eleven-year-old child.

She spotted her mother standing near the window next to Ellen and Sol. Both women were nodding at something Sol was saying. His hands gesticulated as he stressed a point, a habit Lacey always found annoying. Feeling stronger, she stepped further into the room. Immediately, a hand touched her forearm, and she turned to see another neighbor, Raymond, standing alone at the fireplace. The mantel was lined with pictures of Calvin, Darryl, and her. She avoided looking at them directly.

"How're you holding up?" he asked. "Was a little worried about you at the cemetery."

"I'm really sorry about that, Ray. I didn't mean to carry on so. It's just everything caught up with me at that moment and I caved. I should've been stronger."

Raymond shook his head. Tight gray curls peppered his otherwise black hair and moustache, yet his smooth, dark skin belied his fifty-plus years.

"There's nothing to be apologizing about. You're allowed to cry, to scream—hell, to fall out if you need to. Nobody's judging you on that. I just want you to know that I'm next door anytime you need to talk. Don't matter whether it's day or night. Feel free to call me." He took her hand, held it in his.

Lacey nodded with a stiff smile, withdrew her hand tentatively. Although she appreciated the sentiment, she half suspected that beneath his solace was a tacit offer for something more. Since Ray's wife June died a couple of years ago, he had turned his attention on Lacey, which often manifested in a variety of gifts: fresh catfish from his fishing trips; turnips, collards and carrots from his garden; fat, pungent strawberries that he planted every spring. She accepted the gifts with wary appreciation, not wanting to hurt his feelings and yet not wanting to encourage him.

"I think I'll go check on Mama. This whole thing has been really hard on her."

Lacey walked over to her mother, now talking to a woman Lacey recognized as one of her mother's friends. Contrary to what she had told Ray, her mother was holding up quite well. Despite an attack of arthritis that had laid her up recently, Mrs. Dolores Coleman stood her full height. At nearly six feet, she was not a shrinking violet. Although her hair was gray, it gleamed with a sleek metallic sheen that highlighted still-luminous skin. The height was courtesy of Ibo ancestors brought to the South Carolina islands. The cheekbones spoke of Cree and Apache patriarchs who had taken up with a couple of runaway slave women; the slightly slanted eyes came from a particularly industrious Chinese immigrant brought over to work on the continental railroad, who later married a great-great-grandmother and established a business of his own. These traits were from strong genes that never got muted no matter whose line they married into. Calvin's eyes had been similar to his grandmother's; her own were less so. Still, she had the height and bones.

Her mother smiled as she approached. "You feeling better?"

"Wish everyone would stop asking me that," she said softly, knowing she sounded bitter, and totally unconcerned about her mother's friend still within earshot.

"We're going to worry whether you want us to or not. Don't forget, I lost a grandbaby, Estelle a nephew, Joe a great-nephew. We're hurting, too, and we can imagine, if only a little bit, what's going on with you."

"I'm sorry, I didn't mean to sound so . . ." Lacey stopped.

"Angry?" her mother offered, taking her arm, guiding her to an unoccupied corner. Once there, her mother reached out a finger and touched her cheek. "That's normal, Lacey. Still, maybe you should talk to somebody, someone other than family."

"You mean a psychiatrist?"

"Or at least a grief counselor. And don't pooh-pooh the idea before you've had a chance to think it through. This isn't going to go away just by going through the motions. Lace, you need to speak with someone about the whole grief process, not only what you're going through today, but how you'll be feeling a month from now. And I suspect anger is only a small part of it. As much as I loved Calvin, he was your son. I've never lost a child, can't even begin to imagine it." Her mother's eyes welled up. "Oh, my sweet baby." She grabbed Lacey into a tight hug.

The air seemed stagnant, stifling all of a sudden. Despite the chill outside, the room felt as though someone had turned up the thermostat past eighty. She needed to get away from this room with everybody fawning over her like a child. An irrepressible need to scream was growing in her belly, threatening to erupt. She was scared she was going to lose it again. If she did, her mother wouldn't just be recommending a psychiatrist, but an actual stay in a mental facility.

"I'm going to step out back, get some air," she announced unceremoniously as she freed herself from her mother's arms and strode away. She cut through the living room, ignoring the curious looks. The kitchen was empty; she didn't know where Estelle and Mrs. Hampton had gone. There were so many rooms in this house where people could disappear to. She and Darryl had bought it over twenty years ago with the hope they would fill every room with children. That hadn't happened.

Lacey opened and closed the back door behind her, immediately regretting not grabbing her coat. Still, the biting air chilled the hysteria that had been about to overtake her again. She stood there on the wraparound porch, breathing in cold air, grateful for a moment of solitude. The wooden gate along the large yard's perimeter provided some privacy. She gazed at her daylilies, planted just a few weeks ago along the foot of the gate. They were starting to wilt with the cold snap.

She took in another deep breath and realized she smelled a whiff of nicotine. She turned in the direction of the odor. Around the corner of the porch, a white trail of smoke drifted above one of her rose bushes.

"Hello?" she called out.

For a few seconds, she thought the person either hadn't heard her or was refusing to answer. Then a figure stepped from around the corner. She stared as Sean approached the porch, the offensive cigarette not evident. She hoped he hadn't thrown it in a bush.

From the vantage of the porch, she felt much taller than he, as though no years had passed since he was a ten-year-old coming over to ask if Calvin could come outside. He had been a beautiful child, with an adrogyny that could have gone too far to the feminine except for strong bones and a constant surliness. The illusion of the ten-year-old was quickly dispelled as Sean climbed the steps two at a time. Standing next to her, he easily had the advantage of a few inches. No longer gangly, he wasn't overly broad either. He had that combination college-surfer boy look that probably drew many girls (and women) to him. She noted that he was still beautiful without the androgyny that had marked his early years. The surliness was gone, too. But the light blue eyes were the same, so pale they were almost slate. He seemed bulkier in the short woolen coat he wore over his dark suit.

"I didn't know you were still here," she said, self-conscious that she was out in the cold without a coat. She wrapped her arms around herself.

"Are you OK?"

"You know, I *wish* people would stop asking me that!"

He shrugged. "Maybe they're only asking because they don't know what else to say. There's nothing meaningful you can say, especially when . . . well . . ." He dug his hands in his coat pockets, focused his eyes on a point behind her. That was so Sean-like, not ever really looking people in the eye.

"I'm sorry. You're right. I just feel like everyone's judging me because of what happened at the cemetery. Like I'm some loony toon."

"Nobody even thought that. You were grief-stricken, that's all." A pause. "I'm . . . I'm sorry I wasn't here when . . . I'm sorry for a lot of things."

He seemed so sad right then, as though he were about to cry. But then he sturdied his posture, visibly throwing off the grief.

Now, she felt the need to comfort. She reached over and touched his arm. "Sean, Calvin considered you a good friend. I don't know what happened . . . what argument or falling-out you two had, and it doesn't matter now. I'm sure if Cal was still here, he'd be so glad to see you."

Instead of the sadness easing, it seemed to deepen, causing his eyes to darken, pulling at the corners of his mouth.

"I'm not so sure about that," he said, so softly she wasn't certain she had heard him right.

"Sean, what did happen between you two? Did you fight over some girl?"

He pulled his arm away, not abruptly but firmly, indicating his unwillingness to answer or be queried any further. She thought he would head back into the house or just leave the porch, but he stood there looking uncertain, still not looking at her.

"How's Joan doing?" she asked, realizing she hadn't seen Sean's mother at the services or the burial.

"She's fine. She told me to tell you she's sorry she couldn't fly in. She's a manager at a health-care clinic in Vancouver. It's pretty hectic right now, so she couldn't get the time off."

"I understand. I do miss her, though." She smiled. "I especially miss our coffee clatches. She made the best coffee cakes."

A corner of his mouth went up. "Yeah, she still likes to bake. She does a lot of it when she's not at the clinic. She's put on some weight, too."

"Now, you know better than to mention a woman's weight. We middle-aged mothers . . ." She paused, remembering. "Anyway, we don't like to be reminded that we don't look like the svelte young chicks we once were."

"You still do," he said quietly.

"Oh, Sean, that's sweet. But I'm afraid age has caught up with me."

"I don't think so. You're still as beautiful as the first time I saw you." She realized he was finally looking at her, a direct, pale gaze that seemed to skewer her to the spot. She felt uneasy under the scrutiny, as though a continued inspection would reveal the tiny lines at the corners of her eyes or the wider waistline. She wondered at her vanity; she shouldn't even care about such things, especially not today.

"Well, I think I should get back inside. Coming with me? There's plenty of food if you're hungry."

"No, I think I'll head on back to the hotel."

"Oh, where're you staying?"

"At the Maple Motel just off Oak Park Avenue. I'm there for a few days, then I have to fly back to Indiana."

"Is that where you're going to school?"

He shook his head, but didn't volunteer an answer. The following silence extended, became uncomfortable. He had always been cautious about revealing a lot about himself and she saw that, at least in that respect, he hadn't changed much.

"Well, if you want to save the extra change, there's always room here . . . for a couple of days." Even as she wondered at her own impetuousness, she told herself that Joan would have done the same for her had the situations been reversed.

He was half turned to leave but paused, turned back. "I don't think that would be a good idea."

Just as well, she thought. Still . . .

"Well, the offer is good for however long you're in town."

He nodded, then turned and left through the gate. The same entry he had come through and exited nearly a hundred times before.

Chapter 3

Sean stubbed out his cigarette in the ashtray, stood to walk the few feet to the window. Discount rates didn't get you much of a room, and at $90 a day, he figured he was good here for only another day or so. Outside, all there was to see was the motel's parking lot and beyond that an artery leading to the highway. Just past the road sat the overgrown edge of a forest preserve.

He walked back to the bed, sat down again. He couldn't seem to shake this restlessness, and it wasn't just Calvin's death tugging at him. Damn it! Why had she even offered him the chance?

He turned his attention to the television. An old movie was playing, some hackneyed plot about a jailbreak with a then-young Stallone. Guns were blazing, a couple of cars skidded over a bridge, landing in a carnage of warped metal . . . usually enough to pull him in. Still, nothing was keeping his mind occupied. There were too many things plaguing him. He needed to dull his senses, disconnect.

A couple of years ago, it would have been easy. He would've just taken a few hits, zoned out. But that was then. Another lifetime ago. He lay back, arms folded beneath his head, and closed his eyes. And immediately saw her standing there on the porch, lonely and vulnerable. He'd felt her sadness from where he stood, had tried to shield himself from it.

He hadn't known what to say when she asked why he and Calvin had fallen out. What could he say? He definitely couldn't tell her the truth. He pushed away the sudden image of Calvin, his face twisted in anger, his fists striking out. He still felt the explosion of cartilage caving, of blood filling his nose, his mouth. Felt the fists come down on him again and again.

He sat up, shook the memory from his head. He didn't want to remember Calvin that way. Nor did he want to picture him as he had looked in the casket, his usually smooth pallor gray beneath the light brown skin, a gash across his forehead barely hidden with makeup. Calvin had never been that still; it was unnatural. He wanted to remember Cal from the good times, before everything fell apart. He tried to picture his friend running across the basketball court, hovering over the ball, pushing Sean away with an outstretched arm, then bursting forth with lightning strides and landing a perfect shot. There were a million of these memories, and yet he couldn't seem to hold on to any of them. The only memory that clearly stayed with him were those last words: *Stay the fuck out of my life!*

And Sean had complied, his pride and anger refusing to let him walk through that gate again. Today had been the first time in nearly six years that he had been in that yard. Nothing had changed much. Mrs. Burnham always planted the same lilies for spring and tended to those overgrown rose bushes. Outside of a new coat of paint for the porch (always white), everything was as it had been the last time he was there. Hidden by the bushes, a familiar haunt for him and Calvin, he half expected Calvin to slam out of the back door, round the corner, and join him in a smoke.

And when he heard the door open today, he had paused, for a second foolishly believing that the power of his mind had called forth the ghost of his boyhood friend. Then he heard her calling out, mistrust in her voice, and had felt like a boy again, afraid to be caught smoking in her backyard.

Until he remembered he was no longer a boy. Still, he had gotten rid of the cigarette out of respect.

During the funeral and later at the burial, he had deliberately stayed below the radar, not sure how much she knew, or whether she would even want him there. He hadn't given condolences, too much of a coward to approach her directly. He only planned to stay long enough to give Calvin his due, then leave and never look back. But on his way out of the cemetery, he saw her collapse, and instinctively had pushed through the crowd to go to her. After he made sure she was all right, his only thought was getting back to the motel. But when he would have made the turn at Oak Park Avenue, he maneuvered the motorcycle down Madison instead, straight to her house. He still couldn't explain the compulsion. He had paid his respects, and yet he couldn't leave. As though there was something else he had to do. Or say. At the house, he deliberately blended in with the crowd, watching everyone through a filter that separated him from the bodies milling around. On occasion, he spotted her, but she was always with someone—her mother, or one of her friends. There were a few people around his age; he assumed they were friends of Cal from school. He didn't recognize any of them. His and Cal's rift had resulted in different paths, different lives.

He stayed, not sure why. Especially when the room began closing in on him, making him feel claustrophobic. Still, he didn't leave, but instead sought refuge in the yard for a smoke. And then she had come out.

He had pondered her offer all afternoon. It came at him again and again, even though he constantly pushed it away. He did the plusses and negatives in his head, the usual way he analyzed his situations. There were many reasons why he should take her up on it. He could use the money he would save. And it would only be a few days, if that. And maybe, finally, he could find some peace within himself, make some kind of recompense to his dead friend.

Most of all, he could finally dispel the ghosts from his past, cleanse his spirit.

Besides, his mom would appreciate that he wasn't staying at some smelly hotel looking out over a parking lot.

Still, there was one overpowering reason why he shouldn't even think about it. Should stay right where he was.

The screech of a car smashing against a wall at nearly 200 mph, then exploding on impact filled the room from the television, echoing the loneliness that surrounded him.

He sighed, got up, and walked to the closet, pulled out the one suitcase he had packed. And denied to himself that he had made up his mind the moment she asked the question.

Chapter 4

Lacey took another sip, tasted the merlot just beneath the cabernet. The bottle was almost at its dregs. She knew the words to describe it: full-bodied, firm, rich with currant—terms she'd picked up when she joined a wine-tasting class nearly four years ago. It had been in part a lark, in part a much-needed diversion to fill dead evenings. Her first months as an "empty-nester" nearly drove her crazy, and she'd sought to escape from the silence of the house. The meetings had given her a deeper appreciation for wines and she had made some good friends in the bargain. When she'd first tasted the cabernet, she'd fallen in love with it, and had determined to buy a bottle on her first excursion to France. She'd bought this one in particular, promising herself to save it for a special occasion, then decided on Calvin's wedding. She had planned to uncork it at the reception and toast her son and his new bride. Thinking on what would now never be, she sighed, which was followed by a small hiccup.

Downing the glass was a step toward healing, she told herself, then poured another to toast her son's life, celebrate the years he was on this earth, here with her.

Tonight, she was determined to rid herself of sadness and death. For a night, at least, she just wanted to abdicate the position of grieving matriarch, become a living woman again. Wanted to rid herself of everything that reminded her of this last week. Didn't think she could ever look at another rose, nor dress herself in black again. Tomorrow, she'd tear down the rose bushes out back, throw away her funeral dress and the black pumps with remnants of cemetery grass still clinging to the bottom. She'd do anything and everything to stop the pall that oozed from the house's seams, seeped past doorways, through windows. She needed to fill this house with life again—otherwise she would die an achingly slow death.

Lacey pulled herself up from the leather chair, the same one Joe had sat in that afternoon, took a few steps, stumbled, then straightened up and teetered over to the entertainment center. She pulled out a jumble of CD cases, most of which clattered to the floor. Of the few remaining in her hand, she spotted an old favorite—Rufus with Chaka Khan. She put it on, cranked up the speakers, determined to squeeze out the gloom. Immediately, the room rattled to Chaka's explosive voice demanding someone to "Dance With Me." The walls complied, began shaking. She wanted to join them, began moving her hips but couldn't seem to find her usual rhythm, a persistent wooziness in her head messing with her jam. Then, a guitar riff wailed and suddenly she was transported back to a sweltering, crowded dance floor. She saw herself, a teenager again, tight tee and jeans, high heels that hurt her feet, but she didn't care.

With the memory, she finally found her groove, and began moving her hips and arms to the music. The pile of the carpet caressed her bare feet. She leaned her head back, closed her eyes, ignored the tears streaming from them. Opened a smile to the ceiling, then laughed at a remembered joke someone had told her. Eddie somebody. Felt the blast of his breath against her ear as he whispered about how beautiful she was. Years before Darryl, before Calvin. Before responsibilities and disappointments. All there had been was laughter, music, and an unshakable belief of youth never ending.

A bell suddenly joined Chaka's declaration. Damn, she must be really loopy. She didn't remember any bells on the CD.

See . . . there it was again. She stopped, listened. It occurred to her only then that the music was way too loud. And with the thought, she realized sadly that she wasn't a teenager dancing the night away. And that she had neighbors who were very protective of their peace. It was probably one of them standing at her door.

She reached for the controls, turned off the player, then headed to the foyer. She'd forgotten to turn on the hall lights, and cursed as she bumped into the hall table. The pain, crazily enough, actually brought some comfort. She was alive, at least. Not like her son.

When she opened the door, she expected to see a familiar face. Maybe Ray or Ellen. But not his face. She blinked, wobbling. No, not just his, but theirs.

Lacey didn't feel the floor coming up to meet her, but on her slide down she smiled, knowing that she hadn't lost Calvin after all. Because he was standing there in the doorway, along with Sean, both of them looking very concerned. With that wonderful thought, she closed her eyes and disappeared into a welcome oblivion.

Sean bent over her, the second time in several hours. Then he remembered the open door, stood to close it. At least he knew she was all right; the smell of alcohol on her breath had clued him in. As he bent again to pick her up, he remembered other occasions when he'd had to pick up a body sprawled on the floor, passed out from a nightly binge of beer and whisky. But his father had been much heavier, his body an excruciating burden to a young boy. Mrs. Burnham hardly weighed anything as he lifted her into his arms. Her half-opened mouth made her look like a young girl just sleeping, dreaming peacefully. She had changed from her funeral dress and now wore a large, button-down shirt and faded jeans. Her feet were bare.

In the dark hallway, he traced a familiar path to the stairs. Exactly ten steps up. Just like at his old house. Except here, paintings travelled up the stairwell. His mother had never really decorated like Mrs. Burnham, choosing to leave the wall bare. At the top of the stairs, Sean paused, his eyes adjusting to another level of darkness. To the left was Calvin's old room and a couple of guest rooms, if he remembered correctly. And to the right should be the main bathroom as well as the one room Calvin's mother had deemed off-limits. Only once had he and Cal trespassed into no-man's land, on a rare evening when Mrs. Burnham had gone out to the movies with friends. A bunch of loud women who had cackled through the house as they prepared to leave, talking about the actor's measurement, and whether his "thing" was more than any of them could handle. Sean remembered that he had felt his face flushing and had turned away before Cal could see.

He and Cal had listened to them through Cal's bedroom door. Cal shook his head and snickered: "Man, I can't believe them old broads actually talk like that. And my mama with 'em. Damn, you'd think they know they were too rancid for that. Geez. That's just sick." Cal laughed. And Sean joined him more out of solidarity than shared sentiment. At the time, he knew it was naïve to think older people didn't get it on . . . that was, if the man could still get it up. He knew from some of his parents' arguments that his father had had a problem in the sack. Which occasionally added to a combustible fuel of alcohol and violence.

As he carried Mrs. Burnham to her bedroom door, now half ajar, he remembered on that night it had been completely shut as they snuck down the hall. Cal had opened it, waving Sean in with a grin, then switched on the dresser lamp. He beelined to the closet, pulled back the sliding door, brought down a gray tin box. At the time, Cal wondered why most parents always thought their kids didn't know where to find things, as though a locked box on the top shelf of a closet was invisible to curious eyes. Boxes could be picked so easily it wasn't even worth the challenge. Cal had taken out the gun, passed it over to Sean. It'd been a .357 magnum, sleek and gray. He'd held it in his hand, weighing it, feeling its silent power. For a second, he'd thought to aim it, pull the trigger, but then thought that'd be stupid since a bullet could be in it and it might accidentally go off. But Cal hadn't been as cautious, taking it back and aiming it directly at Sean.

Sean had blanched. "Cut it out, man!" He couldn't help the tremor in his voice as he stared at the barrel.

"Man, you should see your face," Cal laughed, then finally lowered his hand. "Ah, c'mon, you know I wouldn't aim a loaded gun at you. My mama don't believe in loading up. Which is crazy, because I don't see a burglar waiting for her to go get her bullets." Cal had placed the gun back into its box, walked to the closet. While Cal set the box back on the shelf, Sean, still recovering from the terror Cal had juiced from him, looked around, his curiosity beginning to subsume his fear. He'd thought how feminine her room was. And that it really didn't suit her. He had glanced at the bed; a thought flitted and he pushed it away. Couldn't go there.

Now the room was in half shadow, but Sean immediately noticed the changes. The bed was smaller, made for one person. The bed a decade ago would have slept two. There had been a vanity then, now replaced with a small bureau. The undrawn curtains and comforter seemed darker in the light of a moon standing guard at her windows. He remembered white lace curtains from before. She seemed to have changed her taste from the dainty feminine décor.

He laid her down gently, and she let out a half sob before shifting into a fetal position. The room felt cool, and it would probably only get colder as the night deepened; he didn't want her waking in the early hours, shivering.

He shifted her body so that he could pull back her comforter, moved her beneath it, then pulled the comforter up to her neck. He noticed a strand of hair trapped between her right eyelids and gingerly pulled it out, then pushed the hair off her forehead.

Depending on how much she had drunk, and what she had drunk, she might be out for hours. Past the dawn.

He should leave, come back tomorrow, since he really didn't have permission to be here. He had tried calling her from the hotel but had found the number changed. He'd hoped that just by showing up, she would welcome him in.

Not having the privilege of any of the bedrooms, he decided she wouldn't mind if he settled on the sofa. He left the room, closed the door behind him, and quietly walked down the stairs. In the living room, he noticed that the sofa was different from the one he and Cal had vegged out on. That sofa had been barely large enough for a teenager to lie around on. This one would suit him and his extra height. He noticed the empty bottle, the CDs lying on the floor. He picked up the discs, placed them in a pile on the living room table. Then he turned out the lights, kicked off his shoes, and settled on the sofa.

He lay there for hours, desperately fighting his memories. Finally, he felt the first pull of sleep as it began to claim him. He let it lead him into a dreamless slumber.

His last thought was that at least she wouldn't have to be alone.

Chapter 5

Lacey felt something dry rubbing against her teeth. Caught between sleep and consciousness, she didn't know if she was dreaming. She struggled to the surface, finally opening her eyes to find the edge of her pillowcase in her mouth soaked with drool. She spat out the offending cloth, rolled her head on her pillow. The simple action sent a blaze of pain through her head. Sunlight drifted around the seams of her damask curtains, illuminating parts of her room, leaving others in shadow. She shifted her body, closed her eyes at another wave of pain, opened them again. Realized she was in her bed, covered with her comforter. Yet she didn't remember climbing the stairs, let alone sliding into bed. As a matter of fact, she barely remembered anything from the point when she had sat down last night with the bottle of wine, intent on dulling her senses. Obviously, she had succeeded.

Seconds passed before she realized she smelled food cooking. Eggs . . . bacon . . . and the deep aroma of coffee brewing. She smiled her surprise. Calvin must be making breakfast. An unexpected treat, since he rarely . . .

Then she remembered. The sudden comprehension hit her with fear. Calvin was no longer here. And though she'd nearly had to push Estelle and her mother out the door yesterday, they would never violate her privacy. Besides, neither of them had a key.

Lacey sat up quickly, too quickly, nearly knocking herself out with another spasm of pain. She shut her eyes for a few seconds to steady her swirling head. When she opened them again, she had only one thought.

She freed herself from the comforter that she'd placed back on her bed a few nights ago after having stored it away with the first break of spring. The room was cold, the sun barely warming it. And she was still dressed. She hadn't bothered to change—or had been too incapacitated. So, how had she gotten up here? Had someone carried her? The same someone now making himself (or herself?) at home in her kitchen? The thought seemed ludicrous.

Lacey hauled herself to the closet, pulled it open, finding strength through her growing fear and anger. Why was this happening? Wasn't it enough that God had taken her son— now she had to deal with this? She was ready to put a bullet through someone's heart if necessary. Where her fear doubted, her anger told her she could do it without blinking an eye.

She pulled down the tin box from the top shelf, nearly dropped it with her fumbling hands, tried to open it but it wouldn't budge. She remembered then that the key was at the bottom of her jewelry box. Cursing, she gathered the box in one arm, fought her lassitude and dragged herself to the dresser. She retrieved the key from a jumble of chains and rings, only to remember that the bullets were in her underwear drawer. She groaned in frustration as she searched beneath a mountain of panties and bras. Finally, her foraging hand felt the small box and pulled it out. It was dented with age; she only hoped the bullets were still good. Did bullets even expire? She shook her head, her fear growing at her total ignorance. This gun business had never been a good plan to begin with.

She loaded the bullets just like Darryl had taught her years before. The gun had been his gift to her for those times when he had to go out of town on business. He'd put it in her reluctant hands, with a "Just in case . . ."

Well, here was the "in case," right now, and she felt totally unprepared for it.

Gun finally loaded, safety off, Lacey walked to the closed door, opened it, and looked in both directions. There was no one there. Emboldened, she attempted to tiptoe to the stairs, but found she had no coordination, and instead settled on just maintaining a light tread. She eased her reluctant body down the stairwell, paused on the bottom step, leaned over to look from the foyer straight through to the kitchen. Still she saw no one. All of the lurking was beginning to make her feel foolish. After all, it was probably only her mother or Estelle in the kitchen, contrary to her earlier certainty. Maybe one of them had had a key made, thinking to look after her. But even that thought made her angry.

The uncarpeted cedar floor leading to the kitchen was cold to her feet. Her whole body felt chilled and it wasn't just the temperature. Fear could turn the blood cold, dry the mouth, make it hard to breathe. She felt all of that as she neared the kitchen's entryway, gun aimed. Because, in the end, she really didn't believe it was her mother or Estelle who had trespassed in her home. She stepped fully into the kitchen, then blinked at the improbable apparition standing at her stove, a spatula in his hand.

"Sean?" Her voice was froggy, croaky.

Sean turned, his eyes immediately going to the gun aimed at him.

"What the . . ." he started.

"What the hell are you doing here?" she asked simultaneously, her anger not eased but only redirected. How in the hell had he gotten in her house?

"Look, could you not point that thing at me? And you invited me—don't you remember?"

Still stunned, Lacey lowered the gun. Her hand was trembling. "I don't remember you coming over. Besides, you said 'no.' I do remember that much." Her head was thrumming.

The color was drained from his face; he tried to smile, but

it came out weak, shaky. "I tried to call you but your number's changed. So I came over and you opened the door, and then . . . well, you passed out."

An image of Sean standing in her doorway began reemerging in her memory. And the fear began morphing into embarrassment that anyone had seen her in that state.

She walked over to the breakfast table, sat down tiredly, the adrenaline no longer pumping through her. She laid the gun down, pushed it away; then, remembering, she retrieved it to lock the safety. She laid it down again. "I don't usually get piss drunk like that, and I've never, ever passed out before. God, I must have been a sight. I guess I should thank you . . . again."

The smell of burning bacon filled the room.

"Shit!" Sean quickly turned to the stove, switched off the burner beneath the skillet. Lacey spotted a plate of scrambled eggs sitting on the counter. Another plate held bacon drying on a paper towel. The smell of burnt meat was making her queasy.

Sean turned back to her. "You don't have to thank me for anything. All I did was carry you up the stairs. No big thing. By the way, I slept down here on the couch. I would have left, but . . . I didn't think it would be a good idea to leave you alone like that."

Lacey blinked at her self-appointed protector. His hair was tousled, a blond strand dangling near his left eye. His blue cardigan and jeans looked unironed but were not entirely wrinkled. "Well, I see you know how to make yourself at home in the kitchen, at least. So, was it Joan who taught you to cook?"

He shook his head. "Nah. I taught myself when I moved out. Got tired of takeout. Too expensive." He walked to the garbage bin, tossed in the burnt bacon, then headed to the sink to wash out the burned residue before returning the skillet to the stove. He placed fresh strips of bacon in it, turned on the burner. The bacon immediately began to sizzle. Lacey half wondered if he had cooked up the whole pack, then felt ungrateful, since he was cooking it for her.

"Calvin never could cook," she said thoughtfully. "I remember trying to teach him to bake a cobbler one time. He turned the oven too high, totally burned up the peaches." She smiled. "It took hours to air out that sickeningly sweet smell. He didn't fare much better with anything else. Except the occasional hot dog and box of macaroni. Those he could do OK."

Sean didn't smile. As a matter of fact, his face seemed to dim. The subject of Calvin was obviously still too raw for him.

"I thank you for going to all of this trouble, but I don't think my stomach can handle anything right now. Maybe just a little coffee."

"An empty stomach isn't good for a hangover. You should try to eat a little something. I looked in your refrigerator for some kind of juice, but I didn't see any. If you want, I can run out to the store and get some orange juice. That's always good."

"You're way too knowledgeable about the cures for a hangover. Hopefully, not through experience."

He shrugged as he turned over the strips. The grease popped, and she remembered the times when the searing bubbles had touched her hands, nearly cooking the flesh. She hoped he was being careful.

"Some experience," he said quietly. "It's not something I'm proud of." He finished up the bacon, then walked to an overhead cabinet and pulled out a couple of plates and mugs. Then found her fork drawer and grabbed a couple. He seemed to have totally familiarized himself with her kitchen. He loaded one of the plates with eggs and a few strips of bacon, then brought it over to the table along with a fork. "Want some toast?"

She shook her head, eyeing the plate that should have been appetizing. The eggs were a perfect fluffy yellow. Much better than any she had ever made. And the bacon was the right amount of crisp, just short of being overcooked. Her bacon tended to be rubbery.

At his urging, Lacey tasted a forkful of eggs. Despite her protesting stomach, she savored the light texture, the dash of salt and . . . something else . . . then identified the extra spice as sage. He really was a good cook. That would be a plus when he married someday. Most women appreciated a man who could share the culinary burdens.

She took another bite, while he poured a cup of coffee and brought it over. He didn't offer sugar or cream, and she didn't feel like getting it herself. She sipped the brew gingerly, found that it was a little strong for her taste. Still, it helped wash down the eggs and settled her stomach somewhat.

He went back to his station at the counter, resting his butt against the edge, half turned to look out the window over the sink. Lacey had the feeling that he was deliberately allowing her space. It was something a servant would do.

"Aren't you going to eat?"

He looked at her. "No, I'll just wait."

"Why? The food's only going to get cold. Stop being so formal and come over and sit down."

He hesitated, then loaded up a second plate, grabbed a fork, and brought them over to the table. He took the seat across from her, peeked at her as he sat down. Even then, he didn't start eating right away. He seemed to be waiting for a cue from her. She took another bite, and was satisfied to see him lifting the fork to his mouth. She noticed that his wrist was bare; he had gotten rid of the ID bracelet with his name he used to wear faithfully.

They ate in silence, and she thought that if she closed her eyes, it might have been Calvin sitting across from her during one of their rare quiet mornings. If she didn't look straight at Sean, she could even pretend for a few moments. She almost felt normal again. No death, no playing the martyr. She was just Lacey, having a meal. Coming down from a high she didn't even remember, sitting across from a young man she had known when he was just a very young kid. From all she had observed in the last few hours, she could say that Joan had raised a sensitive and caring son. That was the only thing a mother could hope to do.

The headache was barely a whimper as she finished her coffee. She put down her cup and found that Sean had been looking at her, probably for more than a few moments.

"What? Do I look that awful?"

"No. I was just remembering something."

"What?"

"The first time I met you."

"Goodness, that was ages and ages ago. I can't even remember."

This morning, the blue of his eyes was less gray—clear, intense, and direct. They nearly bore into her. "I remember you making me pancakes and bacon that morning. When I told you I hadn't eaten you insisted that I eat, said you weren't going to have me running around without a decent breakfast."

"Ahh, the breakfast-is-the-most-important-meal-of-the-day-speech, huh?"

He smiled. "Just about. I also remember how nice you were. And how you told me that I should consider your house a second home." He stopped, considering his words. "I want you to know that I always felt welcome here . . . at least with you. You were always kind to me. And you actually used to take time to talk to me. I liked our conversations. There were more than a few times I really needed them."

Lacey felt there was something else beneath the thanks. She pictured the young Sean, the remoteness she had initially taken as a sign of brattiness. To be honest, she hadn't liked him much in the beginning. But she had sensed that he needed some friendly words and she had given them to him, if only halfheartedly. Now, she felt guilty that she hadn't realized how much those words, how much her "kindness" had meant to him.

"Well, you were a sweet boy . . ." she started, wondering why she felt the need to lie.

He laughed. "I don't think so. My mom used to say that if crankiness ever became a stock, I would have the whole market cornered."

Lacey laughed with him. Joan always had a pert sense of humor. The two of them had gotten on great the first day she stopped by to meet "Calvin's mom." And to see who else was feeding her son. Dark-haired with blue eyes, Lacey had spotted the resemblance. Probably he had taken his hair coloring from his father. It occurred to her that she had never met Sean's father, had only spoken with him over the phone a couple of times.

"You weren't that bad. I just sensed that maybe you had your typical teenage problems. Lord knows, Cal wasn't an angel, either. I think most young people feel they're carrying the world's burdens. Little do they know. You wait until they grow older, learn a little more, and begin to realize how complicated the world is . . ."

"Trust me, I know how complicated the world is, knew it from a long time ago. Age has nothing to do with what burdens you get to carry."

She sat up at hearing the bitterness in his voice. "Of course, you're right. I was being too simplistic. Want to talk about what's bothering you, Sean?"

She should have been used to seeing him shake his head. "Well, thanks again for the breakfast. I'm going to get dressed and make up one of the guest rooms for you."

She rose, walked her dishes to the sink, turned on the faucet.

"I'll get those," he said firmly.

She would have protested, but with a sense that came from seeking beneath the surface of her own son's moods, she realized that Sean needed to continue his role of protector. He was bending over backward to be nice to Calvin's mom. Maybe as a way to mend a friendship that couldn't truly be reconciled, to settle a debt with Cal. She placed the dishes in the sink and turned to leave.

At the doorway, she turned back to him as he gathered up his own dishes. "I'm glad you're here, Sean. And I meant what I said before—this will always be your second home."

"It's not his fucking home!" Calvin yelled at his mother as she passed through him. "He has no right to be here! Mom, God, can't you hear me?!"

But his mother was already ascending the stairs.

Calvin went back to the kitchen entryway, watched as his turncoat friend looked toward the entry as though he actually saw Calvin standing there.

But Cal knew better. Knew that Sean had bored a hole in his mother's back as she left. Could feel the thoughts that his friend was trying to push from his mind.

"Don't you fucking lay a hand on her!" he yelled, but, of course, Sean couldn't hear him.

No one could. He was all alone, caught between two worlds. Where was he? Hell?

Chapter 6

After showering, Lacey pulled on a comfortable gray sweater, another pair of jeans, then went to the hallway closet to get fresh towels and washcloths for Sean. She walked them to the first guest room, the one Estelle used when she stayed over, set them on one of the bathroom shelves. She brought out fresh sheets from the room's closet, remade the bed. Hoped that Sean wouldn't be turned off by the floral pattern on the cover.

Strange, she felt lighter today. The pain would, of course, always be there. It just wasn't as acute today. Maybe her mother was right. Being alone wasn't always good for you. And keeping busy kept her mind away from darker thoughts.

As she finished straightening up, she began to reconsider her aversion to seeing a counselor. But that would come later. It was too soon, too raw. She wasn't ready to open herself up yet, to divulge the pain that had been swirling inside her. She wasn't ready to talk about Calvin . . . not the way she needed to talk about him.

She went back downstairs into the living room. Sean was rooted to the sofa, the television going. A suitcase was parked near the leather chair. The wool coat he'd worn to the burial was thrown over the case.

"Your room's ready. It's the second one on the left, past

Cal . . . past Calvin's room. Why don't you take your suitcase up."

He got off the couch, picked up his coat and case. As he walked past her standing near the entry, he accidentally brushed her shoulder. He turned, probably to apologize. But that small action brought his face just an inch away from her own. She smelled the coffee on his breath, felt his breath on her lips.

She saw him glance at her lips for a second, and in that second she thought he was going to lean in. To actually kiss her.

The thought should have repulsed her.

Instead she felt herself moistening, and that frightened her.

She saw in his eyes that his thoughts were following hers . . . and that he was waiting . . . but for what? He couldn't possibly . . .

She broke the spell, moving back a step. His face was flushed, his breathing unsteady.

"Let me know if you need anything else," she said, then beelined to the kitchen, denying to herself what had just happened. Right now, she couldn't be in the same room with him. Not until she'd gotten the flurries out of her head.

Good Lord—what had she done, inviting him here?

Upstairs, Sean placed his still-packed suitcase in the guest room closet, not comfortable with using any of the drawers. Right now, he wasn't even comfortable being here. He'd passed Calvin's closed door, not daring to look at it. Not after what had almost happened today . . . and what had happened five years ago.

Still, he couldn't stop thinking about what might have occurred a few minutes ago had he not been rooted to the ground.

Had he misread her look? He could have sworn she'd been waiting for him to make a move.

"Forget it, stupid!" he mentally kicked himself. Of course,

she hadn't been waiting for anything but for him to get out of the way.

But what would have happened if he'd kissed her?

So many times, he'd imagined how her full lips would feel beneath his own, how she would welcome his tongue, let his hands roam her curves . . . and downstairs, suddenly it seemed it was about to happen.

He lay down on the bed, realizing that reliving his fantasy had made him stiffen. He was on his way to a full boner if he kept thinking these thoughts, entertaining these feelings he hoped he'd purged from his mind years ago.

Coming here had been a mistake. He was dredging up things that needed to stay buried. He should just go back to the hotel for the next couple of days. After that, he would fly back to Indiana and leave everything behind. He needed to stick to his original agenda.

There were a couple of friends he wanted to see, to catch up on old times with. Suzanne, especially . . .

And there was the house. His old house. He pictured the expansive California bungalow, the garden bed that was always populated with more weeds than the hydrangeas his mother tried to grow. He remembered his basketball court out back, with the bent rim and half-tattered net. He had gotten a lot of wear out of that court. He and Cal.

He hadn't seen his former home in almost a decade. Probably another family was living there now, imprinting it with their own memories, hopefully happier ones than those he and his family had left behind.

Lying on the bed, he felt the walls closing in on him. He needed to get out of here, get on his bike and ride around, clear his head.

He grabbed his coat, headed down the stairs. Even though he knew he should let her know he was going out, he couldn't bring himself to call out.

He opened the door and closed it quietly behind him.

* * *

For most of his life, Calvin had wanted to be a baseball player. Though most people assumed his preference was basketball (he'd had a mean slam dunk), there had been something about the feel of the wood connecting to the ball, the explosive power as it whipped into the distance—sometimes over a gate perimeter to the shouts of the onlookers in the stands— that had decided him which path he would take. He'd had it all mapped out: Little League, followed by a tenure as first-string hitter in high school. And even though Columbia hadn't been his first choice (his mother had wanted him to go to a prestigious school "just in case" he decided he wanted to pursue something other than baseball), the school had had a decent team. And most of all, it was in New York. Home of the Mets. He'd get his degree in business, then head for the minors, probably in Binghamton. Just a year there to prove his skills, pay his dues. Then he would detonate large onto Shea Stadium to the roar of the crowd. And no way would he ever fuck up. Not like Strawberry and Gooden. No drugs, no drama. He'd play until his body gave out, then retire with a sterling record and generations of adoring fans. That had been the plan.

His plan hadn't included an 80-mph, head-on impact with a Buick that appeared out of nowhere. He'd thought he had time to pass the slow-moving car in front by shifting to the other lane, then quickly moving back. He would have sworn there wasn't any oncoming traffic. It had been so late . . . or, rather, early. Nearly three in the morning. But then the Buick rose up on him. He remembered the face of dawning fear on the other driver, a woman. Her mouth formed a perfect "O" as she let out a soundless scream as both their cars met in a deadly kiss.

It wasn't supposed to happen like this. Not this way. Man . . . everything gone in a smash of metal. All his dreams, his plans.

Now, he watched his mother hacking at one of the rose

bushes with the shears, her motions almost vicious. Why was she doing that? It made no sense.

Then again, nothing was making sense.

Like, why he was here instead of . . . where? Where was he supposed to be now?

Heaven? Hell? Lord knew he had earned points for both places. Guess it kind of evened out. Maybe this is where people went when the scales were too balanced, no points favoring either. Maybe they got to walk the earth, tied to their former home, haunting their loved ones.

Only, his mother wasn't aware that her son was haunting her. He'd been here since he felt the car tear him apart. A whoosh, a bright light . . . and then he was here.

Was here when the call came telling his mom that he was gone.

If ever there was a hell, that had been the moment he should have felt the flames. Standing there, watching his mother crumble to the floor screaming, tears and snot wetting her face, he'd never felt more helpless. He'd reached out to touch her, but his hand only met a barrier. He'd tried to tell her he hadn't gone anywhere, that he was still here. But, of course, she hadn't heard him. And then, finally, when she'd gotten up from the floor, she'd walked right through him. So, she could touch him, but not the other way around.

He had visited hell again, watching Grams and Aunt Estelle come to the house, their bodies worn down with grief, aged in a way he had never seen them before. And to see his Uncle Joe cry, a man who had never shown anyone his tears, had made him tremble with fear.

Seeing his own body lying in the coffin had totally creeped him out, as though the body had no right existing without him. And all that makeup they had piled on his face, making him look like a damn fag. Man, he hadn't even looked like himself.

When his mother crumbled again at the cemetery, he'd

been stunned. A woman who'd never left the house with a snag in her panty hose or a wrinkle in her slacks, had sat down in front of everybody like a child, crying, inconsolable. Until Sean . . . He tightened his hand into a fist.

Later, he'd watched from the shadows as everyone gathered at his house—his mom's friends, their neighbors, his friends from school. Jake, Tiffany, Rashad, even Chris had been there, standing together in his living room, looking lost. Which had been weird. Especially, seeing Jake looking down at his feet, not saying a word. Jake, the perpetual clown who had been silent maybe a whole two minutes since Cal had known him. Tiffany looked like a ghost of herself, eyes rimmed with tears, her hair pulled back so tight until the scalp paled against her already pale skin. She and Cal had only been going together for a few months; it'd been too early to admit feelings that he hadn't been sure of, but he'd known that she cared for him. During the funeral and burial, he had spotted Angie and hoped she and Tiffany wouldn't come face-to-face. Not that it had been likely. They weren't the type to talk to one another. Besides, Angie was a long time ago. A quick fling when he was fifteen and trying to prove something to himself.

Calvin walked through the wall into the kitchen and sat down in the chair that Sean had occupied that morning. In the days of his ghosthood (was that even a word?), he'd determined that he could fake out the physical world; chairs would hold him, he could lean against walls without going through them, if he believed strongly enough that he was real. Each day, he learned something else to manipulate. After a few more days, maybe he would be able to make himself real enough to be seen. To be heard. To be felt.

Then he would take pleasure in kicking Sean out of his home. He'd pitch him through the door on his ass, kick the shit out of him. And get him away from here. Away from his mom.

Chapter 7

"Thought I was seeing a ghost. So, why're you here?"

He hadn't expected the hostility. But the look on Suzanne's face was hardly welcoming as she stood on her porch glaring at him. He hadn't even had time to get off his bike and say hello before she stormed out of her door, her arms crossed, posture defiant.

"Why're you so pissed? I just dropped by to say hi."

"OK, so say it and go already. Shouldn't be hard. You're used to doing that."

Her red hair had been cut and was just a scattering of waves and curls around her face. He'd never thought he'd see the day when she would get rid of that curly mane that used to become a curtain in the wind. It had been her signature. The babe with the hair. She used to wrap him in it, entangle him while they were wrapped around each other, warm blue eyes laughing at him. With him.

Those eyes weren't laughing now. Nowhere near it. Were as cold as the wind cutting through his wool coat.

"So I'm supposed to feel guilty about moving out of state."

"No, you asshole! You're supposed to feel guilty about not saying shit about it to me. Not even one fucking good-bye."

"There were circumstances . . ."

"Fuck your circumstances! There's a little invention called the phone or haven't you heard? You shoulda called instead of cutting out and leaving me to . . . well, it doesn't matter, anyway. Nothing about you matters in my life anymore, Sean, so I don't know why you're here now."

"Cal died."

The stone look wavered a bit. "Yeah, I heard. I'm sorry . . . for his mother, at least."

He caught the pause. "What's that supposed to mean?"

She shook her head. "Nothing."

He let it go. "Anyway, I came back for the funeral."

"Why? It wasn't like you and Cal were still tight. As a matter of fact, he used to talk trash about you every chance he got. The guy practically hated you."

Sean unstraddled the bike, parked it at the curb. He walked the path to the first step, keeping his stride casual, but feeling anything but. This whole homecoming was turning out to be a bust. Seems he'd left more than enough bad blood behind.

"I had to pay my respects. Nothing wrong with that."

Her laugh was bitter. "That's more than Cal woulda done for you. Don't know what you did to piss him off, but it musta been something major."

Sean knew she was waiting for him to clue her in. She was standing in nothing more than a red jersey and jeans, seemingly oblivious to the cold wind whipping her now-small curls into a frenzy. He had to push his own hair out of his face. Suzanne waited for something, anything. But there was nothing he could give her.

She must have realized this because she changed the subject. "That your old bike? Thought you gave it to Sam."

Sean nodded. "I did. I'm just borrowing it while I'm in town. He's got a new Harley, anyway."

"Yeah, looks like it's seen better days. Almost ready for the scrap. So, why did you stop by, Sean?"

"Maybe I was hoping that time might have made it easier . . ."

"Easier for what? For you to slink back and apologize?

Uhn-uhn, no way. You don't know the hell I had to go through because of you."

"What hell? What're you talking about?"

She stared hard, then her features gave way to a normal expression, conceding to some internal resolution, leaving him just to look and wonder what she was keeping from him.

"Look, tell me what I did wrong other than leave town? I know I should've called, but you don't know what was going on . . . There just wasn't time."

She gave her head a quick shake.

"Can I come in?"

"For what?"

"To talk, catch up on what's been going on?"

"OK, Sean, here's a quick summary of what's been going on with me. For starters, I got pregnant. Yeah, that's right. But not to worry, 'cause I also got an abortion. Of course, I had to get on antidepressants after that. And right now, I'm trying to get a nursing degree so that I can finally move out of my father's house. Oh, and by the way, the baby was yours. But, hey, don't worry. It's all good now. So, I don't need anything from you. Not anymore. So what's been up with you?"

The rush of words slapped him like a physical blow. There was no ducking them, even if he had seen them coming. But how could he have known? They'd always used a condom. How the hell?

"How . . . when?" the questions stumbled from him, earning him another glare of derision.

"Does it matter?"

"Tell me, dammit!"

He hadn't meant to snap, but shit, she was skewering him for something he hadn't even known about.

"I found out about a month after you sneaked out of town. Of course, I couldn't tell my dad. He woulda just called me stupid. And I *was* stupid . . ."

"But we used protection . . ."

"Obviously it didn't work at least one of the times we got together. Outside of Cheryl, there was no one else I could turn to."

At Cheryl's name, Sean felt his back stiffen. The thought that Cheryl Lansky might have had any say about the existence of his child . . ."

"She the one who told you to get the abortion?"

"So, what if she did? It's not like you were around to help make the decision. Dammit, Sean, I couldn't afford to have a baby. At least Cheryl was there to help me see what I had to do."

"She get you the drugs, too?" Good ole Cheryl, who'd turned him on to heroin and who knew ways to get a whole pharmacy. Who had tried on several occasions to seduce him behind Suzanne's back, and who, no doubt, had run his name into the ground when he was away because he'd had the audacity to say no.

Suzanne's silence answered the question. No legitimate doctor would prescribe antidepressants to a teenager, at least not without her father's consent. And if she'd kept her pregnancy a secret from her father, then she would have had a hard time explaining why she'd need pills. Of course, the doctor could have been part of Cheryl's network of "favor-givers." Sean had no illusions what favors Cheryl gave in payment.

"You don't have any right to judge."

"No right, huh? I guess not. It was my baby, after all . . ."

"But you weren't here." She crossed her arms again, daring him.

No, he hadn't been here. Even though they were broken up at the time he left, he had been responsible for a life. A life he might have been able to save had he not had to leave. His absence had cost him a child he hadn't even known about. The thought caused his stomach to churn with anger and sadness.

"No, I wasn't."

"And no reason for you being here now."

He stared at her for a few seconds. She was aged beyond the few years he had been gone. Her soul was hardened, and he hated that he was the cause. But at least it was good she was trying to make a future for herself so that her life wasn't totally derailed. Maybe one day she would be able to forgive him. Maybe one day he might forgive himself.

"I guess you're right," he said solemnly, softly. He caught a flicker, a softening in her expression. But he didn't stay around to see whether he was mistaken or not. He got on his bike, drove off, knowing that she was still standing on the porch, watching his receding back. Watching him leave her life again for the second time.

Lacey raked up the strewn carcasses of twigs, rose petals, and leaves. She hadn't realized she'd been serious about getting rid of the rose bushes. But after the incident in the living room, she'd escaped to the back porch, and the blood-red of those beautiful petals just mocked her confusion and sadness. She'd retrieved the shears from the basement and had set about doing something constructive. At least, it had seemed so at the time. But destruction was never constructive; in another few weeks, she would regret undoing years of care and nurturing, would miss the lovely scent. She was going to have to rake up this mess, but right now she was too tired.

She walked back into the kitchen, wondering if Sean was still in his room. Or rather, the guest room. Before, when he'd stayed over nights, he'd slept in the extra bed in Cal's room. It seemed strange that he was all grown up now. That he was here without Cal.

That she'd been willing to let him kiss her.

No, she wasn't going to go there.

She left the shears on the counter, walked through the kitchen into the foyer. Checked the living room but he wasn't there.

She spotted the empty bottle from last night, winced at the memory of her drunkenness. The CDs were neatly stacked on the table's edge. Probably Sean's doing.

The doorbell rang, breaking into her thoughts. She went to the door and found Raymond standing there with a grin, a covered picnic basket in his left hand.

"Baked up a batch of blackberry muffins. Made a few too many for myself. Thought you might want something sweet."

She opened the screen door. "Thank you, Ray. Come on in." Of course, she had to invite him in even though she didn't feel like company, and she especially didn't feel like looking into Ray's moon eyes. Although hopefully the circumstances would temper his courting.

She settled him on the living room couch and took the basket into the kitchen. He said yes to an offer of water, and she brought back a long, chilled glass, handed it to him. One of his fingers grazed hers and his smile brightened. She took the leather chair a comfortable distance away.

"How're you doing today, Lacey? Any better?"

"Yes, better. I mean, I'm getting there. It'll take some getting used to."

Ray nodded. "I know what you mean. When June passed, I wandered around the house, entirely lost. I mean, it's a good-sized house, but not too big, you know. Yet after she was gone, it seemed so . . . enormous . . . with me being by myself. Funny thing, though, the rooms themselves seemed smaller, like without June's life in 'em, they'd shrunk a little. I don't know if I'm explaining this right. It was just that nothing . . . nothing was the same without her. Know what I mean?"

Lacey knew exactly what he meant. When Darryl died, things in the house seemed askew, out of place. The bed was too large, rooms too quiet. The quiet had taken on a "loudness" that blared through the house. It was preternatural, unsettling. Eventually, she had found an equilibrium with her home again, but it had taken a while. With Calvin gone now, the house was a stranger again. And she was a stranger exist-

ing within its walls, getting through days and nights, count-
ing down to when she would feel "normal" once more . . . if
she ever would.

"I stopped trying to figure out the whys of anything," he
said. "Some things don't make sense and never will. Like how
fast June's cancer took her away. She hardly had time between
that first pain in her stomach and the doctor saying she only
had a few months. Actually, it was only a matter of weeks.
And with Calvin, well, you wonder why someone so young is
gone, especially when everything was coming his way. He
would have made the majors. I truly believe that."

Lacey didn't have to figure out why her son died. The police report had laid it out very clearly to her: *Head-on crash,
driving south in the northbound lane.* Witnesses were very
unanimous that Calvin had been the car in the wrong. An au-
topsy had at least cleared him of any intoxication or drug
use, but that was cold comfort.

"Yes, he would have made it. If only he hadn't . . ." She
couldn't finish the sentence.

Raymond diverted his eyes. Calvin's fault wasn't a secret.
Still, no one voiced their disbelief that someone supposedly
so smart had done something so mind-bogglingly stupid. At
least, not in front of her. Whenever she thought about it, she
could feel the strains of anger reverberating. Her son was
gone because of his own senseless action. Thankfully, the
other driver had survived. But barely.

Raymond took a sip of water. She saw him peering at her
over the rim of the glass, drinking in her face. She knew he
was calculating the minutes he would stay, the days he would
visit, how soon her loneliness would make her open up, make
her accessible. He was lonely, too—that much she understood. But mutual loneliness was a pitiful reason to let someone into your life, into your bed, with so little in common. As
kind as Ray was, there was nothing that pulled her to him.

Maybe she was superficial, but there should at least be
some attraction between the man and woman. She couldn't

even begin to imagine Ray touching her intimately. But then again, it had been a long time since she had imagined any man touching her.

There hadn't been anyone since Darryl. And after such a long drought, it was hard to remember what it was like to even thirst for it. Hunger for it.

She heard a knock at the front door. She rose, wondering why her mother didn't just ring the bell. Or maybe it was a Jehovah's Witness or someone selling something.

She opened the door to find Sean standing on the porch. She blinked; she'd thought he was upstairs, and for a second she was confused.

"I don't have a key," he said matter-of-factly. His hands were shoved deep in his coat pockets, his hair tossed in his eyes. He looked as sad as he had on many occasions when he'd come to her front porch, seeking shelter in her home from things he never spoke of. That Joan never alluded to.

Without a word, she opened the door to let him in, not questioning why he had left without saying anything. He paused in the foyer for a second, caught sight of Ray, and headed up the stairs.

When she came back to the living room, she could tell by Ray's confused expression that he had seen Sean.

"Isn't that the Logan boy? The one who used to hang out with Calvin?"

Lacey didn't understand why she suddenly felt defensive, why an innocent situation no longer seemed so.

"He came in for Cal's funeral. He won't be staying long."

"Oh. Yes. Of course. That's nice of you to let him stay here." She heard the catch in his voice, the question, the tiny speck of suspicion. She didn't need any of it. She stood by the sofa, looking down at him.

"Thanks for stopping by, Ray. I really appreciate the visit. And thanks again for the muffins."

He sat for a second, not quickly picking up on the subtle message that he was being kicked out . . . albeit graciously.

He could take his suspicions home with him, stew over them, have them for dinner.

When he stood, he took the opportunity to give her cheek a quick peck. "I'll be back by tomorrow. I promise you won't have to go through this alone."

He headed to the door, leaving her speechless in his wake. Under normal circumstances, she would have called him out on his nerve. She was going to have to put a stop to this soon. Although today wasn't the day. She followed him to the foyer, opened the door and stood out of pecking distance.

He hesitated at the door. "Well, then . . . good-bye."

She breathed a sigh after she shut the door.

"I remember him."

Sean's voice made her jump. She hadn't seen him standing on the stairs. How long had he been there?

He came down the remaining steps and stood in front of her. She still had to get used to his height.

"You should remember him. He lives next door."

"He was always getting at me and Cal about the noise we made when we played ball out back. He always seemed so . . . old."

"Well, he's probably just a few years older than me."

"That's not the type of 'old' I mean. There's old like in years, and then there's the type of old that makes you wonder if the person was ever young at all. Old-timey and . . ."

"Sean, I'm not going to stand here and listen to you bad-mouth a nice man."

"So, you like him?" The stress on "like" made the question personal. His eyebrow was raised; the expression made him appear older. She could see the contours he would grow into in just a few years. His was the type of face that would age well, would still have young women fawning when he was well into his forties, fifties. Life was definitely too fair to the male species.

"Of course I like him. He's a very decent man."

"That's not what I meant."

She knew this, even as she answered his question. And why was she even answering? Who she liked was none of his business.

"Why didn't you tell me you were going out?" She assumed her mama-hen voice she often used with Calvin.

"I didn't want to bother you."

"Trust me, Sean. Being courteous is no bother. Next time, just let me know, OK? I don't want to think you're safe upstairs, then find out something's happened to you."

He smiled at that. "I'm glad you still care."

"I've always cared, Sean. You know that."

"Sometimes I did. Other times . . . I got the feeling that it was better I wasn't around. Like you thought I might be a bad influence on Cal."

She was a little startled at how well he had read her those years ago. "If I'd really thought you were a bad influence, I wouldn't have let you near Calvin." Again the lying.

He lost the smile. "Not that it would have stopped Cal. He always found a way to do what he wanted to do."

She stiffened. "You got something to say to me about Cal, Sean?"

That struck him dumb. After a long moment, he simply shook his head.

She didn't like half-assed allusions; they made her angry. No one—least of all, Sean—would tell her about her son. She hadn't worn blinders these many years. Calvin had had his faults, but he hadn't been a bad kid. If anyone had been on a slippery slope downward, it was Sean. And he had the nerve to come in this house and make snide remarks about her son?

Instinctively, she wanted to kick him out. To tell him to go back to the hotel, back to Indiana.

Instead, she took a deep breath. "I'm going to make lunch soon. And my mother's coming over. If you have other plans, let me know. Otherwise, you can join us."

She saw him hesitate. "What're you making?"

"I'm frying up some catfish. My mother usually eats her heavier meals at lunch."

"Yeah, my mom tried that a few times, too. Didn't work, though . . . with her weight, I mean."

Back on safer territory, she let her resentment ebb away. "So, are you staying?"

"Do you want me to stay?" He seemed to now have a habit of capturing her eyes, not letting go.

She knew he was asking about more than lunch. "Yes, I want you to stay."

His smile was back, wider this time. "I guess I'll stay, then."

The smile made his lips come into focus. They were perfectly shaped over a firm chin with just the slightest dimple. A matching dimple marked his right cheek.

The memory of his mouth so near her own came unbidden. She pushed it away.

"OK, then make yourself useful. You can do the salad while I fry up the fish."

"Wouldn't baked fish be healthier?" he asked with a laugh as they walked to the kitchen.

"Smart-ass," she said. Then smiled.

Chapter 8

"Lacey! What happened to your lovely roses?"

Of course, her mother *would* come to the back door today of all days. Which meant she had seen the debris that Lacey meant to rake up in the yard. Her mother stood on the back porch, looking at the mess, her face in shock.

"Come in, Mom. Don't worry about that."

As the older woman entered the kitchen, she immediately took in Sean standing at the cutting island. He had been slicing tomatoes for the salad, but at her mother's question, he stopped and looked at Lacey with a puzzled stare.

"What do you mean 'don't worry about it?' All those beautiful roses, the whole bushes, have been torn down. The porch looks absolutely naked. What happened?" Her mother's eyes were still focused on Sean, as though he were somehow responsible. And Sean was still staring at Lacey.

"I've decided to make some changes around here. Anyway, those bushes were way too overgrown. It's time I planted something new, something different. I'm also thinking about painting the porch, too."

Her mother looked at her as though she had sprouted appendages from the head. Still, the older woman said nothing. She peered at Sean again.

Lacey wiped her hand on the dish towel she had been about to pitch to the side for the laundry. "Mom, this is Sean

Logan. He and Cal practically grew up together. I think you met him a few times when he was younger. Sean, this is my mother, Mrs. Coleman."

Lacey's mother took a seat at the kitchen table, laid her purse to the side. "You're the young man from the cemetery."

"Uh, yeh . . . nice to meet you." He looked uncomfortable, as though slicing tomatoes in Lacey's kitchen was akin to committing some felony . . . or a misdemeanor, at least.

"I see you're making salad," her mother said to him, then turned to her. "Nice of him."

After forty-odd years, Lacey knew the subtext of her mother's benign comments. Just as Ray had done earlier, she was questioning the situation. Lacey couldn't understand what the fuss was about. Sean had been in this house nearly a thousand times, had almost grown up in it along with Cal. There was nothing unusual about his being here.

"Yes, it's very nice of him to help make *your* lunch. You want endives in your salad?"

Her mother cut her a look, the same look she used to give the teenaged Lacey when she'd said something smart-alecky. It used to make Lacey want to slink away, although the stubbornness she'd inherited from her father often countered her fear. She still had that stubbornness, and she held a conversation of eyes with her mother.

"Well?" Lacey pressed for an answer.

From the corner of her eye, Lacey saw that Sean had gone back to cutting the tomatoes. She also knew he was listening intently, waiting for a cue from either mother or daughter to make himself scarce.

"Endives would be fine."

Lacey smiled. "Good. Sean, endives, please. Mom, you can sit here and relax while I get the fish going."

She had the skillet on the range, the fish floured and seasoned. Like her mother used to do, and her grandmother before her, she had also doused the fish in cornmeal for added texture. She poured the canola oil in the skillet, laid the fish in, and immediately the familiar briny, spicy smell began to fill the kitchen. She pointedly ignored her mother, whom she had no doubt was staring from Sean to her.

Why was it everyone's immediate assumption that a male and female staying under the same roof must be sleeping together? And the thought of her and Sean together was ridiculous. She was twice his age, which made him just a kid. Well, not exactly a kid; still, the idea wasn't even to be entertained.

She was simply doing him . . . and Joan . . . a favor. And he was proving useful in exchange.

She turned and found him adding endives to the salad. Then he began slicing up the cucumber he'd retrieved from the refrigerator. His motions were deft, quick. Much like a chef's.

"I spoke with Joe this morning," her mother offered. "He's not doing so well."

Lacey lowered the fire, turned to her mother. "Is it his heart again?" Joe had suffered a mild heart attack nearly two years ago, but with a restrictive diet and regular medication, had just about recovered.

"I don't think so. I think . . . well . . . with Calvin's death and all . . . he's going through a slight depression. That's never good on the body."

"I have to call him. Invite him over for dinner tomorrow, maybe."

"That might do him some good. Still . . . it's going to take some time. For all of us."

Lacey peered at her mother, really seeing her since she had walked into the house. Noticed that her body wasn't as erect as before. Her pallor was a little grayish and there were circles beneath her eyes. She always got those when she wasn't sleeping well.

"Maybe you and Estelle can come over, as well. It'll do us all good to be together. You know."

Her mother nodded, smiled. "I know." Then, looking at

Sean, "So, Sean . . . may I call you Sean . . ." and not waiting for an answer, "where do you usually stay?"

Sean had finished cutting the cucumber and was tossing the mixture. "I stay in Muncie, Indiana."

"And what do you do in Muncie?"

"Mom, lay off the questions, OK? Sean isn't here to be grilled. He came for the funeral and is staying just another day, then he's going back. To Muncie."

Despite her protest, Lacey had been tempted to let her mother continue the questions. Her mother had a way of getting information out of people that would have been suitable to Gestapo tactics. Lord knew, she'd pulled enough secrets from Lacey during her younger years. Had made Lacey's growing up an exercise in evasive maneuvering in order just to have a life. Still, she wouldn't sic her mother on Sean. He was an enigma, but that was his business. If he wanted to tell them about his life, then he would. Still, she had to admit she was curious.

If he wasn't going to school, then what was he doing? And in Muncie, no less. How did he support himself? What plans did he have for the future? Why had he moved from Canada back to the States, away from Joan?

Lacey mentally shook away the questions. It was as though she wanted to step in as a surrogate mother. Because she still needed to be a mom, still needed to care about someone, to watch them become a fully realized adult, to see their dreams fulfilled. She couldn't do that for Cal any longer. And she had to fight the lure of stepping past the boundaries Sean had set, to see him . . . well, happy. Throughout the years she had known him, she'd been able to count on two hands the number of times she'd seen him smile. Even now, she still sensed a deeper layer of melancholy. But then again, that may have been due to Calvin's death. And all those missed opportunities to reconcile.

Calvin had rarely mentioned Sean in the intervening years, and the few times she brought up Sean's name, Cal had snapped at her. And she had snapped back at his impudence. "Why this rift, Cal? What the hell went down between you two?"

But her son had been as reticent as Sean was being.

She had long ago given up trying to find out what had happened between her son and his former friend. Maybe it was for the best.

Some things were better not known.

Calvin Devonne Burnham. A couple of times, he had nearly forgotten his own name. He didn't know whether that was a sign he was moving on . . . or simply fading away. He had given up on the idea of heaven or hell. Yet, if he was to slip into nothingness, he would rather it happen soon. Now, even. That would be so much better than watching Sean sitting with his mother and grandmother at the kitchen table, looking like he belonged there. Belonged in this house. His grandmother was actually smiling at the motherf . . . motherfuc . . . He paused, shook his head. He was losing words. Losing memories. He pressed hard to grab on to one, to anything.

Then, thankfully, they began to come to him, one after another, not fully crystallized, but defined enough to help him focus. He remembered his father pushing him on one of the kiddie swings in Taylor Park. Remembered gripping hard to the chain and laughing harder as he swung to the sky. He remembered his mother holding his hand as they stood in line to get tickets to see a Care Bear movie. He had loved the Care Bears. Although, a few years later he would pretend that he had never seen or read anything remotely similar about fuzzy bears, no matter how much his mother pressed with an "Oh c'mon, Cal, you remember how much you adored the Care Bears?" Thankfully, she had never questioned him about it in front of his friends.

His mother had been cool like that. So had his Gram, Aunt Estelle, and especially Uncle Joe.

He was sad to hear that Joe wasn't doing that well. All because of him.

And Gram wasn't looking good, either. Yet she managed
to smile at something Sean said, and some of her sadness
seemed to fall away.

Sean had a way of making females smile.

Another memory. A party. Cal had been about fourteen,
Sean fifteen. Cal's mom had gone to the movies on one of her
very few dates. Some loser with a balding head, and the mistaken belief that a pink shirt and purple tie meshed. Cal had
waited until he heard the front door shut behind them. He
could hear his mother laughing at some lame joke her date
was telling. He also could tell by the sound of her laugh that
she really didn't find the joke funny, that she was just being
polite.

He'd called Sean minutes after.

"I heard Cheryl's got something on tonight. Bunch of folk
gonna be there. I betcha Suz is, too. Wanna go?"

He'd heard Sean's pause. "I don't think so, man. My father's been at it again."

"More reason to get outta the house."

"Yeah, that's easy for you to say. If my old man finds me
gone, he's gonna explode."

"So, what you do is wait 'til he passes out. You know the
drill. He'll probably be out all night, so you're home free.
Besides, Cheryl's parents are out of town, so you know that
party is gonna go on into the morning. Man, c'mon, let's
go."

"What about your mom?"

"She's on some lame date tonight. Besides, I got the bed
made up with pillows. She'll think I'm sleeping. And later, I
can sneak back in through the window. She'll never know.
C'mon, no excuses, man. Let's go."

It hadn't taken much to convince Sean. Especially if it
meant a few hours away from home, which Cal knew was
pretty messed up. There were things Sean wouldn't let on,

but Cal had figured out anyway. Some really mean bruises Sean had tried to keep hidden that Cal had peeped. Sometimes, they'd be so bad, Sean would wait out the other guys in the showers after gym before he'd take off his clothes.

Cal had ridden his bike over to Cheryl's house, which had been streaming with kids hanging out on the lawn, the back deck, and pool. Lights blazed, music blared, but not to a screeching pitch; Cheryl knew enough not to piss her neighbors off too much—otherwise the cops would be called and there'd be a lot of explaining to do to her parents. Riding up, he saw Sean parking his Honda CB at the curb. The sleek black-and-silver body drew some of the more mercenary skanks looking for a ride later. Sean gave them a ready smile that transformed his face, made him look like one of those Hollywood princes that girls dropped their panties for. And definitely, Sean had the offers. Sometimes he took them up on it, "partaking of the freebies," as Cal liked to put it. Mostly fun fucks, nothing serious, unless one counted Suzanne, the only one that Sean showed any kind of longevity with.

Sean trooped through the groupies to where Cal was waiting.

"Let's see who's here," Sean said, already heading for the door. Cal eagerly followed behind. Although he was a year younger, he stood as tall as Sean, both of them towering over even some of the seniors at Milliard High. Wherever one of them went, the other was expected to be along. Like brothers.

Inside, the smell of marijuana was strong. Couples in some serious lip-locks littered the hallways and stairway. He and Sean nearly tripped over a pair that was lounging on the floor.

Sean looked around and Cal knew he was scoping for Suzanne. No wonder. The girl was a definite babe, with a mass of tangled curls all down her back. She also had a delicious set of nougats that Cal had on more than one occasion imagined sucking into oblivion. But in the mass of blonds and brunettes, there was no sign of a redhead anywhere. One particular blond detached herself from a pawing admirer and headed straight for Sean. She wobbled as she advanced; Cheryl never could hold her liquor well. She had a whole bottle in her hand and had probably already polished off half. She stepped to Sean with a silly grin, her lipstick smudged, her upper lip bruised, indicating she had already been at work.

"Seaaanniieee, heyyyy, so glad you coul' make . . . it," she hiccupped at Sean, then dropped her bottle and reached over greedy hands to attach to his shoulders, placing her stewed breath in his face. Cal could smell her standing right next to Sean, feeling patently ignored. Sean, with a half smile, backed up his face, being diplomatic. "Hey, Cheryl. Cal and me thought we'd check out the party."

"Real party hasn't started yet. Now that you here, we can get it going. C'mon," she nodded to the stairs.

The straps of her small tee-shirt were half down her arms, giving a view of her moderately small but firm breasts. Cal thought he spotted a hickey on one of them.

She was raring to go. One of her hands felt its way down Sean's stomach, attached itself to his package.

"Hey, let's not go there, Cheryl, OK?"

Cheryl laughed. "Oh, c'mon. Suzie Q isn't even here. And nobody's gonna tell." She turned to Cal. "You gonna tell, Cal, sweetie?"

"Who, me? Hell, naw," Cal had offered with a smile, wishing to hell that Cheryl would give him such a reception, drunken or not. He sure as hell wouldn't be turning her down. Which Sean was obviously doing, as he extracted himself from her grasp.

"Maybe some other time, Cheryl. I'm gonna grab me a beer or something. Got any eats around?"

Cheryl looked at him with disgust. "If that's all you came for, you can take your ass back where you came from."

Cal had cursed beneath his breath. He'd wanted to stay long enough to get some action going with someone. Why did Sean have to be a drag and piss Cheryl off? Anybody else would've taken her up on her invitation . . . no big deal.

He could see that Sean was angry. "Hey, you want me gone, that's all you had to say. I'm outta here."

And Sean had walked to the door, leaving Cal standing there, torn between loyalty and the pull of a good time. It wasn't often he got to sneak out to a party. His mother wasn't even home yet. Damn.

In the end, Cheryl decided for him.

"You can leave, too, Cal. Everybody knows you're Sean's right nut. Where he goes, you're right there hanging."

Cal didn't know he had struck out until he saw a trickle of blood running from her nose. Goddamn! He'd slapped the shit out of her.

And it had felt good.

Next thing he knew, Sean had come back and was pulling at his arm. "C'mon, let's get the fuck outta here."

Sean dragged him through the curious bodies gathering around, rabid for a good fight. And both of them left, knowing it would be a long time before Cheryl would want to see either one of their faces around. Which was too bad. Because she threw some killer parties.

And yet, the next day at school, Cheryl had sidled up to Sean at his locker with a large smile, his rejection conveniently forgotten. Of course, she'd ignored Cal standing there.

It was always like that with the girls. There was nothing Sean could do to stay permanently on their shit list. All of them eager to get in his pants, to brag about their conquest.

All of them eager to smile in his face.

Calvin watched his mother as she sat watching Sean. Although she wasn't smiling, the intensity of her look was the same as those on the faces of the girls who used to hang around Sean, hoping he would suddenly notice them. Cal rounded the table to see from an angle, to follow where his mother's eyes held. At times, she seemed almost mesmerized by Sean's eyes as he spoke of his mother and his years in Vancouver. He actually seemed animated as he told about how the winters got so cold there that tears actually froze on your face. His grandmother laughed but his mother remained silent, never pulling away from blue eyes that seemed to focus for uncomfortable lengths of time on her own. Cal felt a tenseness that belied the fact he no longer had a body. It was almost as though he felt the blood rushing to his face, his heart beating faster. If he could still feel it pounding, he would probably now be experiencing tremors as he watched his mother's eyes move to Sean's lips, linger there a fraction too long. If that weren't bad enough, he looked from his mother to Sean and saw that Sean had noticed the direction of his mother's focus before she could recall it quickly. Saw a quiet blush color his cheeks. Then he had the nerve to let his own eyes wander—to her lips. And unlike his mother's nonexpression, Sean's face read like a lurid novel. He let his eyes go farther down, just for a moment, to settle on her breasts.

Motherfucker. The word that had escaped him moments before thrummed in his head. If he didn't stop this shit now, Sean would literally become a mother-fucker, fucking Cal's mother right before his eyes. And worse still, Cal had a gnawing suspicion that his mother would let him.

The thought of the two of them fucking, their bodies pumping together, sweaty and heaving, stopped his breath. Or what passed for breath in his noncorporeal form. He actually felt the coldness of dread.

No, fuck, no! That wasn't gonna happen. Not here, not ever.

Now he knew why he had not gone on to wherever dead folks go.

He was here to stop this unnatural thing that threatened everything he had ever known.

He rounded the table until he stood behind Sean. He stood there, concentrated with all his focus. Then reached out his hand.

And was rewarded when Sean jumped a little. Finally, contact.

Cal tried to do it again, to make Sean feel him. But this time, his hand only went through Sean's shoulder, as insubstantial as it had been before.

Still, he was progressing, if slower than he wanted.

He tried again with his mother. But like the many times before, he was unable to touch her because of that damned invisible barrier. It was as though something was trying to keep him from her.

He walked over to his grandmother, gently touched her arm. And just like with Sean, his hand went through.

That's why he drew back in shock when she suddenly stood up and exclaimed, "Oh, my God! Calvin's here! He's in this room!"

Chapter 9

Lacey sat looking up at her mother in alarm. She'd never seen her so shaken before. Even as Lacey tried to calm her, her mother kept insisting she'd felt Calvin touch her, that he was here in this kitchen.

"I *know* what I felt, Lacey! It was Calvin! He's right here!"

"Mom, please! Sit down! You're imagining things. It has to be the stress from the funeral. Probably the finality of it is starting to set in. I know you want him to be here, Mom. But he's gone. He's gone." Lacey's voice trembled as she said these last words. Just when she thought she was doing better, something stoked up the pain again.

Her mother teared up, but she finally sat down again, her momentary excitement curbed by Lacey's words. Lacey peered over at Sean, whose eyes were wide with concern. He probably thought the elderly woman was on the verge of a breakdown. Between her antics at the cemetery and her mother's outburst, the women of the family might appear weak and simpering to someone so young.

She watched as Sean stood suddenly and walked over to the cabinet and retrieved a glass. He ran water in it, and brought it over to her mother. Her mother's eyes seemed vacant at the moment, but she smiled up at him as he handed her the glass.

"Thank you," she said softly. She had already dried the

tears, but whatever peace she had found these last few days seemed to have deserted her. Her whole frame seemed to be shaking.

"Mom, I think you should stay here for a while, maybe spend the night."

"No, no. I'll be fine. Of course, you're right and I'm just being silly. Maybe it was just wishful thinking. But it felt so real, not just the touch, but the very essence . . . I know, I'm rambling. I'm just tired, I guess."

She tried to smile. "The meal was lovely, but I think I'd feel better if I went home and lay down for a while. Don't worry about me."

"Well, if you think you'll be all right. But I'm driving you home, and don't even bother arguing. You're in no state to be driving."

Lacey realized just how disturbed her mother really was because she didn't try to argue. The mother she had grown up with would have reasserted her independence and insisted she not be treated like a doddering fool. But the woman slowly getting up from the chair wasn't that woman. She was old and she was tired. And she looked defeated. Lacey hadn't fully comprehended until this moment how much Calvin's death had drained from her mother. She had masked her own pain trying to be strong for Lacey. Now she needed to be strong for her mother.

"Sean, I'll be right back. Just make yourself comfortable."

She started to take her mother's arm but the woman just shook off her grip. "I can walk just fine. You can drop me off at home, then drive my car back."

"No, you might need to go somewhere. Although I hope that you just take it easy for the rest of the day. I can catch a cab back."

Her mother didn't protest any further as they headed out the kitchen door. Lacey did her best to ignore the mess still waiting to be raked up out back. That was more than she could deal with right now. Right now, it was just enough to get her mother home safely. Then she had the rest of the night to face.

Another night alone.

Sean waited outside the large brownstone, his motorcycle parked at the curb. He discarded his spent cigarette, lit another. He'd been waiting nearly forty minutes and was beginning to wonder whether he'd missed her. After all, she hadn't known he was coming. Hell, he hadn't known he was coming until the second it occurred to him. Luckily, he remembered the address from that one time he and Cal had driven over to drop something off for Cal's grandmother. He'd waited at the curb then, just as he was doing now. Finally, the door opened and Lacey stepped out. Her mother stood inside talking, her words muted with distance. Lacey gave her a peck on the cheek, then turned to walk down the stairs, glancing either way for a cab. The street was a major thoroughfare and cabs often passed by, but there wasn't one in sight. After a moment, Lacey looked in his direction and saw him waiting. For her. Sean dropped the cigarette, crushed it to the ground.

As she walked toward him, he wasn't sure whether she was glad he was there. Her expression was more puzzled than anything, her eyes a question mark. He found he couldn't pull himself from those eyes. He remembered just before the old lady had started screeching about Calvin that he'd caught Lacey staring at him. And it hadn't been an innocent look. He knew when he was being checked out, and he'd taken the opportunity to let his eyes roam as well. He'd hoped that she picked up his subtle signal. Had begun hoping from that moment that there was something mutual going on between them. But then Cal's grandmother jerked him back to reality, scaring the bejesus out of him with her insistence that Calvin was standing right there in the room. He began feeling paranoid, thinking of the touch he was sure until that moment he had imagined.

He wasn't good around death. Never had been.

"Sean, what're you doing here?" Before he could answer, "I know you're not expecting me to ride on this." She eyed the motorcycle warily, and he could tell she was going to reject his offer.

"It's safe enough. Gets you where you want to go. Besides, I'll let you wear the helmet," he grinned. "Or do you really want to wait God-knows-how-long for a cab? Just say the word and I'll go and meet you back at the house."

She hesitated, looked up the street, probably trying to will a cab to come. Sean waited, hoping, then held back a smile as she finally reached out a hand for the helmet. His smile broke through as she pushed the helmet over her hair. He imagined her with "helmet hair" and thought she would still look good.

She slipped into the seat behind him, her body molding into the contour of his back. The intimacy sent a tremor through him, caused him to stiffen uncomfortably against the crotch of his jeans. He cursed beneath his breath. He was definitely going to have to control his reactions for the next twenty-four hours or he'd never make it.

"Hold on to me," he instructed. And skipped a breath as her arms tightened around his stomach, as her thighs pressed into his own. Her breath fanned against the side of his neck, pricking his nerves. It might have been his imagination, but he thought he felt her hand stroke his stomach. The thought had him almost at a full salute.

He revved the motor and they took off. Cold air whipped against them as he accelerated, the blast nearly stealing his breath. As he drove, his mind barely registered passing cars, signs, and stoplights. At one red light, he had to jam hard on his brake to keep from going out into the intersection. He had never been this off in his driving. But he found it hard to concentrate on anything except the soft body melded to him, and the arms around him.

Twenty minutes later they were in front of her house again. She didn't move right away, which was fine with him. He wasn't in a hurry to be away from her. Even out here in the cold, he felt the heat from her body fusing with his own. One of her hands was still splayed on his stomach. And it wasn't his imagination this time; there was a slight movement, a barely perceptible caress that had him painfully encased, dying to unzip, dying to bury deep inside her. He moved his hand over hers, intertwined their fingers. Heard, or rather felt, a sudden intake of breath on his neck.

"I have to go . . . and rake up out back."

Then suddenly she was off the bike and practically running for the front door. She still had the helmet on.

He sat on the bike, engine off, trying to figure out what to do. Should he follow her and apologize? Not that he could follow her just now, at this moment. He was going to have to sit a few minutes before he could get up. He was that far gone. And the last thing he needed was for her to see how erect she'd made him.

She'd probably kick him out now. Because there was no way to explain away the fact that he had made a move on her. On his friend's mother.

If Cal were still alive, he'd no doubt kill him. As he promised to do several years ago. After . . . Sean squelched the memory. It was too painful still. He couldn't afford to think on the past.

Instead, he closed his eyes and willed his hard-on to disappear.

What the fuck had she been thinking? God! She'd made a pass at her son's friend. At her friend's son. Someone young enough to be her own son. Someone she'd watch grow up, almost.

Lacey pulled the rake through the brambles, stabbing the ground in anger. She wasn't angry at him. No, she was angry with herself, angry at her body's response as she clung to him, felt the musculature of his thigh, the heat of his ass against her crotch. At the way her body throbbed as her hand moved along the hard muscles of his stomach. It hadn't been a conscious action. More like her body had disassociated from her brain and had touched what it'd been wanting to touch since that near encounter in the living room.

At least she hadn't let her hand wander fully where it would have gone before Sean brought her back to herself and her senses. Because at that moment, in view of the whole neighborhood, she'd been willing to give in to an irresistible pull to search out his dick, feel for it through his jeans, unzip him. Her mouth had longed to lick along his ear, as during the ride she'd had to resist placing her cheek along his own. When he'd interlaced his fingers with hers, she knew that he felt the same and she'd panicked.

She had to ask him to leave. She had no choice. Because no way could he stay the night again. Her decision made, she felt some of the anger leave as she held a Hefty bag open to empty a shovelful of limbs and torn rose petals into it.

It wasn't that she didn't trust him. After all, he wasn't the one who had made the first move. It was herself she didn't trust.

Calvin's death had left her more vulnerable to emotions she had managed to avoid or just plain ignore. Like simple lust.

Even though she knew it would be wrong, she wanted desperately to walk into the house, to find him, pull him to her bed, and give in to one of the few emotions she could feel outside of overwhelming grief.

She heard the back door open and close. It seemed she didn't have to go inside the house to find him. He had come out to find her. He still had his coat on. He came down the few steps to stand where she was and without a word, tried to take the rake from her, but she held firm.

"Let me," he said, staring directly into her eyes. He no longer averted his gaze as he used to. But then she'd given him every reason to think . . . to know . . . that she was open to him. That he didn't have to hide his feelings from her. Not any longer.

Maybe she'd known all along how he felt, even those years ago. But, of course, then, she could do nothing. Now was a different situation. And she was scared. She needed to get him away from here . . . away from her.

"Sean, I think it's probably better that you go back to the hotel. I'm sorry." Now she was the one diverting her gaze, focusing on the bridge of his nose, anywhere but those blue-gray eyes.

"Yeah, I figured you'd want me to go. I'm sorry about what happened back there on the bike. It's just that I thought you . . . well . . . wanted me."

She allowed herself to meet his eyes again and her body trembled at the emotion she saw there. They were begging her to fess up, to say she felt the same way he did.

But she was the adult. Or, at least the one with a lot more life experience. He was too young to understand the consequences of what they both wanted.

"Sean, I *am* attracted to you, if you hadn't already picked up on that. And I'm in a vulnerable state right now. That's why it isn't good for you to be here."

"Why? Do you think I'll do something to you?" The question was a challenge.

"Actually, it's because I'm hoping you do something to me that this is a bad idea."

When he smiled, even the little half smile that played along the right corner of his lips, his face transformed into a beauty that was almost transcendent. She'd never seen a boy . . . a man . . . whom she could think of as beautiful.

He closed the space between them and took the rake from her hand. And let it fall to the ground.

This time there was no mistaking his intent as his face closed in, his lips nearing hers.

"Sean, no, OK? We can't do this." She pushed at his chest and he pulled back a little.

"I'm not a child anymore. And this isn't some schoolboy's crush. Tell me, what would you do if I was your neighbor?"

"Trust me, if you were Ray, we wouldn't be having this conversation."

"But if I was his age, you wouldn't be pushing me away, either."

"It's more than age, Sean."

"Then what is it?"

"Well . . . you were Calvin's friend . . ."

"Yeah, but Cal's not here."

She resisted the urge to slap him. "I know Cal's not here! You don't need to remind me that my son is dead." She saw him blanch at her words. She glanced away, focused her eyes on a bank of gray-tinged clouds moving across a slate sky. She couldn't remember the last time the sun had shone fully. Sometime before Cal died. She looked back as he spoke.

"I'm sorry. I didn't mean to sound like I don't care. I wouldn't purposely say anything to hurt you."

After a second, she sighed. "That's not a promise you can make, Sean. You live long enough, you're going to say something . . . do something . . . that's going to hurt someone. That's a given. It's called living."

Instead of an answer, his finger came up, traced along her jaw. Her body stiffened, her crotch clinched. "Living is more than pain or hurt. It's pleasure, too."

His mouth stopped her protest. The sudden heat and liquid of the kiss caused an involuntary moan. She had to hold onto his shoulders to keep from totally melting into him. Through his coat, sweater, she felt the hard tendons of his muscles.

His lips consumed hers. She had no time to catch her breath or to think as every atom of her body responded to his need. He pulled her to him, tightened his arms around her waist, not allowing her any escape. She felt the hard swelling of his penis against her stomach, ached to take all of him inside her. Her panties were soaking with her own need, her walls spasming with anticipation.

She tried to find the common sense she had only a few moments ago, but any trace of it was pushed out of her head as his tongue pushed farther into her mouth, and she found herself sucking it eagerly. It'd been so long since she had been kissed completely. For the first time in days, she was totally here, her body and mind together and not operating separately like a zombie's. His mouth pulled away and she immediately missed it, but then it traced along her jaw, down the crevice of her neck. The feel of his desperate breath against her flesh almost made her come.

Her hands found the top button of his coat, nearly ripped it out of its catchhole. He stepped back to finish her task, his hands impatiently working the rest of the buttons until he could finally rid himself of the woolen barrier. He threw it unceremoniously to the ground.

"Do you want me to go on?" he asked breathlessly.

She didn't know whether he was asking about his clothes or permission to continue what they had started. Either way, her answer was "yes." With her consent, he pulled off his sweater, began unzipping his jeans. As he shed each piece, she realized the madness of the situation. They were outside with the temperature just a little above forty. And here he was, undressing. And now he stood totally naked, waiting for her. Her eyes were drawn to his tumescence. The shaft was thick, the head purplish, moisture already beading.

Suddenly, she felt self-conscious, which left her immobile. He closed in, touched his lips to hers again, softly at first, then with a growing insistence. He took one of her hands, moved his lips to her ear.

"Touch me, Lacey," he whispered. The need in his voice, the way he said her name, was raw and naked. As naked as the skin beneath her exploring fingers—the smooth flesh of his chest over hard and firm muscles; his stomach, lean, just a trace of soft down around his navel; travelling farther downward, the thicker texture of pubic hair, springy between her fingers. Finally, her fingers enclosed the rubbery texture of his shaft, tightened eagerly. His eyes had been closed as he savored her touch, but they popped open as she began moving her hand up and down his penis, setting a rhythm. He moaned as her lips retraced the path her fingers had already taken.

During her marriage, Darryl had often encouraged her to explore him with her mouth and she had halfheartedly complied, more to avoid an argument than from any true desire. Now, she wondered at her eagerness, her craving to taste Sean. She lowered to her knees, felt his hand caress her face as she took him in her mouth. She worked her tongue along the grooves, heard his intake of breath. His scent was heady, the taste of his moisture so different from her husband's. She found herself wanting more of it, and began working her mouth and tongue, drawing him in farther.

"Oh, Lacey . . . oh, God!" she heard him cry out. Her hands moved to his ass—firm, compact—and squeezed the young flesh hard until she elicited another moan, a half-strangled cry. His hand guided the back of her head as she worked him, as she sucked liquid from him, drew life from him.

Without warning, he shoved her away, and she blinked up at him, confused.

"I want to be inside you." It was a demand, not a request. Without ceremony, he joined her on the ground as his hands tugged her sweater over her head. The inferno in his eyes frightened and excited her.

He gave a frustrated groan as his fingers tried to work the front hooks of her bra without success. The sound of his frustration settled her nerves, made her feel in control. She leaned over to him, put her lip to his ear.

"Sssshhh, let me do it." She pushed his fingers away, unhooked the bra, and freed her breasts. Her already firm nipples became even more erect as the cold air hit them. Self-conscious, she worried that he would be turned off by the slight sagging, would begin noticing her other flaws. She wanted to remain beautiful in his eyes, didn't want to see them fog over with the reality of the aging woman before him. But instead of disgust, his eyes shone with fascination as he reached out a hand to circle a nipple, then bent to enclose it with his mouth. He licked it as avidly as she had worked him minutes before.

She moaned as his tongue played along the button, back and forth, stopping in half circles, completing full arcs along the screaming flesh. If he didn't stop, she was in danger of coming, and she desperately didn't want to come now. She wanted to draw out this moment as long as possible. Because she knew that this would be the first and last time she would make love with him. That after today, she wouldn't allow him near her. But today, she would take everything he had to offer: pleasure, comfort, moments free of pain. She knew that in subsequent lonely nights, she would touch herself, think of him, remember the ways he had touched her, how wonderful he had made her feel.

She pushed his face away, forcing his mouth to release her. "Finish undressing me." Now she was the one demanding.

He smiled, laid her on her back as he unbuttoned and unzipped her jeans. He tugged them down to her knees, pulled them down farther, cursed as they caught on her sneakers, which he quickly discarded, then pulled the jeans all the way off. She liked the way he caressed her with his eyes, as though he were staring at a treasure hard-won. He bent to nuzzle her stomach with his nose as he slowly pulled down her panties. The touch was feathery, accented with a whiff of breath that sent tremors through her. His mouth followed the panties' descent, travelling downward until his head rested between her thighs. He flung the panties on the mound of discarded clothing as his tongue found her clit, fastened onto it. He had already brought her too far, too fast, and she cried out helplessly, spasming after just a few flicks of his tongue, leaving her whole body trembling. She moaned in frustration; she hadn't wanted to come so soon.

Sean burrowed his face deeper into her chasm, his hands holding her thighs steady as he licked and tongue-fucked her. Another wave slowly began building, radiating from her core to her extremities—thighs, legs, even her fingertips. She had never orgasmed more than once, had never come close. Only now did she realize that she could . . . that she would. The surge hit hard as he brought her again. Tears streamed down the sides of her face, disappeared into the grass. Crying had become a normal state for her these days.

She felt a cool rush of air as his head moved from her thighs. He easily shifted over her length, her scent on his face, his breath. He positioned his lean frame on top of her, blocking out the cold, giving her his heat.

"Sshh, sshh, don't cry. It's OK." He kissed her softly, gently. Then, "Do you want me to stop?"

Every doubt had been kissed, licked, and stroked away. All she wanted right now was to feel him deep inside her.

"Fuck me, Sean," she ordered quietly. Her choice of words left no ambiguity. There was no wavering, no hesitancy.

He immediately complied by plunging into her as deep as he could go. The sudden invasion forced her to draw in a sharp intake of breath.

"Tell me . . ." he started, but the rest of his words were lost in a tortured sigh as he began a slow thrust.

"What?" she breathed, enraptured by the sex, by the sensation of him inside her finally.

He tried again, his voice strangled. "Tell me what you want . . . fast . . . slow . . . hard . . . soft . . ."

"God, yes," she gasped and he did his best to oblige her, alternating his pace, his thrusts. She barely caught her breath as his varied rhythms shook her, pushed her body into the cold ground. A limb with a prickly thorn had attached itself to one of her thighs, and as Sean thrust repeatedly into her, the thorn became imbedded deeper into her flesh, another invasion. Instead of diminishing the pleasure, the pain seemed to heighten it, every sensation merging with one another. Lips, hands, penis worked her to a final frenzy. Sean caught her half scream with his mouth, sucked it away from her. Fucked the hell out of her, fucked away the pain, the sadness. Kept fucking her until he released deep inside her with a sob. He fell limp, his penis still lodged in her. She throbbed around his pole, pulling the last moisture from him.

She might have lain there all afternoon, well into the evening. Would have willingly stayed on the cold grass with him inside her, both of them clenched together as he breathlessly peppered kisses along her face and neck.

But then a movement in the kitchen window caught her eye. There was a face looking out at her. At them. A very angry face, distorted with a hatred she had never seen before. The scream that would have erupted caught in her throat as she looked at her dead son fuming at his mother and his ex-friend lying together naked.

Chapter 10

"OK, calm down! You're not making any sense!"
"Let go of me!"

Sean tried to hold on to Lacey's arm, but she wrenched free from his grip. He flinched from the anger in her face, at this moment directed at him.

She was in a panic, her clothes disheveled from her hurried dressing after their lovemaking. He'd barely had time to get on his own clothes, trying to rush after her. Bits of leaves and petals clung to her hair. Her eyes darted around the kitchen as though she expected to see someone lurking in the corners. Sean actually saw a shiver go through her before she pushed him away and hurried from the kitchen. The sound of her feet reverberated on the stairs, followed by the audible shutting of her bedroom door. Although not an actual slam, it was loud enough for him to know she had closed it with some force. The sound effectively shut him out, told him he wasn't welcome upstairs. That he shouldn't follow.

He couldn't figure out what had happened. One moment, they were lying together and for the first time in years, he had felt safe. No more running and hiding. No fear. And for the few seconds he'd lain with her, barely recovered from his climax, he'd even thought that maybe he could move back to Oak Park to be near her. That she would welcome him.

Then, without warning, she pushed him off her, looking

wild-eyed as she said something about Calvin in the window. He'd looked in the direction she had been staring, but saw nothing but the empty kitchen window.

Sean kicked at the chair where more than an hour before Calvin's grandmother had sat as she shouted something about Calvin. What the hell was going on?

Calvin. It was always about Calvin. Because of Calvin, his life had been derailed. Well, that wasn't exactly true, but Cal had definitely figured into the reason.

Coming back for the funeral had been a mistake. Suz was right. Cal wouldn't have even bothered. So why had he?

Of course, he already knew the answer. He looked toward the ceiling as he heard rhythmic steps that sounded like pacing upstairs. She was definitely agitated about something.

He needed to do something, anything, instead of just standing here. Maybe she was having another episode just like at the cemetery. It couldn't be easy losing a child. He thought about what Suzanne had told him earlier. He still hadn't processed the information. Hadn't had the opportunity to run through his mind what it might have been like to have a child, someone who looked like him, a little boy or girl with his blood running through them.

Just as well. He would probably have been a lousy father, considering his own role model. Kid was probably better off in heaven or wherever the unborn went.

Something fell over upstairs with a thud. Had she collapsed again? On the hind edge of the thought, Sean rushed to the stairs, taking them two at a time. He came to her door, and without knocking, pushed it open. She hadn't locked it.

Lacey was sitting at the bottom of the bed, her back to the door, her head braced in her hands. She looked up, turned, and he saw that her eyes were brimming with tears.

"Sean, I told you to leave me alone." Her voice came in a breathy hiccup as she turned away.

He stepped into the room, but not too far, choosing to give her space.

"I heard something fall."

She shook her head. "I accidentally knocked over the chair. That's all."

Sean saw a lightweight chair, white with gold padding, a leftover from the discarded vanity set. She had already up-righted it.

"I would offer to go, but I'm not leaving you like this. Lacey, tell me what's going on."

She sniffed, wiped her eyes, half turned to him again. "I told you . . ."

"Yeah . . . you saw Calvin. I'm sorry, but that sounds crazy."

"I guess I'm crazy, then. And maybe my mother's crazy, too."

He took a chance and stepped in farther, neared the bed, but remained standing.

"I didn't say *you* were crazy, just the statement. Your mother probably got you weirded out, that's all. Made you think that maybe Cal was here. Hell, she had me going for a second. But like you told her earlier, it's just everything happening all at once. Not to mention me."

"You?" Now she turned all the way around.

"Don't you think it's more than a coincidence that you and I make love, and suddenly you see Calvin staring out at us? You have to know Calvin isn't haunting you. It's not possible. So it has to be the guilt you're feeling about what we did out there."

He saw the words taking effect, saw her eyes settle on an empty space of wall as she thought over what he'd said. After all, it made more sense than to believe a ghost was hanging around.

"It seemed so real," she said softly, to herself. "He looked so angry."

Sean walked the remaining steps until he stood over her. He reached out a tentative hand, touched her hair. Caressed a bang off her forehead. "Calvin's not feeling anything anymore. He's beyond any pain here on earth. He's at peace."

She nodded her acquiescence. He knew she wanted to believe it. He wanted to believe it, too.

But a nagging suspicion in his soul told him that his former friend was not wandering the halcyon fields of heaven. That he was more likely in torment.

But he would never, ever say that to her.

Sean eased himself down on the bed beside her, casually settled an arm around her. He held his breath, waiting for her to shrug him off, but she just sat there. Emboldened, he pulled her closer, and instinctively her head lowered to his shoulder. He grazed her head with a kiss.

They sat that way until the sun finally set.

Calvin watched them sitting on the bed, hatred seething for Sean, a fiery anger blazing toward his mother. At the moment, he couldn't distinguish between the two emotions.

He still couldn't believe his mother had actually fucked Sean, like a bitch in heat.

He shook the word out of his head. No, he didn't want to be angry at her. There had to be a reason for what she had done. Grief had left her weak and stupid, open to whatever scam Sean was pulling.

And he had no doubt Sean was up to something.

Probably revenge. What better way for Sean to get at him than to bang his mother? Probably had been silently laughing all the while he had been fucking her.

And all that sympathy shit, all of it was nothing more than a play to get into his mother's pants. Though, she'd been more than eager to pull them down for him.

Or rather, let Sean pull them down. The memory seared through him, coursed like blood.

He wanted to kill, needed to kill.

He had to find a way to kill Sean. Before Sean destroyed his mother.

It might take an eternity, but seeing as he wasn't going anywhere, he had enough time in the world.

Lacey woke to rain pounding against the windows. Her head lay on Sean's chest, his arm draped around her. He was asleep, a slight wheeze escaping that was out of sync with the steadier rhythm of his heartbeat against her ear. They were lying on top of the bed, on top of the comforter, still clothed, shoes discarded. She barely remembered drifting off and only had a vague recollection of Sean holding her into the night, softly reassuring her that she wasn't crazy, that she just needed to rest.

As the room had darkened into night and her body tensed up, listening out for sounds that shouldn't be there, she'd asked him when he was going back to Muncie. He had been oddly evasive. She'd reassured him that she wasn't trying to rush him away, but by his silence she'd known that he was also contemplating his departure. What she hadn't admitted to him, had barely admitted to herself even, was that she wished he could stay longer. That she liked having him near. That he'd made her feel life again.

She softly shifted out of his arm and settled on an elbow to study him in the dim light of the muted dawn. She still saw some of the boy in his face, soft in repose, but in the hours since he'd reentered her life, she had begun to appreciate the man he had become. There was a small scar at the crest of his temple, the skin whiter than the rest. A golden five-o'clock shadow graced his chin. Pulled by an irresistible need to touch him, she delicately traced a finger along the line leading from his forehead to the bridge of his nose, felt the tickle of breath as she let her finger wander to his lips, so sensual on someone so young. Giving in to her urge, she bent to plant a whisper of a kiss on his mouth and caught a whiff of her scent on him. Which reminded her that she still had both their scents on her own body.

She carefully moved off the bed, not wanting to wake him,

then stepped into the master bathroom. She closed the door, began pulling off her clothes and dropped them to the floor. Her jeans had dirt smears on the rear and the hairs of her sweater were littered with small twigs. The stained crotch of her panties had already stiffened with her secretions as well as Sean's. A moment from the garden flashed in her mind and it was as though she could still feel him moving inside her, touching her with more than just his flesh. Her body throbbed with the memory. What was wrong with her? She had gone so many years without sex, occasionally satisfying herself in the solitude of her room, and since Darryl's death, that had been all she really needed or wanted. Now she felt like a dewy-eyed teenager going through her first crush. But she wasn't a teenager, although she had foolishly acted like one.

A cold wave doused her momentary heat as she realized just how foolish she had been. There could be consequences to what she'd done. She knew nothing about Sean's sexual history, about the girls and women he had slept with. And she had carelessly taken him inside her body without any protection. With all the diseases going around, that had been a damn stupid thing to do. Another thought shook her, made her pause as she reached for the shower door. Disease was just one of the fallouts. There was another thing to worry about. But at her age, what were the odds? It couldn't possibly happen, not now, not after everything, including losing her only child. Ironic wouldn't even begin to describe the situation.

Lacey shut her eyes for a second, closing out the unsettling thoughts, opened them again to step into the shower. As she closed the glass door and turned on the hot water, she promised herself she would not let her guard down again. Sean would be flying home, if not tomorrow, then very soon. Until he was gone, she would have to be strong for both of them, reset the boundaries. No more rolling in the grass like frolicking teenagers.

She shuddered to think what Joan would say. Joan likely

would cuss her out, yell that she'd betrayed her. And she'd be right. She *had* betrayed Joan. There were unspoken rules between friends, and she had violated a very important one: you don't sleep with a friend's child. She knew that if the situation had been reversed, with Joan screwing Calvin, she'd have had some choice words for both of them.

The water jet shocked her skin with near-scalding heat. She rotated her body beneath the pulsating spray, letting the water wash away sweat, dirt, all evidence of her lapse. Her hair plastered to her face, caught in her eyes as she spread liquid soap over her body, began lathering it into her skin. The smell of vanilla was soothing. Baths and showers were her restoratives. After she'd received the call about Calvin's accident, she'd sat in a hot bath for hours until the water turned cold and she could no longer stand the chill. It had kept her sane in those ensuing hours, had stemmed the impulse to run through the house screaming.

Sanity was what she needed now. There were too many things she had to do. Plus there was Uncle Joe to worry about, as well as her mother. She couldn't afford to indulge in escapism, no matter how pleasurable. What she needed was to get back to normal, to heal.

She couldn't even think about Calvin right now without guilt . . . and trepidation. It had been horrible enough to see him in his grave, but to imagine him restless and wandering through the house, a witness to her every sin, that was more than her sanity could deal with. Sean was right, of course. The angry face in the window had only been her imagination, born of grief and guilt, two very powerful emotions that could play with the senses.

The blast of the water nearly drowned out the opening of the shower door. She stared at him blankly, his sudden appearance not fully registering. When it did, she felt a ridiculously overdue shyness as his eyes travelled along her naked body. She resisted the urge to cover herself with her hands.

"Sean, I'm taking a shower. Whatever it is can wait."

He looked unsure but determined. "Can I come in?" His hands were poised near the hem of his sweater, ready to pull it off.

She backed up against the wall, seeking space. "Sean, I need to be alone right now." But already she felt herself moistening, her body ready to betray her resolve. "Just go back to the room."

"Are you still freaked about what you think you saw?"

"No, Sean, I'm freaked about what we did . . . what I did. And just to let you know, it's not going to happen again. So if you think you're going to walk in here and . . . Sean, please just leave me alone."

She hadn't meant to say it so coldly but knew she hit a nerve when she saw his eyes narrow. The water seemed louder with his silence.

"OK, I'll get out."

And he left the bathroom, closing the door behind him.

She shut the stall door, finished her shower, feeling oddly guilty. But she had nothing to feel guilty about. He'd had no business invading her privacy.

After the shower, she towelled down and put on her robe. When she stepped into the bedroom, there was an echo of silence.

She knew then that he had not only left the bathroom and her room. Knew that if she walked to the guest room, she would find it empty and his suitcase gone.

She wanted to run down the stairs, out the door, call him back.

Instead, she got dressed and went downstairs to prepare for another pointless day.

Chapter 11

Joe Morgan could remember a time when his body worked in synchronicity with his brain. It hadn't been all that long ago, either. His fifties and early sixties had held none of the physical complaints that had torn down the bodies and eventually corroded the lives of his surviving friends. Now coming on the sunset of his sixties, his brain barked orders but his suddenly aged body stubbornly rebelled.

"Get on up, old man," he said aloud. His body tried to respond, but as he moved his left leg, the limb seemed to have forgotten its purpose, hanging precariously over the floor. Joe took all of his mental effort to force it to do what he wanted. Once he had his foot on the floor, he shifted his other arthritic leg, which achingly followed suit after some nudging. Several minutes later he was standing, if unsteadily.

Fifteen minutes later he was in the bathroom trying to steady his trembling frame over the toilet. As he relieved himself, he thought, not for the first time, that aging was one indignity after another that forced one to face up to the cruelties of time. Maybe it would have been better had he shuffled off this mortal coil a few years back when he was ahead of the game. Now he felt just like a doddering geezer, not unlike many of his buddies just before they joined their various subterranean communities.

He would have gladly gone to his maker if he could have

bartered for Calvin's life. It just wasn't right, his still being here when his grandnephew was no more.

Nothing seemed right these days. It was as though all of the life force that had bolstered him these many years had been buried alongside the boy. And now the only thing that tied him to this earth was a paltry assortment of decaying skin and nerves that barely held together.

Joe bathed and dressed, gaining strength with the familiar motions. By the time he settled in the kitchen and made his regular breakfast of poached egg whites, wheat toast, and apple juice (recommended by his doctor), he felt a tenth of his old self, which was just enough to get him through the day. He had just opened the morning paper when the kitchen phone jarred him from his reverie. He rose from the table and moved as fast as he could, which was a little quicker than a hobble. He had set the phone to ring seven times before it went into voice mail. Anyone who knew him knew it took him at least five rings to catch the phone. If they hung up before then, they weren't anyone he needed to be concerned with. He picked up.

"Yeah?"

"Joe?" It was Lacey. "How are you? Mom told me you're not doing so hot."

"Baby girl, your mama needs to tend to herself. She's not happy unless she's worrying about somebody. Been that way since we were kids."

"Yeah, I know, Uncle Joe. Still, I just want to make sure you're doing OK. Besides, I need some company tonight so I hope you haven't made any other plans. How does broiled pork chops sound?

"A whole lot less appetizing than chicken-fried chops with giblet gravy."

"Well, you're not getting any of that from me. Mom wouldn't let me hear the end of it if I served you up that much grease. We're hoping to keep you around for awhile."

"Don't know what for . . ."

"Joe . . ."

"I know, I know. You don't have to worry about me. I'm more worried about how you're doing. Everything OK? Your mama called yesterday, said you've got a houseguest."

A silence that stretched too long. "Yeah, well, he's gone now. Just one of Calvin's friends."

"That boy had a lot of friends. He sure knew how to pull people to him."

"Well, his friend's flying back home today, I guess. Or tomorrow. I don't know. He left the house this morning." Her voice faded on the last words.

"Anything wrong?"

"No. My mind's just wandering. Joe, please say you'll come tonight. I want you and Mom here."

"Estelle, too?"

"Yes, Estelle, too. I need my family around me."

He nodded as though she could see him. "I know, baby girl. I'm still reeling from it all. Seems like only days ago that Calvin and I were out on Lake Michigan trying to catch us some rainbow trout. I never could catch as many as he could. He was good at whatever he put his brain to."

"Well, he needed to have used that brain when driving."

"Don't be angry at him, sweetie. It does no good."

"Then who can I be angry at, Joe? Who? Because I need to feel something besides this pain. Look, don't mind me. I'm just lashing out."

"Well, baby girl, you're more than entitled. Maybe you shouldn't go back to work Monday. It might be too soon."

"I have to go back sometime. Bills aren't going to pay themselves. Besides, I need the distraction. Too much I need to forget."

"You're not trying to forget Calvin, are you?"

"No, of course not. Not him."

"Not him? Who, then? What's going on?"

"Nothing, Joe. Dinner's at seven. Estelle or Mom'll pick

you up around six-thirty. And just to make it worth your while, I'll have a small treat for you. Creamed potatoes."

"With giblet gravy?"

"No. Chicken broth."

"Girl, you sure know how to take the joy outta eating."

"And keep the fat out of your arteries. See you later, Joe."

She'd tried to put a smile in her voice, but it hadn't quite caught. She was trying to be strong for all of them, and she didn't have to be. Yet, no one had been able to convince her of that. She'd been the same way after Darryl had a heart attack at thirty-five. Way too young to be taken, just like Calvin. And yet, Lacey had survived, collected herself, and moved on.

But if anyone were to ask him, he'd have to say she'd never fully recovered, no matter how much time had passed. Survival was just existence, not true living.

She was a young woman, and if he'd said it a number of times, obviously no one was listening: Lacey needed some loving in her life. If she had someone now, instead of going it alone, this bad patch might not be so hard on her. Or at least there would be someone to help her through those nights the way that obviously he, her mother, and sister couldn't.

She didn't have to be alone. Hopefully, one day she would realize that.

"So, where are you now?" his mother asked over the phone.

The question ended on a slight cough, and Sean knew she had been smoking again. She'd told him she was going to quit. Still, he couldn't say anything. He had been trying to quit for nearly ten years.

"I'm just hanging out until my flight."

Actually, he was back at the hotel, having shelled out another $90 for just a few hours before he headed to the airport. This room looked out over the front parking area, but at least smelled of ammonia and Lemon Pledge, which was reassuring.

"Have you run into anybody from the neighborhood?" Her voice dropped several decibels, as though she thought someone might be listening in. She'd become paranoid since he'd told her he was coming back for Cal's funeral.

"Just Sam. And Suzanne. No one else."

"Well, good. It's probably better that way. Too many questions could get asked. So, did you get a chance to talk to Lacey?"

The question prompted a vision of Lacey standing naked in the shower. It was the first chance he'd really had to look at her up close, to visually appreciate every curve and swell. The memory made his breath quicken with desire and pain. She had practically told him to get out.

"Yes, I saw her at the funeral and . . . afterwards. She seems to be doing OK."

"Well, she can't be doing too OK, Sean. She just lost her son. I know how I'd be if I lost you, and it wouldn't be OK. I hope you took the time to give condolences for both of us. I know you, Sean. You'd go to the funeral, then cut out."

"Look, Ma, I spoke to her, all right? She's sad, but she has people looking out for her. She doesn't need me hanging around." That last bit hurt even more. No, she didn't need him around. He was a mistake she wanted to forget.

"No need to snap at me. You OK? The funeral get to you?"

"Well, it was hard seeing him in a casket like that. Just seems weird, you know? And Lace . . . I mean, Mrs. Burnham . . . she was grieving hard. I just wish there was more I could do for her."

"There's nothing you can do. This is something she's going to have to get through in time. So, you'll be back in Muncie this evening?"

"Yeah."

"How's the job going?"

Sean didn't like thinking about his dead-end job waiting tables, even though it was at a high-end restaurant. Still, it let him observe the ins and outs of managing a restaurant. One day, when everything was behind him, when enough time had passed, he might go to culinary school, get a degree, open his own restaurant. Although this was far from what he had planned to do when he was back in high school.

He hoped none of his old friends would ever find out he hadn't graduated. When he left Oak Park, he left more than just his records, his GPA, and his sure chance at an Ivy League university; he left behind the chance to move on with his life. That one night turned his whole life upside down. He'd do anything to go back and change things.

But he couldn't change a damn thing. Mistakes couldn't be undone.

Cal was dead now. Maybe the truth could finally come out.

Yet he couldn't bear to hurt Lacey. And the truth would hurt her.

"It's a job. It's keeping a roof over my head for right now."

"You don't sound too happy about it. You know, you could always move back to Vancouver. There are plenty of jobs here."

The thought had occurred to him more than a few times, especially those nights lying in his dingy apartment decorated with the latest style of peeling paint, listening to the dripping faucet in his kitchenette. It would be so easy just to leave everything behind. To leave the States again.

But he wanted his old life back.

No, that wasn't true. He wanted a new life, a better life. With someone he could love.

"Yeah, I know. Maybe . . . sometime in the future. I have to go now, Ma. I'll call you when I get into Muncie."

He hit the "disconnect" button and dialed Sam's number. He wanted to make sure his old friend was home when he returned the bike. He also wanted to bum a ride to O'Hare. In another five hours he would be in the air, leaving Oak Park behind for good.

All he would have left of this place would be memories.

Some painful. Some bitter. One in particular, disturbing. But then there was one other.

A flash of warm lips and soft skin ran through his mind. Taste, touch, and smell made the memory exquisite.

At least he would have something to focus on during lonely nights. A whole lot better than concentrating on ceiling flakes.

He pushed the thoughts away as Sam answered on the third ring and he began arrangements to get out of town.

Calvin listened to the sound of Uncle Joe's laugh, buttery and thick like the molasses his mother used to pour over his waffles. It warmed his cold soul, made him forget he wasn't part of this world anymore. His uncle looked much stronger than he had when he first walked into the house, almost like his old self. Joe was always in his element when telling a story. Right now he was sitting in his old favorite leather chair in the living room, pantomiming with his hands how Calvin had fought to land a catfish into their rickety boat. It had been on one of their camping trips to Axehead Lake inside the county forest preserve. On this particular trip, the boat had sprung a slow leak that forced them to race back to the bank before they were totally weighted down.

Calvin perked up his ears as he fought for the memory, found it with some exertion, but it was nothing more than a series of black-and-white instances, mimeographed collages that barely came together. Still, he remembered that he had been about twelve. Almost a year after his father died.

"I swear, that boy would not let go of that fish for anything. Here I am, shouting for him to throw it back, and help me bail. And what does he do? He bails out the water with one hand, and holds on to that thrashing body with the other. Put his fingernails right through those scales and refused to let go. And boy, that fish was some angry creature."

Calvin saw the smiles on the women's faces, an eager audience when he was the subject. His mother's laughter warmed him even more. He had already forgiven her for what she'd done earlier today, although he had a hard time understanding why. Most of his anger had dissipated when Sean left the house, sneaking out like the coward he was. Although he had lost his chance for retribution, he felt better knowing that his mother was no longer threatened. That Sean wouldn't be touching her again. Still, part of the anger remained, knowing that he had touched her at all.

"Calvin was always stubborn like that," his mother piped in. "But that's how he got as far as he did. When the school counselor told me he was dyslexic, I almost let that man convince me to put Calvin in a remedial class. But Cal wouldn't hear of it. 'No, Ma, I can do this. I can show them. I'm not a dummy.' He would study extra hours, and worked with his tutor . . . and he kept his word and improved his grades. And all of this while playing ball. I don't know how he did it. But it was one of the things that made me so proud, the fact that he wouldn't just take what life meted out to him. He wanted so much more."

A sudden moan. "That poor baby." Aunt Estelle swiped at a tear.

His mother walked over to her sister sitting on the couch, began rubbing her shoulders. "Stell, we're going to get through this, OK? I'm sure that if Cal were still here . . ." she paused and exchanged a look with her mother. "We just have to go on living. That's what he'd want us to do."

"I know, I know. I don't mean to be such a whiner."

"Estelle, you are not whining. You're grieving like the rest of us. But tonight, we're going to try not to be sad, OK? We're going to think only about the good times, what we had when he was here. And what we're going to do moving forward. Which reminds me, how're the plans for your trip coming along? You're still going, right?"

Estelle touched her hand to her sister's, her mouth pursed. "Who wants to go to Peru this time of year?"

"Well, sweetie, you did. That's why you made your plans

months ago. And I'm not going to let you waste your money sitting at home moping, even if I have to drag you to the airport myself."

"That's right, Estelle," his grandmother said forcefully, half leaning out of her chair. "Cancelling this trip isn't going to bring Cal back, so you might as well go on and have some fun. Just make sure you don't get stung by any scorpions."

"Now, ladies, she don't need to worry about no scorpions. It's them damn mosquitoes with malaria that's going to be the problem," Joe said with an authoritarian's wisdom. Or more like the worldview of someone who liked watching the Discovery Channel.

"Joe, stop that!" his grandmother turned a wicked eye on his grandfather. They were always getting into it. "Don't be teasing her. Besides, malaria is in Africa, not South America. All Estelle needs to do is go and enjoy herself. And don't find any scorpions. Maybe she'll find a nice young man instead."

"Mom," both daughters admonished in chorus.

"You need to stop matchmaking," Estelle said with some of her old sass that had been overshadowed in these weeks. "I'm not going on this trip to manhunt. This is just an educational excursion so I can make a photologue to show my kids."

Estelle's "kids" were her tenth-grade class at St. Augustus.

"I'm not saying anything else," their mother said, her voice peeved. For as long as Cal could remember, their grandmother had been trying to get Estelle with somebody. At least, he sort of remembered other occasions when his grandmother had made a big deal about Estelle's "condition."

"Your mother's only looking out for you girls," Joe said. "'S nothing wrong with that. Both of you need to find somebody."

Cal stiffened, looked over at his mother's expression. But right now, it was neutral. She wasn't giving anything away.

"I'm not thinking about that right now, Uncle Joe. My

only goal in the coming weeks is getting back to normal, finding a way to go back to a job I don't particularly like . . . and finding out what to do with myself for the rest of my life."

"That's what I'm talking about, sweetheart. Life shouldn't be a series of days to get through. There should be some living, some loving involved."

"Look who's talking," Estelle said to him. "How come you never married Ms. Mabel?"

Joe's expression fell and now he looked every minute of his age. Even more so. Something went out of him.

"Did it ever occur to you girls that I might've asked, that she said no?"

Both his mom and aunt peeked at each other, their faces an identical mirror of shock.

"Uncle Joe, I'm sorry. It never occurred to me . . ." his mother started.

"It never occurred to you that this old man had had some heartaches in his life. Mabel was my heart, but in the end, she didn't want to be with me. It's enough to break a man."

"But you never said anything," Estelle said, her tone subdued, chastened.

"I never said anything to either of you 'cause it was my business and I didn't see any reason spreading it all over. Life is what it is—you go on and live with the pain. The one thing you don't do is let the pain take you down. You hear that, baby girls? You can't let anything take you down, otherwise you might as well be in your graves. I learned the most important lesson and it took years for it to get through—you gotta find what makes you happy and hold on to it. Don't let it get away. Mabel left me because I didn't do her like she wanted. And in the end, I had to live with my mistake. What I'm telling you is, don't go making the same mistake I did. Which means that Estelle, you need to stop trying to go it alone like it's the most normal thing in the world. And you,

Lacey, got to stop believing your life ended with Darryl and Calvin. And another thing: if you don't like your job, go find you another one."

"Sure thing, Uncle Joe. I'll just leave my six figures as a marketing consultant and do what, then? Open a cookie shop?"

"If that's what you want. Although, to be honest, baby girl, your cookies are all right, but if you were to go into business, your recipes would need some major tweaking."

"Joe, you know those recipes are mine!" his grandmother exclaimed.

"Ain't going down this road any further, then," Uncle Joe smiled.

"Well, then I think I'll keep my day job."

"Now, don't let me talk you out of doing what you got to do. Do what makes you happy, girl. Life's shorter than you think. We all found that out the cruelest way we could. Ain't none of us thought we'd outlive that boy, and yet here we are and where is he?"

For a second, Calvin thought his grandmother was staring at him. The look sent shivers through him. And his mother looked more apprehensive than sad. Of course, he hadn't meant to scare her. He hadn't realized that she might ever be able to see him. But since then, he had been trying to make her see him again and now she couldn't.

But his grandmother seemed to be able to sense him. Like right now . . .

"I'd hope he would be in heaven. But I'm not so sure anymore," his grandmother said sadly.

"Mom!" his mother said, her expression shaken.

Uncle Joe's face was more hardened than shocked. "What's that supposed to mean? You're not saying that boy went to the other place, are you? 'Cause there's no reason he should be there. He was a good boy, a good son, nephew, and grandson. What more could God ask for?"

"Of course I'm not saying that, Joe. I'm just saying . . ."

she stopped, seemingly struggling for words. "Oh, never, mind. I'm just an old woman with a lot of imagination. It's just sometimes I feel that Calvin never left. Like right now, I feel that he's right here in the room with us."

"Mom, that's crazy." Estelle sat up, looking uncomfortably at her mother, but Calvin saw his aunt begin to peer around as though his grandmother's words had conjured up some unhealthy mojo.

His own mother said nothing, but just looked at her mother sadly, as though she feared her mother was right.

"But Mom, why wouldn't he be able to move on?" she finally asked.

"What are you two talking about?" Estelle got to her feet and walked to stand next to Joe, still seated in the leather chair, seeking reinforcement from the only other one who seemed sane at the moment.

Both his grandmother and mother ignored Estelle. They sought an answer in each other's faces. "Maybe something he needs to still get done," his grandmother offered to her worried daughter. "Have you . . . felt . . . ?"

"Doodo, doodo," Uncle Joe began, mimicking the theme from *The Twilight Zone*. "Y'all starting to sound like you both stepped out of Rod Serling land. Look, there's no such things as ghosts, vampires, werewolves, or aliens. OK, maybe there might be a chance we've had some otherworldly visitors, but by otherworldly I mean a nearby galaxy somewhere. That's more believable than . . ."

"Than what, Uncle Joe? The existence of a spirit? Since that's what we're taught in every church, every denomination . . . that we're more than flesh, then who's to say whether or not a spirit can hang around for whatever reason?"

Uncle Joe stood, angry now. "This is nothing but nonsense. And you got your mother buying into this mess. Calvin is not here! He's in heaven!"

Calvin had been standing near the window, observing from a safe emotional distance. But the emotions in the room flowed through him, empowered him. He backed away, confused. And backed into the marble-topped table holding his mother's favorite lamp. A keepsake from his parents' honeymoon, he had hardly ever paid it any attention. He just knew that his mother loved the intricate shell pattern on the ceramic base that reminded her of Hawaii.

The pattern burst into a thousand little shards as it hit the hardwood floor near the window.

Cal froze, feeling suddenly exposed. Not that he hoped to hide from his family, but he had become used to his invisibility.

But the way his folks looked around the room, then at each other, he knew he was still invisible.

And yet . . .

"What the hell was that?" His uncle's question shattered the shocked silence that followed the lamp's falling to the floor.

His grandmother seemed less disturbed than everyone around her. "You all are going to learn to believe this old lady one day." And she smiled.

Chapter 12

Sean watched as the young woman tried desperately to reason with the screaming toddler. She might have been about nineteen or twenty, although her frustrated expression and pink "Hello Kitty" shirt peeking from beneath a pink jacket gave her a juvenile appearance. She peered around apprehensively, aware of the attention they were drawing. Her hair was dark and mid-length to her neck, her face freckled. But Sean could easily imagine her with flowing red hair and a near-flawless complexion. The toddler, a girl whose face was red and scrunched up in her tantrum, had the woman's features and coloring, but that didn't necessarily mean the woman was the girl's mother. No matter her relationship to the child, she was obviously overwhelmed.

He sat in the terminal waiting area, his battered suitcase taking up the chair beside him. The woman and girl were sitting across from him, pulling his attention despite his best efforts to ignore them. The woman finally retrieved a pink stuffed rabbit from a large carry-on bag and offered it to the little girl, but the girl slapped it to the floor. For some reason, the action made the child scream even more.

Two seats down from them a gray-haired man in a brown tweed jacket and holding a newspaper threw the woman an exasperated look, half turned, seemed about to say something, then thought better of it. He went back to his paper, holding it closer to his face as though hiding the view next to him would somehow muffle the child's volume.

The screaming girl began squirming, shimmied out of the chair, at the same time pulling out of the woman's grasp. She was angry at something and was determined not to be comforted. The woman tried to catch her, but the child evaded her by darting toward Sean. And ran smack into his legs.

"Hey there," he said, grasping the little girl to keep her from bouncing to the floor. She cried louder, pulling away from him.

"I'm so sorry," the woman said as she stood and tried to pick up the toddler. "She's having a bad day." More enraged, the girl began twisting violently, trying to elude capture.

"Sarah, Sarah, stop!"

But Sarah had no intention of stopping. She kicked out a foot, lost her balance, and fell with a thud to the floor. Impossibly, the screams got worse. The elderly gentleman abruptly stood with a huff, and moved several rows away from them.

Sean wasn't sure what to do. For some reason, he now felt dragged into the drama and responsible for calming the child.

Sarah got up again, twisted away from the young woman, and turned to run up the aisle. The whole waiting area sat with expressions of impatience, curiosity, or plain disgust, silently looking on to see how the whole thing was going to play out. Sean felt the waves of judgment directed at the woman and couldn't help but feel sorry for her. Which was why he found himself jumping up from his seat and running after the little girl. He caught her in two strides, lifted her up in his arms and held on tightly to the squirming body. Her screams were shrill knives in his ear. She struck out a hand, connected with his nose, actually causing some pain.

"Sarah!" he said with an authority he didn't feel, considering he was a stranger and had no right to even be holding her.

The timbre of his voice got the little girl's attention as she looked at him with wide eyes. Maybe she wasn't used to being bellowed at.

But just as quickly, she began to scrunch her face up again, ready to let go with another volley of ear-splitting cries. "Hey Sarah," he said in a gentler voice. "It's OK. It's OK. I got you."

The young woman came up to him, but instead of taking Sarah, she held out the forsaken pink rabbit. "This is her favorite toy. Could you give it to her?"

Sean realized that the mother was abdicating her role, and drafting him to become peacemaker. Sean took the toy, feeling little hope that the girl would have changed her sentiment toward the animal. Still, he held it up. "See the bunny, Sarah. Here's the bunny."

She shook her head violently. Well, at least it wasn't a scream, and at least there was some communication going on now. "Don't want the bunny? Then tell me what you want."

The face was contemplative as she looked up at him with teary brown eyes. "Mousey . . ." she said with solemnity.

Sean turned to the mother. "Mousey?"

"Oh, God! I totally forgot. She loves that animal. And of course, I went and left it back at my mother's. What am I going to do?"

The woman looked so stricken, for a moment Sean wanted to laugh. He couldn't imagine a parent this intimidated by a small child. Could never imagine a case where it wasn't the parent inspiring the fear.

He stroked the girl's head, trying to see how long he could prolong this détente. She seemed quiet for the moment, having gotten her message to someone who could understand. All of this because of a missing stuffed animal. The thought triggered something in his brain.

"You know, I think I saw some stuffed animals in a souvenir shop here somewhere. They might have a mouse."

The little girl heard the word "mouse" and actually cracked a small smile. It was obvious who was the boss here.

"But I don't have any more money," the woman whined. "I spent the last on a McDonald's kiddie meal."

Sean sighed. The little girl bopped his nose with her head.

"I think I got a little change left. I'll go see what the store has. Here, take her." But when he tried to hand the child back to her mother, the woman just shook her head.

"Please. Could you keep holding her? She seems to like you and I'm afraid she'll start crying again. We can walk with you."

He looked at the clock over the terminal desk. It was already a few minutes past ten. Their flight was scheduled for eleven-thirty, but the plane hadn't even arrived yet. And there was the matter of his luggage. He didn't want to have to tote both the girl and his suitcase. He doubted the woman would trust him alone with the child while she watched their bags.

"Look, the shop's just past the food court. You stay here and watch my bag and I'll be back in less than ten minutes." Before the woman could protest, Sean hustled Sarah back to her mother, then did a quick about-face in the other direction. Even before he had rounded the corner leading to the food court, he heard the child's wails.

It took him several minutes to find the shop, and when he entered, he immediately saw that the selection of animals was limited. He stared among the assortment on the shelf behind the register, which really wasn't an assortment at all. There were two giraffes, one yellow, the other blue. There was an ugly green frog with a red tongue hanging obscenely from his gaping mouth. He could imagine Sarah's reaction to that one. Somewhere between a wail of terror and a scream of horror. Sitting near the far right edge was a small gray elephant. Not having much choice, he made a quick decision. Even though the elephant wasn't a "mousey," given its size, it might just fool the little girl. He'd have to explain away the trunk somehow. He looked at the price tag: $14.99. He shook his head as he pulled out his last $20, wondering again how he managed to get entangled in someone else's mini drama.

The Asian lady behind the counter smiled as she rang up the purchase. "I'm sure your little one will like it. Cute, huh?"

Sean gave her a half smile as he took his change and the

plastic bag with the elephant. On the walk back to the waiting area, he pondered the words, "your little one." This would be something he would have done as a father, buying his "little one" a stuffed animal, picking her up to comfort her. To calm her fear, her anger.

His dad had barely done that for him. The one memory he had of any real tenderness between him and his father happened years ago, so long ago that he wasn't sure it was an actual memory, but rather some fantasy he'd dreamed up.

There definitely hadn't been any stuffed animals in his house when he was growing up. His father had said they were too "sissy" for a boy. When he was older, his toys consisted mainly of G. I. Joes and Rambo action figures ("They aren't dolls," his father proclaimed) and his father's hand-me-down BB gun. Trying to make a "real man" out of him, his dad had taken him out to open fields and encouraged him to shoot birds with the deadly buckshots. But Sean had deliberately misfired, not caring that his father thought he was a rotten shot. The only thing he came away with from those forced outings was a healthy aversion to guns.

Sean shook the thought away. He didn't like thinking about his dad.

The wail wasn't as audible as he neared the waiting area. Sarah was struggling against her mother, but her motions were halfhearted now. Sean suspected that the girl had simply worn herself out. In another hour, she'd probably be asleep, finally giving her mother some rest.

The young woman looked up with relief when she saw Sean. He took the seat next to her and eased the elephant out of the bag. The disappointment on the woman's face was almost palpable. But Sean held the stuffed animal up to Sarah, who had petered down to a whimper upon Sean's approach.

"Look, Sarah. Look who wants to meet you. It's Mr. Mousey."

Sarah gave the animal an angry look. "Not Mousey!" she declared with finality.

But Sean wouldn't give up. "It is, too. Look, it's a big mousey. With big, big ears and a big nose. Look, he wants to smell you." And he tweaked the elephant's nose against the child's nose. He stopped short of assuming a "Mr. Mousey" voice to get his point across. He wasn't used to entertaining kids, didn't know how to even do voices, and felt a little silly waving the elephant in the girl's face.

But then, a smile began peeking through. She reached out a tentative hand, stroked the elephant's trunk. And laughed. Sean released his grip, and the child eagerly took full possession. Her fascination complete, she sat in her mother's lap, gleefully playing with her new toy.

"Thank's sooo much. You're a lifesaver."

"No problem." He was set to go back to his seat next to his suitcase, but her next question stopped him. "So do you have a kid of your own?"

The question unexpectedly stung him.

"Uhm, no."

"Didn't mean to assume anything—it's just that you seem to have a way with her, so I thought you might have a kid yourself. Sarah doesn't usually let strangers pick her up. She's kinda high-strung, but I guess you've figured that out already. My mother says she's just picky. I don't know what you call it, but whatever it is, I hope she grows out of it soon. I don't think I can take too much of these terrible twos."

"You both'll be all right. Probably mothers go through this all the time. I know I didn't make it too easy on my mother when I was a kid."

"I guess everybody here thinks I'm a bad mother. But Sarah's not always like this. I'm just not good at handling her when she's this way. There's so much you have to deal with with a small kid, ya know? I'm glad I didn't know about all this back when I was pregnant. I don't think I would've gone through with it—I mean, having her."

Sean looked at Sarah, her eyes fighting to stay open. She was beginning to drift off. He thought how providence had worked to make sure she came into this world. And how it had failed with his own child.

"I guess I was too young to be having a kid. I'm eighteen now, but I had just turned sixteen when I got pregnant. Now that she's here . . . well, I love her, even with her temper. She can be quite sweet when she wants to be, though. I just wish she wanted to be a lot more often. Oh, I'm sorry. I'm going on and on and I haven't even told you my name. It's Raquel."

"Hey, Raquel. I'm Sean."

She started in again, laying out her life for him, and he realized that for whatever reason, she needed to unload, and had chosen him as her sounding board. He sat there listening as she related her tale of a teenage dalliance that fizzled out, but not before she was left with her "sweet" little memento. Again, Suzanne popped into his head, and he understood as he listened to Raquel's hardships, that he was forgiving Suzanne right then, that the anger that might have grown and eventually erupted would now never get a chance to truly form.

He faded back in when she asked him a question. "So, do you live in Muncie?"

He nodded. "Yeah," he said halfheartedly.

"Don't sound too happy about it. So, why're you here in Chicago? Me, I came to visit my mother. Your folks live here?"

"No, I flew in for a funeral. In Oak Park, actually. A friend got killed in an auto accident."

"I'm sorry. How old was he?"

"Twenty-one."

She shook her head at the enormity of someone that close to her age leaving this world.

"Wow. So, were you two really close?"

Sean stared at his fingers, his feet, the floor. "Yeah, we were close. Once."

"Drifted apart, huh?"

"Something like that." He didn't elaborate, hoping she would just drop the subject. When he thought about Calvin now, the thought eventually turned to Lacey. And he didn't want to think about her. And yet, she somehow managed to sneak into his mind when he least wanted or expected it.

"So, what're you going to do when you get home?"

The question shouldn't have taken him by surprise. It was just an ordinary, throwaway question. But it forced him to really think about the answer. What was he going to do? Go back to his apartment where he would put away his clothes, then catch a few winks before he drove his old Chevy to Foxfire's and clocked in. Where he would smile, wink at the ladies, take their orders as he evaded wandering hands that "accidentally" found his ass or crotch. If he wanted, he could get laid every night by some of the grander dames with bottomless purses who would probably reward him for an evening well spent. On a few occasions, he had been tempted.

He had even tried a girlfriend or two, but the fit never seemed to mesh. So, the lonely nights.

He was tired of those nights. Of his days.

He was tired of Muncie.

And he didn't want to go back to Vancouver, either.

"I don't know what I'm going to do," he said softly.

A voice came over the intercom. "Flight 366 to Muncie has just arrived. We will be boarding in twenty minutes. Again, we will be boarding in twenty minutes."

"Well, I guess that's us, then. Look, she's asleep."

Sean looked at the little girl. Quiet like she was now, she was the picture of sweetness, like her mother had said. One hand clutched her new friend, and the other was at her mouth while she sucked her thumb in her sleep.

"Maybe one day, you'll have a little girl of your own," Raquel said, looking down on Sarah with a smile.

Sean sat there and pondered the possibility of one day having a family of his own. Of finally being happy.

Forty minutes later, he was still sitting there when the plane took off.

Chapter 13

The walk along the carpeted corridor of cubicles seemed more like a stroll down King's Green Mile. Lacey hated the solemn looks, the solicitous smiles, the awkward silences. She understood her coworkers were simply following some unwritten protocol on dealing with the grief-stricken, but their reactions only made her feel on display.

She breathed a sigh of relief when she finally opened the door to her office and shut it behind her. The glass front looked out on her secretary's empty cubicle. Tanya was usually in by eight-thirty and it was almost nine now. Something must have happened with her car again.

Lacey took the seat behind her desk and peered at the inbox filled with a week's worth of backlog. Even though her body was present, her mind was in various places: standing in the viewing room at Williams Brothers Funeral Home looking down at Calvin's scarred face; shivering in the cemetery as she watched his casket sink below the grave's perimeter; in the backyard seeing Calvin's face through the window; later, in the bedroom, watching Sean sleep and wanting more. She felt a pang and pushed it away. She needed to be here, to get some normalcy, some perspective.

She picked up the overstuffed red folder topping the inbox pile. The Schumann file. She hadn't spoken with Mr. Schumann in over two weeks, but if she knew Carol, Carol would have already gone forward with their promotional campaign for Schumann Foods. Luckily, Carol couldn't take credit for it. Most of the campaign hinged on Lacey's ideas of enlarging the food distributor's Internet site, placing interactive banners on the more prominent portals and search engines, as well as doing a direct mail targeted to supermarkets in New York, Chicago, Vegas, and San Francisco, the locations of Schumann's offices.

When she'd first received the account, she had been pretty excited. It was a major coup to get the multinational distributor as her personal client. But that had been a mere blip in an otherwise uneventful tenure at Meredith Stephens & McCray. Her dissatisfaction had been coming to a head even before Calvin, and now since his death, nothing seemed important anymore. The incentive was no longer there. Just the large paycheck, and she had already concluded that the money wasn't enough.

Still, she looked at Carol's posted notes attached just inside the folder. The largest one read:

> *Lace, we've decided not to go with the interactive site or the mail drop. Just too costly. Bill agrees with me that the money could be put to better use by featuring Schumann on well-placed billboards in key cities as well as doing the TV promo we discussed before. I know you had some problems with it, but in the end, I think the promo will be more effective.*

"Damn it!" Lacey slammed the file down on the desk. She rose and marched to the door, opening it with such force, it banged against the wall. Carol's office was several doors down, and Lacey felt rather than saw the questioning eyes peering up from their computers as she strode down the hall. She consciously slowed her hurried steps, but she knew her anger was visible in her expression and her eyes. Jim, one of the copyeditors, swiveled his chair to follow her progress.

She didn't acknowledge Carol's surprised secretary, nor did she bother knocking before she opened the door. The marketing manager sat demurely, dressed in a Laura Ashley print blouse dotted along the front with small fuschia roses. Most of Carol's wardrobe tended along the line of Laura Ashley or Anne Klein, varying between a garden-tending Stepford wife and an urban sophisticate. The gold-and-walnut pen Carol had received in appreciation from the Ceylas account sat upright in her hand, paused over a proof page. Brown eyes widened at Lacey's abrupt entry, widened even more at Lacey's face. Lacey closed the door behind her, walked to the desk.

"Just read your note in my Schumann file. Who gave you the go-ahead to change the plans? Everything was all set. This is going to put us behind on the clock."

Carol lost the deer-in-the-headbeams look and assumed her usual business demeanor. Despite the neutral expression, Lacey knew the woman was quivering inside.

"Bill and I concluded that we could reach a wider market with billboards and a limited television campaign."

Lacey gritted her teeth. "I seem to remember us having this discussion weeks ago. Television reaches outside our targeted market and will only waste a whole lot of money. And, I'm curious, whose idea were the billboards?"

"Well, I . . . I mean, Bill . . ." Carol's eyes dimmed over. "Bill basically thought . . ."

Lacey shook her head. "Don't even try it. This wasn't Bill's idea. More like *you* whispering in Bill's ear and yanking his balls so he'd get in line behind you, like he always does. One would think you were the EVP, not Bill."

"There's no need to get personal, Lace." Carol's voice rose an octave, but was restrained. Restraint was her trademark. Armageddon could fall right in the middle of the office and Carol would tell everybody just to keep a reasonable perspective.

"Everything was settled and budgeted down to the last cent, Carol. More importantly, the client loved the ideas. So, what did Schumann have to say about the changes?"

"He told us to go with it. As long as it saves him money."

"But it doesn't."

"In the end run . . ."

"In the end run, we will have wasted half a million dollars for old standards. The idea is to target our actual market and not throw money out there willy-nilly, hoping to get a few nibbles."

"Look, Lace, I think I know this business well enough . . ."

"You forget I know this business just a little better as I've got more years here and the MBA in marketing to prove it."

"Lacey, I don't see the need to start comparing résumés. This isn't a slight against you."

"Isn't it? Then why wait until I'm out of the office before you make all of these changes. This is not only a bad move, but it's a lack of respect for my input. After all, this is . . . *was* . . . my account."

"And it still is," a voice said from the door. Lacey turned to see Bill standing in the doorway, a sheen of sweat glistening on his balding pate. He stepped in and closed the door.

"Ladies, I could hear you through the wall, which means we need to watch our voices. Let's just clear the air before this gets further out of hand. Take a seat, Lace." He pointed to one of two chairs fronting Carol's desk.

Lacey's first impulse was to refuse. She was simmering and didn't feel the least bit like playing the cooperative company player. Still, she took her seat and tried to keep her resentment in check as Bill sat alongside her. She didn't have to look at Carol to know that the woman was probably trying to hide a look of triumph. After all, Bill was here now and Bill was going to clear the mess up for her. As he always did. It occurred to Lacey for the hundredth time that there was definitely something going on between these two.

"Lace, I know you're unsettled by everything that's happened in the last few weeks. It can't be easy dealing with Calvin's death. Anything that dreadful is bound to make one lose perspective."

Lacey felt the heat of blood rushing to her face, had to fight to stay in her seat and not pounce. Instead, she took a breath, and spoke evenly.

"This isn't about Calvin. This is about the lack of respect I get around here. The least either of you could have done is consult me before making any major changes to *my* account."

"We had to make a snap decision, Lace, because we had to run the plan by senior management on short notice. This is a major account and we can't afford to blow it."

"So my ideas would have blown the account, is that what you're saying?"

"No, no," came a chorus from both Bill and Carol. "No, your ideas were very good," Bill continued. Carol nodded her head. "But this Internet thing is chancy."

She started to back up her argument with well-established numbers showing how pivotal Internet marketing was to a successful campaign, how peer-to-peer and business-to-customer Web sites could enlarge a customer base and expand good will. But this was common sense she knew Bill, and especially Carol, wasn't really willing to listen to. Their ears were open only to what they wanted to hear.

At that moment, she felt superfluous. Realized that she had been all along. Her decision was made even before she had fully thought it through. She didn't often act on impulse but it felt right, as she spoke to Bill, totally ignoring Carol.

"Bill, I feel it's time for me to move on. There's not much more I can contribute here."

For a second, Bill looked stricken. "Lace, look, you're overreacting here . . ."

"No, no, I'm not. I'm acting within reason. This isn't the first time my ideas have been pushed aside. What am I doing here, really?"

"You're the manager over marketing and a damn good one at that. Which is why you should really think this through before you do something rash."

She felt tired all of a sudden. Tired and sad. Because she realized at this moment that even though she was making a major move by walking away, she didn't feel a thing. No regrets, not even fear. Nor did she feel the relief she had envisioned in her fantasies about leaving her job, breaking free.

Since Calvin's death, her life had been numbed down to an alternating haze of pain and nothingness. Only for a bright second had the fog cleared, allowing her to expand beyond the grief, the void. But that second was gone, too, the memory of it threatening to become subsumed into the emptiness.

She rose from her seat and Bill and Carol stood in concert. They exchanged a look, which was an odd mixture of confusion and intimacy. Definitely something going on there. She expected to see triumph on Carol's face. Strangely, what she detected was something that looked close to fear.

Carol was the one who pleaded. "Lacey, we can talk about this."

She turned to the woman who had been a constant thorn in her side. "That's just it, Carol, we can't." She walked to the door, turned back to Bill. "You'll get the two weeks and then I'm gone." And with that, she closed the door on both of them.

Chapter 14

"You did what!?"

Lacey pictured Estelle's face on the other end of the phone. Her left eyebrow would have shot up and the right side of her mouth would have turned down. That was her sister's usual *You did what!?* look.

Lacey had been home for nearly two hours now. She'd walked out of Carol's office very tired and barely able to complete a coherent thought. To the dismay of her secretary, Tanya, who had finally made it in moments after Lacey had finished her confrontation with Bill and Carol, Lacey grabbed her briefcase, closed her office door, and told Tanya she was going home. She'd left the building as quickly and quietly as she could, ignoring the curious eyes. She would give them their two weeks, attend the endless meetings, answer the repetitive e-mails, deal with the redundant obligations, but not today. She had unofficially designated this "No Bullshit Day" and had observed it by leaving at ten instead of her usual six. Today she was just too spent of energy—physical, mental, and emotional—to deal with anything or anyone.

"You heard me right, Stell. I quit, I resigned, I left."

"You're not going back?"

"That's usually how it's done. You quit, you don't go back."

A long pause. "Well, at least the house is paid for. But still, what are you going to do for income now? Lacey, did you even think this through?"

"No," she sighed. "Something happened today that was the last straw. That, on top of everything else, just made me realize I'd had enough. I told you before how they treated me, almost from the first day. I might as well have been a shadow on the wall for all the appreciation I got. No amount of money is worth dealing with that, day after day. I think the only reason I stayed as long as I did was because of Calvin. But . . . I don't have to anymore."

"Lacey, you still have bills . . ."

"And I'll find a way to take care of them."

"How?"

"You need to know right now?"

"No, *you* do."

"Listen, Stell, I didn't call to get lectured."

Another pause. "I'm sorry, Lacey. But you can't call and tell me you quit your job and expect me to break out the champagne. This is a serious move, and if you don't know what you're going to do, believe me, this will turn around and bite a good chunk out of your ass. You can't even ask for references now."

"I'd only need references if I was staying in the same field."

"So . . . you're leaving marketing altogether? I thought you liked marketing."

"I do, to an extent. I just didn't like the office politics, the pandering, the fawning, not to mention the obsolescence they condemned me to. Or the fact that I barely believed in anything I was palming off on the public. Not to mention all the -isms. And don't tell me to try another firm; they're all the same. Stell, I can do better than this. I know I can. I have to . . . because, I have nothing else."

The break in her voice was unexpected. She realized she desperately needed to get the rest of her life in focus, otherwise she would be totally lost. Walking away from a job that she had begun to loathe was a step in the right direction. Wasn't it?

"Oh, sweetie, don't say you have nothing. Because you have more than you realize. First of all, you have family who love you. Never forget that. Also, you have the brains and skill to do whatever you need to do. You're going to find your way out of this and come through better than before. I know this may sound callous, but your whole world didn't stop with Calvin. Again, I'm sorry if I'm sounding unsympathetic. It's just that I'm worried about you, and don't tell me not to, because I'm going to worry about my younger sister. Remember what you told me the other day? That we have to go on living? Well, let me throw those words back at you because they make a whole lot of sense."

Lacey wiped away the lone tear coursing down her cheek, smiled, and just as quickly lost the smile as the enormity of what she'd done finally hit her. "Oh God, Stell, I *don't* know what I'm going to do." She took a much-needed breath as she fought the onset of panic. "Well, at least I have some savings, but that'll only hold me over for a little while."

"Well, if you need a little extra, I have some money . . ."

"No, Stell. I'm not taking your money. I'm going to do fine . . . once I figure out what it is I'm going to do."

"What is it you want to do, Lacey?"

Lacey started to answer, fumbled as she realized she didn't know. Growing up, she had wandered through fantasies of becoming an actress, a choreographer, and during her more sensible moments, even a doctor, none of which were feasible for a forty-two-year-old woman starting over. She had chosen marketing in college because it had piqued her interest. But now she wanted something more.

"Maybe you can start your own firm."

"And go up against the big firms? No, thanks. I wouldn't last the year out. No, I have to be smart from this point on. But your suggestion makes sense in one way; I'm never going to be happy working for someone else. Whatever I choose, I never want to have to put up with the shit I dealt with at Meredith."

"But, sister dear, you're only going to get another pail of shit. A different pail, but still shit. At least it'll be your own, though, and that tends not to be as putrid."

"Ugh, thanks for that picture."

"Feel better?"

"Yeah, I do. Thanks for backing me up, Stell."

"Well, I'm told that's what sisters do, so I'm sticking with the handbook."

When Lacey hung up, she did feel better. At least enough to push back the panic and know that she would find a way to survive. On her own terms.

Yes, she would survive. She'd lost a husband and her son. This was nothing compared to that pain.

Sam's cot felt lumpy as hell and the smell of gasoline flushed with motor oil stifled Sean's breaths in the claustrophobic room. The lone window was sealed shut, preventing the entry of crisp, lung-cleansing air. Sean shifted off the broken spring that threatened to stab his ass, his mind trying to straighten out the thousand thoughts straddling his brain, jumping around. The wall clock indicated it was almost half past ten. The sun barely filtered in from another dreary day.

If he were smart, he would have Sam take him back to the airport, make up some reason why he'd missed his plane yesterday, and hope a sympathetic agent would allow him to board another flight to Muncie. Then he could forget this lame idea of starting over, stop thinking he could have some sort of life again in Oak Park. As though the last few years could be easily erased. As though what happened that night over five years ago wouldn't begin plaguing his dreams, haunting his steps.

But even that torment would be worth it if only . . . But he knew he couldn't just go back to her, ask her to let him into her life. Into her bed. Especially when she had made it clear she considered him a mistake she'd rather not think about.

The thumps on the stairs outside brought him out of his reverie as the door to the garage apartment opened and Sam walked in with two cans of Budweiser. "You finally up?"

"Yeah. Man, you need to get you another bed. This one's crap." Sean shifted his behind again for effect.

Sam shut the door, walked over to the cot to hand a can to Sean, but Sean shook his head.

"Gonna have a whole new bedroom set one day," Sam said as he settled into a green beanbag chair crisscrossed with black tape that rounded out his minimalist décor of chair, two tables, and cot. A small refrigerator sat on one of the tables. "The bed's gonna have black leather sheets and down pillows. May take some months, but I'm gonna get me some new furniture and gear, too. And the place ain't gonna be some studio, either, man. I'm already eyeing a walk-up in Rogers Park that's pretty sweet. Right near the lake."

Sean half nodded at his friend's ambition for better digs, but doubted that Sam would be moving out of the garage apartment anytime soon. Sam worked as a clerk for a comic book store and he'd hardly be making the kind of change needed to get by in a Rogers Park flat. Still, who was he to burst someone's pipe dream? He had to deal with his own dreams and the minute sliver of hope that somehow he could make his life right again.

He stood, stretched his length trying to shift the kinks out of his back. But the cot had done its work and a stitch of pain ran down his spine. Still, he was grateful for the roof, the bed, the bag of pork rinds Sam had passed to him for an evening's repast. Otherwise, he would've had to crash at the airport. There were too many things he had to do, but the first on his agenda was getting a job. At least a decent job might appease his mom's worry a bit. She hadn't sounded at all pleased during his call to her last night from Sam's parents' kitchen in the main house. She definitely hadn't liked the news that he wasn't leaving Oak Park. That he was going to find a place and try to get his life back on track here. During the long hours before sleep last night, he had even thought about taking a couple of culinary classes at a community college.

"Sean, are you *trying* to tempt fate? You move back to Oak Park, someone's bound to start asking questions. You don't know who knows what."

"Nobody knows anything, Mom. And with Calvin gone . . ."

"Calvin's death doesn't change the situation. It actually makes it worse. With Calvin gone, it'll all be on your shoulders if the police ever found out."

"They're not going to. And nothing's going to happen to me. I can't go back to Muncie, Mom. I'd die if I went back there. And I don't want to live in Vancouver, either. That's your life now, not mine."

"So what's in Oak Park that's pulling you back? Most of your friends are probably away at college. Except . . . maybe . . . oh . . . ohhh, I know who it is . . . it's Suzanne, isn't it? You're starting up with her again." The acrimony tightened her voice. She had never liked Suzanne.

"Mom, you can't believe how wrong you are about that one. And even if I had any feelings for Suzanne, trust me, she wouldn't want me back in her life again."

"You seem so sure about that . . ."

"Look, I don't wanna talk about Suzanne right now. That was over eons ago."

"So what's the deal then, Sean?"

Sean had hesitated, trying to search for any reason that would settle his mother's curiosity. Because there really wasn't any reason for him to move back to Oak Park. The only thing pulling him back here wasn't something he could divulge to her. Not yet. If ever. He'd take that bullet when the time came. For right now, a lie would be easier.

"There's this restaurant opening up here and they're looking to train a couple of sous chefs. I know I don't have the credentials, but if I take some classes, maybe I can work my way up from waiter later on. This is a chance for me, Mom. Don't ask me to give it up."

The silence stretched for almost half a minute, followed by a long, drawn-out sigh. And he'd known by the sound of it that she was about to say OK. "It's your life, Sean. I just don't want things blowing up in your face. We were lucky last time, and I just have a bad feeling about all of this. But if you're determined to stay, all I can say is be very careful. Don't let too many people know your business."

When he'd hung up, he'd stood in the silent kitchen that was a picture straight out of "Old, Used, and Cruddy," a far cry from the tidy kitchen his mother kept back in Vancouver. Or the nicely arranged kitchen in Lacey's home.

It was strange how she was no longer Mrs. Burnham in his mind. He could never go back to that. Back to the point where she had only been a fantasy often visited, then laid away. She'd become too real lying in his arms, and he could never forget the feel of her body, soft and yielding, beneath him.

Sam, cued from the living room by Sean's silence, had come back into the kitchen and led him to his present refuge. Sam had slept in his old room in his parents' house, temporarily relinquishing his tenuous step to full independence—the garage apartment he had barely converted from storage to partially livable space.

Thinking over the lie he told his mother last night, Sean thought of the various restaurants in downtown Oak Park as well as the north side of Chicago. He did have experience enough as a waiter, although he definitely wouldn't be getting any references from Foxfire's. At this point, they didn't even know he wasn't coming back. Melvin, his manager, would be pissed to shit to know he was going to be one man short tomorrow night and would hardly be all that charitable with recommendations.

Still, he was a good waiter. And he might make a good

chef one day. He liked cooking, liked creating something that would make people close their eyes in pleasure. He had been studying recipes on his own for the last couple of years. Had tried them out successfully with his last girlfriend, who'd told him to go for it. So why the hell couldn't he?

He looked over at Sam, who had a silly smile on his face. "Wouldn't believe who I ran into. She was asking about you, too."

"Who, Suzanne?" Sean couldn't imagine that Suzanne would be asking about him, though. Not after that last talk.

"Naw, but guess again, 'cause you close."

It took a second for him to get the clue. "Aww shit," he muttered softly.

"Yeah, you know who," Sam's smile widened. "She heard you were in town and that you stopped by Suz's. She wanted to know if you were still around."

"What did you say?"

"Hey, what could I say? I didn't know your whereabouts were top secret."

"From that bitch, they are."

"Hey, what's with the rancor? You still steaming about her lying to Suzanne about you? Man, you oughta get over that. That's history now. We all grown and shit. And she's still fine as hell."

"And still a conniving slut. She's the one who got Suzanne to . . ." He stopped, not sure whom Suzanne had told about her abortion. "Anyway, man, she's nothing but trouble. And trouble is the last thing I need now."

"Well, trouble may be headed your way. I saw her early this morning at the mart when I went to pick up the beer. She made a beeline right for me, and I knew it wasn't my indelible charm that had finally gotten to her. Her smile was so bright, man, near 'bout blinded me. You always did that something special for her."

"Only because I was the only piece of dick she hadn't yanked around her finger."

"Hey, she's yet to pull my length, either, man. Not that she would ever give me the chance. Now, you . . ."

"Me, nothing. If she drops by, just tell her I'm gone." Sean was already headed for the door.

"And where're you going?"

"Out. I'll be back later . . . not that you're to pass on that bit of news. Just tell her I left town for good."

"That's only going to work for so long if you're staying in town. Cheryl's bound to find out."

"I'll deal with that when I have to, then. Just don't feel like dealing with it now."

Sean walked out of the apartment, nearly slammed the door. Walking down the steps he realized he didn't know where he was headed. Right now, his whole thought was escaping a meeting with Cheryl. It was too early in the afternoon to deal with that shit. Actually, any minute of the day would be either too early or too late. There never was a good time to face off with Cheryl.

He walked to his bike that Sam had retrieved from inside the garage, got on it and revved the motor, still not sure where he was going. He thought for a second before an idea came to him. His foot hit the pedal, and the bike accelerated as he moved forward to what he hoped would be the beginning of his future.

Chapter 15

Calvin watched his mother as she cleaned out the refriger-ator, tossing old food into the garbage bin a few feet away. Right now, she was peering at a head of lettuce whose top leaves had browned around the edges. He watched as she did a mental debate, then whoosed the lettuce into the bin without a turn of her head. So far, she had rearranged the furniture in the living room, straightened up the closets, re-ordered the kitchen cabinets. She was like some dynamo run-ning on an amp high.

She always cleaned when she was upset. And from what he had heard earlier, he knew she was stewing. Damn. She'd up and quit her job at Meredith. He'd never thought she would do something like that. But then again, he hadn't known how miserable she had been. She'd never let on, never let him see how bad it had gotten. All those mornings when she'd had a smile on her face as she grabbed her briefcase and car keys and shepherded him out the door to school . . . all bogus. The few times she had spoken to him about work, she had kept her tone upbeat, but had quickly changed the subject, asking him something about his classes or about his team schedule. Dodges, he knew now.

He leaned against the wall, studying her. Her motions were manic, furious almost. Pain emanated from her. He felt it across the few feet between them. And he wished more than anything that he could walk over to her and hug away that pain. He hated knowing that all the shit she had taken had been on account of him. That she had stayed at a job she despised just so he could have all the things he thought he wanted, things that didn't mean a damn now. The uniforms, the sports gear, the cellphone, the DVD player, the couple of Xboxes, the clothes, the sneakers (Jordans and Nikes, never under $200 a pair), then later a car, used but doable. And of course, there had been his tuition at Columbia and money for books and other things he needed. She hadn't wanted him to have to work to pay for the extras. She'd wanted him to concentrate fully on his studies. Not that he had used the free time wisely. If he'd known just a few months ago what he knew now, he would have hit the books harder, wouldn't have stayed up all hours hanging out with friends, drinking, shirking off. And would have severely curtailed the party-going, where the only studying he did was estimating the probability of getting laid.

She stooped, pulled an onion from the vegetable bin, put it back.

He wanted her happy again. Wanted to see her smile.

What fucking good was it to just hang around here and not have the power to *do* anything? If he could walk invisible into a bank, get into the vault and pull out millions, he would return and just drop the bills at her feet. If he could even extract every memory of him from her mind, make her forget him so that the pain would go away . . .

The doorbell rang. His mother stood, grabbed the dish towel to wipe her hands, then pulled down the hem of the sweater she had changed into along with a pair of jeans. He followed her down the foyer as she walked to the front door. A familiar scent trailed her, although the name of the perfume was foggy in his mind. He had a hazy recollection of buying it for her every Mother's Day. A lame gift—even so, she had taken the gift as though she was receiving it for the first time. Damn, he should remember it, but it was harder now to hold on to his memories. The thought frightened him. Still, he retained the more important ones, the crucial ones that connected him to his past.

When his mother opened the door, he saw Ray standing on the stoop holding another covered container. Hell, it couldn't be more muffins. What was the game with this guy, anyway? He knew for certain the old geezer wanted to get into his mother's panties. The thought was repugnant, almost as foul as seeing her with Sean. Actually, nothing could be sicker than that. He shook away the mental image of his mother rolling around on the ground naked, Sean piling into her like he would have any of the stupid, simpering girls back in high school. A young, tight babe he could understand, but his mother? What the fuck was wrong with Sean?

Ray's smile broadened at his mother's, "Hi."

"Saw your car in the driveway, thought I'd drop by like I meant to yesterday. I apologize for not coming over but errands got in the way. Anyway, I made some of those greens you liked from before. Turnips, mustards, and collards, seasoned with turkey meat. Just like June used to make them."

He knew his mother's fake smile and she had it on now as she opened the door to let in her neighbor. Calvin stepped out of the way, then remembered he didn't need to. No one could feel him—except maybe his grandmother. And Sean. He remembered Sean's reaction when he'd touched him. Yeah, he was sure Sean had felt him—at least that once. That was something he would keep in mind . . . just in case.

His mother took the offering as she directed Ray to the living room. "I'll just put this in the refrigerator. I still have so much food left over from the repast, I'm not going to have to cook for weeks."

"That's good, good," Ray said, settling onto the couch. Calvin stood near the archway entrance while his mother left the room. He watched Ray as the man's eyes wandered over to the pictures on the fireplace mantel. He seemed to be staring at the one picture of his parents together, his eyes measuring the picture as though trying to read something there. Or something not there.

His mother came into the room and Ray quickly averted his eyes, the geezer smile back. Calvin stiffened as he saw the man steal a look at his mother's behind as she sat down in the nearby chair. Wasn't probably the first time the old fool had scoped his mother.

"So, you doing better today?"

His mother nodded. "Yeah, but I still have a long way to go. Thanks again for the greens, Ray. You didn't need to."

"Oh, it wasn't any trouble. It's just a little something to let you know that I'm thinking of you." He paused and his face softened. "As a matter of fact, I think of you quite often, Lacey. I don't know if I'm going to say this right, and I know the timing may be bad . . ."

"Ray . . ." His mother cut off the sentence. Calvin looked at her face, but couldn't read it. Yet there had been a hint of exasperation in her voice. Not that Ray picked up on it. The man leaned forward, his eyes locked in on his mother's face expectantly.

"Lacey, I want you to know that you don't have to be lonely."

"I'm not lonely, Ray. I'm just alone . . . for now."

"Alone isn't good for a young, vital woman like yourself." Calvin saw the man's hand twitch, as though he had to force himself not to reach out to touch her.

"Alone is exactly what I need to be right now. To get my life in order. Ray, I appreciate your concern, but please don't worry about me. I have family and friends if I ever get lonely."

Ray settled back, determination replacing the softness. Calvin saw that the man wasn't going to give up that easily.

"Family's good, friends are, too. But sometimes a woman needs more. She needs someone to talk to about things, intimate things . . . Someone to turn to in the middle of the night."

Calvin laughed, the sound hollow to his ears. This old

geezer was actually making a play, and by the look on his mother's face, it wasn't going over well. Actually, it wasn't going over at all.

"Ray, I want you to know that I like and respect you as a neighbor . . ."

"Lacey, I want to be more than that . . ."

"I know, Ray, I know. But I don't have those feelings you seem to have for me. They're just not there."

Now there was anger on his face, in his voice. "Maybe I'm just not your type. A mature black man isn't to your liking. Maybe you like them paler, younger . . . young enough to be your own kid!"

His mother stood abruptly, nearly knocking over her chair.

"I'm not going to be talked to like this in my own home. Ray, I told you my feelings, and I'm asking you to respect them."

"Yeah, yeah," he muttered as he got up from the couch. "No one has to tell me what's been going on in this house. Yeah, you like being alone . . . alone with that young thug your son used to hang out with. Yeah, that's right, a thug. Both of them were nothing but troublemakers. I always had to get after them."

Calvin balled his hands into fists, wanting to pummel the fool. He was lying! In Calvin's blurred memory, he saw the man yelling after him and Sean, but only about the noise they made playing ball. That was the most trouble they ever caused the fucker. Why was he trying to make it sound like something more?

"I want you to leave, Ray. Now." Her words simmered in the room. When his mother was angry, she didn't yell. Her voice seethed instead. At his tallest at six-foot-two, dwarfing her by a few inches, Calvin had often felt knee-high in the face of his mother's quiet wrath.

"I'm leaving, I'm leaving," Ray muttered, his resentment and anger matching hers. She stood back as Ray walked out of the room, then followed him to the door. She opened it for him, but instead of leaving, he turned to her.

"I wasn't going to say anything, given how your boy ended up. But I think you ought to know that those boys got up to something, something they didn't want the police to know about. And I'm not just talking about their usual tom-foolery. I heard them talking outside one night about how they had to keep quiet about something they'd done. Don't know exactly what, but I do know your boy was angry enough to start in on that white boy with his fists. That much I heard. That much I know. So, if I were you, I'd watch my back around that friend of Calvin's. Might be more trouble than he's worth."

The door slam shook the walls. His mother stood there for more than a second, staring at the closed door. Her body shook. Calvin knew she was playing Ray's words over in her head. As well as his warning.

He felt like his body was shaking, too. How the hell did the old man know? And what exactly did he know?

She released a shaky breath and he saw a tear glimmering in one of her eyes.

"Calvin, what the hell did you do?" she whispered to the air.

Calvin could only shake his head. He pushed away a memory that threatened to rise up and force him to confront it.

But he refused to remember, instead pushing it far down into the recesses of the hundreds of memories that he still retained, that had not floated away to the ether that would eventually swallow everything he knew.

Chapter 16

Sean took in the kitchen setup as the manager, Russ Beam, turned to address the gray-bearded man who had abruptly interrupted their interview. Sean had already pegged the bearded man as the executive chef and right now he didn't look none too happy. Their tones were low, but occasionally the chef's voice rose enough for Sean to figure out that there had been an unexpected menu change, which the chef obviously didn't appreciate. His face was already red from the steamy temperature in the kitchen, but his nose seemed to be getting redder by the moment. Sean peered over to the left where sat an impressive Fortenay stainless steel range with several pans of sauces simmering on its multiple burners. He had seen another one back in Indiana, only this one was top of the line. A station chef stood tending to the sauces while another prepped a large fillet of salmon with basil and garlic. The doors leading to the main dining room were constantly in motion as waiters came in to pick up trays to cart back out to a mostly high-end clientele.

The chef said something in French, something that even a noninterpreter could translate into a hearty "fuck you." Then he turned to the station chefs, barking orders in English with a heavy French accent and a gusto that belied his displeasure. The manager shook his head, then turned back to Sean with a weary smile.

"So, you're Leo's kid? Yeah, I remember you now. It's been what? Seven, eight years? So what's Leo up to these days?"

Sean shrugged. "Don't really know, don't care. He ran off some time ago. My mom and I haven't heard from him since."

Mr. Beam shook his head. "A shame. He didn't seem the type, but then again, what is the type? So, why're you interested in working here? The only position I have open at the moment is waiter, and remembering what Leo told me about you, you were headed off to college. So what happened?"

"Things didn't work out. I left town for a bit, but I'm back and I really need a job. I've done waiting before so I have the experience. If you want, you can test me out on the lunch crowd, let me show you that I can handle the position."

Sean waited the few seconds as the manager contemplated the offer. Visually, the man's face didn't change, but his eyes darted here and there around the kitchen, seeing without seeing before settling back on Sean's face.

"Well, it's $10 an hour plus tips. There's a lot of work, even with the lunch shift. If you can come in tomorrow, I'll give you a dry run—then we'll see how it goes. I trust that Leo didn't raise a fool, which is the only reason I'm giving you this chance."

Sean had counted on that when he remembered the sign in the window he spotted yesterday. Russ Beam had been one of his father's card buddies, coming around the house on Fridays. Sean particularly remembered that the man could go his father beer for beer, followed by a few whisky chasers. His father invariably wound up passed out in the early hours while Beam would stagger out of the house and somehow navigate his car without killing anyone.

"Thanks, Mr. Beam. What time do you want me tomorrow?"

"Be here at ten. We don't open until noon and that'll give me time to go over the main dining room and kitchen duties with you. I'll introduce you to the other staff. Any questions?"

Sean shook his head. Mr. Beam gave him a curt nod and then led him back through the rear door, which opened out onto an alley that by any reasonable standard would have barely passed inspection. The overflowing Dumpster sat too close to the door and garbage littered the walk. Sean could hear the scurrying of four-legged creatures searching out the refuge. Still, he knew from the restaurant's history that it was one of the most thriving bistros in Oak Park. Also, their menu was top-rate, which meant the kitchen staff, especially the chef, knew their stuff. And Sean planned on picking up more than trays if they gave him the chance. He would watch, study how this particular kitchen worked. How the cooks went about their duties. He would feel them out, see if they were open to passing on what they knew.

In a few years, maybe he would even open his own restaurant. If not here, then somewhere where he could finally lay the past to rest and get on with his life. He'd been in a holding pattern too long, never looking forward, but always over his shoulder.

He had gotten used to the running, to the fear that almost seemed normal. Hadn't thought too much about what he wanted to do with the next years; it had been enough just getting through the days. But that hour in Lacey's yard and later in the dark silence of her room had finally made him realize that he didn't want to run anymore, that life could be good again. The way she'd look at him had lessened the deadness. He desperately wanted her to look at him that way again, wanted to feel her touching him, kissing him. The way she responded to him had let him know that she needed him as much as he needed her. They had found something in each other, if only for those few hours. And he knew that he didn't want to walk away from that.

His thoughts were scrambled as he exited the alley onto the familiar downtown square. To the north was the clock tower abridging the elevated tracks, lording over a boulevard with a cluster of stores and cafes lining both sides of the street. On a cold Monday afternoon, the boulevard was pretty much empty except for a few stragglers, including a couple ahead of him strolling down the street, hands interlaced as they peered through the window of a specialty shop. He tried to picture him and Lacey walking casually together, holding hands. And knew that it wouldn't be that simple. There were too many things that separated them. Too many barriers.

Calvin was the main obstacle, even though it had been Calvin's death that provided the occasion for him and Lacey to get together. Yet, even in death, Calvin kept them apart. There were things he could never tell Lacey, things she wouldn't understand—or want to believe. Yet not telling her felt like lying.

But then he and Calvin had always been good at lying. Lying had provided freedom from parents and rules. At the time, it hadn't seemed like a big deal. Slipping out of the house, skipping classes. And one time even slipping into a house where the owner had left the door open. Calvin had found some ready cash and Sean had taken some jewelry and a camera. But the guilt ate at him for days and he tossed the items in a trash bin a week later. He'd never let Calvin talk him into anything again.

Until that one night. The night that changed both their lives and ended their friendship.

Though, if he were to be honest with himself, there was another reason, something that had unraveled everything he'd thought he understood about himself. He never allowed that particular something to settle too long on his brain. It was just one of the ghosts that pursued him. Ghosts he didn't know how to deal with.

Chapter 17

Calvin felt the pull again. It was stronger this time, nearly dragging him from the chair he had been sitting in. He'd first felt it a few hours ago, in the late evening. Now, in the shadows of the night, it was more insistent, threatening.

"No!" he yelled to the silence. He wasn't ready.

The darkness wanted to subsume him, to eat at his flesh, tear at his brain. It was proclaiming him dead, at last. Just when he'd decided that he wanted any existence, even this limited one, it was coming for him. And more than anything, he didn't want to disappear into the ether, into nothingness.

Or plummet straight to hell.

Somehow he felt heaven was out of the picture for him.

He was afraid. He wanted to call out to his mom, but she was asleep upstairs. Besides, she couldn't hear him anyway, even if she had been awake. It had taken her hours to finally drift off. He'd watched as she tossed in half slumber, worry lines evident even in her repose. He had willed her some peace, and finally, just before two in the morning, the tossing had stopped and she had settled beneath the comforter, her breathing a soft whisper in the room.

Only then had he drifted to the living room to wait out the night. For hours he sat, listening to the silence. And then the call, the pull.

Why now? Why not when he first died? Or even at the funeral?

Why now, when he'd figured that it was his mother who was keeping him here? She was the one who needed him. He saw that now. And he wasn't about to leave her. Not when her life was so fucked up, mostly due to him.

As he was lifted from the chair, he grabbed the back, found it tangible in his grip. He closed his eyes and began to will himself whole. But the draw was too strong now. He felt his essence pulling in several directions, threatening to rip him apart. A howl of pain and horror wrenched from his throat as his soul cried out to God or whoever could hear him.

"Please, please! Let me stay! Please! Oh God, Mama!"

At the moment he called out to her again, pictured her in his mind, the pull weakened, and the pain ebbed a little. He thought of her sadness, especially this afternoon. Concentrated on her face, the loneliness and sorrow there. And felt strength returning to his body, which began moving together again until he stood as whole as he had a few moments ago. For right now, he had won. But he knew it was only for the moment.

The call would come again. And maybe next time, it would be too strong to resist. Eventually he would weaken, no matter how much he tried to stay. The force would pull him into eternity. Into the unknown.

His body felt shaky, as though he were standing on corporeal legs that had suddenly gone limp. He felt sweat that was not there, but would have been if he still had a body with glands. His mouth was dry, missing saliva. There shouldn't have been the feel of tears in his eyes, and yet he could swear tears were rolling down his cheeks.

How had it come to this? One stupid stunt and now his soul was in peril.

Worse than that, he had hurt his family. Had sapped their strength and left them limping along.

He walked to the window to look out on a moonlit night. His legs weren't as shaky now, but he found it hard to stand as he touched a cold windowpane, half expecting to see his breath fog the glass.

He had to make things right again. Before he was forced to leave forever. He needed to make his family whole like before, before he went and got himself killed. He needed Joe and his grandmother healthy again and Aunt Stell going on with her life. And he needed his mother happy, most of all. Happier than anytime he had ever seen her. Happier than he had ever made her.

But he might as well be asking for a way to harness the moon. He had never felt all that powerful in his life and he felt even less so in his death. At least when he was alive, he could use his limbs, be heard when he spoke, hold things in his hands.

He looked down at the empty space on the table sitting near the window. The same table he had bumped just a day ago and knocked over his mother's favorite lamp. He could touch things but still didn't know whether he could pick something up.

Maybe if he could hold a pencil in his hand, he might be able to write a note. Convince his mother that it was him, let her know she shouldn't worry. He would lie if he had to, tell her he was at peace. Then maybe he could actually find some peace.

On the edge of the table sat a paperback book that hadn't been there a day ago. Or even this morning. His mother must have taken it down from the shelf. Even in the dark he was able to read the title: *Life's Crises: Getting Past Survivor Mode.* Maybe she had only recently bought it. It was medium-sized, not too heavy.

He reached out, touched it. Felt the slick paper of the cover. Ran his fingers along the edge. Pressed a finger in, feeling the paper settle into his incorporeal flesh. He concentrated hard as he slipped the whole hand beneath the book. He tried to lift it, but only felt the pages flutter as his hand moved through the book instead.

Even that little bit of effort cost him strength. He felt his body trembling again. But he couldn't give up. He would keep at it, even if it took him the rest of what was left of the night.

He reached out a few times more, each time coming away increasingly frustrated. The frustration kept him from trembling, though. It was a strong emotion. He found he gained strength from acute emotions.

As he was about to move his hand beneath the book again, sure he would lift it this time, a movement across the street stopped him. Someone was out there, standing underneath the streetlight just across from the window. At the moment the figure was looking toward the house as though he were studying it. Stalking it.

Even without seeing him fully, Calvin knew who it was.

The thought brought with it a simmering rage that shot fire through him. Right now he felt life coursing in his hatred. He balled his fist, rammed it against the window. And felt the glorious impact of hard, cold pain. He rammed his fist again and again. Felt the window finally smash beneath the blows. Shards of glass flew out of the window while the remainder crashed to the floor.

He heard the abrupt creak of the bed upstairs and realized his mistake.

Lacey shot straight up, adrenaline racing. She sat dazed for a second, unsure what had awakened her. Then a creeping realization brought a verve of dread. She'd heard breaking glass. And it had come from downstairs.

With shaky breath, she slipped out of bed, the cold floor beneath her bare feet shocking her further. Common sense told her to reach for the phone this time, call the police. But instinct told her that what she might encounter wasn't something the police would be able to handle.

Sense warred with instinct as she exited her bedroom. Why was she so sure it wasn't a burglar breaking in?

Because she had seen Calvin's face in the window, that's why.

An angry Calvin, who might have knocked over a lamp and earlier scared his grandmother silly.

Actually, part of her hoped it was a burglar, because she wasn't sure she could deal with the other situation. Still, she continued down the hallway to the stairs.

Near the bottom her courage abated, abandoning her to pure fear. She shivered as an unexpected draft met her. From her vantage, she could peer into the living room and saw the drapes billowing, dark, ominous shadows moving in the moonlight. She could also see a jagged break in the window, the source of the cold air. She stood still, not sure what to do. Maybe someone had been trying to break in after all. Maybe they were somewhere in the house even now, skulking around in the dark. And she was standing here, vulnerable.

She turned to go upstairs, regretting her decision not to call the police. She was halfway up the landing when the doorbell rang. She turned, but didn't move. It was almost dawn; the sun hadn't even risen. There was no way anyone was dropping in for a visit. At least not a friend.

"Lacey! Are you OK in there!?" boomed through the door.

Sean. Her momentary relief quickly morphed into anger. What the hell was he doing breaking her window?!

The question was on her lips as she rushed down the stairs to unlock the door. She jerked the door open but Sean didn't give her a chance to ask anything.

Instead, he rushed past her to the living room, looking around as though expecting to find someone there.

"Someone's in the house. I saw him. You have to get out of here, now."

He caught her arm and started to navigate her toward the door, but she pulled away.

"What do you think you're doing, Sean? Why did you break my window!"

"That's what I'm saying! Someone broke your window, and it definitely wasn't me. I saw it when it broke. I saw a fist ram against the pane. If it wasn't you and it wasn't me, then someone else is in your house and we're not staying around to find out who. We can call the police from outside."

A book flew through the air, missed hitting Sean by a fraction of an inch. But Lacey felt the breeze of it flying by. Then the lamp table near the window crashed to the floor. Wood splinters flew in several directions.

"Oh, shit! Oh, shit! What the fuck is going on?!"

Lacey had no more doubts about what was happening and who was doing it. She also knew her son's temper. Remembered the many times she had had to make him take a time-out because he was so quick to strike out rather than to think a problem through.

And the problem right now was Sean standing here in this room. No longer letting doubt block her emotions, she could feel the electricity in the room. The hatred.

"Sean, you're right—let's go."

Now she was the one pulling Sean's arm, but even as they headed for the door, she felt a rush of air, heard Sean's sharp intake of breath as he doubled over.

"What the . . . Oh God!" Sean crumbled to the ground. Lacey felt a whirl of wind around her and heard the incredible sounds of impact even as she watched Sean contort in pain from invisible blows. He couldn't defend himself because he couldn't see who to defend against.

"Calvin, stop it! Stop it now!" she yelled to the son she couldn't see, the son she had been mourning just hours ago.

Sean was balled up in a fetal position trying to protect his body, his hand lifted trying to fend off the attack. But his efforts were futile.

In the dimmed room, everything was a blur. Her senses were heightened by fear and horror. This couldn't be her son doing this; Calvin had never been this violent, no matter how angry he had gotten. But she knew in her soul that if she didn't get Sean out of here now, Calvin would kill him.

She bent over Sean's crumbled body that was no longer writhing in pain. Instead, he lay motionless and, for a moment, her heart stopped. Then she looked closer and saw that he was still breathing, although he had been knocked out. In the muted light, she saw bruises forming on his face. She had to get him help, but first she needed to get him out of the house. She grabbed his arms, hoping to drag him across the floor, when a fist lammed into her arm. She stopped and looked around in shock. Had Calvin meant to hit her? The thought was frightening.

She waited out an immeasurable few seconds, holding her breath. But no more blows rained as she shielded Sean with her body. Calvin had stopped—for the moment. She grabbed the opportunity to reason with him.

"Calvin, please, let me get Sean some help. Don't do this. This isn't you. You couldn't hurt me—or Sean—no matter how mad we've made you. And I understand why you're mad. But it's my fault, not Sean's. Please."

The electricity that had been so tangible a few moments ago seemed to ebb in force—as though Calvin had stepped away from her. From both of them.

Sean stirred at that moment and his eyelids began fluttering. Her relief that he was coming to was intensified by her worry that Calvin would continue his attack if he saw that Sean was conscious.

Sean was fully awake now, looking up at her, confused. He opened his mouth to speak, but she shook her head. "Don't talk," she whispered. "We need to get you out of here."

He moved slightly and she saw him grimace in pain. Calvin had done some damage. She hoped there were no internal injuries.

And as much as she was worried about Sean, she was even more worried about her son. About his soul.

Why wasn't he at peace? Why was he haunting her?

Lacey managed to get a shoulder beneath Sean's arm, but found it hard to leverage his weight properly. Still, he was able to move some on his own and that helped as she walked him out of the living room. There was no more sign of Calvin now and she prayed silently that he would just let them get to the door.

"I'm OK," Sean said as he stopped to shift his balance away from her and walk on his own. He hobbled the rest of the way to the door and she followed, her eyes wandering from side to side, fearful of another attack. As she passed the table where she kept her mail and purse, she grabbed the purse before she opened the door and led Sean outside.

The air was brittle and numbing with only her pajamas for cover and her feet bare, but right now she would rather brave the cold than go back into the warmth of her haunted house.

Haunted by her son. A son she didn't know, because in death, Calvin had become a stranger, not the boy she had raised.

"Lacey, what the hell is going on? What happened in there?"

She looked up at him. His face was pale beneath the bright porch light, making his bruises stand out even more. She traced a finger along the edge of one. He closed his eyes and shivered and she realized it wasn't from the cold. She brought her hand down.

"Sean, you can't ever come here again. Do you understand? What were you doing out here in the first place?"

When he opened his eyes, she saw varying emotions, including guilt. "I couldn't sleep and . . . I needed to talk to you."

"Talk? At this time of morning? Sean, why didn't you go back to Muncie? I thought that's where you were going when you left without a word." She hadn't meant for the last to come out like an indictment.

"I started to, but changed my mind. Answer this question, Lacey—do you *want* me to go home?"

She couldn't believe he was asking her this. Not now. Not with Calvin running amok inside her home.

"What I want isn't going to be—now or ever. You want to know what happened inside, Sean? Calvin nearly killed you, that's what happened. The same Calvin that watched us fucking out back. My son. The child I thought I raised to be a loving and kind young man. I don't know what's going on with him."

Sean's head shook slowly. "That couldn't be Calvin. He's dea . . ."

". . . dead. Yes, I know that all too well. I was the one who had to bury him, remember? His body may be in the ground, but obviously his soul hasn't moved on. It's right inside this house and it's . . . he's . . . angry. I felt him. I felt his fist just like you did. You still want to say it's my imagination? Sean, trust me, I didn't give you those bruises on your face. You didn't see him—but you felt him, didn't you?"

He nodded reluctantly, his eyes looking away from hers. Because looking into her eyes might make him acknowledge a whole lot of stuff he didn't want to believe. She could see the fear now. They were both afraid of someone they shouldn't be.

"You can't go back in there, Lacey," he said after a long pause.

"I don't plan to. At least, not tonight."

She reached into her purse and pulled out her cellphone. "I'm calling my mother, letting her know I'm driving over. How did you get here?"

"The bike." He pointed his head across the street where his motorcycle lay against the curb. "I guess I better get back to where I'm staying."

"No, Sean, I don't want you driving the bike. Not tonight. As a matter of fact, I think I should take you to the emergency room."

Already he was shaking his head. "No, I can't afford to be holed up. I start a new job tomorrow."

"Sean, you can't possibly go to work in this condition. If you could see the marks on your face . . ."

He smiled a little. "I've worked with worse injuries than these, trust me. I'm just a little sore . . ."

"You were knocked out! You could have a head injury."

She saw the unyielding obstinacy that she had seen in

Calvin so many times. He wasn't going to be talked into any-thing he didn't want to do.

"Where're you staying?"

"With a friend. Over his garage, actually."

She sighed. "OK, then, at least let me drive you. You can leave the bike here until . . . until you're better."

"No, I need the bike to get to work. Sam—my friend—won't be around to take me and I don't want to wait on pub-lic trans. I can't afford to be late my first day."

"What time you have to be there? Where is it, anyway?"

"No, I couldn't ask you . . ."

"You don't have a choice. You try to get on that bike, I'm going to stand in the street and make you run me over. And I don't feel like dying tonight. I don't want to think what could happen with you on that bike in your condition. I couldn't bear it if . . ."

She stopped herself from finishing the sentence. The thought of Sean in a casket sent a pain through her heart.

He reached out, touched the hair near her brow. He un-derstood what she wouldn't allow herself to say.

His finger grazed her skin and a tremor shot through her. She wanted more than anything to rest her face in that hand. Especially now, when she needed some comfort. But she couldn't afford to let herself go—for both their sakes. So in-stead, she pushed his hand away.

"No more of that. We can't ever . . . do that again."

He took his hand away. Reluctantly.

"At least say you're glad I didn't go."

"Why? What's the point, Sean?" Sadness edged her questions.

"Because I don't want to feel I'm making the wrong choice by staying here."

"And you're staying here because of me?"

"Yes." The answer came too quickly, too firmly for her. She didn't want this. How had she let this happen?

It seemed more like months than days since she first saw Sean in the cemetery. She'd thought then that he would come and go, and that in her mind, at least, everything between him and Calvin would be resolved.

How could she have expected everything that'd happened? One indiscretion, an hour of allowing herself to feel something besides pain, the one joy she'd had in weeks—and now everything had become so complicated. No, "complicated" was too lame a word for what was going on. There was no word for this. Any of this.

"Sean, please don't overhaul your life, not for me. If you're staying here, it should be something you want to do . . ."

"But this is what I want to do. To start my life over. Actually, just to start it—period. To get it out of neutral."

"Neutral" was an interesting adjective to describe the life of someone so young. Neutral was what her life had been. Was. But then, neutral had been so safe and normal.

"What are you going to do about him?" Sean asked unexpectedly. She noticed his voice had lowered a decibel.

"What do you expect me to do? Exorcise him? He's my son. I'm going to try to give him peace so he can move on."

"How?"

"I don't know how," she said sadly. "Anyway, it's cold out here. I need to get you . . . home. And I am taking you to work tomorrow, right?"

"Yeah," he said with the ghost of a smile.

She beeped her car parked in front of the house as they walked to it. Sean got in gingerly, indicating that he wasn't as well as he was claiming. As she opened her door, she took one look at the broken living room window. For a second, she thought she saw something moving. But then shook off the thought. The possible reality that her son had come home to stay was still too discomforting.

Well, at least she didn't have to worry about burglars. She was sure Calvin would take care of anyone who traversed that doorway.

She shook her head at the lunacy of her life, got into the car, and drove off.

Chapter 18

"What the hell happened to you?" Russ Beam asked, warily surveying the damage on Sean's face.

Sean had his lie ready. "I had an accident with my bike yesterday. Some car cut me off and I swerved into a line of garbage cans. It's nothing. The bruises should be gone in a couple of days." At least he hoped they would be.

Russ Beam cocked an eyebrow.

"Don't try to bullshit me. I've seen enough fights to know what type of bruises I'm looking at. Someone whaled on you, which means trouble, and I don't need any trouble around here."

"Look, Mr. Beam, whether you believe me or not, there's not going to be any trouble around here. At least, not from me."

"Well, what the hell am I supposed to do with you? I can't have you walking around the customers, looking like you just rolled in from a bar brawl. This is a classy place and people are put off by shit like this."

"OK, I know it looks bad, so maybe I can help out in the kitchen until my face heals up. Please, I really need this job."

"Yeah, and I really need a waiter. Look . . . I want to help, I do, but I don't think this is going to work out."

The anger was immediate. Just when he was about to get his life together, something had to come and fuck it up. No, not just something. Calvin. It was bad enough that he'd fucked up Sean's life when he was alive. Now he was reaching beyond the grave with the same shit. No matter. He wasn't going to punk out and walk away . . . not this time.

Sean saw the kitchen staff pretending not to listen, even as the chefs went about the business of preparing the lunch menu. He also noticed that none of the staff had the time to clean up the floor or workspaces.

"Tell you what. You don't have to pay me for these days and I'll still help you out. You need someone to at least sweep up the food on the floor, not to mention out back where you got all that garbage on the ground. That's never good . . . someone might call it in to the city inspector." He let that last hang.

Russ's eyes hardened. "You threatening to report me? Listen, you fuck, I'm not going to be threatened by some punk . . ."

"Hey, I'm not saying one thing or another. It's just that I've seen restaurants closed down for weeks, months even, because they didn't have their stuff together. The word doesn't necessarily have to come from me. All I'm saying is you got yourself a waiter . . . in a few days. Since you lasted this long without one, those few days shouldn't matter. In the meantime, you got someone that's going to keep you straight so no one *can* report you. Especially not me."

The manager stood there, looking like he wanted to bust his ass, but Sean held his ground. After a few moments of the standoff, Russ cracked a smile. A small one, but at least it broke some of the tension.

"Yeah, you're Leo's kid, all right. You got your ole man's devious ways. Leo knew how to rob the shirt right off your back and leave you wondering what happened. All the time smiling in your face. I see he taught you well."

"He didn't teach me a damn thing. Whatever I learned, I learned on my own. If you've ever been desperate, then you know the street I'm standing on. I'll do you right if you give me the chance. That's all I'm asking."

"All this just for a waiter's job? You aim low in life, kid."

"You don't know where I'm aiming."

"Got plans, huh?"

"Yeah. I plan to open up my own restaurant one day. And I plan to learn from the best."

Russ Beam raised an eyebrow before breaking out in a gut-shaking laugh that startled some of the younger chefs. Maybe they'd never heard him laugh before.

"Man, you got some balls, I tell ya, fronting me off like this. Well, OK, then. Get to sweeping, mopping, washing, drying, and whatever it is you think you can do. And I hope to see all of this here sparkling like the Hope diamond in a few. Oh, and another thing," he raised a finger in Sean's face, "that ground out back better be clean enough for me to eat off of when you're through, you hear?" The finger came down. "And don't worry, I'm no slave driver. You'll get paid for your efforts."

Russ indicated with a nod of the head that Sean should follow him. He led him to an anteroom near the back of the kitchen where all the cleaning implements were kept, then left him on his own. Sean took off his coat and placed it on a hook near the door, then grabbed the first broom he saw. He sighed. This was shit work, he knew. But at least it had bought him some time. Time enough to heal and get back on track.

He began sweeping bits of lettuce, parsley sprigs, chicken bones, and other discards lying on the floor into a small pile. Kitchen floors hardly ever stayed clean unless someone was constantly on top of it. He knew how hard it was, and that it really didn't indicate overall dirtiness. He'd basically been bluffing about snitching to the city. But he'd been desperate.

That bit about his being like his father had dug into his flesh. He hated any resemblance to the man who'd raised him. Who had beaten him and his mother. And who had ultimately made his life the mess it had become.

The only thing that raised his life above an absolute shithole was knowing that he had this small talent for something he loved doing. And there was his mother. Their relationship had its share of rough patches, but she had tried to protect him, at least, even though she often failed.

And most of all, there was Lacey. The thought of her sent a tremor through him. He had taken a chance coming to Calvin's funeral, but he had never thought or hoped anything like this could happen. And yet it had.

This morning, she'd picked him up like she'd promised, pulling up in the driveway according to the directions he'd given her the previous night. And he'd watched her eyes taking in the small garage, the dingy second-floor windows above that faced out onto the sparse backyard, before those lovely dark eyes came to settle on him. He knew she thought the place was shitty. Yet, she'd said nothing as he got into the car. He had been curious why she wasn't at work, but it was none of his business. He was just glad for the ride. And for the little time alone with her, even though in a few days he would be OK enough to ride his bike and this would end.

He'd been reticent about the new job when she'd finally asked, embarrassed to tell her that he was just a waiter. He was sure there were plenty of guys who'd be all too willing to wine and dine her, taking her out to the same fancy restaurants where he could only bring them their plates. He didn't have the money or the experience she probably wanted from a lover.

Still, he was sure no one would ever love her the way he did. If she would let him.

One day he would prove that he was worth loving . . . to himself and to her.

Calvin be damned. As he already was, it seemed.

He still couldn't wrap his mind around Calvin being a

ghost. Things like that just didn't happen. Weren't supposed to happen.

Thank God he'd never encountered any other ghosts. Ghosts who would do more damage than the beating Calvin gave him.

He pushed the broom around the stations, circumventing the head chef, who patently ignored him as he barked orders. Still, a few of the other chefs nodded acknowledgment, indicating that everyone in this kitchen didn't have a bug up their ass. He nodded back, knowing he was going to need a friend or two around here if he was going to succeed with his plans.

Maybe he was only chasing a dream. But it was his dream, something to hold on to.

And his dream included Lacey.

She hadn't expected the kiss. Neither had he. He hadn't planned it. When she'd turned to him in the car to ask what time she should pick him up, all he could see was her lips, parted slightly and moist from when she'd flicked her tongue over them. It was an unconscious habit. He'd first noticed it years ago, when he had sat watching her on the sly, fascinated by her beauty, drawn to her kindness.

Instead of reaching for the car door, he had reached over and touched her lips softly with his own and had felt her surprised intake of breath. He didn't know how she would react, hadn't even thought about it. It seemed everything he did with her was instinct, a driving impulse that wouldn't let him just sit quiet. Not anymore. He had felt her stiffen, but she didn't pull away, even as he became bolder and pushed his tongue in. The kiss lasted only a few seconds, but it had sealed something between them.

Because when he pulled back, he saw her desire and knew that it was far from over. And he finally knew at that moment that he had been right not to get on that plane to Muncie.

He was going to be with her. Even if he had to send Calvin to hell to do it.

He hoped it didn't come to that.

* * *

"You think he's gone?"

Lacey glanced at her mother before continuing her inspection of the living room. It felt silly looking into small crevices, but she didn't know where ghosts hid out.

"No, I don't," Lacey answered. "He's still here somewhere."

Her mother shook her head in amazement as she stood near the broken window that Lacey had just nailed over with wooden slats. Lacey had already put in a call to a repair service that morning from her mother's house.

"I don't understand why he would act out like this. Why is he so angry?"

"I don't know, Mom. Maybe he's just trying to find his way out of this world."

She wouldn't ever tell her mother the truth. There was no reason to worsen a bad situation.

"You know what you need to do, don't you? Get a séance together. Maybe Calvin has something he needs to say. Maybe then he can move on."

A séance. Not that the thought hadn't crossed her mind in the straggling hours before the sun shone unwaveringly into her mother's guest room, bringing none of the warmth the light promised.

But she didn't think she needed a third party to talk to her son. Hopefully, all he needed was to hear her voice, to hear her expiation. To hear her say it was all right for him to move on, that he didn't need to stay. Not for her sake.

And that what happened with her and Sean would never happen again.

But was that a promise she could keep? This morning's kiss had floored her. Not just the surprise of it, but the overwhelming response it triggered. She knew she was still attracted to him, had feelings for him, even. But she'd thought what happened in the yard was simply her reaching for a touch of life to push away the death that had enclosed her.

She truly believed that except for Calvin's death, she would never have fallen into Sean's arms.

Until that kiss. Now she forced herself to remember the discomfort she had felt that one day years ago when Sean had stood next to her, making her realize just how tall he'd gotten. How his chest and arms had broadened. And how easily she could fit into those arms. The thought had frozen her to the spot, made her feel more than a little guilty. She knew women, a few of them her own friends, who fantasized about being with young men—boys, even—but she hadn't been one of them. That day she had shaken away the nascent and disturbing feelings Sean had evoked in her.

That was then. Now all of her defenses seemed to have evaporated when she could least afford to be this vulnerable.

"So, what about the séance?"

"No, Mom. At least, not yet. I think we can communicate with him without bringing in some strange person."

"Calvin! Calvin! Do you hear me? This is your grandmother!" For some reason, her mother was shouting up to the ceiling, as though Calvin hovered above them.

"Mom, I'm pretty sure he can hear you and that he knows you're his grandmother."

"I'm just trying to get his attention," the older woman said as she bent heavily to pick up a stray piece of glass. Lacey walked over and gingerly took the shard from her mother's fingers. She'd thought she had swept up everything.

She stood for a second, listening out for any strange sounds. Maybe he was in another room.

But most likely he just didn't feel like making himself known.

Or couldn't.

Last night, she had felt the electric charge of his rage. This morning, she'd been through every room in the house, including the basement, and had felt nothing. No charge, not so much as a static cling. Just a quiet, empty nothing.

She didn't have to think hard to figure the difference between night and day. Last night Sean had been here. And Calvin's rage had been palpable. And therefore, Calvin had been palpable.

Today he was without his anger. Which meant he could be standing right next to her and she wouldn't feel him.

"Calvin," she said softly, almost to herself. "I love you. I want you to have peace." She listened. Her mother listened. Silence.

"Séance?" her mother tried again.

"I'll know by the end of the week. I have to give him time to gather himself."

"Gather himself? What's he got to gather? He's spirit, honey, nothing more than mere air. It should be easy for him to fly to heaven."

"Maybe he's confused right now."

"You may be right about that. Someone needs to lead him to that light like in that movie *Poltergeist*."

"This isn't the movies, Mom. This is real life. And we have a real-life ghost, who happens to be my son."

"It's too bad his father wasn't waiting for him . . . you know, to lead him where he needs to go."

Lacey shuddered to think about Darryl still hovering around. Not after what had happened. She felt guilty enough as it was, with her son having been a witness to her weakness.

"Darryl's long gone. Unfortunately, Calvin's on his own now," she said sadly.

She hated thinking of Calvin so lonely, so angry, so lost.

How could she possibly help him? The haunting could go on for years. And even if she moved, she'd feel guilty for abandoning him.

No, she had to stay and deal with this.

Just as she had to deal with her feelings for Sean.

"Well, we might as well tell Estelle and Joe that Calvin plans on staying a bit."

Lacey looked at her mother like she'd lost it. "And you know exactly what they'd say. You know how they looked at us that day we even mentioned that Calvin may still be around."

"Well, we have proof now."

"We have a broken window, a few thrown books, and . . ."

"And what?"

Lacey left the question unanswered, thinking of Sean's bruised face.

"Whatever we do, we're going to have to do without either Joe or Stell's participation. Especially with Joe's health doing so poorly. The shock of it—that is, if we could even convince him—would send him straight to the other side."

"You're right, I guess," her mother said sadly. Lacey knew she was worried about Joe. "So, what're you going to say to him when you do this talking?"

"I don't know."

"Well, for starters, tell him that we all love him. And we just want what's best for him. And if he wants to come visit me, he's always welcome."

Despite herself, Lacey chuckled. Just as quickly, the mirth died away.

"Calvin, where are you?" she asked beneath her breath.

Of course, she couldn't hear his answer.

"I'm right here, Ma! I'm right here! Can't you feel me? I need you to feel me, to hear me. I'm so sorry, I'm so sorry. I didn't mean to hit you."

But no matter the rush of his words into her ear, she couldn't feel him. Not now, anyway.

If guilt could have taken him on, he would have been long gone.

Last night, he had totally lost it. As much as he thought he hated Sean, he hadn't thought he would ever hurt him like that. But last night, he had wanted to kill him.

Why couldn't Sean just leave his mother alone? Why was he all up under her, stalking her early in the morning?

A memory came to him, one he didn't want. But one he couldn't push away.

Sean's garage. Or rather, Sean's father's garage. Sean on the floor working on that old bike of his.

"Man, you should just get a new bike. Don't know why you're holding on to it like it's your mama's tit and she's got the last bit of milk."

Sean smirked as he tightened a spark plug with his wrench. "You know what they say about mother's milk being good for you."

"Ugh. You're just foul."

"Who's foul? You're the one who brought the metaphor up."

"Metaphor? Man, stop pretending like you actually learned something in English class."

Calvin stood quiet for a moment—then a thought crossed his mind and he did a mock shudder.

"What now?" Sean looked up at him.

"Just imagining your mama's tit."

"Hey, fool, keep your mind off my mother's body. How'd you like me talking about your mama like that?"

"Yeah, I wish you would be thinking 'bout my mama's body. I mean, that'd be sick, man. Hey, guess what? That old dude next door with the sick wife, I caught him scoping my mom the other day. I mean, c'mon, he's as old as air and had the nerve to be looking at my mom's ass like it had 'lollipop' written all over it. And the thought of anyone wanting to get with my mom—God, the thought makes me wanna puke."

After a few moments, he realized Sean wasn't saying anything. He looked down at a slow bloom coloring Sean's face. God, he was actually blushing.

"What, did I shock you?" Calvin laughed.

Sean still didn't say anything for a few moments, and then he asked, "You really don't see your mom, do you, Cal? She still has it going on."

"Yeah, but she's gotta be about thirty-something. 'S about

time she hung up the see-through panties, know what I mean? My dad's been gone forever, and even if he were here, man, oohhh, just foul, you know?"

"Well, what if your mom found somebody—you know, someone she liked . . . and who liked her? Wouldn't you want her to be happy?"

"She's already happy. She has me, doesn't she?"

Sean got up from the floor, walked around his bike to inspect it. "Yeah, man, but you can't supply all her needs."

"Yeah, and I suppose you can, huh?"

Silence. A disturbing, long silence. Then a thought came and Calvin stiffened.

"Man, you better not be thinking about my mom like that. I'd kick your ass."

Sean sighed, almost an admission. "I know you would, brother, I know you would. No, I wouldn't play you foul like that."

Still, for the rest of that afternoon, Sean was unusually quiet. And that disturbed Calvin. Because, what if?

Standing now, watching his mother leave the room, his grandmother behind her, Calvin remembered other times that he'd thought nothing of. The way Sean's eyes would peer up at his mother when she walked into the kitchen, then quickly look away as though he was embarrassed to have her see him looking. The way he always seemed to take her side whenever Calvin recounted an argument between him and his mother, the way he always found a reason to be around when his mother got home from work.

Calvin realized how dense he'd been, too damn focused on his own world. But suddenly he realized something.

He'd assumed that Sean was getting revenge against him by going after his mother.

But he'd been wrong. Very wrong. It was much, much worse. Sean was in love with his mother.

Strangely, the thought didn't bring the usual anger. Instead, it stabbed him with fear. A fear nothing like the fear from last night. And yet the fear was the same. The fear of disappearing into nothingness.

If his mom let Sean into her life, she'd soon forget about him. Forget that she'd ever had a son. And he'd fade away forever.

He couldn't let that happen. Wouldn't let it.

Survival was all he understood now. And he knew what he had to do. Hurting Sean wasn't the answer. That would only turn his mother against him.

But there was another way he could stop Sean.

To pull off his plan, he needed to be able to do what he tried to do last night and halfway succeeded. He needed to be able to hold things, specifically a pen or pencil. He knew now that he could make things move . . . if he was angry enough. Now to figure out how to do it without the anger.

He was going to leave his mother a message. About Sean. Then he'd watch with satisfaction as his mother told the motherfucker to get out of her life for good.

Chapter 19

"Well, well. Look who's back in town. And playing in the garbage. Seems like old times."

The mocking voice grated into his peace. He'd almost forgotten that he was behind the restaurant out back, surrounded by overflowing garbage bins. The monotony of his motions had lulled him into a semiconscious state where his mind was away from his body and his body was on autopilot.

He might have had prior nightmares of meeting Cheryl Standler in an alley, with her standing there laughing at him, but reality had added a few details. A rake in his hand, the bottom of his jeans soiled with egg yolk, his jacket stained with something that might have been mustard; he wasn't sure.

He stopped and looked at the apparition approaching him. He didn't need to ask how she'd found him. Sam could never keep his mouth shut, and Cheryl was too adept at getting any information she wanted.

She still had the looks, but age and overindulgence had worn down the softness. Unlike Suzanne's hair, Cheryl's grew down her back. It didn't flatter her face, though, which, as always, was enhanced by a battery of makeup. Alcohol was hard on the looks after a while.

She stopped within a hand's length of him, staring at the bruises on his face.

"Goddamn, what happened to you?"

The question went unanswered and she just shrugged. "So, you came back from your hideaway to what . . . sweep garbage? Sean, I'm disappointed. I was so sure you would be doing something more worthwhile . . . like working in a filling station. Ah, but yeah, those are basically self-serve now. Damn, automation has knocked you out of a job and down to . . ."—she looked around the alley—". . . this."

"You finished? I've got work to do." He went back to raking, pointedly ignoring her.

"Hey, I'm just stopping by to say welcome back. I'm sure Suzie Q was glad to see you."

He stopped and stared her down. "Yeah, I heard how you helped her. Thanks, thanks a lot."

The smile left quickly. "Hey, don't blame me for that. Suz needed help, and you weren't around to clean up your mess, so don't start acting all wounded now."

"Cheryl, why is it that you're always butting into other people's lives? What, servicing the lowlifes in town not keeping you busy enough? And why the fuck do you get your jones bothering me?"

He expected some half-assed smile with an equally smartass answer. What he saw made him pause. Cheryl stood naked, her face as open as an unassuming child's.

"You know why, Sean. You always knew. Even when you were with Suz, you knew. Still, I stepped back . . ."

"Is that what you called it? Stepping back? Cheryl, you only stepped back far enough to try to get your hand on my zipper. So, you still giving free blow jobs?"

Again, she surprised him with a look that said he had struck her, almost physically. Damn it. The girl was actually making him feel sorry for her.

"It was more than that."

"Why me?"

"Because . . ."

"Because what?"

"I don't know, Sean. It just was. It still is. And all those other guys before, they weren't anything. I just needed someone to hold me . . . and you never would. Ever. I always hated Suz because she never appreciated what she had. I would have given anything to have been her those years ago. But you never gave me the chance. You just blew me off, treating me like I was nothing but shit."

"Cheryl, I didn't treat you like shit. You treated yourself that way. If I didn't get up in your face saying what you wanted to hear, it's because I wasn't going to lie to you, not like the others did."

"You, don't lie?" She smirked. "So, Mr. Tell-It-Like-It-Is, why don't you tell me why you really left town. And don't give me that half-assed answer you gave Suz. Something was up, and it had to be really bad for you and your mother to just up and leave like that. I know someone who worked at St. Anne's and she said your mother gave barely a day's notice and then—poof—both of you just gone."

"What, you writing my life story now? I'm warning you, Cheryl, back off."

"Or what? What're you gonna do, Sean? Kill me?"

Sean's hand tightened around the rake handle until an errant splinter punctured his flesh. He didn't answer her, just let the question hang. It was a disturbing silence and she sensed it. A slow realization made her eyes widen.

"Nah, you couldn't," she finally said, more to herself than him. "You're not capable of anything like that."

"You don't know what I'm capable of, Cheryl. That's why I'm telling you to lay off. For both our sakes."

Just then the back door opened and Sean turned to see Russ step outside. "You almost through here? I'm not paying you to flirt with your girlfriends."

Before Sean could speak up, Cheryl did. "I'm not his girlfriend. I'm just an old friend passing by. I'm going . . . for now."

She turned, took a few steps, then turned back. "Glad to see you coming up in the world, Seanie."

"So, what d'you do to her?" Russ asked, looking at Cheryl's figure with an appreciative half smile as she walked out of the alley and turned south onto the boulevard. He turned back to Sean. "You usually have this effect on folk?"

Sean sighed and shook his head. "I'll be through here in a few."

"Good, because I need someone to unpack some boxes that just arrived. And there's more mopping to be done. Antonio just broke a jar of saffron and it's all on the floor."

"I'll get on it."

"I'm sure you will, kid."

Sean waited until Russ had shut the door before he parked the rake against the wall and pulled the splinter from his hand. A bead of blood pooled from the wound and he sucked it. The pain was muted by the cold.

Cheryl's words echoed in his head. "You're not capable of doing that . . ." The way she had looked at him, just for a second . . . like it had only occurred to her at that moment that maybe she had sized him up all wrong, that she didn't really know him at all.

And she didn't. No one did.

No one knew what he was capable of.

Including him.

Joe looked at his niece as she stared at the glass repairman replacing the window. She hadn't answered his question, not head-on. And the answer she did give just didn't make sense. Something was definitely going on.

"So, you tripped and the book flew right into the window?"

"That's what I said."

"Uh-huh."

His tone made her turn her head.

"Joe, why don't you believe me?"

"Because you're not being straight with me. You forget I know when you're not telling the truth. Remember the time when you were sixteen and you snuck out to that party your mama told you you couldn't go to? Remember how you took your mama's car and banged it up good? And the cock-and-bull story you told her about a girlfriend taking the keys behind your back and getting into an accident? Your mama bought that story and still doesn't know the truth today. But you and me had a little talk back then, remember?"

Lacey sighed. "I remember, Joe."

"You couldn't pull one past me then, and you're not pulling one on me now. I may be an old man, but I've as many years of experience on you today as I had nearly twenty-five years ago. Now, what's going on? How did that window really get broken?"

He watched her expressions morph from one thing to another. She was debating with herself on something, on whether to tell him that something, and on how much to tell him. Whatever it was, it must be bad.

"Joe, you'd hardly believe me if I told you the truth."

"Try me."

"I want to tell you—really I do, Joe. Mama thinks I should."

"And I always believed you should do what your mama says. Now, tell me."

The repairman interrupted. "All done here."

Lacey took advantage of her reprieve, gathered her purse and pulled a wallet from it.

"How much again?"

"Four hundred."

Joe whistled beneath his breath. "Costly accident, that. Make sure you don't go hurling any more books again."

Lacey paid the man and led him to the door. He heard the door close and took a seat, waiting for her to come back into the living room. Instead, she just stood in the foyer looking in, looking around like she was searching something out.

"Let's take a walk, Joe. Outside."

He got up as slowly as he had sat down. His arthritis was flaring up again, and his knees weren't really up to any walking. Still, he sensed she needed to get out of the house, so he followed her to the door and they both grabbed their coats from the coat tree.

They walked down the street toward the corner. She slowed her steps, letting him keep a comfortable pace. He realized just how old he felt. He wasn't much longer for this earth, and it saddened him. He was like these trees he was passing, between seasons, life hidden beneath the weariness of a winter that's been too long. What little life that remained was subsumed and he was tired of constantly trying to push past the decay. There were no more springs for him. No illusions about righting past wrongs, undoing mistakes, or rewriting even a part of his life. He would just have to be satisfied with what had come and gone.

After all, living was full of mistakes.

"Well, are you going to talk, or are you going to walk an old man into the ground?"

His niece pulled her woolen coat lapels together, keeping out a brisk wind. And remained silent for the beat of a few moments.

"Joe, do you believe in the supernatural at all?"

"Supernatural? Are we back on that again?"

"We were never off it, Joe. If you would just listen, and don't let your usual stubbornness get in the way, maybe you'll open your mind to things. Lord knows I had to." She paused, stopped her steps as she turned to him fully. There was fear in her eyes, fear and sadness. "Calvin is in the house. He's come back."

Joe felt his eyes blinking rapidly. They tended to do that when he was caught by surprise.

"What do you mean, he's come back? You mean, like a zombie?"

"No, Joe. I mean like a ghost. He's in that house. For all I know, he could be right here, even, walking alongside of us."

"OK, baby girl, you're not making any kind of sense that's logical. I know you wish the boy was here; I do, too, but he's gone on and you just have to accept that."

She gave him a sad little chuckle. "I wish it were in my head, Joe. I wish it were just my imagination so that I could take medication or pills or something to get over this. But if I didn't believe in ghosts before, last night made me realize just how wrong I was. It was Calvin who broke the window. He threw things around the room, even attacked his friend Sean."

"Sean? That white boy you let stay with you? I thought you said he was gone."

"Well, for some reason he came back last night. And Calvin beat him up."

Joe flicked his left ear with his gloved hand. He never could hear good with that ear.

"You say what now?"

"I can't even tell Mama this. But it happened. Sean was here last night, and out of nowhere, something . . . someone . . . started pummelling him, and I have good reason to know it was Calvin. Because I saw him a few days ago."

"You saw him?" He flicked that left ear again.

"Yes, I saw him looking out at us through the kitchen window . . . at me and Sean . . . after we . . . in the garden . . ."

He was hearing things and then he wasn't. Too much was coming at him at the same time, so he didn't know what the hell she was trying to say.

"OK, you need to finish that sentence for me. You *think* you saw Calvin, looking out on you and Sean after you . . . what now?"

"After . . . we made love. In the garden out back."

He stared at her but she refused to meet his eyes. The long, drawn-out silence between them made him realize that she was waiting for him to have his say.

"You telling me you and that boy . . ."

"He's not a boy, he's a man."

"A very young man, not much older than Calvin, so that would make you what, around his mama's age?"

She didn't answer. And he didn't trust himself to say anything just then. A seagull cried out as it flew overhead and he followed it with his eyes, absurdly wondering why seagulls were called that if they stayed inland all the time. He looked at Lacey again and saw that she was near tears. He had hurt her.

"Lacey, baby girl, I'm sorry. Sometimes I talk too fast and say things off the top of my head. I didn't mean to judge you like that. Your business is your business. Besides, you're still an attractive woman. The only thing is, I wonder why you didn't choose someone more fitting."

"You mean someone my age?" she sniffed as she wiped away a tear. "Look, I know it was a dumb mistake. And, of course, I can't ever tell Mama about it. I don't know why I let it happen. I was feeling lonely . . ."

"Of course you were," he offered, trying to mend fences. "I guess it's understandable. Hell, men do it all the time, so I guess you women are due. But now, back to the real issue—what did you mean when you say *Calvin* beat him up?"

The tears were gone now. "Just what I meant to say. I saw Calvin in the kitchen window . . . watching us. And he was so angry. At the time, I convinced myself that I had only imagined him standing there. But now I know I wasn't seeing things. Mama felt him, too. And last night, he actually threw things—he, he broke the window . . . he was just so mad. I could feel—I mean, actually felt—him standing near me. And I saw Sean being beaten with invisible blows. I felt the air current, I heard the blows, and most of all, I saw the bruises form on his face out of nowhere. Joe, you say you know when I'm lying. Do you think I'm lying to you now?"

Joe sighed as another layer of tired settled on him. He was much too old to start believing in weird things. It put his preconceptions about the afterlife—about life, even—in a flux.

Yet, he looked into his niece's eyes and knew that she wasn't lying. And neither was she losing her mind. Still . . .

"I don't know what to say to that, girl, I really don't. But if what you say is true in any way, then we've got a problem."

"Don't I know it. I never thought that I would be afraid of my own son, Joe. But last night, it was like he was a stranger."

"Well, maybe he'll settle down now. You know, if this thing between you and that boy is through, then maybe Calvin will just . . . move on."

"I hope so, Joe. I really do. I not only felt his anger last night, I felt his pain. I really hurt him and I would die before I did that again."

"I know you would. So, are you still afraid? Can we go back to the house? You think Calvin'll be throwing any more books around, because I really need to sit down."

She looked at him, worried, took his arm as they turned back to the house. "Joe, please tell me you're seeing a doctor. I know how devastating Calvin's death has been for you, and I probably shouldn't have even told you what I just did. You don't need to be worrying about me; you need to be taking care of yourself."

"Baby girl, you have to understand that the doctor can only stretch out my years for so long, and then it's time for me to move on. I have to move on just like Calvin has to. When it's our time, there's no rewinding. And I hope you can let me go when I do cross over."

She stopped and hugged him tightly. "Joe, don't ask me to do that. I don't think I can let go."

He laughed gently. "Lacey, in order for you to go on, you have to let go. And I love you, too, baby girl."

He wiped a sudden tear from her face. He was going to miss her when death did finally come for him. He was going to miss them all.

Chapter 20

He saw her car pull up and she waved for him to get in. He had been standing in front of the restaurant, psyching himself against the cold, dragging on the smoke from his cigarette. He was tired and dirty, although he had done his best to clean up. He didn't want her looking at him with disgust.

He tossed the cigarette and got into the car and was immediately surrounded by her intoxicating scent. She had changed from this morning's jeans and a black coat. Right now, she wore tan wool slacks and a cream-colored, woolen mid-length coat. Her hair was pulled back into a ponytail with a gold butterfly barrette. Just like this morning, she only wore a smattering of makeup. And she was more beautiful than girls like Cheryl could ever hope to be.

"Sean, we have to talk."

His heart lurched at her tone. She was going to tell him that she couldn't pick him up anymore or see him again.

"If I'm going to drive you around, you can't be kissing me. You can't be touching me. Is that clear?"

His relief was palpable. "I'm sorry. I won't do it again."

She pulled out of the parking space, and soon merged into the rush-hour traffic, which was still heavy, even at nearly seven.

"So, how was your first day on the job?" She kept her eyes

on the car ahead, which every few seconds kept putting on its brake light, causing her to have to stop at intervals. He stared at her profile as he spoke.

"Shitty, for the most part. But nothing I'm not used to. They have me in the back until my bruises heal up—then I'll start the actual waitering."

"But, what do they have you doing now?"

He hesitated, then swallowed his discomfiture. "Basic stuff, you know, mopping, sweeping, stuff like that."

"Oh Sean, I'm so sorry. I feel like this is my fault." She glanced at him, then trained her eyes on the street again. A flurry of honks indicated the mood of drivers impatient to get home. The darkening evening was punctuated by street lamps as well as the ambient lights from restaurants and shops still open. It seemed overly busy for a Monday evening.

"It's not your fault, Lace." He was silent as they turned down Lake Street. "That was some weird shit that went down last night." He had refused to think about Calvin for most of the day, but now he was forced to, was worried about her being in that house tonight, alone. "Are you going back there?"

She didn't answer right away. "I don't know. I may, if it's quiet. He doesn't seem to have a problem with me."

His slight laugh was bitter. "Yeah, it's me he wants to kill."

"Sean, I don't think he was trying to kill you. He was just angry—at both of us—for what happened. I don't know what it is about the male gender, so possessive about every little thing. He's settled down now."

"So have you thought about what you're going to do—about him?"

"Do? I guess I'll have to learn to live with him. After all, I've lived with him for most of his life, except now he won't be running up my food bill."

"Lacey, I'm serious. You don't know how dangerous he is right now. What he did to me . . ."

"He'd never do that to me, Sean. I don't believe it. Are you *trying* to scare me?"

"Yes, if it'll make you see reason. You may have been his mother, but you don't know the half about your own son."

"And I suppose you do, Sean." The anger was soft, her voice tight. He hadn't meant to make her angry, yet he seemed to be pushing her buttons lately. At least when it came to Calvin, whom she didn't really know and didn't want to know about. Unfortunately, if his ghost was hanging around, she was going to have to deal with some truths.

"Why don't you tell me?"

"Because I can't tell you, Lacey. I can't. But you saw a little bit of the real Cal last night."

She shook her head, had to stop short for a red light that she hadn't been paying attention to. He bounced forward and realized he hadn't buckled his seat belt. He put it on.

"Then if you can't tell me, Sean, stop all of the insinuations. I'm fucking tired of it."

He was quiet the rest of the ride home, feeling her anger, trying to fight his own. Because in the end, no matter what, Cal would win. He'd keep them apart any way he could. Sean knew that much.

She pulled up into the drive in front of the garage. There weren't any lights on in Sam's house. Even though the comic book store closed at six, Sam had said something about a Trek convention being held at the Congress Hotel, so he'd probably driven into the city. And Sam's parents were always out until they dragged themselves in from whatever bars they had hopped for the night. Cold stone alcoholics. Just like his father. He wouldn't be staying here long.

She sat with her hands on the wheel, looking straight ahead at the peeling garage door. He knew she was waiting for him to get out.

"I'm sorry I made you angry. Just forget what I said."

She turned to him and her eyes were unreadable.

"I can't forget it, Sean. Because I need to know. I need you to tell me what you know about my son."

The request tripped him up and his hand froze midway to the doorknob. "Lacey, that's not such a good idea."

"Sean, please stop protecting me."

He tried another tack. "It's too cold out here to sit and talk. And you'll run your battery down with the heat. Maybe some other time."

She shut off the motor. "Then we'll talk in your place. I'm assuming they have heat up there."

He didn't want Lacey to see the hole he was living in, even if it was a temporary setup. It was bad enough she knew that he was sweeping to earn chump change and that she probably saw him as nothing but a loser dropout.

"You don't want me to come up?"

"It's not a nice place to visit. Old, ratty furniture . . ."

"I've seen ratty furniture, Sean. Lived with it myself when I was away at school. There's nothing to shock me. And I don't judge you by it. I wish you'd stop judging yourself."

He wanted to hold on to this second. He wanted to be able to replay this moment again and again whenever he began to feel his life was shitty. He wanted to remember that Lacey thought more of him than he'd ever thought of himself.

"OK, let's go up."

He got out of the car and waited for her to join him.

Lacey settled uncomfortably in the partially deflated bean chair, wriggling against the irritating beads that bit into her behind. She wrinkled her nose at the faint odor of gasoline. Sean stood at a small tabletop refrigerator and pulled out a couple of bottled waters. He walked over and handed her one. She wasn't thirsty but took it anyway, not wanting to insult him. If she had figured anything out about Sean Logan, it was that he had more than a little bit of pride going on and sometimes that pride got in the way.

He opened his bottle as he sat on a dingy cot covered with a dingy blanket and took a sip. She hated to think that he slept here, but going back to her house was out of the question. Maybe she could put him up in a hotel.

He looked at her and those gray eyes penetrated. She uncomfortably thought of how they caressed her in the garden, even as his hands . . .

"What do you want to know about Cal?"

She had the question on her lips and the possibility of answers frightened her. Still, she asked it.

"What is the worst thing you know about my son? The worst thing you know he's done?"

If it were possible for eyes to be open and yet close up, then his eyes were doing that at this moment. His whole body seemed to close off from her, move back in response. She knew then that he wasn't going to answer her—or at least tell her the whole truth.

"He . . . uhm . . . he used to get into some stuff that might not have been entirely legal. Both of us did."

"Did he deal drugs?"

Sean shook his head. "No, no, he didn't."

She allowed herself a small measure of relief before asking: "But he took them, didn't he?"

He nodded, sparing her the words.

"Heavy?"

"Not really."

"Describe 'really' for me, Sean."

"Some marijuana, a little hash . . ."

"Shit," she said beneath her breath. "Coke?"

Again he nodded. "Not too much. Just a couple of times. I didn't want to get too deep into that stuff. I knew too well what that shit did to people."

"So, he wasn't a regular user?" As though it would be all right if her son had only been a hobbyist with his drugs.

"We did it at parties, mostly. His main thing was drinking. He did a lot of beer, some whisky . . ."

She listened, incredulous, and wondered where the hell she had been. Yet she knew the answer. Working overtime, trying to make more money so her son could have better things, better objects. But what he'd really needed, she hadn't given him. She had failed him somehow.

"And that's the worst—the worst you can tell me?"

Sean was quiet for a moment. "Yeah."

She watched him, but he kept his eyes averted.

"Will you tell me the whole truth one day, Sean?"

He closed his eyes and shook his head. "Don't ask me anything more, Lacey. Don't make me say things we'll both regret."

Her heart plummeted. "So, it's that bad, then?"

His silence indicted her son and herself along with him. What had Calvin done? And how could she have been so blind?

For the second time today, she felt tears flooding up and she cursed them. Cursed herself. Crying now wasn't going to do one bit of good. And she realized that maybe Calvin wasn't at peace because he needed to atone for something he'd done in this life.

She hadn't realized that Sean had gotten up and walked over to her until she felt his finger trace a tear, wipe it away. That mere touch made her breath pause. She stared up into those eyes that could mesmerize without even trying.

By the way he was staring at her, she knew he was going to break his promise. And she knew that she was going to break her own, the one to herself and to Calvin. He bent to kiss her. It was a butterfly touch of breath and lips, followed by a slight flick of tongue along her bottom lip that left a wet trail in its wake. Her body throbbed, mocking her supposed resolve, overriding her guilt and common sense. Still, she held firm for the few seconds it took her to open her mouth and invite him in. Without permission from her conscience, her hand reached up and raked his hair. Pulled his head closer.

He yanked her up in one motion. Grabbed her to him so

tightly that for a second she could barely breathe. She gasped and he relaxed his grip around her waist so he could pull back to unbutton her coat. She hadn't bothered to take it off because she hadn't meant to stay very long. Just a few questions. That's what it was supposed to have been.

What it was now was his hand wandering along her ass, gripping, squeezing, kneading. His kiss was rougher, desperate. Fear drove him, she understood. Fear that this might be the last time.

She knew it wasn't.

She knew also that everything that said this was wrong was a lie. This thing between them had been a long time coming and she understood that now.

She didn't protest when he picked her up and carried her to that horrible-looking cot. He laid her down gently, almost reverently. The cot was lumpy, but it was going to serve its purpose. It had been made for just this moment. Waiting for two eager bodies to cover it, to strain its coils, make music of its tired creaks. He lay down beside her, heat emanating from him, pouring over her.

He wasn't hesitant as he had been in the garden. His hands were much more assured, removing her blouse, her bra with a hurried ease. When she was fully topless, his lips hovered for a second and his warm breath on her nipple caused it to lengthen, become firm with anticipation. He started to touch down, then stopped. Those eyes pierced her again, almost silver in the dim light from a naked bulb overhead.

"You want to do this? I mean, with everything that's going on?"

She thought about Calvin at home. Thought about never making love with Sean again. Guilt and need fought each other. But tonight, one would win. "Yes."

She wouldn't hurt her son again. Deliberately. He would never know or find out.

God, she needed this. She inhaled a shaky breath as Sean touched her with his lips. Drew a nipple in and touched it lightly with his tongue, wetting it. She pulled him closer, desperately wanting to merge into him, disappear in his arms. He responded by sucking harder, almost bringing her pain.

His hand moved down her stomach, to the button of her slacks. One-handed, he released the fabric, found the top of her panties, moved past it. Traveled down her stomach to the crevice of soft flesh he was searching for. He found it wet and waiting.

His fingers explored her while his thumb set its aching rhythm on her clitoris, seducing her, readying her entrance for him. He started slow, gentle, and she moaned at the eddies moving upward, outward to her whole body.

Frenzied, she unzipped his jeans, searched him out, found him hard and moist at the tip. Enmeshed in the fabric of his briefs, she set a pace, catching up to his rhythmic ministration, her hand dewed with his dampness. His breath quickened on her breast as she tortured him.

He moved up, caught her lips again. This time, she took the lead, capturing his tongue, sucking his liquid heat, drinking him. He moaned her name against her mouth, so much desire muffled in the strain of his voice.

She broke the kiss so she could tug at his sweater, pull it unceremoniously over his head. Now he was as topless as she was, and she wanted to pay him in kind, licking her tongue over a firm pebble, feeling him shudder with the touch.

She stopped, looked up at his face, savoring his male beauty. Wondered, as she stroked the curvature of his jaw, why he'd never taken advantage of it. Most guys his age would have, with thoughts of easy money walking down a runway or posing for the pages of a magazine. But then again, that had never been Sean. He always denied his looks as though he were ashamed of them. She ran her thumb along his full lips; he captured it in his mouth, bathed it with his tongue. Then set about giving her a full baptism along her whole torso, down her stomach.

He stopped long enough to discard her pants and underwear. He unzipped and pulled off her boots, then threw them to the floor. Then shed the rest of his clothes. He hovered above her like a living David.

He moved up, settled on her eyes, locked them to him. "You're beautiful, you know that?" he said softly, mirroring her own thoughts about him.

"No, I've never been beautiful, Sean. You just see me that way because . . . I don't know why."

"No, I see you clearly, Lacey. Always have. And you've always been beautiful."

She had to turn away from the sincerity because she saw that he really believed that. Such was the optical illusion of youth. But his eyes made her feel she was the loveliest woman he'd seen, and she would accept that gift for now. Fantasy ruled tonight; she didn't have to deal with reality or those things beyond reality. She just wanted to be wanted, desired . . . loved. She'd missed that for so long.

"I want to be inside you," he whispered against her ear. "I need to be inside you."

She smiled. "Come on in, Sean." He shifted to move on top of her, and she wrapped her thighs around his back. He pushed into her and she'd thought she had been prepared, thought she would be used to his being inside her. But it was as though he were entering her for the first time. She had forgotten how the tremors set off when he rubbed against her walls, first so slowly that it hardly felt as though he were moving. Her chasm contracted tighter, tighter, and he exhaled a groan against her ear.

Her hands needed to hold him and they moved softly over the tight mound of his ass, squeezed the firm flesh as he had done to her earlier. He ground his pelvis into hers, moving in and out, in deeper still, until he could go no further. She gasped as he touched a place that set her trembling. She wasn't a virgin by far, but shit, she had never felt anything like this before.

The trembling wouldn't stop, as the intense friction grew

and settled through her. She gripped his arms, holding on desperately, felt his muscles straining as though they wanted to burst through his skin. His face was contorted with the pain of his pleasure, the striving to a climax.

The cot shifted with their bodies, moved across the floor as he rode her faster and faster. Suddenly he lifted up, pulled her up with him, enclosing her in his arms, his hands pushing her ass and pelvis into him. She grasped him to keep from sliding down his sweaty torso, her legs pinned around him. His mouth caught hers, wouldn't let go. They were one body, moving with one motion, their trek punctuated by the slapping of flesh, the groan of the cot, a wind now beating against the one window. His back was hard against her thighs; there would be some bruising. Glorious bruises.

"I love you," was a blast of heat in her ear, a gasp, a whisper, a promise. And she believed him.

That spot, that wonderful spot . . . out, out, damned spot—no, in, in, damn it . . . God, she was quoting Shakespeare. She would devour him if she could. She tried to swallow him whole. And heard his answering cry. In the chill of the room, she felt as though her flesh were on fire.

She couldn't wait for him. She had to come now. The rumble was explosive through her, taking her breath, merging her senses. Even when the rumbling finally ebbed, she was still shaking. She held him close, letting him have all of her. He was the devourer now, his mouth, hands touching and tasting where they could, even as his penis expanded, filled every bit of her until he could hardly move.

He cried out. The hot flood washed up into her. The stream traveled from her canal, moved upward. She felt the heat in her stomach. Her walls squeezed him harder, harder until his strength was sapped and they both collapsed onto the shaky cot. It bounced, but held sturdy. She gripped him as they both gasped for air, their pulses racing. Her blood pounded in her ears.

She closed her eyes, waiting for her body to settle back

into some normalcy. Then his lips settled over hers, so softly, such soft kisses, his finger stroking her still-tingling nipple. And the throbbing in her crotch grew, expanded.

"Stay with me," he said between breaths, between kisses. "Tonight. Just tonight. I won't ask anything else of you."

She moaned his name, giving him his answer.

And he replied with a deeper kiss, giving both of them time to recover, to prepare for a sleepless night.

Calvin waited. The paper lay on the table near the new window. The pen lay beside it.

She would see it, if not tonight, then tomorrow. Strange. He'd thought she would be home by now, but it was way past midnight. He'd probably freaked her out too much, and she was staying with Gram again.

So he would have to wait. Quietly. Patiently. Until she came home.

At least the void wasn't calling tonight. Maybe it had given up.

Maybe he could stay.

And maybe his mother would finally welcome him home.

Maybe it could be a little like it was before.

Before his accident. Before that night five years ago.

Before everything had changed.

Maybe.

Chapter 21

Lacey felt every strain, every pull of her tired muscles as she fought with the key in the door lock. The sun was up fully now, and she'd just dropped Sean off at work.

Sean. She had to stop and catch her breath. Every pore of her body called out, wanting more. Only her poor body didn't know it couldn't take any more. She needed sleep.

She needed to get her life in order.

She needed to settle matters with her son. She only hoped he couldn't smell Sean's scent all over her. Both of their scents.

Was Sean mirrored in her face for Calvin to see? Was he in her eyes? She'd checked her reflection earlier in her compact. Her lips were bruised. And there were other more intimate bruises all over her body.

She had betrayed her son once more. And couldn't seem to regret it right now. She only regretted that things were as they were, this enmity between two young men, both of whom she . . . loved? The thought that she might have opened her heart to Sean was a new, growing realization.

She opened the door and settled against it once it was closed. She looked around the foyer, half expecting to see her son standing there, his face full of accusation. She waited. Nothing.

She headed for the stairs, the thought of a shower compelling. She had to lose Sean's scent. Had to lose every evidence of her betrayal.

A sound in the living room made her pause on the first step. Something had fallen—or been dropped.

She didn't want to go in there, didn't want to have a confrontation right now. But somehow she knew that Calvin wanted her to go into the living room. Was beckoning her.

She walked in, fear edging out the residual pleasure that still nagged at her crotch. Nothing looked out of place. The only thing she saw was a pen on the floor near the table that Calvin had thrown over the other morning. The pen in itself wasn't unusual.

Except there shouldn't have been a pen there. She kept all of her pens in the small office upstairs. She was anal like that.

She walked over to the fallen pen, picked it up. It was her favorite black point that she had last seen lying beside her computer. She looked around the room again. Nothing else seemed weird. And yet, right now she felt she was being watched.

She half turned to walk out of the room, pen in hand, when she spotted the torn sheet of paper on the lamp table. It was from her yellow pad upstairs, even though it hadn't been there yesterday. There was handwriting on it that wasn't hers. Still she recognized it. Calvin's.

The writing was shaky, as though his hand hadn't been sturdy enough to write. It must have taken a lot of strength for him to do this.

She picked the paper up and her heart jumped.

She closed her eyes, wishing the words away. But when she opened them again, the accusation was still there.

"Sean is a murderer."

She placed the sheet back on the table. Now her hand was shaky.

Sean is a murderer. Why would Calvin write that? Why? Even as she asked herself, she knew she didn't want to know the answer. Either her son was a liar—or her lover was a killer.

Right now, Sean's scent seemed to permeate the room. It was all over her.

She raced up the stairs to the bathroom, loosening her clothes as she went, determined to wash herself clean and guiltless in the shower.

An hour later, she sat on the corner of her bed wearing her terry cloth robe, the torn message in her hand. She needed to talk with Calvin. She wanted to talk with Sean. And she was unable to do either. So had Calvin's attack on Sean been an attempt to protect her? Was this the secret between them, the reason their friendship had ended? Calvin had witnessed Sean killing someone, but had kept quiet about it.

Her mind was muddled. She still didn't want to believe that she had misjudged Sean so completely. She felt foolish, violated even. If Calvin was telling the truth, she had spent the night with a killer. She remembered Sean's reticence, not just last night but the whole time he had been here. Had wondered why he kept making insinuations about Calvin while keeping quiet about his own past.

Yes, she had been reckless. And stupid.

How much did Calvin know and how much was he involved? She needed to find out.

The one thing she knew was that she couldn't ask Sean. How do you work those questions into a conversation: *Did you kill someone? And why?*

She didn't think he would hurt her. At least she felt that he wouldn't. But she also knew her feelings were getting in the way. They were blinding her. She didn't know Sean. Not the real Sean, not who he was, what he had done in the past. Yet she could recount every freckle and scar, could describe down to the minutest detail the way his taut skin stretched over muscles and sinew, how his fingers tapered perfectly, the fullness of his lips, the slate of those incredible eyes . . . Eyes of a killer? Her stomach turned.

The phone rang and she picked up the extension on the bedside table.

"I want you to meet me at Vincenzo's in an hour," her

mother said without her usual greeting. "I have someone I want to introduce you to."

Lacey scoped the tables of the restaurant, trying to spot her mother. Dark paneling, red leather booths, and black-and-white photos of Italian immigrant families graced the walls, creating a warm, open atmosphere. And the food was supposedly spectacular, she'd heard.

But she wasn't the least bit hungry. The hostess came up to her and she gave the woman her mother's name.

"Oh, yes, right this way."

She followed the hostess past the noonday diners. En route, she noticed a fortyish woman dining with a man around Calvin's age. Son . . . or other?

The hostess led her to a booth near the rear where her mother was seated with a woman. Her mother smiled as she beckoned, and the hostess placed another menu on the table, then left. Lacey took the offered booth seat next to her mother.

"Sweetie, I think we have found some help. I want you to meet Mrs. Carmen Carvelli. She's a psychic."

Lacey blinked at the introduction as she looked at the woman. Fiftyish, attractive, and stylish, she was hardly how Lacey would picture a psychic.

"I know, I know," the woman said with a throaty voice. "You don't do psychics. Don't believe in them. But then again, you probably never believed in ghosts before, either." She reached her hand across the table. "Nice to meet you, Lacey."

Lacey took the hand and shook it weakly as she sat down. "I'm sorry for seeming rude . . ."

"Don't worry about that. You've been through such a horrible experience, losing your only child. And then from what your mother has told me, you've been going through something just as unsettling . . ."

Her mother piped in. "I met Carmen last year during a

seminar on the paradigm of theology, psychology, and para-psychology . . ."

"Paradigm?" Lacey mouthed to herself. "I didn't know you were into all of that, Mom."

"I'm not, actually. It's just that the seminar was held in Oak Park, it sounded interesting, and besides, I had nothing better to do that evening. When I thought about who might be able to help us, Carmen popped into my head."

The woman nodded. A pair of diamond drop earrings glinted.

"Your mother has an open mind, which is always refreshing. Much of the world around us goes unobserved simply because people refuse to take a step outside their skepticism, their comfortable little boxes."

Lacey, aware of the other diners, lowered her voice. "So, you've dealt with ghosts before?"

For the first time since Lacey sat down, the woman appeared less confident. "Not really. But I've read up enough on them to be able to give you some advice. First of all, your ghost . . . son . . . is angry. We need to figure out why. His anger is obviously anchoring him here to the between, the plane where he is subsisting."

The words seemed nonsensical, except for the fact that they were true. Calvin was neither in this world or fully in the next. He was in a state of "between."

"Do you know why your son is angry?"

Lacey shook her head, refused to look the woman in the eyes. It was her imagination, but it appeared as though the woman was seeing through her. Inside her.

"I think you do." Not an indictment, just a matter-of-fact statement that put Lacey on her guard.

"Why would I know? I wasn't with him when he died. He must simply not want to move on."

"Yes, but that's not enough to keep him here. Something, someone is anchoring him. If it were a love interest, some girl, most likely he would be haunting her. As it is, he's haunting you. A mother and son tend to be close. I know I'm close to mine. And I can sometimes tell . . . a prescience . . . when something is going on with him."

"Carmen's son and daughter-in-law live in the historic district over on Forest," her mother interrupted. "Carmen was telling me about the home he built. Sounds lovely."

"Trust me when I say I know that circumstances that affect the child can also haunt the mother. My son and his wife, although she was his girlfriend at the time, went through something last year that defied logic. Even being a psychic, I had to fight my own skepticism. This thing might have destroyed him, almost did. I'm hoping now that we can save your son. But before we do, you have to start telling the truth. Why is your son so angry, Lacey?"

Lacey fidgeted with the napkin. Luckily their waiter came. "Ready to order now, ladies?"

All the while the waiter took their orders, Lacey felt the psychic's eyes on her. They never wavered, even when the woman pronounced her own order to the waiter, that included a linguine and clams in white sauce, sauteed spinach, and a glass of Chianti. Lacey wondered if her mother was picking up the tab on this. Lacey could only stomach a salad; her mother ordered pasta alfredo.

The waiter left and her reprieve ended. "You know, don't you, Lacey, but you're afraid . . . and ashamed . . . to say."

Lacey cut her eyes at the woman. "I have nothing to be ashamed of." She felt her mother looking on in confusion, but for one of the few times in her life, her mother held her tongue.

"Exactly. You have nothing to be ashamed of. Not in front of your mother and definitely not in front of me. I see someone . . . young . . . handsome . . ."

"Oh my God, it's that boy, isn't it?" her mother said suddenly, her octave level above normal. A couple of women at the next table glanced over. "I knew something was up between you two. I could feel it. And Calvin . . . well, no wonder."

The moment was surreal. Here she was, with a psychic and her mother talking about her dead son being angry over her young lover. If a book was written about this, it would most likely be shelved with the absurdist literature.

"Lacey, how could you . . ."

"Mom, would you please lower your voice. Nothing is going on . . . anymore. It won't . . . because it's over. So, if Calvin was angry about that . . ."

"Oh, he is very angry about you and your young man. And I can tell that you're confused. As is your son. He's very confused, and it's only going to get worse. I can't see the past always, but I do get glimpses into the future. Not too much, just enough to let me warn you. Things aren't the way they seem. There are clouds of anger and fear hovering over you, your son, your . . . friend. If those clouds aren't cleared, there could be tragedy for you, for all of you. I think the decision is yours, though. You're the catalyst for what's happening now . . . although all of this is arising out of something in the past. Something dark. There's also someone else . . ."

"Lacey, another one?" her mother exclaimed, then took a drink of water.

"No, Dotty. This is someone close, but not in that way. An older man. I can't see him clearly but he's going to be pivotal."

The food came and a large Caesar salad was placed in front of Lacey. She pushed it aside. Her mother didn't seem at all eager to start in on her pasta. Mrs. Carvelli didn't have the same loss of appetite. She set on the clams and linguine as though she hadn't eaten in a while.

"Uhm, this is very good. Although I might have added a little more wine." Then she took a sip from her glass of Chianti. "Uhm, very good."

For a second, Lacey thought she'd been forgotten.

"You left your job recently. Don't worry about that. You're going into business for yourself . . . something dealing with food, but I can't see further than that. But remember, that's just one possible future."

"And what's the other future?"

But Carmen Carvelli would only shake her head, stabbing at a clam with her fork. "We'll pray that this particular cup will pass you by. You've been through enough. I'll say some words over my rosary tonight."

Her words didn't comfort Lacey. Actually, her stomach was tighter than before. She pulled out her wallet and put down a fifty to cover the meal. Mrs. Carvelli shook her head again.

"I'm paying for myself, so you don't need that fifty."

"I insist. Thank you for your . . . advice." Lacey left the fifty on the table and rose. "Mom, I have to go. I have a phone call to make."

Her mother looked distressed. The psychic's prediction wasn't sitting too well with her, either.

"Are you all right, Lacey? Don't you want to stay and finish your meal?"

"I'm fine, Mom. I just have to go."

As she left, she barely acknowledged the hostess, who wished her a good afternoon. If the psychic's predictions were right, there wasn't going to be anything good about her afternoon, nor her subsequent mornings and nights.

Outside the restaurant, she pulled out her cellphone and dialed, then left a message.

She really didn't need to speak with him. The message that she couldn't pick him up would be enough.

On her way home, she remembered that he still had to pick up his bike.

He was going to have to work out some arrangement. Maybe his friend could drive him over. Sometime when she wasn't at home. When she was somewhere else and didn't have to look into his eyes. And wonder about all the things those eyes have seen.

Chapter 22

Sean was cleaning one of the convection ovens when Emilio gave him the message.

He stopped, rag forgotten in his hand. "And she didn't say anything else?"

"No, man. Just told me to pass on the message. Your lady, huh?"

Emilio was one of the sous chefs and was responsible for the inventory. As such, he and Sean were often the ones unboxing, checking the incoming products to make sure everything was in that had been ordered. Also, he was the only one to work closely with Jean Dubec, the head chef. In these two days, Dubec had only acknowledged Sean once and that was when Sean's mop had inadvertently connected with the chef's shoe, leaving a water mark. By the look Sean received, he might as well have been a bug dirtying up the kitchen floor.

During the early morning, when his back had begun to hurt from all the hauling, lifting, and mopping, he'd asked himself several times whether it was worth it. Compared to this, his old job wasn't all that bad. But then, images of the previous night would come to him—Lacey, her brown skin dewed with sweat beads that he had eagerly licked off, her breath calling to him, her hands around him, stroking—and he knew it was worth every bit of the drudgery.

And now she had given him this message without any explanations.

"Did she sound angry?"

"Nah, she sounded normal. Just said you had to find another way to work. That she wouldn't be available. And one other thing, man?"

Sean felt his heart racing. "What?"

"She said don't call her back. That she didn't want you to. Fight, huh?"

Sean shook his head, too stunned to answer. What had happened in the few hours since they were apart? After last night, he'd thought that things were set between them, that they were going to find a way to work out the Calvin situation.

Calvin. That was it. Somehow he had gotten her to change her mind.

He threw the rag down, turned to Emilio. "Tell Russ I have to go."

"Man, I don't think you wanna do that. Especially since Russ is still interviewing. Just in case you didn't work out, you know?"

Sean said nothing more as he walked to the closet and grabbed his coat. He had to find Lacey, find out what had happened. If she didn't know by now how he felt, he was going to make her understand.

Even if he had to tell her the truth finally.

He wasn't going to let Calvin win. Not this time.

The cab fare came to just over $25. He had thirty, a small advance he had coaxed out of Russ yesterday before he left. Usually he tipped, but he needed some change to hold on to. The driver didn't look too pleased as he got out.

His bike was still parked across the street, which wasn't surprising. It was too old and worn for anyone to seriously consider taking it. Besides, in this quiet neighborhood, everyone looked after their neighbors. A few people were probably peeking out at him right now.

He walked to the door and rang the bell. No answer. He rang again, listening out for any sound of movement inside. Maybe she was hiding from him. The thought sickened him. He knocked, first gently, then harder and harder until his knuckles burned in pain.

He wasn't going away until he spoke with her. The only way to do that was to get inside. He noticed that she'd had the broken window fixed. He would find some other entry. Maybe around back.

He walked to the gate leading to the yard. Walked the path that led to the stairs. The porch looked bare, naked without the rose bushes. She must have pulled up the roots because there wasn't even a branch left.

He couldn't look at the ground without remembering. Those memories were all he had to hold on to now. He walked up the steps, stared into the window, trying to see between the gap in the curtains. His vision was limited to the kitchen table and chairs and just a bit of the hallway beyond.

He tried the door handle but it was locked. He remembered that she also had a dead bolt on the back door. He didn't want to break a window, but there was no other choice.

Even if she wasn't home, there was someone else here he needed to speak to. Someone else he had to make understand. He wasn't going away this time. And he wasn't running. No matter what Calvin decided to do to him.

He took off his coat, wrapped it around his fist, broke through the window to the left of the door. He knocked away the jagged shards sticking up, reached in and turned the lock. Then pulled the window up and crawled in.

He stood in the warm kitchen for a second, listening out. If Lacey had been home, she would have come in by now at the sound of another window breaking. Nothing. She wasn't home.

But he knew who was. And he waited.

"Calvin, I'm here, man. You got something to say to me, c'mon!"

The answer came in a sudden gut-wrenching punch to his midriff that knocked the breath out of him. He doubled over in pain.

He held that position for a few seconds, waiting for the next blow. It didn't come. Obviously, Calvin was waiting, too.

Almost a minute passed before Sean allowed himself to straighten up. He half expected to see Calvin standing there. But there was no other living being in the room.

"Cal . . . listen to me." He found it hard to catch his breath. "You can beat me, probably kill me. It's not going to change the fact that I love her. And anything you do is just going to hurt her."

A vise settled around his throat, began tightening. He couldn't expand his chest to pull in breath. He clawed at the invisible hand, but, of course, there was nothing there but his own skin. In a few seconds, he was going to pass out. In a few minutes, he would be dead. Even as he fought for breath, he began to release the life in him. But it really didn't matter if he survived, since he'd lost the only bit of happiness he'd managed to glean out of twenty-two years. His life passed before his eyes, the pain, the failures, the meaninglessness. And then she was there before him. Like an angel.

"What the hell? Sean! What!?"

Before he passed out, he realized that she wasn't a dream. She was actually here. His angel.

"Calvin, let him go! For God's sake, stop it!" she screamed.

Sean's body collapsed to the ground and she ran to him. The skin around his mouth was blue, but a flutter of breath touched her skin as she placed her hand to his nostrils. His eyes remained closed. He was passed out.

She started to rise to head to the kitchen phone to call 911, but a sudden hand on her arm stopped her. Sean was waking, coughing. He placed his other hand around his throat, feeling for something that was no longer there. He didn't appear to see her as his eyes wandered the room.

"He's not going to hurt you again, Sean," she said quietly. "Are you, Calvin?" she said to the silent room.

"You're going to let me get him out of here. And you're going to stop this."

She didn't know who she was more angry with. Sean, for obviously breaking in and putting himself in danger? Calvin, for almost killing Sean? Sean's strangling sounds had alerted her as she came through the front door, and she'd run to the kitchen, not knowing what to expect. The sight of Sean turning blue, clawing at his throat, had chilled her blood. Anyone else would have thought he was choking. But she'd known immediately what was happening.

For the second time in days, she helped Sean to the door. She unlocked the back door and led him outside.

The cold air seemed to revive him but he still needed her support to stand steady.

"Sean, I told you not to come back here. You know you upset him. He's not like this with anyone but you. Are you trying to rile him?"

Sean, almost half dead a few moments ago, came fully alive with anger. "Why are you always protecting him?! You saw what he did!"

"He's my son! What do you expect me to do? Especially when you keep provoking him?"

He shifted away from her supporting arm. "I provoke him just by being alive. He wants me gone from you, and you're letting him win. That's why I came, to find out why you all of a sudden decided you don't want to see me. You told me not to even call you. Why? After last night . . ."

"Say that louder. I'm sure Calvin couldn't hear you in there. As for the why, obviously you've encountered the reason. Isn't that enough? You might have died just now. Let it go, Sean. Just let it go. You need to go home to Muncie, Vancouver, wherever. Just as long as it's away from here."

He winced as though he had been slapped.

"My home is here."

"No, it isn't. Not anymore. And I can't do this again. Don't make me choose between you or my son. Because you know what the answer will be."

His face paled as he stared at her. He reached out to touch her cheek, but she jerked her face away. "Please go, Sean. There's nothing here to keep you."

She saw the words settling in, saw the light in his eyes extinguish. But she couldn't help him. She had to protect herself and her son.

"I'm not coming back," he said softly.

"I understand. Please don't."

She turned and went into the house, locking the door. The kitchen was quiet; she didn't know if Calvin was standing there or not.

"He's gone now for good. Please, try to find some peace, Calvin. For both our sakes."

He tried not to see the tear trailing down his mother's cheek. She couldn't possibly be crying because of Sean. What could he be to her but some quick fuck?

And she wasn't going to make him feel guilty, either. Sean deserved just what he got. Breaking into his house, telling him that he was hurting his mother. Like Sean could possibly know what's best for her. If he'd spent this much time protecting his own mother, maybe her ass wouldn't have been beaten as much.

Calvin had felt sick when Sean actually said what Calvin had already figured out—that he loved her. God, it was sick. Especially since Sean didn't know what love was, had never known what it was to have to sacrifice for it, to be torn by it. Not like Cal's heart had been.

He closed his eyes, tried to remember when he'd first realized. The first time the thought had come to him after he had thrown away the delusions and stopped denying it to himself. But that night, that one horrible night . . .

His mother was talking to him now, but it was as though he were sealed in a vacuum. The words fell empty in the room. She shook her head, threw up her hands, and stormed out. She was angry . . . angry at him. He was going to lose her anyway.

All because of Sean. Why did Sean have to come back and confuse everything? Bring back the memories that death should have erased?

The sound of gunshots blasted inside his head. He saw the body falling, the look of surprise on the man's face just before life left him forever.

It had happened so fast. Two shots and it was over.

A body lay on the ground as he and Sean stood near the trees . . . old, dark trees that hid crimes and sins. This wasn't supposed to have become a place of death, but by the end of an hour, it had become a makeshift cemetery.

The body was still there, probably. He hadn't heard anything about it ever being found.

The note hadn't been enough. Wasn't enough to keep Sean away. Sean would find his way back here, find his way back into his mother's arms, and that uncontrollable rage would come over Calvin again, forcing him to do something he really didn't want to do.

He had to tell her where the body was. She needed to see for herself. The bones of the dead man would tell its tale, show her who Sean really was. Any feelings left would die there next to that grave.

He drifted upstairs to her study. He had another note to write. A longer, more complete one.

Chapter 23

Sean didn't even bother to go back to the restaurant. The job was as good as gone anyway, not that it mattered. Not that anything mattered.

He sat on the stairs leading up to the garage apartment, his coat lying beside him. His bike was parked in front of the garage door, looking abandoned. It would be, soon. He was going to leave it with Sam.

He thought of his options, none of them good. The last thing he wanted to do was have his mother wire him money, but there was no other way. His ticket to Muncie was no longer good and all of his money was gone except the five dollars he had held back from the cab ride.

He still heard Lacey's words echoing in his ears: he didn't belong here. This wasn't his home. Maybe he would take her advice and go back to Vancouver. Vancouver was all right, and the prospects were probably better there than they were in Muncie. Muncie had just been a lark, an appeal from a friend who lived there and who later moved, abandoning Sean to the emptiness of a place without family or friends.

He touched his neck again, took a deep, cleansing breath just because he could. The cessation of air was a nightmare he would have for a long time. He almost died today. And what was scarier than the thought of his actually being dead was the knowledge that at some point he had stopped caring, stopped believing in anything good.

Then Lacey had come into the kitchen and saved him. At least, his body. She might just have destroyed his soul, more than Calvin ever could.

When he looked up and saw Cheryl standing just inside the yard, he let out a small, bitter laugh. God was playing with him today. He'd often wondered whether God had a sense of humor and had decided that if He did, it must be a sick one.

She was walking without her usual vixen stride. She actually looked humble as she walked to the stairs, then stood at the bottom looking up at him.

"I went by the restaurant today. They told me you'd been fired."

"Yeah," he said, retrieving his pack of cigarettes from his coat pocket, pulling one, lighting up, then putting the pack away again. He was going to have to quit the habit one day. Today wasn't that day, though.

"I'm sorry. It wasn't because of me, was it?"

"Cheryl, contrary to those voices in your head, not everything is about you. I got fired because of me."

She put on her "sexy" smile. "Well, it wasn't a big loss. You can do better."

"Let's see, according to you I'm only fit to pump gas and sweep alleys."

"I was just being a bitch that day. You always bring that side out of me for some reason."

"Lucky me—I don't even have to try. So what're you doing here? Come to gloat some more?"

She edged up a couple of steps until she stood a hand's reach away from him. "Does it look like I'm gloating? I'm trying to be nice."

"Cheryl, 'nice' doesn't work well with you. Besides, I don't need your sympathy. Like you said, I can do better."

"So what are you going to do now? Leave town?"

"That's none of your business."

"Don't be mean."

"You don't seem to understand anything else. Why don't you just go?"

She reached out a hand to touch the hair on his forehead. He jerked his head back, and she brought her hand down.

"Do you like being alone all the time, Sean? Even when you were with Suz, you never seemed to be . . . I don't know . . . actually there . . . with her. With any of us. It was like you were always somewhere else. Did you ever find anyone, Sean? A girlfriend, someone?"

"Cheryl, why are you so worried about my love life? You need to worry about your own. I don't happen to see you with anybody, or are you running around on somebody?"

"There's no one because I've been waiting . . . for you. Waiting for you to come back and see that I'm still here. And you know what, Sean? I'm always going to be waiting, because there isn't anyone else for me."

Sean swallowed hard at the rawness of her words. He would have given anything for someone else to be saying them to him right now.

"Cheryl, I'm sorry. I don't feel that way about you. So please stop waiting, because it's not ever going to happen between us."

She smiled, then said softly, "That's what you think, Sean."

Before he could move, she grabbed his cigarette, threw it to the ground below, and pressed her lips hard against his. She slipped her tongue in before he could stop her. Her hand reached down below his belt, grabbed him through his jeans. Squeezed him in a way that suggested years of practice, of knowing certain pressure points to push a guy's buttons. She was pushing his now.

Sean's knee-jerk contempt ran headlong into his wall of pain and was jolted back. A few hours ago, he would have pushed her away, slammed into the apartment, and locked the door. But he found himself frozen by her lips and hands, both of which were creating a refuge from Lacey's rejection. She unbuckled his jeans, pulled the zipper down. He felt the warmth of her skilled hands touching his startled flesh, which bucked and hardened under her ministrations.

He was almost gone. Almost. But then she whispered in his ear, "I love you, Sean."

The breath against his skin transported him back to last night, a millennia that was only hours ago. Lacey's breath, her smell, her touch . . . so different from Cheryl's. Cheryl, who wanted him more than anything, who would probably give him everything . . . and yet he didn't want her gift, no matter how freely and eagerly given. Nothing could erase Lacey from his flesh, tear her from his heart. Not the warm kisses Cheryl trailed along his face, her soft moans, the deft hands working him harder. He hadn't realized how much the mind could be in conflict with the body, and for a second, as he felt his blood rushing through his veins, he thought his flesh would win out. But his soul called out for another. And just that quickly, his burgeoning desire was dampened, and his body responded.

Cheryl pulled away as she felt his tumescence decrease. "What's wrong? What am I doing wrong?" He heard the desperation in her voice.

"It's not you, Cheryl," he said quietly. "It's not you."

"Then who, then? And don't say Suz, because I know you haven't been around her since the day after Calvin's funeral."

He raked his hair with his hand. "It's nobody. I told you I just don't feel that way about you."

"You did a second ago." Tears welled in her eyes. "Why aren't I ever good enough, Sean? Is it the other guys? I promise if you let me in, there won't be anyone else. And I have trust money from my parents. You could move in with me until you find a place. I could take care of both of us . . ."

"Cheryl, I don't want to be taken care of! I'm not some fucking gigolo." He stood abruptly, pushing her away. Surprised, she nearly toppled backward, until he reached out to grab her. When he tried to let her go, she refused to release his arm. He broke her grasp with his other hand, then started up the stairs.

"Don't walk away from me, Sean! Why can't you see there's no one else who's going to love you like I do? Why can't you see . . ." The last ended on a half sob.

He didn't say anything as he looked down at her, trying to find the words that wouldn't inflict the pain Lacey had laid on him.

She wiped her tears and as she stared up at him, her eyes shone an understanding that was absent a moment before. "God, you're gay, aren't you? That's why . . . of course." Her voice hardened with derision. "No wonder you could never love Suz or any other girl who thought they had a chance."

"Is that the best excuse you can come up with? Why not just accept the fact that I'm not turned on by you. That it takes more than tits and ass to get my attention."

"Then what is it, then? You like kiddies or something? Like Michael Jackson?"

"You're sick," Sean said, took the last two steps in one stride, opened the door, and nearly slammed it behind him. But even the closed door couldn't drown out her fury.

"No, you're sick, you pervert! Something has to be wrong with you!"

The words brought up a memory, another voice, almost the same words. A misunderstanding that he had tried to straighten out, to keep it from blowing up before it was too late.

But it did blow up in his face.

Something hit the door hard. He walked to the window, looked out, saw Cheryl standing with a shoe in her hand. Both her feet were bare. From his vantage he could see her other shoe had landed on the porch. She threw the other one at the window, but luckily it missed.

His anger flared and for a second he thought about opening the door, grabbing her, and throwing her down the stairs. The image of her tumbling body was so sharp in his mind that it brought with it a dread that he would actually do it.

He couldn't afford to lose control, to be responsible for someone's death. Not like before.

He walked deliberately to the chair and plunked down, sat quietly waiting for Cheryl's tantrum to end, for the vile accusations to stop.

They went on for nearly twenty minutes before she finally tired and left. Even after she was gone, the ensuing silence held echoes of her anger. Her pain.

He sat there until the sun went down and the darkness blotted out the shadows and finally closed off his thoughts.

Joe dreamed of Mabel again. Soft, laughing eyes and caramel skin, silky and sweet to touch and taste. She'd reached out for his hand and he had taken it, surprised that the skin of his own hand was no longer spotted or wrinkled, but supple and smooth as it had been when he was young. Laughing, he pulled Mabel into his arms, feeling the suppleness of her hips against his, her breasts melding into his chest. This was how it was, how it should have been for the rest of his life. He felt the streaming sun around them. His bare feet was tickled by the grass all around in the lush field.

Mabel reached her petite arms around his broad chest, clasping him in a sweet vise. "Oh, Joe, I never should have said no to you. But you know how stubborn I can be. I forgave you a long time ago, but my pride won out, and cost us both so much. But it's all behind us now. C'mon with me, Joe. Let's start again. Let's be good to each other."

Her clinch tightened, robbing him of breath, but he didn't care. Mabel was in his arms again and she loved him still, wanted to be with him. And he would stay with her as long as she would have him. Forever, if need be.

Then Mabel was gone from his arms, leaving the mammoth pressure against his chest, his heart, as though an elephant had parked itself there. He sought to draw in breath, but the pain wouldn't let him. He woke completely, felt the moisture of sweat running down his face. How long had he been asleep? He didn't want to be here in this lonely bed. He wanted to go back to the field where Mabel waited for him.

He tried to roll over, found that he couldn't. The tightening pain was robbing him of his strength.

By the time he realized what was happening, he didn't even have the ability to move. He lay there on his back, the ceiling his only purview. And he began to wonder about all that lay waiting for him on the other side.

He should have been afraid, but fear wouldn't settle on him. Just a strange expectation, edged by his pain.

He could barely pull in any breath at all. That was all right, though. Soon, he would be with Mabel. Soon, he would leave this tired, broken-down body and be able to walk without aches, to run, to be young again.

A regret stabbed him as the pain reached down to the core of his spleen, threatening to rip it all to pieces. Dotty, Stell, and Lacey . . . his three girls, as he sometimes called them. He would give anything for them not to have to deal with another loss.

But it couldn't be helped. He closed his eyes, waiting out the pain, the little twinge of fear that had suddenly come up on him. He waited out the fight. And when it was over, he moved to the light, ready to go home. Ready to go to Mabel.

Chapter 24

Lacey maneuvered the Lexus through a bend of trees on the north side of Thatcher Woods. The sun was nearing the horizon line, its halo an orange blaze that didn't provide much light in the patch of forest. The road was unpaved, rocky, and she heard the pelt of rocks flung against the car. An unexpected branch scratched at the roof, a squeaky, ugly sound.

At some point the road would become unnavigable and she would have to get out and walk. For now, she inched along, no longer blinded by her tears that had been intermittent for hours.

She and Estelle had gone to the morgue that morning and made arrangements to have Joe's body transferred to Williams Brothers—the same funeral home that had handled Calvin. Her mother was too overwhelmed after finding her only brother lying in his bed, his eyes half open, his hand clutching his chest. A heart attack. Lacey couldn't help wondering whether he'd suffered long, or whether the death had been a quick one. The news had nearly rendered her inert, unable to think, even. But she had offered to take care of matters, fearing for her mother's already shaken health. If she lost her mother now, she didn't know what she would do.

Her own heart was stretched beyond breaking. Joe was gone. Joe, who'd been there her whole life. Joe, who had given her her first driving lessons at nine, who had taught her to fish at seven, who had taught her to fight off bullies with a swift right knuckleball. Who had even taught her to make apple cobbler better than her own mother could. Joe, who had always been there with his own time-earned wisdom, parcelling out common sense when hers had seemingly taken a vacation. Was it only just a couple of days ago they had gone walking together? He hadn't been well even then, but she'd thought that he just needed time to recover from everything that had happened in the past weeks. Damn, he was only sixty-six, much too young to go, especially when people were living well into their eighties and nineties.

Her guilt gnawed at her stomach. She'd been wrong, telling him about Calvin. Maybe the truth had plagued him, caused him to worry, and exacerbated his already tenuous health. Following so close on Calvin's death, confronting something so unbelievable might have been too much for him. The combination of guilt and sadness sapped her spirit and left her just a shell going through the motions now. Still, she moved on until she came to a stop just near the lake. She had gone online and surveyed maps of the area to flesh out the sparse information.

The written note she'd found in her study had described a band of trees that stood along the bank of the Des Plaines River. The swamp oaks matched the description. Yet, the directions were so brief, there really was no way to know the exact place.

As she stumbled on a patch of uneven dirt, she asked herself why she had even come. Why she needed to know. And with Joe's sudden death, why it still mattered.

But it did. She needed to see for herself. To know the truth of the secret Sean had been holding back from her. Of a night five years ago.

She walked carefully, treading along the trail paralleling the water. Overgrowth of trout lilies and bloodwort snagged at her pants leg. After five years, the makeshift grave would be overgrown also. The place was secluded, dark, quiet. A good place to hide a body.

She had not known Sean's father, except through the bruises she sometimes saw on Joan's face. Joan had casually explained that she was "accident prone" and always refused to talk when Lacey tried to push further.

Joan had obviously been embarrassed and for a while had stopped talking to Lacey after she slipped a brochure on domestic violence into Joan's purse.

So many times, she'd thought it would be good for Joan and Sean if the man simply disappeared from their life. Then one day he did. Supposedly with some young blond Joan said she saw him around town with. Lacey had breathed a sigh of relief, thanking God that the man was finally gone.

Now, she held her breath, praying to God that she wouldn't find the man himself. But Calvin's note put together the many pieces of a puzzle that had plagued her since Joan and Sean suddenly left town. And it explained why Calvin had cut all ties with Sean before that.

Death was a schism that tore at lives and wrecked souls. And a shared secret over a violent death could definitely murder a friendship.

It had been her gun that took this man's life. Sean had shot his father down in cold blood with her gun after he and Calvin lured him here to these woods. She couldn't reconcile that her son could have been party to such heartlessness. And his soul couldn't rest until the crime was exposed.

She stopped just at the edge of the water, trying to picture that night in her mind. Tried to see the two boys standing here, the gun in Sean's hand, as a faceless man stood trembling, waiting for a bullet to rip his soul from his body. She imagined the report of the gun in the silence of the dark woods, saw the body falling. Saw her son and his friend—her lover—standing over the man. Had Sean even felt anything when he killed his father? She couldn't imagine the hatred that had brought him to that point, or the skewed loyalty her son had shown, standing with his friend over a dead man. But guilt had finally worn away that loyalty.

She searched the trunks of the oaks standing along the bank, but the sun was almost set, the light nearly gone. She cursed herself for forgetting to bring a flashlight, but she had been overwrought and had wanted just to get this over with. She hadn't planned this well at all. If she didn't do this now, she might not ever get the nerve to come out here another time. She stood trying to adjust her eyes to the growing dimness. Then remembered the tiny flashlight on her keychain and retrieved the keys from her purse. Going slowly, she traced the thin laser beam along the lines of the trunks, looking for a telltale sign of a bullet hole. Sean had shot more than once and one of the bullets had lodged into a tree trunk. That much Calvin had divulged.

Minutes passed, and the surrounding area was soon covered by a curtain of night. Frustrated, she stopped aiming the beam, took a breath. Tried not to think about Joe, about Calvin . . . about Sean. She was the only one who could bring this crime to light, the only one who would. Sean certainly wouldn't.

She just wanted to find the body and let fate lead where it would. She couldn't bring herself to name him, to point the accusing finger. Maybe he would leave town, go somewhere where no one could find him. And he would be gone from her life for good.

She continued, steadying herself against a trunk, running the light up and down in lines. The beam was thin but intense and illuminated the gnarly bark of the trees. She walked around, aiming at all angles. Along the fourth tree, she found an indentation, small, round. Perfectly round. She closed in, aiming the beam steadier on the hole. Even in the dark, the metallic gleam of metal shone under the concentrated light. She'd found the stray bullet.

They had decided on this tree because it was marked. If ever they needed to find this particular place again, they would know it, first by the cluster of the trees, then by the lone marked tree, the bullet its signature.

According to Calvin's note, the body was buried just beneath this tree. They had used a trowel Sean's father had carried in his car and had dug just deep enough for the remains not to be disturbed by wildlife. Lacey hadn't brought anything to dig up earth. She just wanted to find the tree, to write the anonymous note designating the area so that the police could find the body. She couldn't become involved more than that because there was no way to explain how she knew the information. She could very well become a suspect.

If the body was found, maybe Calvin would be able to get redemption and move on. He was the only one who mattered in this mess. She couldn't allow herself to feel anything for anyone else. As much as her son was to blame for his part of this, she held her own measure of guilt. She'd left Calvin to his own devices, trusting him more than she should. Than a good parent should. Someone more intuitive would have picked up on the signs she had missed, signs that might have allowed her to prevent this.

She tracked the beam down, noting the bare earth that was a telltale sign from the flora-covered dirt all around. She bent down to look for any more signs, anything else that marked the grave. Something glinted among the straggle of indistinguisable plants near the base of the tree. She pushed them aside, felt something cold and metallic. She pulled at it, but it was snagged in the stems. She tore at the plants, pulling them up by the roots, loosening the object from their hold.

The metal was cold in her hand. She focused the beam on it and her heart froze. It was Sean's ID bracelet, the one he always wore years ago, the one she noticed missing from his wrist just last week.

She hadn't wanted to believe it. Even after finding the stray bullet and bare earth that indicated a disturbance in its depths. She hadn't wanted to believe it of her son. Or Sean.

But the bracelet was evidence that Sean had been here. Just

as the bullet told of the violence done here. Calvin hadn't lied. Not this time.

She found that she was trembling. This time it wasn't the cold, because the temperature, even this late in the evening, was in the lower fifties. Spring was trying to come in at last. The warmer temperature, the cloudless skies in the last few days, should have been a harbinger of new beginnings.

And yet her life kept ending over and over again. And she didn't know how she was ever going to move on from here.

She pocketed the bracelet, knowing that she was tampering with evidence. Knowing that she was probably aiding a murderer.

Her heart didn't tell her it was wrong.

Sean looked at his face in the mirror. The bruises on his face were lightening, but there was still a dark mark around his throat. He turned on the faucet and the cloudy water gushed out with a protesting groan. He held his hands beneath the icy rush, splashed his face, turned it off.

The small half bath in the garage apartment was barely large enough to move around in; he didn't see how Sam did it with his wide frame. Well, Sam would have his bathroom back soon, and Sean would be on his way to Vancouver in another couple of days. His mother said she would be able to scrape the money together by then.

He'd pay her back somehow. Yet he owed her more than that.

She'd been glad to know that he was coming to Vancouver; she'd never wanted him to go to Muncie in the first place.

He went into the other room, grabbed his gray sweater off the bed, pulled it on. It would be too warm for today, but he hadn't packed too much, not having thought he would stay more than a few days. So much had changed since then. Including the weather. The sun played havoc with the grime ingrained in the wood and floor of the room, brought everything into a dirty relief.

He was putting on the only pair of sneakers he'd brought with him when Sam came in without knocking.

"Sean, your mother's on the phone. Take it in the kitchen and try not to be too loud. My mom's in the living room on the couch. She's not feeling well."

In Sam parlance, "not feeling well" always meant a hangover, whether he was talking about himself or his parents. It was the middle of the week; but then again, his own father had found a reason to drink every damn day of his life. Called it "smoothing out his nerves." The booze had let him deaden the world around him so he didn't have to deal with his disappointments. At other times, the alcohol fed his anger, turned everyone into enemies. A conspiracy of feminazis, faggots, and liberals who made the world worse for real men like him. And Sean and his mother were a part of that emasculating world.

Sam opened the door to the kitchen and walked in, treading lightly. He could hear the news blaring from the television in the living room. A couple of beer cans sat on the stained counter. The wall phone was off the cradle, swinging on its twisted cord.

He picked up the phone. "Hey."

"Hey, yourself. Good news. I was able to get the rest of the money. I'm going to wire it to the Western Union—you remember, the one on Madison—later this afternoon, so be there early tomorrow to pick it up. Sean, it's going to be OK. Everything's going to be fine."

She paused. "So you're not going to tell me what happened, what made you decide to come on home?"

"There's nothing to tell."

"Don't tell me it's nothing. I can hear it in your voice. Something happened. You know what—never mind. You never could open up, Sean. And it's my fault. You always had to keep your secrets . . . our secrets, and now you have to keep another one. I'm sorry I didn't protect you like I should have . . ."

"Mom, stop it. Nothing was your fault. Anyway, that's all

in the past. You've got nothing to be sorry about. Once I'm back in Vancouver, I'll settle in, find something."

"And stop wandering? Sean, I want you to be happy, no matter where you are. If you can't find that in Oak Park or Muncie, then I hope you can find it here. But don't just come back because you feel you have nowhere to go. You have to go where your heart is."

Sean felt a stab of pain. He had already followed his heart and it had led him absolutely nowhere.

"I'll be home soon," he promised before he hung up.

He stood there for a second, staring blankly at the phone, trying not to think about his heart. About Lacey.

". . . and in other news, an unidentified body was found on the edge of the Des Plaines River on the northern tip of Thatcher Woods. Police were led to the remains by an anonymous tip . . ."

Sean had been about to turn toward the door. Now he stood listening, his blood turning cold.

". . . are treating this as foul play. The body has been sent to the morgue to determine the cause and time of death. Police refuse to speculate this early on . . ."

Sean waited until the news report ended. He raced out the door and didn't bother about the noise as he let it slam behind him.

Sean hadn't realized he was heading to Suzanne's house until he got to the corner of Lake. The big, yellow Tasty Dog sign was still there, declaring a new spicy taco in red lettering. The smell of grilled burgers teased his nose as he waited for the signal to change. Years ago he and Suz would hang out there, waiting for her father to leave so they could go back to the house and make out. They would fill up on halfway-decent cheeseburgers and onion rings along with bottles of Pepsi. The guys hanging around would talk a little louder, start ragging on one another in a game of one-upmanship, trying to get Suz's attention. But they had been invisible to her.

He'd been able to talk to her back then. Not about everything, but at least about some things. Other things she had figured out on her own. And she'd told him that whenever he wanted to tell her everything, she would be there.

He didn't know why he needed to talk. Or what he wanted to say.

He resisted calling his mother, although he was going to have to before the day was over to let her know what was going on. To get prepared. If they made an identification anytime soon, it would only be a matter of time before the police started putting everything in place. Even Cheryl had been curious enough to go through the effort of checking up on his mother. They weren't safe, not anymore.

They had done everything wrong. He realized that now. If the police ID'd his father, Vancouver wouldn't be far enough to run. They would soon trace his mother, who was living there under her maiden name, and would extradite her back to the States. He should never have involved his mother at all. He should have just taken off, and not let her know where he was so the police could never charge her with being an accessory.

But when his father had gone missing for two days and his mother had started worrying and talking about calling the police, he'd confessed everything to her. Surprisingly, she had not condemned him. She'd barely said a word of mourning, either. Instead, she had sat down with him and they'd both decided on what they would do next.

Calvin had been the wild card; if he said anything, then Sean would have gone to jail. His mother had decided not to trust Calvin.

How had they found the body? Had a wild animal dug up the bones? Or maybe the rain had worn away the topsoil; he and Calvin obviously hadn't dug deep enough. Hell, they hadn't been prepared to dig at all. That hadn't been the reason they were there, and what had happened hadn't been planned.

He swerved the bike around the corner, rode three blocks until he sat in front of Suzanne's. The bungalow had a brick wraparound, yellow dormer, was staid and unremarkable, as were most of the homes along the street. Most of the families here were working class: civil workers, secretaries, nurses, construction workers. His own father had been a site foreman. Good enough money when combined with a nurse's income. Suz's father owned a hardware shop downtown. And her mother was out the door by her daughter's fifth birthday.

He wondered what their child would have looked like. Whether it would have been a girl or boy. And would it have been happy growing up in this house.

It was late in the afternoon and he hadn't even tried to call. He knew by looking at the house that it was empty. Her father would still be at work right now. And Suz always had the living room TV going, drowning out the silence. The tube, visible through the sheer curtains, was dark.

Still, he sat there remembering the good times that he had managed to grab for himself. Making love to Suzanne had been a large part of those times. She had been so open to him, trusting, making him feel that he was everything she needed. And he'd liked the worship. Liked the way she would look at him and make him feel, for that moment, at least, that he was something more than he could ever be.

And he'd held on to her, not hoping for more than that. His father had taught him not to reach too far or you'd topple over. Better to settle down and reach for the accessible. But that philosophy had turned his father evil. Or maybe he had been that way all along. His father had grown up in a juvie home, and his parents hadn't cared much about retrieving him once he got out. Lovelessness could turn anyone evil.

As Sean sat there in front of Suzanne's house, he realized she wasn't the one he wanted to talk with. He wanted to reach out to someone, confess everything, but Suzanne's face wasn't the one that kept popping into his mind. He saw Lacey's eyes clearly, saw them looking at him expectantly as he quietly told her everything. Saw those same eyes harden and look on him with the same contempt she would have for a murderer. And about the other . . . she would simply brand him a liar. She would never want to hear that about her son.

His mind was muddled as he sat on his bike, as he tried to sort out what he'd heard on the news. Hadn't there been something said about an anonymous tip? A tip from whom? No one but he and Calvin—and his mother—were supposed to have known where that body was.

Maybe animals had dug the bones up—because surely they would be bones by now—and a passerby saw the remains. Then called it in anonymously because he or she didn't want to get involved.

That's what had to have happened. No one still alive would have told.

The thought bloomed further as he began to understand the depths of Calvin's hatred for him. No—no one *alive* would have told. But someone dead might have. If that someone could now communicate with . . . Lacey. The anonymous tipper?

No. No, he didn't want to think that. She wouldn't have. She couldn't have turned him in.

And yet she hadn't turned him in. Yet.

How much had Calvin told her? How much had she told the police?

He hit the gas, pulled off, readying for another confrontation with the woman who had told him two times to stay out of her life.

She didn't want to see him, but he didn't care this time. He had to know if she was the one who had called the police. And if so, why she would risk sending him to prison.

Obviously, she didn't know the full truth.

Only the things that Calvin had fed to her.

If he was going to prison, she was going to hear everything, not the half-assed version from Calvin who would rather send him far away, if not outright kill him.

Chapter 25

"**Y**ou ever want to just leave, get away from all this shit?"
Calvin threw in a three-pointer, stepped back, and smiled. "Man, whatcha talkin' about now? Oh, are we having one of those deep 'meaningful' talks again? Look, if you don't want to shoot ball, then let's get out of this sun. I'm about to fry."

Sean took the ball from Calvin, pounded it against the surface of the driveway, aimed at the hoop, missed.

"Besides . . ." Calvin wiped the sweat from his face with the end of his tee-shirt . . . "I told you what you had to do. You don't owe nothing to nobody. Your ole man's never gonna stop using you for his kung fu practice doll."

Sean shook his head. "I can't leave my mom, no way . . . not with him. He'd turn everything on her, blame her for my getting away."

"Man, what you oughta do is wait one night when he comes stumbling drunk up your driveway and be there waiting for him with your bike. You know, swerve into him. I'm not saying do any permanent damage, just enough to incapacitate his ass for a while."

"Man, you and your lamebrain ideas. You know he'd put me under the jail and pour the concrete over my body."

"Then I don't know what to tell you, man. You always talking smack about leaving and then you don't. You can't do

*this, you can't do that, you can't leave your mama . . . So
what you gonna do? Just hang waiting for him to kill one of
you?"*

"It's not that serious."

"Yeah, not yet. He just hasn't reached his zenith yet. Ole
boy's gonna get in his zone one day, start whaling on either
you or your mama, won't know when to quit. And then I'm
gonna be looking at you in your casket. Now, is that serious
or what? Or if that don't get you, imagine your mama in a
casket. I like your mama enough that I wouldn't want to see
her like that. I know I sure wouldn't want to see my mama
like that."

As though his words had summoned her, his mother came
out the back door and stood on the porch.

"Calvin, it's getting too hot out here. You and Sean come
in and get something to drink."

Calvin grabbed the ball from Sean, who had gone all sta-
tionary, frozen with an odd look on his face. He wished Sean
wouldn't be so intimidated by his mother. All the time, he either got quiet or started blushing. Like he was doing now.
His already heat-flushed face seemed to go all shades of red.

"C'mon in, let's grab some food and play Nintendo or
something. Mom bought me some new games." They started
toward the porch. "You know, if you don't want to deal with
that shit tonight, you can stay over."

Sean said nothing, just stared ahead at Calvin's mother.
Gave her a nod as they reached the door.

"You look nice today, Mrs. Burnham."

She smiled, reached over and brushed a bang off his forehead. That made him blush more. "You have to stop compli-
menting me, Sean. My head's going to start swelling and I
won't be able to wear any of my hats."

She smiled, he smiled and got even redder. Calvin just rolled
his eyes, thinking how much of a suck-up his friend was. At
least where his mom was concerned.

"So, you're going to stay over or not, man?"

Sean started as Calvin's mother disappeared through the door, nodded.

"Yeah, I'll stay."

Lacey felt more than saw him approach. She was putting the keys in the car door, ready to get in. She didn't even jump when his hand clasped her arm.

"Why did you do it, Lacey?"

She didn't need to ask what he was referring to. He'd seen the newscasts, had figured things out for himself. His suspicions would naturally point to her. She should have been afraid, but strangely, she wasn't.

She turned to him, looked up into his face. She'd expected to find anger, accusation. Instead she saw hurt.

"Let me ask you the same question. Why . . . no, how . . . could you do it? I don't care how much of a bastard your father was, Sean, you had no right to kill him."

"Is that what Calvin told you? Did he tell you whose gun it was? Calvin used to carry your gun sometimes in his backpack. He used to say it was for protection."

A motion caught her eye. She turned to see Ray standing on his porch, gawking at them. She hadn't seen him since she kicked him out of her house days ago. And, of course, now he would have to be outside when Sean decided to spill his guts.

"We are not talking about this, not here, not now." She lowered her voice. "And yes, I know you used my gun, the gun that Calvin handed to you. And I know he's paying for it right now. His soul won't rest until your father is laid to his own rest."

"Lacey, do you know what you've done? To me? To my mother?"

"What does this have to do with Joan? She's in Vancouver . . ."

"Where the police will be tracing her, thanks to you."

His voice was growing louder and Ray was still watching.

"Get in the car, Sean. Right now. If you insist on broad-casting this to the entire neighborhood . . ."

Sean started to protest about leaving his bike, then looked over and saw Ray. He didn't say another word as he walked to the passenger side and got in. She got in, strapped in, took off.

"Where're we going?" The anger was still in his voice.

"To Williams Brothers. My uncle died yesterday morning. I have to finalize arrangements for the funeral tomorrow."

She saw the double take. "Shit, Lacey, I'm so sorry. He was such a cool old guy. I always liked him. I didn't know he was that sick."

She held back the tears. Crying would come later. And her grief would be with her indefinitely. Right now, she had to deal with the issue of Sean, of Joan, of Calvin.

"How much did Joan know about this?"

Sean sighed, moved closer to the door as though to put some distance between them. "Not everything, just enough to get her into hot water with the police. Aiding and abetting after the fact. She didn't think I could beat a rap, since we buried the body. It was a stupid thing to do. But it was an ac-cident, Lacey, I swear it . . . and it was Calvin's accident, not mine."

Lacey felt as though someone had punched her in the stom-ach. "Wait a minute. Calvin said . . . wrote . . . that *you* were the one with the gun. You shot your father because you were tired of him abusing you and your mother. I understand that, Sean, why you thought you had to do it, but stop trying to blame Calvin for this. Why on earth would he want to kill your father?"

For a long silence, Lacey thought he wasn't going to speak. And when he did, she wished she could take back the silence and undo the words.

"Because he saw me and Calvin . . . together. He followed us. And we were . . . Calvin and I . . . were . . . Anyway, my father started calling us a couple of faggots, and he started hitting me like he usually did anyway. Calvin tried to make him stop, and he turned and took a swing at Calvin. That's when Calvin pulled the gun from the book bag he'd been carrying. He shot at him twice. He missed the first time, but the second bullet caught my father in the face."

It was strange how her world kept spinning out of control, and the more she tried to rein it in, the greater the velocity increased until it threatened to crash into a ball of flames. The fire was all-consuming; she could feel it in her heart, her stomach, her extremities.

She stopped the car suddenly, causing a Honda behind her to stop short with a squeal.

"Get out! Get out now!"

"Lacey, you said you wanted the truth—well, I'm giving it to you."

The sound of his voice was a fury in her head.

"I don't know why you're lying, Sean, but I don't want to hear anything else from you. Now get out."

"Fuck no! I'm tired of you putting on these damn blinders whenever the truth gets a little too uncomfortable for you! And I'm tired of pussyfooting around about Calvin! I don't know why you can't see him the way others did. He definitely wasn't the choirboy you keep trying to make him out to be."

"Don't you think I know that! But what you're telling me is that you and he . . . were what . . . lovers? Oh my God! And then you come after me? That's sick!"

"It's not what you think."

"Then what the hell is it?"

Cars were honking. The Honda behind finally swerved around them into the northbound lane, the driver stopping for a second to throw a birdie before he squealed off. The other cars followed suit, some drivers throwing angry looks. She didn't care.

"We need to get out of this traffic," he said, sounding reasonable when everything was as unreasonable as could be.

"If you don't get out of my car, I'm just going to sit here."

"OK, then. You'll sit here and listen to me."

"I don't have time for you. I have to be at the funeral home in a few minutes."

He sat, staring out the windshield, his face obstinate, unbudging. He wasn't going to leave and she couldn't hardly force him out.

"Fuck it, then," she said and began driving again blindly toward hell. All during the ride, pictures of Sean and Calvin played in her head, memories tripping over themselves. The many times . . . too many, in retrospect . . . they had been alone in Calvin's room with the door closed. She had thought they were just being teenagers, closing out the adults in their lives. She had done the same thing when she was a teen. Still, what had they been doing in that room? She couldn't go any further with the thought. It was too disgusting.

When they reached the funeral home, she pulled into the lot, turned off the engine. She sat silent for a second, staring at the side wall of the mortuary displaying the WILLIAMS BROTHERS sign in large lettering and just underneath in smaller letters REASONABLY PRICED. ALSO HAVE LAYAWAY PACKAGES. And the reality of Joe's death hit her again. She felt tired and beaten. Life had defeated her at last.

"What else do you have to tell me, Sean?"

"Are you going to turn me in . . . to the police?"

She shook her head, then remembered. She reached for her purse, dug deep inside. "If I had wanted to turn you in, I could have, but I didn't. I also could have left this for the police to find. It was over the grave you and Calvin dug."

She pulled out the ID bracelet with Sean's name etched into it. "You were very careless that night. Both of you."

He looked at the bracelet as though she had pulled some extraordinary magic trick, then reached for it. He stared at it for a moment before pocketing it in his jacket.

"Thanks," he said quietly, his eyes taking in the same wall. They didn't want to look at each other. Couldn't.

"So now I'm an accessory after the fact. Just like your

mother. And now we all have our little secrets, don't we? Calvin and his little notes."

"Why are you still staying in that house, anyway?"

"Because Calvin would never hurt me. Anyway, I haven't heard or felt anything since that day when he . . . attacked you. Nothing except this note."

"Maybe he's gone."

She shook her head. "I don't think so. But if he is, hopefully he resolved what he needed to do. Just like you'll have to do one day. You have blood on your hands just like he did, and until you come clean, it's going to stain your soul."

"You won't believe it wasn't me. And I guess you want me to go to the police?"

"Sean, you do what you feel you have to do. I hope this doesn't hurt Joan."

"You should have thought of that," he snapped suddenly.

"I guess I wasn't thinking about covering your ass. I was thinking of setting my son's soul free. Seems we have different priorities."

She opened her door and got out, waited for him to do the same. When he did, he walked to her side.

"You can take the bus back. Here." And she began reaching inside her purse to find bus fare for him.

"Keep your money. I don't need it. I don't need anything from you." He had never looked at her so icily. His eyes froze her where she stood. For a second, she thought that he could actually hit her.

Instead, he turned and strode down the street, his blue jean jacket flapping in the wind. And strangely, she thought that he should be wearing his woolen short coat, even though the temperature was turning warmer.

She would never stop caring about him, she realized. Even after what he had done to his father, to her son, to her, even.

She headed to the door of the funeral home, determined to shut Sean out of her mind, out of her life.

Chapter 26

Joe was the one who taught him to straighten out his throws, showed him how to hold the ball across the seam. His dad had started him off, but he'd never had the patience with a ten-year-old who decided so late that he wanted to join Little League. Then one day his dad was gone. So it was Joe who took him through his drills, teaching him to swing through. Shy and stumbling at first, Calvin had flourished under his uncle's tutelage. But the power came later in high school as his arms developed, as his eye learned to hone in on the ball. And Joe was still there, giving him tips, pacing him. "Steady, boy, steady. You don't want to swing too fast, or too low. And don't curve your wrist so much."

Joe had taught him nearly everything he needed to know to get him to first string, to get him a full scholarship. Joe was the one who had told him to set his sights beyond the horizon.

Joe had also told him not to park on stupid. To know there were always, always consequences. "There's a formula. Says that for every action, there's a reaction. That's not just science, that's life. You act a fool, foolish things are going to happen to you."

Calvin had never paid as much attention to that lesson as he had the others. If he had, it might have saved his life. Growing up, he'd made a lot of wrong choices, never sure which road to go down. His mother had tried to give him an internal compass. Had talked to him about drugs, about girls, about the choices his father would have made. But in the end, he'd followed his own way, especially as he got older. He was always quick to act, overcome by his own anger, the fury inside his heart.

Even now, he tried to remember those times when he had struck out without thinking, but there were too many memories tangled together that it was hard to pull out just one to examine. Though his memories were less clouded now, they were often disconnected, telling only a part of the story, just like spliced scenes of an abstract movie. It was too confusing at times. At least the void seemed satisfied leaving him alone for right now. So, he had time to think about Joe. To remember Joe.

Joe, who had died a lonely old guy, alone in his bed. Calvin had always wondered why Joe lived alone, had never married. He hadn't been a bad-looking guy, and he'd known so many things that he never ran out of conversation. Knew how to keep house, cook, wash, work on his old Cadillac. Any woman would have been glad to settle down with Joe.

Remembering, it occurred to Calvin that Joe might have been gay. But he had never picked up those kind of vibes from his great-uncle. And hadn't there been a woman once, someone he had loved a long time ago when Calvin was just a boy? Not that having a girlfriend meant anything.

Still, there were ways to tell.

Just as there were ways to hide. Even from yourself.

In his teens, thoughts would come, but they were easily brushed away. But then he'd find himself dreaming, wondering. Soon the wondering invaded his waking life. Tormented him, driving him, daring him.

And so one night, he had walked down a road he had never anticipated taking. And having taken it, he found he couldn't turn around and go back.

Because by then, a man lay dead at his feet.

A man who had known about Calvin even before Calvin figured it out himself. Even as he hid it with girlfriends . . . Angie in high school, Tiffany in college. Hid it with bold remarks about tits and ass . . . about what he would do to Suz, to Cheryl, if given half the chance. But his strutting had been a mask, and he had taken off that mask only once in his life.

And shit-assed fate had fucked him up at that too-painful moment. His heart already wounded, he looked up to see Sean's father stepping out from behind some trees.

"I always knew your ass was a fag! Two faggoty-asses fucking in the woods!"

Calvin closed his eyes, shutting out the picture of the hatred on the man's face. Blond like his son, his features were harsher than Sean's, worn with cynicism and despair. Why had he decided that night to come after them, the one night when Calvin opened up his heart, spilled his feelings . . . only to have them thrown back in his face?

"Faggot!" he could hear the man screaming as he pummelled Sean, as he turned on Calvin . . .

And then the sound of a shot, followed by another slicing through the silence of that serene place, the place he had chosen because no one could witness, could run back and tell his mother. He had never wanted her to find out.

Would Joe have been disappointed in him? His grandmother, Aunt Stell? And what about his mother? How would she have felt to know that her lover was someone her own son had loved? Would she have allowed Sean to fuck her had she known? Would she have even cared? He knew now why Sean had rejected him. He could see it with a clarity that had been missing for so long. But what was more painful was the way his mother looked at Sean, how she protected him from her own son. As though Sean meant more to her than Calvin.

Even as he thought this, he knew he wasn't being fair. Of course, his mother would protect Sean, she would protect anybody from an attack. Calvin realized his anger stemmed from so many things . . . from rejection, from loss, from jeal-

ousy, even. He was jealous of both of them because they were finding something together that he never had and now never would.

A light distracted him from his sorrow. He was sitting on his father's old stuffed chair in the basement, a repository of discarded clothes, furniture, sports gear, and relics of his childhood. In the cool darkness, the glimmer wavered just off to the left, near the washer and dryer. His heart jumped . . . but then again, it couldn't, it just felt like it had. The vortex was coming for him again, he knew it. Except it wasn't like the void he had encountered before. The light was warm; he could feel the warmth emanating, even from the distance. It was a welcoming feeling.

The initial fear fled as the light moved toward him.

And he decided at that moment that he was ready. If the void wanted him so badly, he wouldn't fight it this time. He would go into the light, into eternity.

The light was right in front of him now, and strangely he felt a quieting peace, almost as though the light was comforting him. Maybe his soul was ready to accept what death had to offer.

He waited for it to draw him in, to absorb his energy, to shuttle him to the hereafter.

Instead, it began morphing, widening, taking on the definition of a man. A man he knew well.

And suddenly Joe was standing in front of him. But it wasn't the Joe he knew, the Joe of just days and months ago. Here was a younger Joe, a Joe long gone before Calvin was even born and only seen by Calvin in pictures.

The voice spoke even before the body had fleshed out entirely.

"Boy, you and me are going to talk." The voice was young and strong. And angry.

Chapter 27

She couldn't bring herself to go to another repast. She just didn't have the strength to be "strong" again. She was being a coward, she knew. And she was abandoning her mother. If not for Estelle taking over, she would have gone to the gathering at her mother's house and taken her place as the mournful niece and dutiful daughter. But Estelle seemed more than willing to stand in for both nieces.

"If you don't want to go, sweetie, I'm sure Mom will understand," Estelle had whispered as they filed out of the funeral home. Lacey looked over at her mother, who was dry-eyed and holding up well. She'd used up her supply of tears in the couple of days after Joe's death. And Lacey had in turn whispered to her mother her desire to sit this one out. Her mother had turned to her and with a half smile said, "I understand. This has to be so hard for you. Especially with everything else that's happening."

Yes, it was hard. She had lost her son and her favorite, her only, uncle. Those by themselves would be enough to stress a body. But that her son's soul was trapped—"trapped" was the only word for it—in her home had her existing in an up-turned world where nothing seemed reasonable anymore. She no longer felt comfortable there. Every creak, every unexplained sound put her on edge, even though Calvin was remaining scarce these days. Still, as much as she wished Calvin would move on to everlasting peace, she was afraid that his soul was unprepared for the next life and that when he finally did pass on, his sins would still be attached to him.

Because of Calvin, her life was on hold. She couldn't even think about her stalled career, her financial question mark, not to mention the emotional lapse that had shoved her into Sean's arms, a lapse she had only begun to regret. Sean had murdered his father, no matter what he said; she refused to believe that Calvin was capable of such an act. And Sean and Calvin had been more than friends. There was no way she could reconcile that fact in her mind with the man . . . the boy . . . who had held her, caressed her, pushed himself inside her.

She drove aimlessly, seeking distance from her life. A temporary escape, if it could even be called an escape. Just a dulling of her mind and senses, a distraction from her thoughts. She was on the Eisenhower headed in the opposite direction where Calvin, and now Joe, lay buried. The burial was almost a blur now. There had been fewer mourners than were at Calvin's funeral, which made sense as Calvin had been young and popular. Most of Joe's friends had died before him. Only a few of his neighbors and a couple of men with whom Joe had served in Vietnam stood at his graveside after the minister had said the final prayers. The military pallbearers had played "Taps" and sounded off the guns. The flag was presented to her mother.

Among the few mourners had been an unfamiliar man dressed in a gray suit with a white carnation in the lapel; her mother identified the stranger as Joe's regular pool partner. The two would often double team the younger guys at the community center where Joe hung out. And would beat them soundly.

So much about Joe she loved, and so much more she had never known. Joe had lived a simple life. Not one of quiet desperation, as had so many men like himself, older, grayer, without dreams realized and goals met. Instead, Joe had lived a life of acceptance, making the most of the hand that life had dealt him. No bitterness, no hatreds. Nothing but love. And she would always remember that.

She didn't realize she was on autopilot until she pulled up into the parking lot of the Oak Park Conservatory. She had often gravitated here whenever she needed to think, to sort things out.

It was late Saturday and the sun was clear, warmer. A golden bloom to match those within and without the glass building of the conservatory. A few people milled about outside; most of the visitors would be inside walking among a select collection of exotic flowers and plants. Along the outside perimeters, purple crocuses and yellow begonias bloomed in profusion.

She locked up her car and walked to the entrance, wondering at her need to be among flowers when she really should be at her mother's side, honoring Joe. But then again, Joe had loved flowers, had kept a beautiful garden in his yard. He would never have done what she did to her roses, no matter the circumstances. He would never have allowed death to subsume the life around him. Joe had respected every aspect of life, including the end of it.

The temperature felt around 70 degrees or higher within the glass house, and the air was moist and pungent with the attar from hundreds of flora. Paths led to various marked sections—the Fern House, the Prairie Patch, the Tropical House. She headed to the Tropical House, her favorite exhibit. Inside were collections of Hawaiian orchids, tropical climbers, anthuriums, and economic plants like cacao, coffee, and papaya. The smell was luscious, transporting her to an island in the tropics. Off to the east of the room she heard the gurgling of the small waterfall.

There were only a couple of people wandering around the paths, which gave the much-desired illusion of solitude. She wandered over to the stone bench beneath an areca palm arbor not too far from the central lagoon filled with tropical fish and spanned by a rustic bridge. Surrounding the lagoon were banana plants and lady, fishtail, and Chinese fan palms. She sat down and closed her eyes, letting the sounds of water lull her into a remnant of the peace she was seeking.

But that peace was cruelly interrupted by an unexpected voice.

"Lacey." It was a warm whisper near her ear. And she opened her eyes to look into gray, almost silver ones.

Sean hadn't planned to follow her. Actually, he had wandered the whole night riding his bike, refusing to think about the future or whether he even had a future now. Sometime in the early morning, he had found himself parked a block down from her house, not fully knowing how or why he was there. He certainly had had enough of getting his ass kicked by Calvin. Still, he sat there until the sun came up. He knew he had things to do so that he could get out of town quickly. Especially if the police started closing in. He still hadn't picked up the money his mother wired him a full two days ago. He should be thinking of saving his own ass, and keeping his mother out of trouble.

Still, everything was Lacey in his mind. He just couldn't seem to let her go, even though she had so easily dismissed him. He couldn't stop seeing that look on her face when he told her about Calvin. And as much as he wished he could just walk away, he didn't want to leave it like this between them.

He watched her get in her car around nine, and kept a distance behind her all the way to the funeral home. Even then, he hadn't planned to slip into the viewing room, slip into one of the back pews. Or follow them to the burial later. But he had, keeping a distance from Lacey and her mother.

When he saw her car go the opposite direction of the line of mourners, he wondered where she could be going. After twenty minutes, he almost decided to turn back, chalking the day as another day lost. What did he expect her to say to him, anyway? Did he really expect her forgiveness? Did he really want forgiveness for simply telling the truth?

But now he was sitting next to her, trying to think of words to say to counter the look she was giving him. The look had quickly gone from surprise to anger.

"Why are you following me? Can't I have a little bit of peace?"

"I promise you I'm not stalking you. I just didn't want to leave it like this, like it is between us now. I don't want you to hate me."

She stood. "Sean, this isn't the time. We just buried Joe and I don't want to talk about you and Calvin, not today."

"I had to let you know that it never went that far between me and Cal. It was just a kiss, that's all."

She grimaced and turned away, started walking toward a dark alcove of overhanging fronds. He hurried after her, grabbed her arm. She shook him off.

"Lacey, won't you even listen?"

She kept walking. "I heard you very clearly yesterday, Sean. You told me my son was a murderer and that you two had a thing together."

He kept after her, talking to her back. "No, that's not what I said. Yes, Calvin shot my father, but it was in self-defense. And nothing happened between me and Calvin. I didn't feel the same way he did. He caught me off guard and I told him 'no.' I told him I was in love with someone else. I just didn't tell him who. That's why he wanted me out of his life. Because I didn't . . . I couldn't . . . love him . . . at least, not like that."

She faltered in her step, but just for a second. And in that second, it seemed she was going to turn around to say something to him. But she kept walking, disappearing around a bend. Even with longer legs, he had to half canter to keep up with her.

"For God's sake, Lacey, stop running from me!"

That made her turn at last. "I'm not running. Don't you

understand, Sean? I'm trying to get away from all this death. My son is gone—my uncle, whom I loved dearly, is gone. And one day soon, I may wake up and find my mother gone, too. I'm tired of everyone leaving me."

He wanted to say that he wouldn't leave her, but that would be a lie. He had to leave, even if he didn't want to.

"All I want to do is just have a moment, just a minute or so, to not have to think about what I've lost. I didn't even want to have to think about you, about us."

"Because the thought of us disgusts you?"

He saw the tears rimming. "No, because it doesn't disgust me, even though it should. Because I want to not think about you anymore and it's not working. Even knowing what I know. And now I feel sick that I might be the one to have put you in harm's way."

She was a few steps away from him and he approached her slowly lest she start to run again. But she stood and waited. He reached out a finger, stroked away a tear. She didn't flinch, but stood motionless as though she didn't know how to respond.

He heard steps around the bend coming toward them. He didn't want any interruptions, not now.

They were just steps away from a waterfall. Behind it was an aperture, visible only from an angle and large enough for the both of them to fit inside. The only problem was that they would have to partially pass through the spray. He wasn't even thinking as he grabbed her hand, began pulling her toward it. He expected her to protest, but she said nothing as she allowed him to lead her away from the encroacher.

She was almost near the fringe of the falls, when she realized where he was taking her. She began to pull away, but he tightened his grip, pulled her into the alcove, getting them both wet in the process. She spluttered the water out of her mouth, moved a soused bang from her forehead.

"Are you crazy? Why did you pull me in here?"

"Because I don't want to be interrupted again."

The aperture provided them slight breathing room only. Sunlight filtered into the otherwise dark space through the glass roof, streaming through the artificially fed water, lighting the curves of her face. A lovely face frowning up at him.

"This is ridiculous. I don't know why you keep pressing the same points. So, you and Calvin weren't lovers. That doesn't change anything between us."

She changed her tack, her voice taking on a falsely calm tone. "Look, Sean, I understand that you have a crush on me, and I'm flattered. And I'll take the blame for letting things get out of hand between us. I was grieving and not thinking clearly. You have to know that none of this would have happened except for Calvin's death. I don't feel the same way you do, so, please stop trying to make this more than what it was. And even that little bit, I don't feel anymore."

"So you don't feel anything for me?" he challenged.

He couldn't see her eyes clearly, but he saw the moisture of her lips as she licked them. "No, I feel nothing."

She licked her lips again. He could feel her breath. It was quicker, a sign that she was nervous. She was uncomfortable with his body pressed into hers. He could feel her shifting, trying to put space between them. But he didn't want space. He leaned into her, his chest pressing into hers. He could feel the soft mounds of her breasts.

"Sean, stop it!"

He should stop. He should just leave and get the fuck out of town. And he was going to. Eventually. Later. Right now, he wanted to be here. He wanted to be with her for the last time. Because he knew he would never see her again after today.

He pressed his lips into hers, pushed his tongue inside her mouth. Felt her quick intake of breath, her shortened inhales as he moved his tongue along hers, licked the contours of it. She tried to say something, but the sound was muffled against his mouth. He wanted to kiss away her lie, to make her take back her words.

His hand reached between them, moved beneath the stern

gray blazer, felt the satin of her white blouse. He worked the jacket off her shoulders, felt it fall to the ground, felt the satin that was the only barrier between his hand and the silk of her skin.

His hands shifted to the buttons on her blouse. She placed restraining hands on his chest, and he thought she was going to push him away. But they just rested there as though they didn't know what they should be doing. As though she didn't know what she wanted.

But he knew what he wanted. Had known a long time ago, when he would watch her sitting reading a book or making dinner. Or the times when she would be carrying laundry from the basement. He would rush and take the basket from her hands despite her protest. She'd only thought that he was being courteous. But he would often find ways to be close to her without her knowing how much her nearness moved him, fed him. Made him want to get even closer to her.

Like now. He could smell the soft scent along her throat as he curved his tongue down the path leading to the open spaces of her blouse, down lower still to the smooth skin between her cleavage.

She tried to stifle her moan, but he heard it. Felt the trembling of her body. He knew she wasn't fighting him, but herself. She wanted him, even though she didn't want to. And she felt something for him, though she would deny it to the world. She didn't want to split her loyalties, didn't want the conflict that would erupt if she were to let herself believe anything he said at this point.

He knew she didn't want to have feelings for him, that she preferred that he had pulled the trigger that night. She could sleep more soundly and send Calvin off to heaven. And leave him in hell . . . or prison.

The thought made him angry. And like her, he didn't want to want this, to want her. She had betrayed him, and worse, put his mother in danger.

But his body couldn't help wanting her. He needed to be

inside her right now. And she didn't protest as he unbuttoned the slacks, shoved them roughly down over her hips, navigating as best he could, given the limited space. Then came her panties, a light band of lace and silk that at any other time he would have taken pleasure in touching.

He unzipped his jeans, freed himself, shifted his hips until his engorged penis met the warm crevice between her thighs. Shifted more until he felt the telltale moisture of her capitulation. She gave a sharp cry as he pushed into her without warning. He thought he had hurt her, but then she arched her back to give him fuller entry and he moved deeper until a spasm sucked him in further.

They stood motionless, connected for a few seconds, listening to the sound of the water that gated their private nook, kept out eyes that might pry. They heard the sounds of footsteps as someone rounded the curve of the path. Could hear the intermittent snatches of voices muted by the rush of the falls . . .

". . . just an interesting collection of dieffenbachia . . . and that waterfall is absolutely lovely."

"Yes, it is. Oh, and look over there, isn't that a bunya-bunya tree?"

"I believe it is. Let's go see . . ."

And with that, the voices receded to see their bunya-bunya tree. All the while, Sean moved slowly in her, all the while she held to the lapels of his jacket, biting her bottom lip so as not to scream out. He slid a hand to cushion the flesh of her behind that was being pressed into the stone. He grabbed the soft mound, squeezed it as he squeezed against her, moving a little farther up her canal. The feel of her was painfully exquisite . . .

A spasm shot through her as he moved a little more. She buried her face in the crook of his neck, touched her lips to it. How could she have fooled herself so completely, believing that she could just move him out of her brain, her heart, even knowing what she knew? But to be honest with herself, she didn't know what she believed anymore. She only knew that right now she loved the feel of his flesh melded inside of her, the tangle of his hair between her fingers, his own fingers moving a pattern across her ass, making her throb even more.

She had fallen. There was no way she could deny it or understand how it had happened so fast. Her heart knew, her body expressed it even when her mind tried to refuse it. She hadn't wanted his love, didn't think she needed the touch of anyone. She had done so well for so long.

Why did he have to come into her life and disrupt the little sanity she had managed to hold on to?

Sean's hands moved to her thighs, shifted them up, cueing her to wrap them around his waist. She tightened them around his back, scraping a knee against a jutting rock in the process. He quickened his rhythm, pounding into her harder and harder, his breath hot against her cheek. "Oh God, Lacey, why are you sending me away?"

"I'm sorry," was all she managed to whisper. "I didn't mean . . ."

His next words nearly shattered her, even as his body tried to split hers apart. "When I go, come with me." He barely could speak between hushed breaths.

She couldn't answer.

Outside, another set of footsteps sounded near. Too near. He stopped the thrusting, waiting. Her heart was in her throat, the fear of being exposed competing with her hunger for him. She looked up, saw his eyes concentrated on her face. She touched a hand to his cheek. He lowered his lips on hers, softly.

The footsteps moved away at last and he took up a slower, aching rhythm that only seemed to make her body burn even more. She needed to come, wanted this to last, wanted it to end, wanted to merge into him, wanted to run from him, wanted him out of her life, wanted to wake up next to him every morning.

This schizophrenia was tearing her apart, endangering them both. Putting her son's soul in peril.

Why did she always have to choose?

"Come with me," he said again, and began moving faster, as though she would give him the answer he wanted if he filled her with mind-numbing pleasure.

And for a second, just a second, the pleasure seemed to push reason to the side, made her almost say "yes."

But in the end, she came with a moan muffled against his neck as she held on to him tightly, her thighs a vise around his back and hips, nearly impeding his motions.

But he was younger, with more resistance to his climax. And he settled into her, grinding their bodies, churning their juices, urging her to a second orgasm. In a matter of minutes, it came and ebbed. And still he pounded until she had to grab the cheeks of his smooth ass to try to make him slow down, to give her a chance to recover. But he wouldn't; he was possessed with having her, marrying their bodies despite the distance she tried to put between them.

She felt another swelling, felt his body tensing. He was going to come this time, ride it with her. They were both gasping, oblivious to caution, single-mindedly intent on the pleasure. Even with the water pounding in her ears, she heard the slap of flesh against flesh, smelled the scent of sex infused in the close opening, felt the muscles in his back flex, the shadow of growth on his cheek chafing her skin as he rubbed his face against hers. Then she felt the moisture of his tongue on her lips as he licked them, then swallowed them into his own.

She nearly blacked out from all the sensations overwhelming her when she climaxed with him, both of them squeezing the other so tight as though their lives depended on it. They were left shaken and wet, from their mingled sweat and the water spray. He continued to hold her, his hand rubbing her back as though to comfort her.

Minutes passed before they finally separated. She slid her legs down, got her footing. Her slacks and blazer lay on the ground and got tangled on the heel of her shoe. She picked them up and found that they were damp. They were going to look a sight but she didn't care. He zipped up his jeans, then helped her with her clothes. She wondered if she was going to make her escape, but he grabbed her arm when she would have left.

"You're just going to leave it this way? Leave us this way?"

"There is no us. There's just this, always this. Maybe I'm in love with the fact of a young body against mine. Maybe it's just an ego thing, I don't know. But Sean, there's no us."

She left him standing there, stunned. Before she hit the full force of the downpour, she turned. "You shouldn't stay in town long." Then she ran through the stream, found a slippery foothold on the path that led to the front entrance. She patently ignored the looks from a couple walking up the path.

She had been cruel, but she needed to be. She needed him gone from her life and she didn't seem to have control of her emotions or her reasoning. All common sense left when she was around him. If she didn't stop this now, it would become messier, more entangling. Yes, she hoped he would leave. For their sake.

There was no future for them. As it were, he was in danger from the police. Because of her.

And even without the police, what did he have to offer in a relationship? He was unemployed, penniless, seeming to have no ambition. And he was so very young.

But he loved her. And despite everything, she felt the same way.

She thought she heard footsteps behind her and she turned, hoping it wasn't him. But it was just a woman and her child, a little boy enamored of a palm tree frond that dipped low to the ground. The child was tugging at it while his mother tried to persuade him to let go.

She didn't see Sean anywhere. He was probably still in the aperture, waiting for the right moment to come out.

Waiting for her to leave.

More curious eyes followed her as she left the building.

Chapter 28

*J*oe examined his nephew as though seeing him for the first time. Which was actually the case, since seeing a body was a whole lot different from seeing its soul. He had fully expected to be joining Mabel, but obviously the powers at hand thought he was still needed here.

There was such anger in that boy, it was almost visible around him. No way could he enter eternity like that.

Joe knew the why of the anger. Knew that it couldn't be easy for his nephew to watch his mother fool around with his old friend. Boys were possessive of their mothers in that way. No one was good enough, sometimes not even the daddies. Still, he had to stop this mess and move on.

"You can't stay up in here. This is your mother's house you're haunting. Don't you think it's about time for you to move to your own place?"

The levity was lost on his nephew.

"I'm not leaving until Sean is out of her life. He has no business touching her."

Joe circled around the ironing board that stood a few feet from the washing machine. Nothing in this basement had changed for years. That was the problem sometimes. Change was hard, and those who faced it were too resistant to it at times.

But life couldn't go on without change. Neither could

death. Calvin could stay here for an eternity, pestering his mother and those who moved in after her. Or he could accept that a change was due, that he had to move on. That we all did.

"*Sean is no longer your business. And neither is your mother. Sometimes in loving someone, you have to let them go. You have to let them go on without you, live their lives the way they're meant to. Love is not selfish, and you're being self-ish.*"

"*You don't understand, Uncle Joe. Sean's a murderer! He killed his father! I saw him!*"

Joe watched his nephew carefully. He had known when Lacey used to lie as a teenager trying to break free from the rigidity of her mother's rules. There was a way she moved her mouth, a way she shifted her eyes that would let him know she wasn't telling the truth or was only telling a partial truth.

Calvin had the same mannerisms growing up, the same cues when he wasn't being forthright. He had never really grown out of them. Joe would joke with him about his need for a good poker face.

Either the boy had found his poker face in death or he was telling the truth.

"*You know this for a fact, then?*"

"*Yes!*"

Joe had thought that it was Calvin he had to deal with and had thought that the ladies in his family would be all right. But if what Calvin was telling him was fact, then maybe he was here to help Lacey see the truth, to help Calvin get her away from Sean.

"*So how're you going to go about all of this? It's not like you can pick the boy up and carry him away from your mother.*"

Calvin smiled a mean smile. He had never seen that look on him before.

"*Oh, I can pick him up, all right. If he comes through those doors again, I'll not only pick him up, I'm going to toss his ass around like a ball. I'm gaining strength. You'll see. After a while, you can pick up things, hold them in your hand."*

"Well, I don't plan to hang around that long. Some of us have places to be. But I'll admit that we can't let this thing go on between them."

"It won't. I made sure of that. I wrote Mom a note telling her everything that happened and where the body was buried. And I know Mom. She won't hold on to that secret. She'll tell the police. Maybe even turn Sean in. At least, I'm hoping that's what she does."

He looked uncertain as he walked toward the stairs leading to the main floor, and looked up them as though he saw his mother standing there. "Yeah, she'll turn him in. If not, I'll just have to think of something else."

Joe walked over to his nephew. "You have to let go of that anger, Cal—otherwise, it's going to destroy your soul. And trust me, you don't want that. It's enough that you get him away from your mother. That you let her know. She's a sensible woman and she's not going to do something stupid. But this vendetta, it's as though you hate him, and not just because of your mother. I know you two used to hang out together, and that you stopped being friends. Whatever that is, just let it go now. It's not doing you any good. And it's not doing your mother any good."

Calvin turned to him, his eyes bright with emotion. "You think I'm not good for my mother?"

"How can you be good for her, Calvin? Your mother deserves to mourn you and bury you and go on with her life, knowing that you're in a better place. But she doesn't have that right now. All she has is the knowledge that you're haunting her for whatever reason. That's bound to make anyone get the heebie-jeebies."

Calvin dropped his head, for the first time showing some repentance. Joe put a hand out to touch his grand-nephew's shoulder, not knowing whether he could actually touch another spirit. Found that he could.

"*Calvin, have I ever led you wrong? I've always tried to give you good advice, but you haven't always taken it. But I'm begging you now to take my advice and let your mother go. Make your peace with God and go into the light. I'll walk with you.*"

Calvin turned to him, tears in his eyes. "*I don't think it's the light that wants my soul, Joe. The only thing after me is a darkness that wants to swallow me whole. And I can't go. I don't know what's waiting for me on the other side.*"

Joe felt a horrid burning where his stomach should be. Almost like an ulcer, and he wondered whether the spirit "remembered" things its body had gone through. He'd never had a full-out ulcer, but whenever he was under stress, he could feel the slight burning along the lining of his stomach. But nothing like this.

He didn't want to think of Calvin in that place. Whatever the boy had done in his life shouldn't deserve everlasting torment.

"*Joe, do you have trouble remembering? You know, things about your life?*"

An unexpected question. "*No, I seem to remember everything I put my mind to. I remember you as a child, even your mother. I can recall days as a kid myself, running alongside your grandmother, playing in our yard down in Alabama. Why? Do you have trouble remembering?*"

Calvin nodded. "*Sometimes. I just thought it was part of being dead. But maybe it's just those like me, those who aren't going to a good place.*"

He sounded so mournful, Joe put his arms around his shoulders. "*I won't let that happen, Calvin. Even if it means we have to stay here until . . . I promise I won't leave you until we find some way to straighten this mess out.*"

Upstairs, Joe heard the sound of the door opening, then closing.

"*Your mother's home. Let's not do anything to upset her*

*while we're here. She's had a stressful day today. They gave
me a great funeral. That girl could always put things together
last minute. She probably needs to rest right now."*

*Calvin looked up the stairs, and then, just like that, drifted
up through the door, away from Joe.*

Joe just shook his head. "Hardheaded boy."

Sean closed his suitcase, looked around to see if he was
leaving anything. He still had to pick up the money. He hadn't
called his mother and there was no way she could reach him.
She probably was starting to worry about why he hadn't gotten the money, why he wasn't on his way home now.

But he would be soon. He didn't know how to tell her that
she might have to give up her life, pull up stakes and move
again. That was going to be hard. She had settled in, liked
her job. There was even a guy she went out with every now
and then, although Sean hadn't met him and probably never
would now.

His mother had found some happiness. And he had taken
it away. Or rather, Calvin and Lacey had. Even with the
thought, he found that he couldn't be angry with her. The
anger was totally with Calvin.

Calvin had never forgiven him for his rejection. Never forgave him for not returning the kiss, but instead pushing him
away. He'd thought Calvin was kidding.

He sat down on the cot, ran his hand through his hair.
Remembered Lacey doing the same thing only an hour or so
ago.

He could have followed her, but didn't. And he understood
a little what Calvin must have felt—to be so ultimately rejected. After she had left him in the conservatory, he had
waited until he thought no one was near, then had wandered
out from behind the falls, wet, chilled even in the high temperature of the glass building.

He heard the knock and for a second thought it was Sam.

But Sam wouldn't knock. Sean walked to the door to peek out the window and blinked. It was Suzanne. What was she doing here?

He opened the door.

"Hey."

"Yeah, I know. What am I doing here?" She looked uncertain about her own question. She looked thinner with her shortened hair, and dressed in a blouse and jeans. She was still beautiful, but he knew one day the beauty would fade and life would catch up with her. He wondered whether she had anyone new in her life. But he had no right to wonder that. Neither did he have time to rehash old times.

"What happened to your face?"

"Nothing. Don't worry about it."

He stepped back to let her come inside, but she shook her head.

"I'm not here to visit. I would have called, but I didn't want to talk with Sam's parents. They can be a trip sometimes. I just wanted to let you know that the police were by my house earlier today. They were asking questions about you and your mom. Sean, those bones that were found in the woods—they say they belong to your dad. Did you know that?"

Sean's pulse raced, but he kept his face emotionless. "Why would I know that? My father left us . . . at least, that's what I thought." He was trembling inside, but his voice had sounded normal enough. He just had to keep cool, just chill. Until he could get out of the city, out of the country.

"So, what did you tell them?"

"Well, I was going to tell them I hadn't seen you. I mean, no matter what went down between us, I don't want to see you get into that kind of trouble. I remember my cousin Ron. He wound up doing nearly ten years for a robbery he didn't even do. You know how it is. They have to close a case and will do whatever it takes, even if that means putting somebody innocent behind bars."

"So did they believe you? I mean, about my not being here?" The look in her eyes froze his heart. "What happened?"

"Cheryl. She was at my house when they came by. Like I said, I would've told them that you weren't here. But Cheryl had to open her big mouth. What the hell happened between you two, anyway? She was absolutely beaming when she told them how you and your mom left so quickly after your father disappeared. Told them how you and your dad argued a lot, how it got violent sometimes. Said that you started acting suspiciously around the time he disappeared. Even said that she heard you threaten his life more than a few times. She put a whole lot of thoughts into their heads. I came by earlier to warn you, but you weren't here and neither was Sam. I think the cops are going to get a warrant or something. They'll probably be coming by, if not today, sometime soon. So, if you had any plans about staying, I wouldn't, if I were you."

"Thanks, Suz. I appreciate this." His breath was shaky.

She started down the stairs, stopped. "Sean, I think I understand why you had to leave . . ."

"Suz . . ."

"I know, I know. Your father left and and you don't know what happened to him. Still . . . I know how much of a bastard your dad was, Sean. I remember the cuts and bruises. I remember how much he drank, the names he would call you. I just wish you had trusted me with the truth when you left town for whatever reason. No matter what happened, I would have kept your secret. Things might have been different between us. A lot of things."

And maybe his child would be alive. But he had no time for regrets. Not now.

After Suz drove away, he grabbed his suitcase, headed out the door and down the steps. It was going to be tricky navigating the bike with the case, but he was going to have to. He'd pick up the money, then head to the airport, see what flights were going to Vancouver. He'd have to hope there were seats available—otherwise, he could be on standby and that wasn't good enough.

Maybe he should ride to Union Station, take the first train to Seattle, then catch a bus to Vancouver.

He was getting on the bike, struggling with the suitcase, when the back door to the house opened. Sam stepped out, his usually amiable smile gone. He threw a guilty look at Sean as two men followed him out of the house. They were both in suits, but Sean knew who they were. Suits or uniforms, detectives and cops all had that look about them.

Suzanne hadn't been fast enough. Or maybe the police had followed.

He took a deep breath as the men approached. The taller one was obviously going to take the lead. He looked like Mr. Kapawski from junior high. All hard lines along the brow, jaws tense. A wannabe drill sergeant. The older, shorter one kept a neutral expression. He probably was the one to look out for.

Sean paced his breath, but a bead of sweat broke out on his forehead. Sam looked unusually ruffled as he disappeared back into the house.

"Are you Sean Logan?" the first detective asked.

Sean half nodded, not trusting his voice.

Then the other one piped in. "Son, we'd like to ask you a few questions. About your father."

"You going somewhere?" The Kapawski lookalike was staring at the discarded suitcase.

"I . . . uh . . . flew in for a funeral. I'm on my way home."

"Well, I'm sorry but we're going to have to delay you for a little while. How long has it been since you saw your father?"

Sean shrugged, his stomach burning. "Probably five, six years ago. When he left my mom and me. Haven't heard from him since. Why?"

"You obviously haven't been checking the news," the

"kinder" detective interjected. "I'm sorry to have to tell you, son, that your father's dead. His body was found buried out in Thatcher Woods—we were able to identify him with dental records. Needless to say, he didn't get there by himself. We need to talk with you, maybe find out what might have happened. We'd also like to speak with your mother. Is she in town, too?"

"No, she's not. And she doesn't know anything."

"What is there to know? Let me rephrase that. What do *you* know?"

He took a breath that stopped at his throat, refusing to fill his lungs. "I don't know anything about it."

"You don't seem broken up about the fact that your father's dead."

"That's because he's been dead to me for a long time. Even before he left us."

"Is that right?" the younger detective asked, his brow going higher, if that were possible. "Why is that?"

"Because he was a shit of a father and husband, that's why. So, no, I'm not crying any tears over him. How did he die?"

Smooth, he thought. He was actually getting a flow. He could do this. Mix the truth with the lies, keep it simple. And he'd have to believe it himself. He didn't kill his father. That was the truth. His father had been a world-class dick. Another truth. And he didn't care that he was dead. A lie, but he had gotten over it a long time ago. But for a second, he saw his father lying on the mossy ground, his left eye staring up at Sean, his right eye blown a few feet from where he lay.

"The coroner has the body right now, so there's no official COD—that's cause of death. But I can tell you that he has a large hole in his face which I'm thinking might have had something to do with it. Now, right now, what we need to do is get an official statement from you regarding the period leading up to your father's disappearance. So, if you wouldn't mind, we'd like you to come with us."

The burning in his stomach was a five-alarm fire now, but he tamped down the rising panic, concentrating on his mantra, *Just keep cool, just keep cool.*

"Am I under arrest?"

The older detective shook his head. "No, son. Like I said, we just need to ask you some questions. This shouldn't take more than an hour. Now, the car's out front so we can cut around this back way."

The detectives took up positions to the front and back of him. Not that he was even tempted to run. He couldn't outrun a bullet and wasn't about to try.

He saw Sam peeking out of the kitchen window. Sam shrugged with a look on his face that said, *Sorry, man.*

Sean didn't blame Sam. His friend hadn't had any other choice.

There was only one person to blame for all of this.

And he wasn't ever going to have to pay for any of it.

Chapter 29

Lacey listened to Bill's message on the answering machine. He was several words short of outright begging her to come back to Meredith Stephens. Obviously, Carol wasn't holding up her end of whatever bargain they had struck together. Too fucking bad. There was no way she was going back there.

"We... I mean, I... miscalculated how strongly you felt about the Schumann account. And, in retrospect... we... I mean, I... think that your original ideas might have been on point..."

She shut off the tape. There was only so much bullshit she could handle in one day. Bill never respected her weekends when she was working for him and now he calls on a Saturday, the day she buried her uncle. *And just hours after you fucked Sean, even after you kept telling yourself... and him... that it was over.* She placed the mail in her hand on the hallway table.

She should call her mother, just in case she needed anything. She was tired, though. The sex had used up the last of her reserves.

She was a stupid woman, she'd decided on the drive back to the house. Actually, she had been driving for nearly an hour, not eager to come back. And in that time, she had scolded herself. How else to explain her lack of self-control?

At her age, she should be past acting on impulses, giving in to her basest desires.

But whenever she was near Sean, all reason seemed to leave her. It was the way he looked at her. No one had ever desired her like that; it was intoxicating in itself. Add to that the attraction that pulled at the both of them. And the affection that had somehow grown into something more on her part.

She kicked off her shoes, headed to the kitchen to get a glass of water. After which she would go upstairs, take a shower, and then collapse on the bed for a much-needed nap.

She knew she was ignoring Calvin. That had become her habit of late. Just pretend that he wasn't here. It was her way of not dealing with the problem at hand. She didn't need to think of Calvin just strolling around, ready to write one of his little notes that would tear her world apart.

She was on her way to the kitchen when two things happened. The phone lines rang, and a sound came from down in the basement. The basement door was in the hallway, just at the kitchen entryway.

The phones in the foyer and kitchen were pleading. The machine would get them.

She stood still, waiting for another sound. But there was nothing. She heard the answering machine kick in, heard her voice asking the caller to leave a name and number.

She nearly jumped when Sean's voice answered her own.

"Lacey, I'm in jail. The police are holding me on suspicion of my father's murder. Someone's been talking, a girl I knew in high school who has a grudge. She told them how I left town after my dad disappeared. She's been saying some other stuff, basically lies, telling them that I threatened to kill my father for hitting my mom. So, they're keeping me here, talking about circumstantial evidence. I don't know what evidence they think they have. I didn't know who else to call. I couldn't call my mom. Please, Lacey, I need you. I didn't do it, I swear. No matter what Calvin says."

He hung up and she stood unmoving, her heart torn. Sean was in jail because of her.

She turned and screamed.

Calvin, just a wavering shape, but truly her son, stood in front of her.

He opened his mouth and a whisper touched her ear: *"Are you going to do it? Are you going to help that mother-fucker?"*

"Oh my God." How was he . . . how?—"Calvin, why are you doing this?"

His mouth moved again, but no words this time. The look on his face said everything, though. It was pure hatred. Hatred for Sean, even for her.

He swung at the wall and she heard the boom of its force.

He had gotten stronger. Strong enough to make himself seen at last.

He reached out, touched her. And she felt it. He gripped her arm tightly. She actually felt pain.

He wanted her to choose.

He was her son. She had given birth to him, cuddled him, raised him, grieved for him. He was a part of her, a part of Darryl, whom she had loved, at least at the beginning. Calvin had always been her first choice.

And yet she heard herself say with a force she would have used for an adversary: "Let me go. Now."

He released her, but his eyes blazed.

"You don't ever touch me like that again, you hear me? I don't care how you feel about Sean. And I don't care that you're not part of this world. I'm still your mother, and death and eternity doesn't change that. You wanted Sean in jail, and you got what you wanted. Like you always do. But it's time to realize that other lives are just as important as yours."

Calvin stepped back, his form wavering even more. Before he faded out, she saw the chastened look on his face. He looked too much like an eight-year-old who had just been scolded by his mommy.

She grabbed her purse and keys off the table and walked to the door. Before she left, she turned to the empty room.

"Calvin, I love you. But sometimes you make it so hard. I'm just trying to make things right again, so please just, just . . ."

She didn't know how to finish the sentence. Actually, she wanted to tell him to just go away. But how could a mother ever say that to a son? So she left it unsaid.

She closed the door behind her, wondering, not for the first time, if she even wanted to come home again.

The smell was always the same. A mix of shit, piss, and sweat from unwashed bodies and unclean mattresses. The walls wore various stages of chipped paint. It was hard to tell the original color. Maybe a pasty green or something equally institutional. He knew those colors well, and the Maywood lockup wasn't any different. He had been in lockup a couple of times in his life, although basically juvie stuff.

Those instances paled to the reality of being locked up with real felons. He could hear the calls and raucous laughter as the sound of a man screaming in agony filtered down the corridor of cells. He didn't want to know what might be happening to the screaming inmate. The guards didn't even bother responding.

This is how fast a person could go from being "a person of interest" to being the number one suspect.

As much as he wanted to fault Calvin, Cheryl's mouth had provided them reasonable suspicion. He had the feeling she had done some "elaborating" for it to have gotten to this point. If she were right here now, he'd have no problem committing murder. Damn bitch was always a thorn in his side and now she had succeeded in crucifying his ass.

"Say, cherry, it don't do no good hanging off the bars. Nothing to see out there, anyway."

He turned to find his cell mate awake, a short reused cigarette propped in his mouth. He was gray enough that he didn't have anything to prove. He eyed Sean with more curiosity than rancor. Still, Sean was wary.

"Don't call me 'cherry.' I'm just trying to get some cleaner air. It smells like shit in here."

The man laughed. It was a hoarse sound not helped by the cigarette. "Yeah, well, what the fuck do you expect it's gonna smell like when they got the shit can right in the room with ya, and the plumbing ain't been fixed for years. So, if I were you I'd work on getting used to it."

"Yeah, I don't have to get used it."

"Right . . . because you're not gonna be here for long. Uh . . . huh. I said the same thing to myself the first time. Can't remember how long ago that was. Stop deluding yourself, cherry. You're most likely looking at a view that you gonna be seeing years and years from now. So what they got you in for, anyway?"

"Murder," Sean said after a pause. He still couldn't believe that he could possibly go to jail for years for his father's death. The whole thing seemed too surreal, something out of a nightmare.

The guy whistled through his teeth, through the cigarette. "Yeah, buddy. You might be smelling shit for a while."

"I didn't do it."

"Yeah, and I didn't do my ole lady. She just fell down those steps by her lonesome. I'm just a socially misunderstood Joe who didn't have the money to get a good divorce lawyer or defense attorney. So guess where I am?"

Sean stared into the empty cell across the corridor, wished he was in there for right now. Instead of locked up with a self-professed murderer.

He could only hope that Lacey had gotten his message. That she would come. Although there wasn't much she could do until he had his bail hearing. Still, it would do him good if he could just see her face.

But maybe she didn't care enough to even come.

"So, was it worth it?"

Sean turned back to the man. "Was what worth it?"

"Killing whoever you killed."

"I told you I didn't kill anybody! It was someone else."

"It always is. You didn't answer my question."

Sean started to protest again, then thought better of it. He didn't need to make any enemies up in here.

"They found my father's body and the police are trying to pin it on me."

"Now, why would they want to do that?"

"Because they don't know the truth."

"And did you try to give them the truth?"

"No," he said, wondering at his candor. "Not that they would believe it, anyway."

"And why wouldn't they?"

"Because the one who killed my dad is dead. That would be too damn convenient for the cops. Wouldn't look good on their records. They need a live body, and I'm it."

"You got a point there. So, were you and your dad close?"

Sean leaned against the bars, his eyes trained on something crawling on the wall just under the barred window. Right now that bug was luckier than him.

"Close as his fists. That's the main thing I'll remember about him. And you know, for all that, he wasn't an evil guy. Just a pissed-off-at-the-world loser who couldn't find anything worthwhile outside of a bottle of beer, a poker game, his television shows, and maybe an occasional fuck. When someone decides his family is to blame for his lack of luck, then shit's bound to happen."

"What about your ma?"

Sean shook his head adamantly. "She doesn't have anything to do with this. No matter what happens to me, they're not going to touch her. I'll see to that."

"That's not exactly what I was asking. So, you got rid of him for your ma?"

Sean slammed a fist against the bar behind him. "I said it wasn't me."

"Well, if that's true, then all I can say is I feel sorry for your ass. Really I do. Because innocence don't even come into play here. It's all a game, you see, of who lies better, who puts on a more entertaining show. Now, the thing you got going for you is your surfer-boy good looks. If that jury is full of women, you may just have a ticket out."

Surfer-boy good looks. That about summed up his whole worth. His looks had gotten him over a lot of times. They were why Cheryl professed to loving him and then turned him in when he couldn't say the same. Why girls smiled his way, women tried to give him money, and some men threw signals. People wanted to get with him.

For some that would be a boon, something to encourage and exploit. For him, it had been a bane, a fucking thorn that nagged in his side.

It had gotten him laid plenty of times. And hardly any of those times had brought him anything more than a transitory satisfaction. They had fed his body and ego. But not until a couple of weeks ago had a sexual encounter actually touched him deeper than his flesh.

Would she come? Would she help him?

She had every reason to resent him. And maybe he had been nothing more than a quick lay, some hard flesh to make her forget her grief. And the sad thing was that even if this was the case, he didn't care. He'd rather have had those few moments with her than a lifetime of beautiful women throwing themselves his way, offering up their bodies and nothing more.

She had to come.

"You all right over there?"

Sean nodded distractedly. He felt the first nagging of his bladder, and eventually he knew he would have to use that fetid bowl or burst his insides. Still, he would hold off as long as possible.

He would have to spend the rest of the weekend here.

"Did you ask for a lawyer? You know they have to get you one if you ask?"

"No. Not yet."

The cell mate sat up slightly, for the first time his expression showing something other than boredom. "Well, what the hell you waiting on? For the heavens to drop one at your feet? Don't you know anything? Nobody's gonna offer you any help in here, especially not the cops."

"I called somebody."

"Yeah, well, unless that somebody is a lawyer, he ain't gonna be much help to you. They can't even get you out until they set bail. And you haven't even had your bail hearing, right?"

"I think it's scheduled for Monday."

"You think? You better find out. I hope this somebody knows how to pull some strings. And another thing. I bring this up with any young blood that comes up in here or is headed down to Statesville. You don't want to stay too long in here, especially if you're a hardbody like you. Everybody knows what goes on, nobody cares. The guards don't stop it; it's not worth their time or trouble. And unless you can protect yourself, I can guarantee you that somebody's gonna try to punk you out. It's just par for the course. That's why I'm telling you, get you a lawyer or somebody with some way to get you out of here."

Sean turned again to the corridor, tightened his grip on the bars. Tried to even his breathing, slow down the pace of his heart, which was racing out of control.

He closed his eyes and when he opened them the guard was standing there looking at him like he was an idiot.

"Logan, you got a visitor."

And his heart began beating even faster.

The guard pointed him to a chair on the other side of the table and he sat down. It seemed eons since they had made love, but it was only a few hours. He should have been on his way out of town, either to Vancouver or Muncie. He shouldn't be sitting on the other side of a prison table, looking drawn and sullen. She had sacrificed him because of Calvin.

"What happened?"

His face turned to thunder, but he kept his voice modulated, too aware of the guard standing in the corner. "What do you think happened? If you hadn't let Calvin jerk you around and called the police, none of this would be happening. I would have left your life like you wanted, like Calvin wanted. So, is this what you wanted? You're so afraid of your feelings, you would rather use Calvin as an excuse to get rid of me?"

She felt her own anger rising. "You actually think I wanted you in jail?" she asked, a little too loudly. She lowered her voice, tried to calm down. "Look, it's too late to undo what's been done. We have to see what we need to do to get you out of here. So, have they set bail yet?"

Sean shook his head. "Monday."

"Do you think you can hold out until then? I have some money and hopefully it won't be that much."

"I wouldn't count on it. I'm going to need a lawyer. You wouldn't happen to know someone?"

She nodded. "Yes, I think I do. I'll call him tonight. See what we have to do next."

He nodded, looked down at his hands folded on the table. His hair seemed longer, the bangs nearly hiding his right eye. He seemed so lost, and she was reminded of the sad boy he used to be hiding out at her house, although at the time, she thought he was just visiting. In a way, she had let him down back then. And she hadn't done much good for him lately.

"Even if you bail me out, that's not the end of it. And it's not just me. They could come after my mother. Cheryl saw to that."

"Cheryl? Who's Cheryl?"

"Someone who loves to make trouble for me. She'd obviously love to see me under the jail at this point."

"And this Cheryl did what?"

"Blabbed about me and my mom leaving town after my father disappeared. That was enough to set the cops after me. They questioned me for over an hour, and I could tell they're not going to go after anybody but me. And if there's a trial and the jury finds me guilty, I'm looking at some hard time. Maybe twenty, thirty."

"You're not going to prison."

"Yeah, well, you don't know that, do you? You don't particularly believe in my innocence, and you know me. So how are twelve strangers going to cut me a break?"

She couldn't answer him. Because he was right. He might very well go to prison, and for a long time. If she could take back that call she made, she would. She hadn't thought they would make the connection to Sean, and if they did, it would be way after he left town. She had even worried that they might trace her through the call, come after her. She had weighed those possibilities against Calvin's predicament and had decided to risk it. To risk Sean.

He reached across the table to touch her hand.

"Hands to yourself!" the guard barked, and Sean slid his hand back to its former position.

Sean waited a few seconds before speaking again. "Lacey, I need you to know that I didn't do this. But there's no way I can convince you. And the only other person who could have helped me can't . . . even if he was willing."

Lacey put a hand to her forehead to rub away a growing ache. The stress was catching up with her.

"Sean, they have no evidence. You know that." She looked at him pointedly and he nodded. Both of them were thinking of the bracelet. That surely would have been the death of his case.

"The attorney I know is very good. He'll get you out of here and then he'll do his damnedest to make sure this doesn't go to trial. And even if it does, there's enough reasonable doubt in your favor. You just have to have faith."

Throughout the whole visit, his eyes had been unfocused, looking down at his hands, at the wall beyond her head, even at the bridge of her nose. An old habit of never looking her squarely in the eye.

But now he was looking at her directly, his silver-gray eyes unwavering.

"You have to have faith, too. Faith that I'm not lying to you, not now. That I've told you everything about that night."

She drew in a slow breath, let it out. And decided at that moment to believe him. Totally.

And to finally admit that Calvin was lying. And that the redemption she was seeking so desperately for her son was not within her power to give him. He had to find it for himself. Only then could he find peace.

She reached across the table and took Sean's hand, intertwined their fingers. The guard didn't say anything, but kept his eyes focused on their hands.

"I believe, Sean. I do. I think I always did. I just didn't want to face the truth."

He nodded, tightened his fingers around hers.

Then said softly, "I love you."

She didn't return his declaration. She couldn't. Not now. Not yet.

All she could do was smile sadly.

"I'll get you out of here," she promised before signalling the guard that she was ready to leave.

Chapter 30

"Do you remember that game at North Trier about five years ago? Man, that was something."

"Yeah, you hit four homers that day. I remember. That was the game the Columbia recruiter saw, made them want to sign you up. See, you haven't lost all of your memories. You still have some good ones. So, when you think about it, you had a good life, Calvin. And you have your mama to thank for that. That's what you need to focus on."

Calvin didn't say anything, looking away at the ravaged rose bush. When had that happened? This was the first time that he had been able to go farther than the walls of the house. Joe had helped him, somehow not as limited by boundaries as Calvin was. Or had been.

Calvin was encouraged by this. Maybe, just maybe, he could go farther than the house. Get even stronger.

"I appreciate my mom and everything she did for me, Uncle Joe."

"Do you? Then let her go. Let go of this life, boy. You're holding on too hard. And there's nothing that should be keeping you here."

"There's something..." Calvin said, his resentment rising. Why couldn't Joe just leave him alone?

The thing is, he felt his uncle's love, felt it encompass him just as his mother's had done when he was alive.

He had been luckier than a lot of his friends.

Than one friend in particular.

In his whole life, no one had ever hit him. All of his pun-ishments had amounted to withheld privileges and ground-ing. All of it earned and deserved.

He remembered the many times he had felt bad for Sean. Remembered the helplessness of not being able to help. The bruises, the cuts. One time a split lip. Another a dislocated shoulder.

His feelings of friendship and empathy eventually began turning, became something else. Something he had tried to brush off. But it had grown beyond just thoughts . . .

"We can go away together . . ."

The words came back at him with a clarity he hadn't expe-rienced since dying.

"What are you thinking about, boy?"

Calvin looked toward the fence surrounding the yard that separated it from the alley. So near, so far away. For a time in his life, everything had seemed attainable.

"You loved someone once, didn't you?" he asked his uncle.

Joe nodded. "You remember her? I'm surprised. She died when you were maybe nine, ten." His uncle stared off into his own space, his spectral eyes glittering as though picturing her standing in the yard. "Never thought I'd see her again. She was the last woman I gave my heart to. But that was all I was willing to give. I wasn't one to settle down, and by the time I'd figured out that she was the one I wanted, she de-cided not to take a chance on me, told me that we could be friends. She got breast cancer years later, a horrible death. I always imagined after she died that she would be waiting for me when my time came . . . and she is, she's up there waiting for me to cross over. But I won't, not until I see you into a peaceful eternity."

"I don't have a peaceful eternity waiting for me, Joe. Nothing but darkness and loneliness. It's so cold, even. Is that hell?"

Joe's eyes dropped. "I don't know. Tell me, Calvin, is there something you've done, something you need to get off your chest, or more like your soul?"

Calvin turned away.

"You can turn away from me, but you can't turn away from the truth. If there's anything, anything at all that's weighing you down, holding you to this earth. I can't say that I was perfect, by no means, but whatever faults I had, I had to eventually own up to them. Does no good hiding them from others, and not from yourself. 'Cause there's always someone who sees, who knows. So, maybe you need to do some owning up. And maybe I'm here because someone has to hear you tell it."

Calvin tried to push it all down. Flashes, images, words mixed and merged, filling in the voids that had plagued him, eluded him. Joe's words were a catalyst that provided the cohesion to set things in place. And his sin began playing in his head, and he realized his mistake as he realized the truth.

"Uncle Joe, I didn't mean for it to go down like that . . ."

Joe perked up. "What, son? What went down?"

"It wasn't supposed to happen like that . . . I don't know . . . I thought that Sean was the one . . . but I'm not so sure . . ."

"Just take your time, Calvin, let it come to you. You've been hiding from it for too long . . . I have a feeling even before you died."

Calvin turned to his uncle, looked into eyes that held no judgment. "I killed a man, Uncle Joe. It was me, not Sean. I was the one. I killed Sean's father . . ."

The sun was a ball of fire, a supernova drawing to its final death of the day. The light was muted in the cluster of trees and growth, the river sparkling through at intervals. This was his place, his private haven where he came to get away from things. Where he came to think.

He watched Sean pitch a pebble along the surface of the

water, watched the ripples form, then ebb away. Sean turned to him then.

"So, why did you want to come all the way up here? What's going on?"

Calvin resisted the urge to turn away from his friend. It had taken him all night to get the courage just to invite Sean to this place. He had chosen it for just this day. For this moment.

He took a deep breath. "I've come up with a plan."

"A plan? What're you talking about?"

"You're always talking about getting away. And you know nothing's ever going to change. And I was thinking . . . well . . . that maybe you're afraid to move out on your own."

Sean was already shaking his head. "I told you I can't leave my mother . . ."

"But maybe your mom's staying around because she doesn't want to leave you here. But if you were gone, then she would be free to leave your dad. Maybe you're the one holding her back, man."

Sean paused in his task of rock skipping, his eyes paused also as the thought penetrated. It was obviously something he had never considered.

"So, you wouldn't just be freeing yourself, but your mom, too."

Sean pitched the rock in his hand, turned to Calvin. "He'd hurt her."

"Well, maybe my mom could help. She knows all these shelters your mom could go to. Your mom could hide out, maybe move, even. He wouldn't be able to find either one of you. After a while, he'd just give up. Probably drink himself to death, since neither one of you would be around to stop his ass."

"I don't know, man . . ."

"You know, you're like a broken record on this. Anyway, don't you want to get away? There're places we could go . . ."

"We?"

Calvin saw the opening, but wasn't certain he wanted to go all the way through. An owl hooted, too early in the day. But the sun was beginning to set now.

"Yeah, well . . . I was thinking that it could be the two of us. That way you wouldn't have to do this alone. We can go away together . . ."

"But why would you? You've got everything going good here. You've got the grades and the skill, and you know you're going to get that scholarship, sooner or later. Besides, you have your mom here . . . and she's . . . great. So why the hell would you give all of that up to come with me?"

The coming darkness gave Calvin his courage. In a few minutes, it would be hard to picture Sean's face, to see either disgust . . . or something else.

Why was he doing this? What did he think Sean was going to say? "Yeah, yeah, I feel the same way. Let's get together?" He should just fake out and tell Sean he was kidding. But instead, he felt an urge to finally get this over with. He was going to have to take it slow, ease it out.

"Because . . . you know . . . I'm your bud, so you know, we stick together. After all, you'd do the same for me."

"Don't be too sure about that," Sean said with his usual half smile.

Calvin heard a rustling. Probably an animal. But now he was on his guard. He didn't need anyone coming up on them. Especially not now. That's why he had picked this place.

He moved closer to Sean, stood face-to-face. Sean stared at him, puzzled.

"So you're going to tell me what this is all about, what's going on? Why do you all of a sudden want to leave town? Both of us? And to go where?"

Calvin shrugged. "Anywhere, anywhere you want."

"OK, you're strange right now, you know that. You're tripping me out."

"Sorry, man. Not trying to faze you. I know I'm going about this all wrong . . ."

"Going about what, man? C'mon, stop hanging on to it like some day-old bread. Just throw it out there."

The knot in his throat made him almost choke. He had to get his words out, but didn't know how. So he pushed them past the knot, pushed them out of his throat, past his mouth . . .

"Sean, I think . . . I think I may be a queer."

"What? C'mon, what are you talking about?"

"Man, I know I'm queer . . . I mean . . . I'm gay, I'm gay."

Sean took a step back, and the motion was a stab wound to Calvin. Cut him deep. Because even though the light was dim, he could still see the look on Sean's face. And it wasn't an accepting one. More like discomfort, shock.

"OK then, you're gay. And you're just now knowing this. I mean, what about Angie?"

"Man, fuck Angie!" Calvin laughed. "Actually, I have, but I don't, man, it just wasn't what I'd thought it would be. I mean, we were together a few times and it was like I was just going through the motions. I swear, one time, man, couldn't even get it up. There she was, all naked, titties in my face, and I didn't even want to touch her. That's when I began to wonder."

Sean shook his head. "That doesn't mean anything. It just means that Angie doesn't shake your bone."

"But that's just it, man! I mean . . . I finally had a chance with Cheryl. She was drunk as a wino, but horny. Remember that party, man? When I hit her after she dissed me? Then we left. You went home . . . but I didn't. I didn't want to go home . . . I wanted to be out. So, I hung out behind the school. And then I went back to the party . . . to see if it was still going on. It was almost two, maybe three. There were just a few kids left. Some of them passed out in the living room. Hell, the door was wide open. And I went inside. I thought, you know, maybe I should just go home. Nothing was going on, so I walked to the door. And then Cheryl was standing there on the steps. I was about to go, but she called me back, smiled, and told me to come up. She could hardly walk up the stairs, but hey, I figured, you know, why not?"

"Man, I don't want to know this . . ."

"No, I have to tell you, OK? Because then you can know the whole reason why I'm telling you this. Why I asked you here."

"Cheryl, she's all comfy cozy with me. Took off her clothes, man. And she's laying there, telling me to c'mon, let's do it. That she knows I want her. And she's purring, like a damned cat, reaches out to touch me . . . there . . . through my pants. And . . . absolutely nothing. So, she gets mad and tells me to get the fuck out. And I leave. Man, I was so scared that she was going to tell everybody, but I guess she was so drunk she forgot about it. Anyway, after that day . . . and after Angie . . . And then there were other things, other times when I did get turned on . . ."

"So, you had two bad episodes and all of a sudden, you're gay?" Now Sean was angry. "Is this what you had to tell me?"

Calvin half turned, leaned against a nearby tree. "No, that's not everything. After Cheryl, I thought, OK, there's something wrong with me. And that made me realize there's only one person who's ever made me feel something, any-thing at all. And I've tried to tell myself that it's nothing, this thing I've been feeling for a long time, maybe even since Little League, ever since I met you."

Sean put his hand up. "Whoa . . . uhm . . . wait a minute. This is . . . I mean, this isn't . . ." He waved his hand as though sweeping something away.

"Yeah, I know, I know. But think about it. You don't hang around the honeys, either. And I know they would have dropped their panties in a hot minute if you even looked their way. And even with Suz, I can tell that you're always holding something back. It was like we're going through the same thing."

"No, man, trust me, it's not the same thing. It's not what you think at all. I'm sorry if I did something or said something that made you think that I felt anything like that. Look, this is coming out of nowhere, Cal. I mean all the times we were together, you never said anything . . ."

Calvin began pacing back and forth in front of the big tree, the tree where he had come so many times before to think about his growing feelings.

"I didn't know, or I pretended not to know, what I felt. But now that I do, I just can't pretend anymore, man. I needed to tell you how I feel, and maybe see if you could possibly ever feel the way I do. I mean, I know maybe not now . . ."

Sean didn't answer, instead looked away toward the river, a dark, moving snake with glints along its back. His silhouette was thoughtful, and at that moment Calvin knew that Sean was thinking it over. Thinking about him.

Right at that moment, he wanted to know what it would be like to touch his friend intimately. To know what his lips would feel like against his own.

He moved quickly and placed his mouth on Sean's. Sean stiffened and he felt his hand come up to push him away.

"Fucking faggots!"

The scream came from Calvin's right. The boys pulled apart as a figure emerged from a cluster of trees. The light was dim, but Calvin could see the enraged face of the man. And recognized the slurred voice. How the hell had he followed them?

Sean's father immediately went for his son. "I knew your ass was a fucking sissy! All this time hanging out with your faggot friend! I knew something was going on between you two!"

"Hey, you don't understand . . ." Sean began, but didn't finish as his father's fist shot into his belly, making him double over. He pulled back his fist again, landing an uppercut to Sean's face.

"Stop it!" Calvin screamed, rushing to pull the man off his friend. Mr. Logan was a few inches shorter than both of them, but the bulk of his body was pure muscle and he easily shoved Calvin aside.

Sean's father turned his hatred at Calvin. "Keep your damn nigger faggot hands off me! I'm going to take care of you later!" The words were a promise.

Sean, standing upright again, threw a fist, and connected with his father's jaw. Punched him again.

"Keep your hands off him!" he warned his father.

Mr. Logan laughed. The sound was evil. "Taking up for your girlfriend? Well, at least you can't say I didn't teach you to be a gentleman." He grabbed Sean's arm, began twisting. He was going to break it. He was going to break Sean down. Hurt him beyond just a beating.

Calvin remembered his book bag lying neglected just beneath the tree. He unzipped it, pulled out his mother's gun.

Sean was on the ground now, writhing in pain. Mr. Logan's fist was aimed at the back of Sean's head. Sean reached for it with his good hand and he and his father began to struggle.

Calvin held the gun, but he didn't think he could use it. The thought of actually pulling the trigger made his stomach flutter. Maybe he could just scare him, then.

He walked up behind the man, tried to reach for a flailing arm, made contact, but was easily thrown off. But he had gotten his attention. The man leaped up in a sudden motion, his arm raised. Calvin moved back out of the way, but the arm shot out, stunned his jaw. And his body flinched, as did his trigger finger.

The thunderous sound seemed to come from all around him. Went through him. He felt splinters fly from the tree where the bullet hit.

"You fucking monkey! You limp-wristed fag!"

The man must be crazy. Who would advance on someone

with a gun, someone who had already shot off a round? As he got closer, Calvin smelled the alcohol. Crazy and drunk.

He raised the gun again.

"Don't make me kill you!"

"Cal . . ." he heard Sean's pain-anguished voice. It was a plea.

"You know you're not going to pull that trigger again. You don't have the balls."

Calvin didn't know what happened next. One minute the man was in front of him, and then he jerked back and fell to the ground. It was so unreal, as though everything after that was happening in slow motion. As though it weren't happening at all.

It was a dream. A nightmare. It had to be.

"Man, what the fuck did you do?! What the fuck did you do! You killed him!"

The words came from a distance, and yet they were near him. Sean was standing up now, holding his wounded arm, looking down at his dead father. His dead father with a bullet in his forehead.

"Oh, man—oh, man!" The moan was of a boy who had lost a father, of someone who had witnessed a crime.

Calvin felt his life drifting away from him. He was going to go to prison. He was going to lose everything. And his mother would know that he was a murderer.

Only he hadn't meant to kill him. He had never meant to kill anyone. He felt tears lodging in his eyes. The dark world became blurred.

"I don't want to go to prison, man. I can't. I won't survive there. We got to go. We got to leave." It was the logical thing to do. They could run now, be together. He had killed for Sean, for them. Sean owed him.

"Are you crazy?" His friend's pitch rose several levels. "We can't just go, we can't just leave him here. The police are going to figure it out! Man, what did you do?!"

Calvin let the gun drop to the ground. Grabbed the collar

of Sean's tee-shirt. "I'm not going to prison. I'm never going there. We're going to take care of this now."

"And how the fuck are we going to take care of it?"

But Calvin didn't have an answer. Then he looked at the river.

"We can throw him in the water. Maybe he'll sink to the bottom."

"Sink? Man, don't you know that bodies float? He'll float downstream and somebody'll find him. And guess who they're going to come after? Me. Especially once they get a good look at the damage my father did to me. They're just going to assume I did it."

"And you'd turn me in, wouldn't you?"

Sean didn't answer. Didn't move. Just looked down at his father.

"He probably brought his car here."

"So, what're you saying? We should take your father's car and go?"

"No, that's not what I'm saying. He keeps tools in the car. He has a shovel back there. We're going to have to bury him."

Cal understood, began nodding. "Yeah, yeah, that's what we'll do. Then we'll put my bike in the car. You drive it. I'll take the motorcycle. You get to my place, get the bike. We'll hang out, pretend everything's cool. That's it. Nobody'll ever find him here. It's too secluded. And, and . . . uhm . . . we'll . . . they'll think he left your mother. He just up and left. I mean, you said there were rumors about other women, anyway. See? It works out, man, it works out!"

Both of them, stunned, bruised, and beaten, buried Sean's father, followed Calvin's plan.

A couple of hours later, they were standing in Cal's yard.

Sean was paler than usual. A bruise was forming underneath his eye. And he was looking strange.

"I don't think I can do this."

Calvin, for the first time that night, feeling in control, felt that control begin to slip away. "Well, we already did it, man. You're neck-high in this shit, man, so you better keep quiet. Don't go getting weak on me. If you'd been man enough to leave in the first place, none of this would have ever happened."

"Man enough to be your hole? Is that what you're saying? You know, you're pathetic. You want to talk big, act big, but deep inside, you know you're a little prick who doesn't even have the courage to stand alone. That's why you were always up under me. You think I could have ever gone with you? Even if I flowed that way, man, you wouldn't have been my choice . . ."

The words drilled inside his head, tore through his heart. He flew at Sean, began hitting him, his fist a rapid ball of molten iron. The pain in his knuckles blazed, felt good. At first, a stunned Sean stood there, as though he would take the beating. But then he grabbed Calvin around the throat, threw his fist, connected with Calvin's nose.

The pain brought back his senses, brought him back to his mother's yard, to the image of his friend standing in front of him, his nose bleeding. It looked broken. His own nose was dripping blood.

But more painful than that was the look in Sean's eyes. Hard and accusing. *You killed my father.*

And he knew he never wanted to look into those eyes again.

"Get out of here. Keep your damn mouth shut and never come back here again. Or it's on."

The hardness wavered for a second. Then Sean turned his back and walked out of the yard. A few weeks later, he and his mother were gone.

Chapter 31

Lacey hung up her cellphone. Martin Leonard had agreed to take Sean's case and would be meeting with him tomorrow. She'd agreed to pay whatever fees were required. And she would be there for the bail hearing Monday.

Everything was set. She sat in her car, waiting. For what, she didn't know.

Maybe waiting for the courage to go into the house. Just like the other times she had waited.

A bump on her window startled her. Ray stood outside, a basket in his hand. She sighed. She didn't feel like dealing with Ray today. Still, she opened her door, got out.

"Ray," she said tersely, then regretted her tone when she saw his eyes lower in discomfort.

"Ellen told me about your uncle. I came over to say I'm sorry for your loss. And I also want to apologize for my actions these past days. I'm foolish, is my only excuse. I had no business talking to you like I did, talking about your son that way, either. I know these here jars of peach preserves are a poor exchange to make amends, but they're from June's recipe she left me."

He handed the basket to her, his eyes now asking for forgiveness. She gave it to him with a nod. "Thanks, Ray. I do appreciate the gesture and I'm sure I'll enjoy the preserves. June was an excellent cook."

He beamed. "That she was. You know, she thought you were a good cook, too. She loved that vegetarian lasagna you brought over to her when she was ill. And the soups. Sometimes her appetite wasn't right, but she was always able to eat your offerings."

The compliment managed to pierce through her sadness. June had been a sweet, docile woman, genuinely suited to Ray's sometimes grumpy personality. She missed them as a couple. Remembered the woman's last year of pain. Everyone had some sorrow. Life seemed to require it.

"I hope everything gets better for you, Lacey. I truly do." With that he turned and walked to his house. He seemed stiffer, older than he had just a week ago. But a week seemed like a lifetime.

She breathed in the courage she needed, walked to her own door. Hesitated, then put in the key and turned the lock. She waited near the door after she closed it.

She'd rehearsed the words she would say to her son. Words she hoped would let him know that she would always love him, but that she couldn't aid him in his revenge against Sean. That he needed to stop lying. That would be the beginning of his redemption.

She needed to see him. To look into his face.

Most of all, she needed his words in writing.

If he wouldn't do it for Sean, then hopefully he would do it for her. And most of all, for himself.

She took a deep breath and called out his name. And waited.

"She's calling you, Calvin. Go to her."

"You want me to tell her the truth? I . . . can't."

"She'll understand, Calvin. She's your mother. She loves you."

"How can she understand when I don't? I don't know why I didn't remember what happened. I didn't think it was me. I didn't think that I could do something like that."

"*So, you wanted to remember it wrong so you wouldn't have to deal with the guilt and the pain. But don't you see, it's that guilt that's grounding you. And then you went and made things worse. You killed the boy's dad . . . and I understand why you had to do it. You were protecting yourself. But you allowed your love, your feelings, feelings that were honest, you let them twist into something hurtful and hateful. You held on to that hurt for so long that when you saw him again . . . when you saw him with your mother . . . you lashed out to hurt him back. To make him feel the pain. Because he loved your mother instead of you.*"

"*I wanted to destroy him for wanting her and not wanting me,*" Calvin said softly, almost to himself. The realization should have felt better, but it didn't.

He felt his uncle's hand on his shoulder. "*I know. But his love was never yours to have. And it's not just the gay thing. What he feels for your mother probably has been a long time coming.*"

"*I know that now. I don't know when it happened, but it happened a long time ago. I thought he was hanging around me because of me. You know, our friendship. I don't think he even realized it.*"

"Calvin . . ." his mother's voice was near the basement door. He looked up the stairs.

"*It's time to go to her, to settle this.*"

"*Yes, I guess it is.*"

"*Do the right thing, son. Do the right thing.*"

Calvin let himself lift up, let his mother's voice pull him to her.

She sat waiting in the living room, in the leather chair Joe had designated his own during his visits. She stared at the pictures of her family on the fireplace mantel.

Darryl stared out at her from a twenty-year-old picture. When she first met him, he had been handsome, with a complete sense of himself, already pursuing pre-law. That confidence, more than his good looks, had drawn her to him. A seventeen-year-old high-schooler enamored of a twenty-two-year-old college student. Her mother hadn't been able to dissuade her from marrying him on her eighteenth birthday. Only with the experience of age did she realize how young and stupid she had been. Darryl had been good to her, but not good for her. He hadn't been willing to let her grow into womanhood. He had married a girl and had expected that girl to remain throughout the marriage.

She hadn't been ready to be a mother, but had done the best she could for her baby son. Had tried to raise him to be an upstanding, honorable young man.

The young man who stood next to her now, his form wavering. He looked so much like Darryl. And her.

He wavered out, but she knew he was still there next to the chair, looking down at her. So she spoke to the empty air surrounding her.

"Calvin, I want to apologize to you. Apologize for not doing enough for you. I don't think I was ever a good enough mother . . ."

The air around her seemed to move. He was agitated.

"I think I put my own ambitions before your needs. I think I realize now that I basically bought you off with things, and trusted you too much to raise yourself. I know I did the things mothers are supposed to do. Drove you to your games, threw you birthday parties, fed you, clothed you, even kissed you good night. I asked about your friends, hoping that you were not hanging with the wrong crowds . . . but that wasn't enough. When you needed me, I was working late at the office, trying to keep on the fast track. I was thinking about promotions when I should have been wondering whether you were really home, whether you were doing your homework, whether you were staying away from drugs.

"I should have talked to you about sex, and I didn't. I gave you the pat answers about being in love, but Calvin, I didn't know what that was. I loved your father, but I don't think I was ever in love with him. I never gave myself time to find out. So, how could I have told you what it would feel like, how it could make you feel so wonderful one moment, then nearly crush you the next. Sean let me know some things, and others I'm just figuring out. I'm sorry I wasn't the type of mother you could come to and tell me things, tell me how you felt. I wouldn't have judged you. You were my son. I would have loved you no matter what. And that love was always unconditional, even if you didn't know it or feel it."

She felt a tear stream down her cheek.

"I saw your anger, and at times, I saw your pain. It started with Darryl's death, and I thought I could rein you in just with words. I thought I could make you forget the pain of losing a father so young. I had your grandmother and aunt, and Uncle Joe to help me. But it was me you needed, not the me I gave you, but all of me."

She stood up and took a shaky breath. Faced the vibrating air. "You think you hate Sean. But that's not what you feel. Not really. Even now. Oh God, I wish I could make it all right for you, Calvin. You may think life cheated you out of love, but you don't realize how wonderful it is that you could feel love. That you found you had the capacity for it. So many people leave this world never truly loving or reaching out to someone. You were man enough to reach out to someone, to try to find happiness. That took a lot of courage. And even if that love wasn't returned, it doesn't diminish the fact that you did love. And that you realized it before you left this world."

She walked over to the table near the window where her writing pad lay next to a pen. She turned and spoke to the empty room.

"Talk to me, Calvin. Talk to me like you've been talking to me. I know I didn't listen to you enough before, but I want to hear you now. I want you to tell me what you want, how I can help you now. Most of all, I want you to talk to me about

Sean. About how you felt about him. How you still feel about him, even though you don't want to. I understand now."

She walked away from the table and continued out of the room. Air wavered as he materialized near the corner of her eye but she didn't stop. She wanted him to be alone with his thoughts, she wanted him to reach inside himself. She wanted him to admit the truth to himself. So that he could admit the truth about other things, including that horrible night when Sean's father was killed.

He had to exorcise his own demons or he would be doomed to walk this world, haunt this house for however long this world turned. And his hell would be hers to endure also.

She hoped he would release them both.

Sean stared up at the bottom of the bunk above his head. His cell mate, who had finally identified himself as "Rudy, just Rudy"—was asleep, his sonorous snores rupturing any hope of rest. Sean pulled on the cigarette stub that Rudy had passed to him.

He thought of his call to his mother that afternoon. They had allowed him the extra call after he told them that she would be worried about where he was. It had been painful hearing her cry.

"How did this happen?"

He'd paused. "Someone found the body. They identified him and the police started putting things together. And please, Mom, don't say too much over the phone, OK? I don't know who might be listening. I just wanted to let you know I'm going to be all right."

"Sean, don't bullshit me. How are you going to be all right behind bars? You're locked up like some criminal. Look, don't worry. I'm coming down there and I'm going to get you out somehow."

"Mom, don't. You know it's too risky."

"I don't care about the risk. I'm coming down there, and there's nothing you can say to stop me. And then I'm going to find you a good lawyer."

"I already got a lawyer . . ."

"I'm not talking about some public defender. Lord knows, with our luck you'll get someone just out of school."

"No, he's not a public defender. He's a friend of Lacey's. I met with him today."

"Lacey? You called Lacey? Why?"

"Because . . . because I figured she could help. She knows people. And don't worry about the money. She's covering that."

"I don't understand. We could be talking about a lot of money here. Why would Lacey do that for you?"

He was tired of the lies. Tired of having to keep secrets. "Because she and I . . . we got close. You know, Calvin's death and other things . . ."

"Close? What do you mean, 'close'? Are you saying what I think you're saying?" He heard the incredulous tone, knew that it was a second from going from shock to anger. "Are you two screwing each other?"

"It's not like that. I . . . love her."

"You love her? Sean, she's my age, give or take a year or two. What the hell are you doing, getting involved with Calvin's mother? You know, I always knew you had a crush on her when you were a teenager, but I would have thought you'd grown out of that. And what the hell is she doing sleeping with you? It's sick!"

"It's not sick! And it's not abnormal or perverted. She's a woman and I'm a man . . ."

"Barely."

"Weren't you the one who said that you wanted me to be happy?"

"Oh God, Sean, you had to know I didn't mean something like this . . ."

Before Sean could say another word, the guard came up behind him. "Time's up."

He could barely get out a "'Bye, Mom, don't worry . . ." before the guard took the phone out of his hand and hung it up.

Another foghorn boomed through the cell. He turned on his side, pressing an ear to the stained pillow, trying to muffle at least half the noise.

But even without the snoring, he would have had trouble sleeping. His mother was angry and scared and he didn't know what she would do at this point. The last thing he needed was for the police to go after his mother, but she hadn't sounded reasonable over the phone. She was going to do what she wanted, especially since she now knew about him and Lacey. He should have kept his damn mouth shut.

He closed his eyes. And Lacey was there with him. In the cell, sitting next to him, stroking his cheek, her perfume chasing away the other smells. He felt himself finally being pulled under as he imagined her lips moving on his, imagine her saying those words he hoped to hear one day.

Even if he couldn't have her in real life, he could be with her in his dreams. He reached for her, closed his arms around her, felt her body meld into his. Felt her breath against his ear as she kissed him. Then began to whisper, "Sean, I want to tell you something, I . . ."

A rumble tore through him, drowning out the words. And he awoke, back in his filthy cell, lying on a filthy cot, listening to Rudy's snores.

Chapter 32

Ten o'clock Monday morning, Lacey sat in the back of the District 4 Maywood courtroom watching as another defendant was brought before the judge. This one seemed to be in his late thirties, early forties, balding. His hands were handcuffed behind him. A very short man in a gray pinstripe suit stood beside him. He looked like a kid dressed for Sunday school.

Lacey's hand nervously tapped her purse as the anticipation of seeing Sean similarly trussed up ate at her stomach. Especially since he was innocent and she knew it, but couldn't prove it. Not yet.

She had driven early to the Maywood courthouse, which served several suburbs, including Oak Park. She had her checkbook, ready to write out whatever amount the judge designated.

"OK, we have Larry Welch, is that correct?" the judge asked, and without waiting for an answer, "I see the charge is attempted murder." He peered at the man from behind wire-rimmed glasses. His weary, drawn face and steel gray hair said that he'd been sitting on the bench for too many years. "What are the circumstances, counsel?"

"Self-defense, your honor," said the attorney. "The victim pulled out a knife and my client was forced to defend himself. We ask that he be released on his own recognizance."

The judge looked over at a blond woman, dressed in a conservative dark blue suit. She stood at another table. "Do you have anything to add?"

Lacey could only see the woman's face from an angle, but she appeared to be smirking. And the smirk was in her voice as well as she said, "Your honor, Larry Welch, the defendant, has a history of 'defending' himself. In 1993, when he was sixteen, he shot and killed his friend Jamie Stapler. He claimed then that the victim had attacked him with a knife and that he'd had no choice. Ten years later, in 2003, a bar fight ended with Mr. Welch taking a bat to one of the patrons. Luckily, the victim here, Curtis Williams, survived. Again, Mr. Welch claimed self-defense. Your honor, Mr. Welch is either the most put-upon victim or is a man out of control who thinks nothing of taking a life. The state asks that bail be denied in this case."

The judge looked back at the defendant. "Didn't quite make your ten-year interval this time, Mr. Welch? You weren't due another killing until 2013. Well, seeing as you seem to be a man of habit, I'm denying the bail request and order that you be remanded to the Maywood lockup until a date is set for your trial."

They escorted Welch out and she had to sit through four more defendants before the door opened and Sean stepped into the room, led by a bailiff. His hands were cuffed, just like all of the ones before him, but she felt better seeing Martin right behind him, looking cool and confident in a blue Brooks Brothers. He never underdressed for any occasion, something she had figured out about him back when they were students at Howard University. Even then, he was given to wearing cashmere sweaters and slacks instead of tee-shirts and jeans. The other brothers ragged his natty style, called him an "oreo" and a "nerd," but he'd had no problem getting the girls. Except her, of course, because she had been married at the time. Though that didn't stop him from making moves. But what started out as mild flirtation evolved into a friendship that lasted twenty years. Right now, Sean was looking straight ahead, but Martin found her with his eyes and gave her a brief nod before both he and Sean walked to the front to stand before the judge.

The prosecutor was flipping through a folder, opened it. She looked at Sean as he approached the front table. She wasn't smirking this round.

The judge also looked at Sean, sized him up in the white shirt Lacey had bought yesterday and passed to him through the guards. He wore his regular jeans, though. The judge looked down at the papers a clerk passed to him, read over something, then turned his attention to Martin. "Are you representing this young man?"

Martin nodded. "Yes, your honor. I'm here to address the issue of bail for Sean Logan. There is no reason for him to remain locked up. He is not a danger to society and has not ever had a felony charge brought against him. We request that he be released on his own recognizance or be allowed to issue a signed promise of appearance. Denying that, your honor, we also request that bail be set no higher than $10,000."

"Your honor," the prosecutor piped in, "this man is suspected of brutally shooting his father in cold blood, then burying his father with no more thought than he would give to an animal. And given the fact that his residence is no longer in this state—as a matter of fact, the defendant and his mother moved to Canada shortly after the disappearance of the victim—the defendant poses a great flight risk. We are at risk of losing jursidiction if another country is brought into play here."

"Your honor, again, since my client will plea his innocence at the arraignment, he is not going to risk having federal agents coming after him in Canada. Therefore I am asking that he be released to his own recognizance . . ."

". . . not going to happen," the judge broke in. Lacey felt her heart jump, but Martin looked unperturbed.

". . . or again that bail be set at a reasonable amount, your honor," Martin continued, as though he had not been interrupted.

The judge shook his head. "Given the severity of the crime and the fact that Mr. Logan has dual residency in two countries, I think it best for all concerned, as well as for the process of justice, not to provide temptation to our defendant here. Whether he is innocent or guilty will be decided in a court of law, so we want him to be there. Given the risk factor, I am denying bail."

Lacey heard a gasp and looked up. Joan stood just inside the room near the doors. Lacey hadn't noticed her.

Joan's dark, curly hair was streaked with gray, her face fuller and more lined. She wore a blue blazer, powder blue blouse, and navy skirt and they hugged the extra pounds she had put on since Lacey had last seen her. Joan clutched a purse to her chest, her expression showing utter devastation. The same devastation Lacey felt.

Lacey watched Sean's mother, unable to break her stare. Joan must have felt the touch of her eyes, because she turned and caught Lacey in mid-stare. Then the expression went from shock to disgust with a downturn of her mouth and a shift of her brow. That's when Lacey realized Joan knew about her and Sean. For how long? Not that it mattered. She might have had similar feelings for any of her friends if one of them had gotten with Calvin. To the mother, women like Lacey were users looking for a revitalized youth through the hard flesh of their sons, their babies.

But Sean was no baby. And she was no user. As much as she might regret losing Joan's friendship, she made a conscious decision at that moment that she would no longer regret what had happened between her and Sean. They were two adults who were pulled to each other, first by circumstances, and then by something much more undeniable.

The bailiff was leading Sean back to the doors, Martin following. Martin's face was lost in thought and Lacey knew he was already planning in his mind for the battle ahead. He looked much like a platoon leader calculating where the next booby trap lay, even though he had warned her this morning over the phone that it was more than likely bail would be denied, given Sean's having lived in Canada, even though he had moved back to the States.

Sean was passing by and he did look at her then. He tried to smile, didn't quite make it. And then he looked up to see his mother standing there.

"Mom," she heard him say quietly as the bailiff led him past his stricken mother, not giving him time to utter anything else. Martin mouthed something to her, but she didn't quite catch it. She would call him later and find out what was going to happen next.

And then the door closed behind them and they were gone.

The next defendant passed down the aisle between Joan and Lacey as Lacey stood and moved toward the aisle, toward Joan. But Joan turned her back, opened the door and walked through it.

Lacey decided to follow, to have it out with Joan now rather than later.

Joan was already halfway down the hall, looking left and right as she went, trying to see where they had taken Sean. But he was no doubt already on an elevator down to the lower level where they probably had a transport waiting to take him back to the county lockup.

Joan stopped at the bank of elevators and pressed the "Down" button. When she looked up and saw Lacey headed in her direction, she turned her back.

"Joan, don't ignore me. I'm your friend." Lacey stopped next to her.

Joan turned then, thunder in her face. "What kind of friend fucks another friend's son? Yes, Sean told me and I'm just sick thinking of you two together. What were you thinking?"

The word "fuck" startled an elderly couple standing a few feet away. The gentleman took his wife's arm to move her away as he glared at Joan.

"You have a right to be angry at me, Joan."

Joan stepped closer, her body rigid with anger. "Yes, I have a right to be angry at you, as well as that damn son of yours who started this whole mess. Between you and your son, you've managed to fuck my son in every possible way. What, you're trying to rediscover your youth? Well, let me tell you, that's all over. So you might as well end it with my son now and let me do what I need to do to salvage his future."

Surprisingly, anger began pushing away her guilt. "No, Joan, this mess started with your crazy husband stalking our sons and attacking them. Calvin acted out of fear and was trying to protect himself and your son."

"Yeah, but whose idea was it to cover it up?"

"And who went along with the cover-up? And made things worse by moving away? You could have stopped this a long time ago, Joan. So don't stand here trying to blame everything on Calvin. And as for me and Sean, he's an adult and we both made choices. That's what adults do. And we don't have to run to our mommies to get permission."

Joan stepped to her and for a second she thought the woman was going to slap her or worse. Her hand was balled into a fist, so the thought had occurred to her.

But the hand never came up. Instead, a tear trickled and Joan's body began to shake. "Oh my God, my son's going to prison."

Just that quickly, her anger and shame were gone. Fear and pity took their place. Fear that the woman she still considered a friend was right, and pity for a mother who might lose her son. She knew all too well how that felt.

When she reached out and pulled Joan into her arms, Joan didn't shrug her off. Instead, her lover's mother placed her head on Lacey's shoulder and sobbed.

"What am I going to do?" she whispered in tears.

Lacey held her friend in the hallway milling with people. The elevator came. And then it left. And they still stood. And they both cried.

Chapter 33

Calvin found it odd, and at the same time strangely comforting, to be standing in front of the basketball hoop where he had spent so many hours of his life. As good as he had been at the game, it hadn't occurred to him even once to try to aim for the NBA.

Sean had brought the subject up one time when they had taken a breather from one of their vicious games of horse, where the penalty for a miss was a ball thrown at the crotch. Hearing Sean's suggestion, Cal had vehemently shaken his head: "Uhn-uhn . . . Too glutted. I'm good, but I'm not shit against a lot of those players. I'd fade into the background too easy and people won't even know I'm there. I couldn't take that. I want people to see me, up front and center. That's how it'll be when I'm holding that bat, when I swing. Just me, gravity, and force."

Then this must be the hell he had tried to avoid his whole life. Becoming invisible, fading into the background where no one can see or hear you.

He wanted out of this hell, out of this limbo.

He wanted to go forward, on to whatever lay ahead. Nothing could be worse than this.

He and Joe had spoken all night about his decision, but in the morning, when Calvin had come back from a bout out-

side, Joe wasn't there. For a horrible second, Calvin thought he was alone again. But later he found Joe in the garden out back, stretching, walking around. Anxious and aimless, ready to move on.

And it seemed Joe couldn't move on unless he moved on.

And his mother was providing the way out.

The pen and paper were still there in the living room, still untouched. An informal confessional made up of pages and ink. Something on which he could purge his sins.

And save both people he loved.

He would have to lie. But hopefully God wouldn't hold that against him, seeing the bigger picture of absolution and redemption.

Joe was away again, already tiring of this pale existence. Waiting for Calvin. As his mother was waiting. And even Sean.

He wandered through the walls, into the house, thought himself into the living room, next to the pad.

He picked it up and dated it. Two days after the killing.

He then began a tale that he hoped would set himself free.

The note was waiting for her when she arrived home from the courthouse. As she had hoped it would be. She picked it up and read it aloud for her and for Calvin. After she was done, she nodded. Hopefully, this would be enough.

He sat watching the inmate staring at him, as the man bit into the desiccated meat loaf hanging off his fork. A similar meal sat before Sean. The meat was congealed and the thick, lumpy gravy made the meal particularly unappetizing. A limp piece of broccoli sat off to the side of the plate. Sean forced himself to eat, just as the other men ate it, because there would be nothing else for the night and an empty stomach became a painful nuisance in the early morning hours between meals.

As he ate, his whole body was tense, primed for something

to happen. The man had been staring at him too long. And Sean couldn't read the look. Every situation, no matter how innocuous, could easily turn into something else.

"That's Romero," Rudy said close to his ear as he sat next to him. "Whatever you do, don't be alone with him. He's always scoping the new blood in here. Let me tell you, this isn't Joliet; in some ways, it's worse. At least there they have more guards to keep the prisoners righteous to a degree. Around here, it's too easy for things to happen, you know what I mean?"

Sean didn't answer him. He didn't have to. Both of them had heard the screams that the guards ignored.

Sean knew that no matter what, nothing like that was going to happen to him. He'd die first. And he'd make sure to take the other guy with him.

The guard called an end to mealtime and the inmates lined up to be led back to their cells. Sean stood behind Rudy, his stomach protesting the digestion of the tough meat. He held his offended stomach and started the orderly march out of the cafeteria when he heard someone yell out, "C'mon, motherfucker, I'm ready for you . . ."

The men in front of him stopped short, including Rudy, as one of the guards yelled out, "What's going on back there?" The guard moved from the front of the line as two inmates began fighting, one pelting the other in the face, blood already running down.

The other guards joined the melee, pulling the attacker off his quarry. The men in the line began hooting and yelling, egging the fighters on. A fight was a worthy distraction from their minute-by-the-hour boredom.

Someone pushed into Sean and he stepped back on someone's toe.

"Hey, pretty boy, trying to get close to me?" a voice asked, much too close to him.

He turned to find Romero in his face, a grooved scar cutting from the bridge of his nose to the middle of his left cheek. The scar was vicious and the rest of his face was no less intimidating. His eyes were dark, both in color and the reflection of the soullessness behind them.

Sean stepped away but Romero closed the gap. He smelled the fetid mixture of meat and, interestingly, alcohol on the man's breath.

"I'm not trying to get close to you. You're the one stepping to me. And I'm telling you to step back."

Romero smiled. "Ugly words out of such a pretty mouth. So, I better step back, huh? What's gonna happen if I don't?"

In his couple of days and nights, Sean had learned fast enough. Rudy had clued him in on some things. Including the inventive ways to protect yourself.

Dinnertime last night hadn't been a waste. Purloined plastic cutlery can be shaped just right, and a spoon can be honed to get a deadly edge to it. That edge was at Romero's stomach now, hard enough for him to feel it. It wouldn't take that much to push it through the flesh.

"I can carve a scar to match the one on your face. Or I can see how slow or fast you bleed. It's up to you."

The guards had finally gotten the melee under control. Hardly anyone was noticing the interaction between Sean and Romero. Their tones were low, but Romero heard what he needed to. And Sean was relieved to see the unpleasant surprise in the man's eyes. Was even more relieved when the inmate took a couple of steps back.

"We gonna meet again, don't you worry. Keep your hardware. It's not gonna do you that much good when me and my crew get through with you."

Everybody was herded back in line. Rudy had moved behind him.

"I saw that. Nice front. But I tell you, you better hope you get out of here fast. Romero doesn't scare off easy. And now he's got his scent on you."

Sean breathed in an angry breath, concentrated on pulling that anger in. Because right now he wanted to find Romero and shove in the makeshift knife. But now wasn't the time.

He didn't know if he could actually kill someone. But what Rudy said was right. If he didn't get out of here soon, he would be forced to either kill or suffer something worse than death.

But there was no way out for him. Not until the trial. And even then, there was no promise that the jury was going to believe him.

He could be facing years of Romeros. His stomach turned, almost causing him to lurch up his undigested food. He swallowed hard and kept up with the line.

The Assistant DA's eyes were glued to the letter. Her nameplate read "Andrea Curtain." Her glasses kept sliding down and she pushed them up at intervals. Dark-complexioned with hair unusually lustrous, she would have been attractive except for the extreme scowl on her face. She finished the letter and all but glared at Lacey.

"Interesting that this letter showed up just now." The tone was accusatory. But then, those in the prosecutor's office were honed by suspicion and cynicism. Serendipity wasn't something they believed in. Especially if it arrived at the eleventh hour, just in time to exonerate someone they had set their sights on.

"I couldn't bring myself to go into his room until just the other day. He died almost two weeks ago and the loss is still raw. It's been hard dealing with his death."

The woman placed the pages of the letter down on her desk, sat back in her chair, and rubbed her forehead. Obviously her day had just been shot to hell.

Lacey continued. "I knew immediately by what Calvin described that it was the body the police found in Thatcher Woods. It was hard for me to read, and at first I didn't want to believe the things I was reading. But that is my son's handwriting. I can testify to that. I just don't want an innocent man to go to prison for something my son did."

"Was your son given to documenting his crimes?"

Lacey felt one of her nerves snap. "My son was basically a good person. This was an extreme circumstance, obviously. He felt he was being threatened out there alone. I knew about Mr. Logan's drinking habits, how he abused his wife and son. His showing up at the woods . . ."

". . . and why do you think he did show up, after your son? Was there bad blood between them?"

"I wish I knew. There're a lot of things I didn't know were going on in my son's life." Lacey cut off, closed her eyes, feeling the truth of her words. "A lot of this might have been avoided if I'd taken time to talk with him, find out what was happening with him. I'm sorry I can't fill in the blanks here. I just know that my son wrote down what he did, maybe because the guilt was too much for him. And I just can't sit by and let an innocent man be blamed for something my son did."

The Assistant DA sat quietly, focusing her eyes off to the left where a couple of cabinets stood against her office wall. Lacey peeked at her watch. It was almost noon. A full day since she saw Sean at the bail hearing.

The woman took one more stab at salvaging her case. "How do I know this letter isn't some ploy to get the defendant off?"

"Why would I sully my son's memory? It's going to be hard for me to hear his name connected to this killing. Some people are going to assume he murdered the man in cold blood. But I truly believe he was acting in his own defense."

"We're going to need other samples of your son's writing . . . to see if it's authentic."

"I figured you would. I have some of his old papers from school. You can also check with Columbia. I'm sure they have his writing on file."

The woman was staring at her again. "I'm still suspicious

about the timing. It's too convenient that it totally clears the defendant. As though it was written for this specific purpose."

"Ms. Curtain, the letter is authentic. And let me ask you something. Can a dead man pen a letter?"

Of course, the woman had no answer for that one.

Chapter 34

The clock was heading on to 11:45. As much as his stomach was growling, he didn't want another confrontation with Romero. This morning in the shower had been hazardous enough. Sean couldn't be sure who was one of Romero's crew, who might sneak up on him and shiv him from behind.

No one had his back, not even Rudy, who was a survivor, and surviving meant not putting your nose out for other people.

They were in the cell and Rudy was snoring. Again. The man's waking hours were few and far between. Sleeping away the day seemed to be his way to cope, his way not to think of endless days behind these walls. Or the walls of Joliet, the downstate prison where most of the convicted were warehoused. Sean wished he had Rudy's capacity, because his own thoughts were beginning to torment him. Memories of his mother crying, of Lacey sitting there looking devastated, of Romero's threat . . . all of it fought for position in the upper regions of his mind. And all of them had to be pushed back. He lay on his back, his arm over his eyes, trying not to think. Trying not to fear.

The sound of the cell door opening made him sit up. Was it lunchtime already?

"Logan. C'mon. We gotta go."

Sean felt his heart jump. "Gotta go where?"

The guard smiled hatefully. "Someone wants to see you."

Sean hesitated. Rudy had stopped snoring, which meant he was awake.

"Where're you taking him?" Rudy asked. The suspicion in his voice mirrored Sean's own.

"You know what's good for you, you betta just mind your business."

Rudy didn't say anything as the guard took Sean's arm, none too gently. The vise tightened as he began leading Sean down a corridor. The men behind the cells began making kissy noises and Sean's stomach plummeted.

Especially as they turned down another hallway, this one lined with doors to closed offices. And at the end of the corridor, Romero stood before an open door to a secluded room.

Sean pulled back against the tenacious claw around his arm. The guard was obviously one of the crew Romero had bragged about. He probably had more guards in his pocket.

The man was practically dragging him now and Romero was smirking at his struggle. Sean's fist flew into the guard's belly and the man bent over. Sean thrust a knee up into the man's jaw.

Romero flew at him while the recovered guard returned the sock in the belly, his fist knocking the breath out of Sean's lungs. Romero had a real knife against Sean's back.

"We're not gonna have any more trouble out of you now, are we?"

Both men were dragging him now, but Sean was causing them some pain. The knife pricked through the prison shirt to his skin, sliced through some flesh. The pain was minimal compared to the fear.

They had him just a few feet from the room. The open door revealed an office with a table and chair and nothing else but solitude. This was where he would die, then.

"What the fuck is going on down there?! Abernathy, what

are you doing with the prisoner?" The angry voice blared from down the corridor.

Romero let him go just that quickly. Sean turned and saw the reason why. The assistant warden with a pair of guards. Rudy had pointed the man out the other day.

Abernathy, the guard who had been bought for a price, stammered, "We were . . . uhm . . . having some trouble with the inmate."

"*We?* Who the hell is *we?* All I see is another prisoner, and that better be a lollipop in his fucking hand."

Sean jerked his arm out of the guard's clutches and began walking toward his salvation. At least he hoped it was. He spoke up.

"The guard was handing me over to Romero. You figure out why."

The disgust was evident on the assistant's face. It seemed he wasn't in on the dealings that went on around here. "Take Romero back to his cell," he told one of the guards.

The guard started to approach. That's when Romero made a quick shift and put the knife to Sean's throat for the men to see.

"We're not going anywhere. This wasn't my doing."

"All right, Romero. Easy now. You don't want to make things worse than what they already are."

"And how much worse can they get, Landers?" he addressed the assistant. "I'm already up for trial. My third time out. Since you all think I killed before . . . and I didn't kill those women. But see, y'all are forcing my hand here. You want this boy to live, you gonna do what I say to do. Abernathy!" he called to the guard. "Give me your gun!" But Abernathy stood still, his face registering confusion. The guard knew he was drowning in shit, but he also knew the rules of self-preservation.

"You're on your own, man," the guard said.

And with that, Sean took a chance. Stepped on Romero's instep hard, felt the wonderful contact of breaking bones. As

Romero screamed, Sean ripped the knife out of his hand and drove it into the inmate's side.

Romero crumbled to the floor, clutching his wound.

"OK, get down there," the warden directed the guards. And they came with guns drawn on both Romero and Sean. One relieved Abernathy of his weapon.

Sean held up his hands, closed his eyes, and wondered what other levels of hell he was going to have to deal with.

But then the assistant warden walked up to him.

"It's OK, son. You're getting out of here."

Sean opened his eyes to see that the warden was telling the truth. "You've been cleared. We were coming to get you, anyway. Your cell mate told us what was happening. You better thank your stars or whatever god you serve that luck was on your side today."

Sean couldn't help the tear that ran down his cheek. Or the sob that tore from him.

It was over.

His mother was waiting outside the open gates. The guard signalled him through with a "Good luck." Not all of them were bad.

He had never been held so tightly.

"Oh, my sweet baby!"

He usually resented that designation, but he held on to his mother just as tightly. He would never take her for granted again.

When he pulled back, he just wanted to know, "How did you do it? How did you get me out?"

He was puzzled by the unreadable expression that came over her face. Something like a grudging resentment. "It wasn't me. It was Lacey. She called me to let me know that she'd spoken on your behalf. Something about finding a letter from Calvin. He wrote it, confessing to shooting Stan. He didn't even say you were there. Why would he do that? And when did he write that letter? It's so strange."

Sean didn't answer. He grabbed his mother again, held her tightly, closed his eyes, and thanked those stars the warden had been talking about.

Then sent a silent thank-you to someone who was no longer here.

"C'mon boy, it's time!" Joe yelled, his face beaming as he pointed to a corridor of light that for some reason was fronting the garage beneath the basketball hoop.

Calvin shook his head. "You go on, Uncle Joe. That light's not for me. It couldn't be."

Joe walked over to him, treading through the flowers edging the walk up to the back porch. Of course, the flowers didn't bend.

He took Calvin's arm. "It's for you, too. It's time for us to go on home."

Calvin closed his eyes, wishing it were so. Hoping, but knowing that his hope was futile. "Why would heaven even want me?" The question came out a sorrowful moan.

"Because you're loved, son. You always were. You just have to let yourself know that. No more guilt, all right? No more shame. You're free, Calvin. Believe it, you're free. Now c'mon, just take my hand."

Calvin felt the warmth of Joe's hand. Wondered had it always been this warm.

He started toward the light, then thought of something and stopped.

"I have to say good-bye to Mom. I have to let her know how sorry I am for what I put her through. Her and Sean."

Joe smiled softly. "I think she already knows, Calvin. I think she knew when you wrote that letter. And I think she's not going to be surprised that you're gone."

Calvin nodded and let Joe lead him toward the light.

They entered.

So warm, so beautiful, so peaceful, so everything . . .

He smiled as he entered eternity.

Chapter 35

Lacey ran the scrub brush against the kitchen floor. The smell of baking pecan ginger cookies in the oven provided a strange counter to the lemon Pine Sol permeating the room. Her back and knees ached, but that was good.

She was only starting to recover, just a bit. The last few days were pushed away by the mania of cleaning the house from attic to basement, baptizing it anew. Getting rid of the sadness, finally.

Her son was gone. And she could mourn him all over again. But she chose not to. Because she knew in her heart that he had gone to a better place, a better man than when he first left this earth.

Maybe Joe had been there to greet him on his way over. But that was probably just a fantasy.

The doorbell chimed at the kitchen door. When she looked up and saw a face at the door's window, she felt her heart jump . . . apprehension and pleasure. But she pushed the pleasure away as she got up and went to let Sean in.

No more sweater or jeans. Dressed in a light blue dress shirt and gray slacks that would probably be uncomfortable in the eighty-degree heat, he seemed older somehow. Or maybe the days locked up had aged him.

They had barely spoken since he was released from jail, except for a call last week when he thanked her. He had sounded so strange that she hadn't pressed him about what he'd been through. She was just so glad he was out of there.

She was glad he was here, for however long that was. "C'mon in," she said as she stepped back to let him enter.

His smile didn't quite make it to his eyes. "I smell cookies. And . . ." he sniffed . . . "Pine Sol. Cleaning?"

She pulled off the rubber gloves. "And baking. Trying my hand at something."

"Something new?"

"Yeah. Contemplating going into business. My mother's recipes."

"What about your job?"

"Gone, all gone, as of a few weeks ago. I left. I couldn't take the crap anymore."

"Good for you."

He was standing too close to her. Too close. She turned toward the oven. "I hope so. Right now I'm in the market for a kitchen. City zoning codes and stuff."

"Smells like they're ready to take out."

"Hmm—forgot you know your way around the kitchen. Let me just go and get them . . ."

She didn't know why she was so nervous. She pulled open the oven door and only as her hand reached in did she realize she had forgotten the oven mitt.

The shock of the pain caused her to cry out. And Sean was there, pulling her to the faucet. He ran the cold water over the seared fingers.

"So stupid!" she yelled as the cold water hit, feeling like slicing knives.

"Shhh, got to let it run a few minutes or so. Got any ibuprofen?"

She nodded, forcing her mind to suppress the pain.

"What are you doing here?" she said between gritted teeth. She didn't mean the question to come out as rough as it sounded, but the pain was speaking.

His attention was absorbed by her burns. The fingers were

welting and red. And she needed the ibuprofen now. He got them after making her promise not to take her hand from beneath the running water.

A half hour and several ibuprofen later, she was at the kitchen table, looking across at him. It was as though time had shifted back to their breakfast together. That seemed years ago.

"So, why are you here, Sean? You're free now. I would have thought after everything that has happened, you'd want to get the hell out of town."

"Yeah, well. That's what my mother wanted. For me to leave, go back with her to Vancouver. I told her no."

Almost like the first time, his eyes skewered her, wouldn't let her go. She was uncomfortably aware of the impression of shoulder muscles, the delts visible through the light material of his shirt.

"What are you planning to do now?"

"Lacey, how did you get him to do it? To write that letter?"

She stroked her injured fingers, gingerly testing the skin. It was scabbing. "He did what he knew was the right thing to do. He had his ways, but he wasn't evil. And I reminded him of your friendship . . . and his love. In the end, he decided to free all of us, including himself. He found redemption in the end, and I'm glad for that."

"I am, too," he said softly. "Lacey, I want to start my life again. You wouldn't believe it, but I got my job as a waiter back at the restaurant. Had to do a lot of convincing before Russ took me on. Since I'm all healed up, I'm waiting up front. I even found a place, so I'm out of the garage apartment."

She nodded. "Sounds like you're moving forward."

"Lacey, I don't plan to stay a waiter. I have plans for my future. And I know what I want. That's the only thing that's kept me going these weeks. Coming back here was the best thing to happen to me. And I don't care about the shit I went through. The price was worth it . . . if you say that there's still a chance . . . for me and you."

She stood abruptly, nearly knocking over her chair. "Sean, don't do this. I'm glad you're getting your life together, but it can't include me. What happened between us came out of painful circumstances. And besides, I really regret hurting Joan the way I did. She didn't deserve that . . . from either of us."

He stood and walked over to her. "We had a talk. And she understands . . . well, as much as she can . . . that I'm not going anywhere. And what I feel for you isn't a crush or something that's going to fade away with time. I've been carrying this for years, and it's not going away. I tried to go on with some type of life, but I failed at it. Lost my ambition, lost any sense of myself. I was just existing. God, I hate to say this, but Calvin's funeral, finding you, saved me."

She didn't have any words. What did he want from her? No way could they become a couple. The world wasn't ready for them. She wasn't ready for them.

"Sean, I did wrong by my son. I'm not going to mess up another young man's life. I would be robbing you of your youth. You may think you want to be with me, but in a few years, you'd regret it, especially as the wrinkles and grooves began wearing on me."

"I don't give a shit about that . . ."

"So, you'd love a gray-haired ole woman . . ."

"And by that time, I'll probably be going bald myself. So what of it? People age."

"Sean, why do you think you love me? Because I was nice to you?"

"Hell, you weren't all that nice. Not all the time, anyway. I know you thought I wasn't all that good for Calvin, and that a lot of times you only tolerated me being around. But the other times, you cared, I know you did. You made me feel like something more than what I was. Everybody was all about my looks and that got played out really fast. All the girls throwing themselves at me. But I just wanted someone to see me, really see me. And you did, more than my mother, more than Calvin, more than anyone. You talked to me and I could feel you, feel you were lonely, too. We were both reaching out, looking for something. Lacey, this thing may have started as a crush . . . but by the time I left town, it wasn't a crush anymore. But I never thought I would ever have a chance to tell you. And these weeks . . . when I wasn't getting my ass kicked . . . they made me lose my breath. I didn't know that life could feel this way, that it wasn't just something that zapped everything from you and beat you down. That it could actually build you up, make you feel good. And I don't want to give that up. I want a chance with you. I want to be happy, maybe even have a kid or two. You're talking about wrinkles and getting older . . . I'm talking about my life."

He put a hand to her cheek, stroked it. The pain from her fingers was quickly forgotten. She couldn't feel anything but him. She could love him if she'd let herself. And he was asking her to let herself.

"I can't. It wouldn't be right. I mean, Calvin loved you . . ."

"And I loved him . . . as a friend. And I'm sorry I hurt him and I wish to God I could take it back. But I can't. Just like I can't undo all of my mistakes. I can just try not to make any more. Well, at least not make any stupid ones that'll get me behind bars again."

"That was a nightmare," she said. "I couldn't stand the thought of you in there."

"We can agree on that, at least. I don't think I can keep standing here and not touch you."

"Sean . . ." she protested.

"No. Not right now. I don't want to hear the reasons. I just want to feel you. And I think you want the same thing."

He pulled her into his arms, and she let him. He held her close, not doing much but enjoying the closeness.

When he kissed her this time, it was with something more

final than their previous kisses. And she imagined years of the same lips, the same touches . . . and thought that it could be good between them.

As the kiss deepened, she forgot about Joan, about all of those who would look at them sideways, make comments.

He pulled back and she saw desire in his eyes. And she knew they would be making love soon.

She took his hand, led him out of the kitchen, through the foyer to the stairs. She wanted this time to be in the bedroom, wanted to baptize her sheets with their sweat. Wanted to know what it would be like to wake up next to him tomorrow and not be afraid of the aftermath. Maybe this time, she would actually remember the condoms she had bought after their first time together. Maybe even then anticipating more between them.

As they walked up the stairs together, something occurred to her.

"Sean, you ever thought about working for yourself? As a cook?"

He paused, smiled.

"Why?"

"I was just thinking. Maybe you can help me start up my business. I was thinking pastries, or something along that line. Maybe you have some recipes of your own?"

He just shook his head and laughed as he followed her up the stairs to her room. He was still laughing as they closed the door.

Please turn the page for a
titillating look at Alison Kent's
THE PERFECT STRANGER.
Available now from Brava.

"You're not pregnant." The dress hung blade straight to her ankles, not an inch of rounded belly between shoulders and knees. Jack couldn't even think to move.

"Your shorts." She held out one hand.

"Uh-uh. No way. You drag me out here, posing as a pregnant woman, no, a pregnant *wife* needing my help, and you want me to give you my drawers? I don't think so. In fact, I'm outta here."

Jack started walking.

"You've been in the back of the cart three days, *Señor* Briggs."

Jack stopped walking.

"We followed a road that leaves no trail. I'm the only one who knows where you are, the only one who knows how to get you safely out of here. You give me the shorts or we both die."

She'd walked toward him as she talked. A step for every two or three words. She stood close enough that all he had to do was reach up and push the hood off her head to see her whole face.

The machete tip inches from his nose dissuaded him.

One day, lady. One day, Jack thought, stomping to the far side of the cart where he shimmied out of his shorts. She caught them, and Jack grimaced as they went up in flames.

He unrolled the canvas knapsack, shook out the paper-thin tunic and trousers and draped both over the edge of the cart. They looked as bad as his fatigues. Butt naked, he stifled his complaints and dressed.

The fit of the shirt left much to be desired. The frayed sleeves barely hung to his elbows. And she'd been right about the length. The hem only hit his waist.

He struggled into the pants; the legs ended a good six inches above his ankles. The flax chafed every part of his skin that wasn't already raw. Hands out in surrender, he walked around the end of the cart and headed toward the fire.

"You've got me. I'm who knows how many miles from who knows where. These clothes would scare away a scarecrow. And even if I were to try and walk out of here, I'd no doubt lose my toes to jungle rot.

"Don't you think it's about time you let me in on the conspiracy? It's not like I'm the father of your *baby*. In fact, I'm beginning to wonder whether or not I'm your husband."

Heedless of her blade, Jack grabbed her wrist and drew her close. "How about it, *Señora* Briggs? Married or not?"

"Yes, I'm married." Eyes burning bright, she jerked away and lifted the machete. The tip of the blade caught the tie at her throat and nicked open the ragged neckline. Grabbing both sides, she jerked and pulled. The hooded dress fell to her feet.

She kicked the pile of cloth away, then bent to scoop it up. Dropping the burlap squarely on the flames, she defiantly faced him down covered head to toe in a black habit and veil.

"But not to you."

Jesus H. Christ! He was married to a pregnant nun.
Wrong, Jack. You're not married, and she's not pregnant.
But she was a nun.

She was also china doll exquisite, a testosterone fantasy that sucker-punched Jack in his near-empty gut. This woman had kidnapped him, taken ten years off his life with the wife and child routine, burned his clothes, refused him a bath and still he wanted to see her naked.

She was centerfold material, as close to perfect as a female got. Except for the tiny scar that bisected the arch of her right brow. And now that he looked closer, he wasn't too sure about her eyes.

It wasn't the exotic almond slant, or even the seductive get-me-drunk-Jack Daniels gold. No. It was the way she'd seen a lifetime of too much, the way she saw too much now. Those eyes scared him.

No soft-voiced china doll should be so tough, so world-weary, or so wise. She was all three. She was also a nun. And she was as Caucasian as he was.

Ignoring the machete she wielded like a sharp tongue, Jack glared down. "So, *Sister Señora* Briggs. Guess the marriage certificate was a fake."

She glared back, the fire in her eyes a one-hundred-proof whiskey burn. "Yes. But it was necessary."

 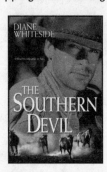